TERROR'S MASK

Other Books by Don Otey

Minerva's Net

Dread and Breakfast

Tank Hill

Guild of Deceit

and soon to be released:

Then The Stillness

(A Civil War Novel)

TERROR'S MASK

Don Otey
Author of Minerva's Net

This is one of my ~~[illegible]~~ earlier novels, I have published a total of 16 in all. Enjoy. They are all listed on internet.
at iUniverse

Don Otey

iUniverse, Inc.
New York Lincoln Shanghai

TERROR'S MASK

iUniverse books may be ordered through booksellers or by contacting:

iUniverse
2021 Pine Lake Road, Suite 100
Lincoln, NE 68512
www.iuniverse.com
1-800-Authors (1-800-288-4677)

ISBN-13: 978-0-595-39560-6 (pbk)
ISBN-13: 978-0-595-83960-5 (ebk)
ISBN-10: 0-595-39560-0 (pbk)
ISBN-10: 0-595-83960-6 (ebk)

Printed in the United States of America

This novel is from Dan Cooper to his three partners Pat O'Leary, Jud Black, and Jim Barnett. By other names they are three real people who I'm proud to call friends. You're a bunch of nut cases, guys, but you're great pals.

ACKNOWLEDGEMENTS

For all my friends and family who have offered encouragement for my writing efforts, I express my gratitude.

To my wonderful wife, Jo Ellen, I want to say you are the most patient woman on earth. And, like Ellen Cooper in this novel, you know how very special you have always been to me.

NOTE TO THE READER

Before you begin *Terror's Mask,* please allow me to set the framework of this novel.

The story centers on four main characters. I tell the story from each of their perspectives. Most of the chapters are in first person with the chapter name identifying the narrator of that chapter.

CHAPTER 1

Pat O'Leary

I look into Celia Grant's sad blue eyes. It breaks my heart.

"Dengue fever?" She wails. "How could Kenny come down with dengue? He hasn't even been out of the country."

We're sitting in a stark waiting room outside the isolation ward at Fairfax Hospital. I never liked being around hospitals under any conditions. Today it's really grating on me watching this beautiful woman suffer. Inside that ward her only son, my good friend Kendrick Grant, is fighting for his life.

Celia's a strong woman and a fine doctor, but she's coming apart, on the verge of hysteria. She starts to speak and her voice trembles. There's a look of helplessness about her as she stands and moves over toward the stack of magazines on the table. She fumbles with them pretending to be interested. I take it as a sign that she needs a moment to compose herself. I want to say something, put my arms around her, try my best to ease her pain, but I don't know how to begin.

After a long, tense moment she regains control and preempts me. Walks over to where I'm sitting, brushes away a wisp of blonde curl, and looks down at me.

"Now I see why Kenny wanted you to get involved, Pat. I can read your thoughts. You're nearly as shaken as I am. I think he's special to both of us." Her voice trails off into a whisper.

"Well, your son had a lot to do with our early success at COB Software several years back, Celia. He was exactly the kind of brilliant young man we needed to add some spark and a note of sanity to what we were trying to do. Kenny had an endless supply of enthusiasm and the smarts to back up his ideas."

"He always told me you were more than a boss to him. Kenny described you as a big old, lovable lug of a guy with a heart of gold. Apparently he was right."

"Yeah, well I cease to be a nice guy when my friends are in trouble, Celia."

Lovable lug? I think. Hell, I'm just a fun-loving Irishman in a less than svelte 250 pound package. But Celia's obviously going through pure agony with her son lying down the hall fighting for his life. Who wouldn't hurt a bit watching a mother agonize like this? Besides, I reflect to myself, Kendrick Grant is a talented young man who made his mark as a member of our staff not so long ago. Right now I'm really hacked off at what life has dealt him at the outset of a bright career.

There's a moment when I can't bear to watch what's happening to her. I look away from the tall blonde lady and walk across to the window, trying to collect my thoughts. Outside the building people are going about their business; cars hurry in and out of the parking garage. A helicopter sets down on the emergency pad and attendants rush out with a gurney. I noticed a pronounced chill in the air earlier as the Virginia countryside braces for a late snowfall. But tomorrow is Saint Patrick's Day, so this could be winter's last blast. Inside this room, though, the walls are closing in on a couple of puzzled people. A valued friend in the full bloom of his productive years is fighting for his life against something called dengue fever—I'm not even sure what that is—and I'm asking 'why him?'

"You said he asked for me, Celia?"

She dabs at her eyes and nods. "He said, 'Call Pat O'Leary. He'll know what to do.' Kenny was already in poor shape by the time I picked him up at Dulles Airport. Stared at me through hollow eyes and looked terrible. I did a quick assessment and drove him straight to the hospital."

I have to admit I'm stumped. Kenny hasn't come around more than three or four times since he worked summers for us after high school and his first year of college. He's a busy young man so I can understand that. My partners and I at COB Software knew the first time we saw him that he was a talent waiting for a chance to break out. The kind of eager youngster you couldn't help liking. Since then he's earned his PhD and has a couple of patents to his credit.

"Tell me what he's been doing, Celia. What's he working on now?"

"Don't know much about his recent activities, Pat. He telephoned me last month and seemed very excited about a new job with some electronics company out west. He came home for a short visit. I saw him off at the airport, and he's called me several times since then. But every time I tried to sound him out on the particulars of his work, he was, well, he was, evasive."

"Let's start with whatever you can tell me—where he was flying and the name of his new employer."

She shakes her head and lights a cigarette. I look around for someone to appear and demand she put it out. But she's the doctor and this is her territory. I guess she knows how far she can push.

Celia leans back and thinks about my questions; exhales slowly.

"You know, he didn't even mention the name of the company he was joining. Said the work was something he was excited to get started on, but that's about as specific as he was. Now that I think about it, there was a note of uncertainty even though he sounded enthused. Didn't feel like I should press him."

"And the flight was bound for where?" I ask.

"He was flying to Los Angeles. Guess that's where he's been calling me from."

"It's a start. You know we'll do everything we can to get to the bottom of this, Celia. Kenny is our friend. He more than pulled his share of the load when COB Software was a struggling startup company. Kenny was always offering innovative ideas, and he worked like a plow horse. We owe him."

"He said you gave him company shares that were quite valuable by the time you sold the company."

"You met my partners, Jud Black and Dan Cooper, some time ago. We made our fortunes, sold out, and retired with more than we'll ever need. I'm glad the stock came in handy for him. We're not about to forget people like Kenny who helped us succeed."

Finally I see a spark of hope in her eyes. She reaches out to touch my hand.

"Thank you, Pat. Kenny told me many times what a dynamite team you folks at COB made at whatever you set out to do. Always said it was the encouragement he got from you that really kick-started his career."

"What I can't get through this thick skull," I tell her, "is how Ken's illness and his new job are connected. I mean, he's there only a month, stays in touch then suddenly flies home with dengue fever? It's mind boggling."

Her voice trembles, and I see a look bordering on panic. "When Kenny called he was at a Dulles baggage carousel. Said he needed a ride home. When I got there he really looked terrible, Pat. Kenny's not the kind that lets his appearance go. He was rumpled and shaggy, hadn't shaved, looked downright grimy. What's worse is that if I hadn't brought him straight here to the hospital and raised billy hell with everybody to get the staff moving, he could be in even worse shape."

She's pacing nervously and lights another cigarette with the butt of her first one. I caution, "Better ease up on those things, Celia. Have a seat and let's talk this through."

I get a nod of reservation, and she stubs out the new smoke and takes a seat.

Celia Grant is a remarkable woman—beautiful and smart. Tall and shapely, must be five nine in heels with long hair the color of spun gold. Celia's pushing fifty, probably a couple years my junior, and with her natural beauty she could be making her living as a model. But she's also a fine medical doctor with a solid reputation in disease symptomatology and communication, a much sought after lecturer, widow of a former U.S. ambassador, mother of one.

She's stopped talking and is staring down at her lap, twisting a handkerchief in her hands. My guess is that her mind is down the hall with her only child, so I don't intrude on her thoughts. Finally Celia breaks her concentration, turns her attention back to me and continues.

"Fortunately, I'd seen the symptoms too many times, so I could do a rapid diagnosis. I spent way more time than I care to remember looking after dengue patients when my husband was in his diplomatic post in Asia. The effects of a wide variety of diseases in that part of the world take down whole communities, often without warning. I saw some ugly scenes that would tear your heart out."

"Hang tough, lady. Kenny used to tell me how strong willed you are. Said he hoped some of your attitude had rubbed off on him."

Her eyes light up again, and she actually manages a chuckle. "Bet he didn't say strong willed, though. Hard headed or stubborn as a mule is closer to the truth."

"Give me a number where you can be reached, Celia. I'll get my partners together and go to work on this problem. We'll go balls to the wall…I mean…"

Celia laughs out loud. "That's the kind of enthusiasm I love to hear. When can I sit down with you, Jud and Dan and get moving?"

"Well, I'm the only one here right now. When we sold out I moved to Maryland and opened a bar."

"And the others?"

"Oh, Jud lives here but he's in Florida visiting Dan at the moment. Dan went south and became a writer. He took retirement seriously."

"So you'll help?"

"I'll call them tomorrow morning and ask them to pitch in. We needle each other a lot, but when the chips are down, there's no better team anywhere than the three of us. Why don't you and I plan to meet in Frederick at my bar, the Slante, as soon as I can get them up here. I'll call you."

She stares at me, tears of anger welling up. "We'll nail the scum that did this to my Kenny."

From the look I get from her, my face must register how shocked and puzzled I am at her sudden outburst of raw anger. She has fire in her eyes.

"Why would you say that? You think this was intentional? That somebody infected him with dengue fever on purpose?"

"Pat, I've checked it out in the lab. This infection is a strain of the virus I've never before encountered. Dengue fever results from being bitten by a particular species of mosquito that isn't native to this country. The fever isn't contagious, so we're only keeping Kenny in isolation to give him intensive care. It normally isn't fatal and runs its course in two weeks at most unless there are other complications. But in Kenny's case it appears to be stronger, virulent, almost as if it's poisoning all of his body's systems. We're dealing with something entirely new and frightening."

"What tipped you off that you were dealing with dengue?" I ask her.

"He showed up with an elevated temperature and severe pain behind his eyes. Kenny kept grabbing at his upper arms and legs like he was experiencing muscle pain. Those are all clear signs of dengue."

"But they're treating him now, aren't they? I mean, surely he's going to be all right."

"We're giving Kenny medicine for his fever and trying to build up his resistance. He's barely holding his own, and the dengue is fighting us very hard. If it progresses to the hemorrhagic stage, I don't know if we can cure him in time. There is no vaccine. The best we can do is keep him sedated and pump him full of nutrients."

I'm almost afraid to ask. "What do you mean by 'hemorrhagic'?"

"In extreme cases the patient's blood vessels begin to collapse. It causes bleeding beneath the skin and nasal and rectal bleeding. At that stage the patient enters what we term DHF, dengue hemorrhagic fever. There's about a 20 percent morbidity rate with DHF."

"But you said this virus normally plays itself out in time."

"Pat, I think this is a manmade super strain we're dealing with, some kind of genetic alteration produced in a laboratory. No telling yet how persistent or critical it may be."

"Damn, do you realize the implication of what you just said, Celia?"

"I understand perfectly, and it scares me witless. We could be dealing with a serious threat to all of us. From what I saw of the effects on Kenny, this form of dengue is faster-acting than I've ever witnessed. He could have been to the DHF stage in a matter of days. The unknown strain could be altered to become contagious and may have a much higher fatality rate for all we know. If such a strong, fast progressing mutation of the virus were to be spread somehow to the general population, we could be facing a full-scale outbreak on a level it's hard to imagine. It could turn into a pandemic that would kill thousands, maybe even millions, before we could get it under control—*if* we can control it. Kenny must have stumbled onto the source. We have to find it before it's too late."

Chapter 2

Jud Black

"I've been thinking," I tell Dan, "there's a lot of scamming going on; computer crackers are misusing their skills against unsuspecting victims. Now we know first hand that it can be downright deadly as it was for your friends. There has to be more we can do to stop the scams."

We're on our way back to Tampa, driving through a central Florida night with star-filled skies. My pal Dan Cooper is worn out, so he's dozing while I do the driving. Our first venture as computer sleuths has turned out to be almost more excitement than either of us could handle. A couple of scary adversaries were playing mind control and remote assassination using the Internet in a scheme they called Minerva's Net.

That pair of bad actors cost Dan two of his closest friends their lives and almost took his wife Ellen. He called me in to help and, as of tonight, Minerva's Net is out of business. We're bruised and battered, physically and emotionally tapped out, but enjoying our hard-earned victory.

Dan and I make an illogical but effective pair. He's in his early fifties, six feet and weighs maybe 180 pounds. Has gray eyes and graying hair. I'm thirty-six and stand six-two bootless. I have dark eyes, a long, black pony tail and a brow ring. Dan's a logical-minded electrical engineer. I'm an independent music composer and performer with my own label and I'm also a pretty fair computer jock. In spite of our outward differences, the two of us hit it off from the outset, and our minds have this eerie way of meshing.

Dan struggles upright in his seat and stares at me. I think I've grabbed his attention. "Run that by me again, Jud. What do you mean 'more we can do?' Like what?"

"They're giving the computer world a rotten name and causing way too much damage. Somebody's got to go on the offense against these dudes. This early retirement is more boring than I thought it would be. We both have loads of time on our hands, and we've got the computer smarts to take them down. Might as well be us that take the initiative."

"You mean like as regular work?" Dan asks. He's awake now for certain. "What would we do, hire out as computer private eyes?"

"Something like that," I tell him. "I've been talking to Pat O'Leary. He wants to know what we're mucking around with down here in Florida. Pat's getting fidgety playing host at his Irish bar. Told me he misses the way we used to put our minds together to kick ass in the software business. He wants to get involved in some real action."

"You're serious, aren't you, Jud?"

I break out in a broad grin.

Dan says, "Oh, no. Here it comes. I know that sneer. This is Dan Cooper, buddy, the guy who knows the kinds of off-the-wall, twisted things that go on behind that innocent grin."

"Listen, pal," I tell him. "Since we sold our business and became retired guys with lots of money and entirely too few challenges, it just hasn't been the same. I need something to get my teeth into."

Dan's been living here in central Florida writing and enjoying life. I keep busy by doing programming gigs putting together cutting edge software like the home security system I'm about to finish. Pat finally got his wish to become an Irish barkeep, moved from Virginia over to Frederick, Maryland and opened the Slante. It's probably the best place on the mid-Atlantic coast to get a mug of real suds to wash down some rib-sticking authentic Irish food.

"You and I did make a super team taking down some pretty twisted folks," Dan says. "Felt like old times pitting our wits against unknown odds and working our way through some rough times."

That about nails the way I feel about it, too. We've always clicked as a team. He had a military career then went to work in industry where I worked for him before we formed our own company with Pat O'Leary. Since retiring, Dan's become a fiction writer with some good credits. He refers to me as a free thinker; guess that's a compliment.

"By my watch, Dano, it's now past midnight. Just turned Saint Patrick's Day. What say we wake up the old Irishman and make a business proposal? I even have a name—COB Investigations."

Dan smiles. We made our fortunes with a startup company we named COB Software for the three partners—Cooper, O'Leary and Black. Three guys on one hell of a roll that set the software world back on its heels. The big guys eventually felt the heat and made us an offer we couldn't refuse.

I watch him rattle my proposition around in his engineer's brain, and I can almost hear the gears meshing. He peers out for a long minute at the pine trees whizzing by the car's window then he turns to me and poses a question.

"You want to make the call or should I?"

* * * *

We pull into Dan's driveway in Trinity, a quiet community north of Clearwater. It's way past one AM. Hardly a sound. Just the palm fronds rustling in a steady breeze. We pull into the garage and I make a beeline to the fridge for a cold Murphy's Ale. This has been a long night I'm ready to put behind me. I reach up and gingerly touch my branded cheek where someone I need desperately to put out of my mind left deep, raw fingernail tracks and some even deeper emotional scars. Guess I fall too easily. She was beautiful and smart as hell. But she was on the wrong side of the law—driving people to fatal accidents through mind control. Who knows? Maybe I would have been her next victim.

"You sure you don't want to wait until morning to call him, Jud? We wake up Pat at this hour and Judy's gonna have both our hides. Maybe we should hold off and catch him at breakfast."

"Where's the fun in that?" I ask and grab the wall phone. Punch the speaker button and start dialing. Dan shrugs.

A sleepy Pat O'Leary answers after three rings. His voice is heavy with sleep and sounds more than a little testy.

"Top o' the mornin', mister O. Got your green hat and socks on?" There's a long interval of dead air.

"Jud, you're a mental case," Pat eventually booms back at me. I'm holding the receiver away from my ear and smiling at Dan.

"You know what time it is, Black?" Pat snarls.

"Yeah, it's St. Pat's Day, and you're already one beer behind, O'Leary. Rise and shine."

I hear a voice in the background and Pat tells me, "Hang on, nutso. At least let me take this phone into the living room."

There's a lot of shuffling and a delay. I grin at Dan and give him one thumb up. He answers with a choking gesture. It's about time I put the phone on speaker and let him share the blame.

"Okay," Pat finally says, "what's so damn important it couldn't at least wait until sunrise?"

"You wanted to know what I was doing in Florida. Thought it was time I told you. Dan's listening in on the speaker."

"Hey, Dan," Pat says. "You're supposed to be his keeper while he's down there. Think he's slipped the reins. Jud's been so close hold about what you dudes are doing I'm beginning to think it's something that's *both* immoral *and* illegal."

"Hi, Pat," Dan answers. "Actually, we've been kicking some butt. Uncovered the wildest scheme you could ever imagine for stand-off assassinations. Just delivered the killers to the gendarmes tonight. Jud looks like he's been through World War III, and I'm beat to a frazzle."

"So why aren't both of you curled up in a corner somewhere sleeping it off while I recover from a long night standing over a hot bar?"

"Because we have something important to bounce off you, mister barkeep. This could be the best offer you'll get all year."

"Shoot, stick," Pat replies. "Looks like I'm already up for the day, anyway."

"Yeah, well, you needed to be up boiling cabbage and getting the corned beef and green beer ready," I throw out at him. "Leapin' leprechauns, big guy, you keeping banker's hours?"

"Got something you can hit him with, Dan?" Pat wants to know. "Give him a good shot for me."

I motion to Dan and poke a finger at my chest. He gestures for me to take over.

"Seriously, Pat," I say, "you sounded like you were spoiling for some excitement the last time we talked. So am I. This may be the perfect answer."

I let that hang for a second then give him my pitch. "What would you say to the three of us hanging out a shingle and starting something called COB Investigations? Knock down computer crackers and scumbags misusing their computer skills."

"Interesting, Jud. In fact, I was going to call you today…at a more respectable hour, of course. You remember Kenny Grant?"

"Sure," I answer. "How's he doing?"

"Lousy. I spent a long time with his mom at the hospital yesterday. Kenny's seriously ill. Has dengue fever."

"Whoa," Dan blurts out. "What the hell is that, and how did he get it?"

"That's what Celia Grant wants to know. You met her when Kenny was at COB. She's a doctor but his illness has her stumped. Mentally, right now she's in a pretty rocky state. Kenny went out west to work for an electronics outfit and came back a month later sick enough to die. I know he's been doing some pioneer work in super small computer circuits. Could be related somehow."

"Sounds to me like we have our first job as computer snoops," I tell them. "Even if this turns out to have nothing to do with his work, it's a way to get COB Investigations rolling. I say we give it a go."

There's a brief silence then Dan nods his agreement.

Pat chimes in. "COB, huh? That name brought us phenomenal success the first time around. Why not? Count me in. When can the two of you get up here?"

"Hell, I can be there by tomorrow, Pat. Get some brews cooling. First I need a few hours in the sack to let my body catch up. Dan and I will tell you about our caper down here, and you can fill us in on the situation with Kenny."

Pat asks, "You in, Dan?"

"All for it," he answers. "Let me talk to Ellen about traveling. She's due out of the hospital today."

"Hospital?" Pat shrieks. "What the…?"

"That's part of the story Jud's talking about. Our sleuthing damn near cost me my wife, but they paid dearly for that mistake."

"Hey, you guys really have been up to your keisters in trouble, haven't you? Most excitement I ever see these days is tossing a rowdy drunk out of the Slante."

I look over at Dan and he's lit up like a marquee. Think he's finally come out of his funk and is back to his lovable old self.

Dan and I shake hands. I tell Pat, "We're gonna have a cool one here to seal our…what?…repartnership?"

Both of us are too charged up over the prospects of the new company to call it a day. Considering all we've been through since this morning—yesterday morning now—that's a heavy dose of adrenaline.

We walk out onto the patio and sit by the pool.

"That fresh air is a real kick, partner," I tell Dan. "Tastes almost as good as the Murphy's."

"Coming from you, that's a real testimonial, Jud."

"No fooling, good buddy. I was beginning to have my doubts we could wallow through this mess and survive. Chalk one up for the good guys." He makes an invisible mark in the air.

We launch into a marathon session. Recap the whole escapade we've just been through. Maybe it's more to put it to rest than anything else. Then we reminisce about our days at COB and have some laughs over the goofy things we pulled and still had success at every turn.

"Guess we had more than dumb luck going for us, Dan. We're pretty awesome when we put our heads together, particularly with the Irishman to keep us headed in the right direction. I am stoked by this new undertaking. Can't wait to get started."

A couple of brews later, we're about to wind down, though. I look at Dan and say, "Man, I'm whipped. Feel like a tongueless man at an icicle licking contest."

"Going soft on me, Jud?"

"Not yet, pal. But I could if I hang around this Florida living and healthy food long enough. Think I'll book an afternoon flight to Virginia then curl up in the back room for a few hours."

"Sounds like a plan to me," Dan answers, and I can tell he's about to bomb out. "I'm supposed to pick up Ellen at the hospital after lunch and bring her home. Better get in some snores myself. I won't wake you in the morning. Lock up when you leave and I'll see you soon."

Dan shakes my hand and staggers off to bed.

I book my reservation and slug down the remains of my third bottle. Then I find the bed and crash.

CHAPTER 3

Dan Cooper

We're sitting in the morning room of our Florida home. I'm sharing breakfast with my wife and soaking up the glorious central Florida sunshine as we've done nearly every day for the past six years.

This is such a perfect weather day that we've opened the sliding doors in the family room to let in the fresh air. An overnight shower has left the taste of spring and scent of tropical flowers.

But this morning is different for a much more important reason. Ellen's frightening hospital ordeal is finally over, and she's back home in Trinity with me.

I look across the table at my bride of 30 years. "Never quite realized how special this time of day was to me, Ellen, until you weren't sitting there across from me."

She looks up and trains her brown eyes on me, the ones that turn me all mushy inside. "For a while, I wasn't sure I'd make it home. But you stood by me, Dan, and kept me going when I most needed you." She reaches out and takes my hand in hers.

Guess the definition of contentment must be something like what I feel when I realize the most precious woman in the world still chooses to share my bed and table. I've been her willing slave ever since I laid eyes on this little five-three charmer.

A pair of long-legged gray cranes struts by outside the patio screen. They briefly look our way and give us their throaty warble. Then they move along, very much at home. After all, this is their turf and we're the intruders.

"See, Wilt and Gertrude even came by to welcome you home. Think I saw Gertie smile, and I know Wilt winked at you. They both look relieved."

"They're not half as relieved as I am, Dan. I really wigged out in that hospital. But let's put it behind us and get back to normal. Life is too wonderful to dwell on the past."

When we sold the business in Virginia and came to Florida, it was to fulfill a dream we'd talked about for a long while but thought was far into the future. My success with Pat O'Leary and Jud Black in the software business sped up our migration south when I was able to retire in my late forties. The years since have been all we could ever want. Our daughter, Danielle, is in Virginia, happily married and working at a job she loves. The dark-haired beauty holding my hand makes every day a new delight for me.

"How are you feeling, El? Anything I can get for you?"

There's that crooked little smile that says she's about to zing me.

"Knock it off, Cooper. Don't treat me like I'm fragile. I'm perfectly all right. Okay?"

"Well. I just thought…"

"I know," she says. "I love you, but you worry too much. How are we going to control your blood pressure and blood sugar if you fret so?"

Jud Black and I got ourselves involved in exposing some brilliant but twisted criminals after they caused us to lose two of our closest friends. We uncovered their master plan—something one of them called Minerva's Net. They turned on us before we could manage to put them away, and I almost lost Ellen. I brought her home from the hospital only yesterday, and I'm still queasy about how close I came to being without the person that keeps my life glued together. But she's being straight with me. I see the sparkle is back in her eyes, and I know everything's going to be fine.

"Jud left rather suddenly, didn't he?" she asks. "Were there problems at home?"

"No. We talked to Pat O'Leary. Jud flew home to help him with something."

"How is Pat?"

"Oh, you know the Irishman. He's happiest when he's busy. Spends most of his time at the Slante."

"And Judy?"

"Okay, I suppose. She'd probably like to knock me on the head for waking her and Pat up before daylight yesterday."

"Sounds like a stunt Jud would be involved in. Want to tell me what that was all about?"

I'm trying to ease into what I have to ask her, not wanting to face it but knowing I must. And I can tell that, as usual, I'm not fooling her one bit. She knows something's eating at me. She pours another round of coffee, and I feel her eyes boring holes through the top of my head. By the time she returns to her seat I know the jig is up.

"Spill it, Dan. You act like you're trying to tiptoe through a mine field. What is it?"

"Well, the three of us are thinking seriously about starting a new partnership." I stop at that.

"You're treating me like a china doll, buster. I really am back to normal."

Ellen props one elbow on the breakfast table, opens her palm and curls her fingers. "Wanta try me two out of three or would you rather open up?"

"Okay. I'm just having a hard time getting the picture out of my head of you lying in the hospital. Never been so scared and totally confused in my life. I could never go it alone, baby."

She leans in and kisses me.

"There's something you want to ask me. Go ahead."

"We want to go into business tracking down and solving computer crimes. Jud, Pat and I. All of us have more spare time than we can handle, and it's not the type of thing a lot of people are into. But it's a service that's sorely needed."

She chews on that for awhile and starts to slowly shake her head.

"You all have new lives going, doing the things you've always dreamed about. Why mess with success?" she says.

I'm ready for that.

"Pat's bar will probably run itself now that he has it organized to suit him. Jud only programs for kicks, and I'm between writing projects. Thinking about doing a novel describing how we cracked Minerva's Net, but it's too soon. Want the whole caper to jell in my mind for awhile first."

I look away and stare out the morning room window. Think about what I've just laid on Ellen so soon after her last experience with my playing sleuth. Maybe it's not fair to put her through the self-generated danger that could develop. I'm about to rethink the whole proposition when she answers.

"The way you guys click, anything you do should be a huge success, Dan. Is this venture what I've heard you call 'white-hatting'? Helping expose hackers for companies with big computer systems?"

"It's a lot more complicated than that, I'm afraid. This is about putting criminals away like we did with the pair that was killing people using the Internet. But my last outing landed you in the hospital. I still have some doubts about this. Could be dangerous."

After that last statement I realize my heart is pounding at double time even though I'm holding my breath waiting for her comeback.

"Taking a risk never stopped you before."

Why did I ever doubt what Ellen's reaction would be?

"This is also personal, El. Our first case involves Kenny Grant. You remember him. He was a summer student hire at COB. He's now a PhD with a world class reputation."

"His dad was a senator or something, wasn't he?" she asks and clears away my cereal bowl.

"Ambassador. His father died two or three years ago. Kenny's mom called on Pat for help. Her son's in the hospital with something called dengue fever, seriously ill and fighting for his life. Appears that in some weird way, it could have to do with his job at an electronics firm out west."

"Then don't look back, Dan. I really am fine, and you'd never forgive yourself if you didn't help out one of your folks. You guys treated your employees like family. That's one reason you were so successful."

She's right, of course. We three guys carry on a lot, pick at each other, toss around good-natured insults, but I couldn't have asked for two better business partners than Pat and Jud. Everybody at COB knew the company was a team effort and they were each an important part of it. The big Irishman tends to keep Jud and me on the level when we spin off center, and he has a real knack with people. Most of the folks we hired would have followed O'Leary into the jaws of hell if he asked.

Ellen's positive reaction makes me feel much better about the hard decision I'm about to make, but it has to be one that doesn't jeopardize her recovery.

"Come with me to Virginia, Ellen. Visit with Danielle and Rick. Your daughter can keep an eye on you while I'm running around. I'd feel much more comfortable with you up there. This thing with Kenny Grant is something we can't turn our backs on."

Ellen hesitates, but I know she won't turn down the opportunity to see Danielle.

She doesn't need to know just yet that my partners and I may be in a race against the clock to stop a dengue epidemic.

CHAPTER 4

The sun rises with a fury and another relentlessly hot day begins in the desert. A man of small stature with rippling muscles stands alone in the dimly lit *dojang,* his private training room. As on every morning, he practices the *poomsae,* those ritual forms and movements that have become his religion. He moves with grace and speed, exhilaration rushing through his straining body.

Kim Yung lunges and thrusts, spins and rises high in the air. In his mind he pictures foes falling before his flawless kicks and punches. Standing shirtless he pauses to admire his body, the olive skin glistening from his efforts, his coal black hair shining. Age is revered in Kim's homeland, and he has yet to pass his thirty-fifth birthday. But he is determined not to be ignored, cast as a lowly operative to fulfill the purposes of the corrupt regime in Pyongyang. Soon the world will know and fear the name Kim Yung.

The walls of the *dojang* fail to repel the heat of another blistering day. The heat that seeps in is a good test of his endurance, he thinks, as he feels the beads of sweat on his skin. He scans the room. The floor is fully covered with a thick padded mat that extends a foot up each wall to meet mirrored surfaces that reflect Kim's powerful moves. The implements of his art, the swords, spears, and knives, are positioned at the ready. High on each wall sit the masks that denote the martial arts styles he has mastered. The lion and cobra assess Kim's every move, the tiger and hawk pass their judgment, the grinning Javan war mask demands perfection.

A padded human mannequin roughly the size of a full-grown man stands near one wall. The figure is slightly bent with age. It greatly resembles the North

Korean Communist Leader who he deeply detests. Kim Yung takes two lightning paces toward the dummy and flies through the air, whirls in a powerful spin kick. The stationary figure's grinning head yields to Kim's foot, spins away and strikes the mirrored wall with a sharp crunch.

"Know your fate, despised one. Kim Yung will have his day."

A slender young woman with the face of a child and the lithe body of a seductress glides silently to the center of the mat without prompting. Her raven black hair is swept atop her head, but Kim pictures it falling to its full length, sweeping to her waist. Almond eyes, smooth skin, long, velvety fingers. She fills the room with her beauty and her subtle fragrance. He knows that beneath her long robe her body is oiled and glistening and awaits his touch to bring it alive.

She hands him a towel, half closes her dark eyes and tilts her head downward. Kim swipes the towel across his chest. Dabs his upper torso and tosses the towel away. She offers refreshment.

"Leader, you are quicker than the wind. Your power would vanquish the worthiest opponent."

He admonishes her in a soft tone; places one finger to her delicate lips. "I have cautioned you before, Lotus. Do not address me in that manner. Only one may be called Leader. I am not that one...yet."

"Forgive me, master. How may I atone?"

She lifts her eyes, showing regret for the displeasure she has caused, begging to be absolved. He quaffs his thirst from the earthen jar, empties the vessel over his head and bends to set it at her feet. Then Kim rises and looks into her pleading eyes; softly strokes her cheek.

Her velvety hand is soft as he strokes it then slowly and deliberately curls her fingers back upon themselves. She kneels before Kim, suffering her pain in silence. The woman is defenseless, at his mercy. Lotus knows that with a single swift move Kim could break the joints if he chose. Instead he eases the pressure and bends to kiss her fingertips.

"I forgive you, Lotus. But you know that a disciplined mind must accompany a trained body. The *hwa rang do*, the flowering manhood of Korea, taught me this lesson. It is my duty as your master to administer to you the rigors of control and patience. You understand, of course."

The beautiful Lotus Blossom rises at his urging. She looks at Kim through wet eyes.

"Yes, wise one. I understand."

"Then call me master—*sah bum nim*—as I call you *chagun kkot*—my little flower."

"I obey, *sah bum nim.*"

He reaches out and parts her bright, embroidered robe with both hands and lifts it from her silken shoulders. She stands proudly before him, her body bare and lovely, glowing beneath his sweeping gaze.

"My perfect Lotus Blossom, you may prepare my bath. Then you have permission to seek my pardon and my favor in your own special ways." She bends to sweep the robe up from the floor.

"I will be honored, *sah bum nim.*"

Kim's eyes devour her beauty. One day he dreams he will ascend to power. Then all the worldly possessions of his homeland will be his to do with as he desires. A dozen maidens as beautiful as Lotus will attend to his every wish. The land of the morning calm will be Kim's realm. As his forebears, the *Silla*, reunited Korea in the seventh century, Kim Yung will achieve his destiny and bring together all of the Korean people. The Communist fools believe their threat of nuclear mastery frightens the world. They will come to know the true unbridled power of the new science that evolves even now in this desert oasis. They will be banished and Kim Yung will be the Leader.

Kim's musings are interrupted by the embarrassing intrusion of Lee Hwan at this unguarded moment. The indiscreet underling will pay for his poor timing.

Lotus clutches her robe to her body and shies from Lee Hwan's gaze. She turns slowly and walks away, her robe held closely, her bare back turned to the two men. Kim admires her youthful form and firmness. His fatigue fades away, and he feels the rise of passion.

"Beg pardon, master," Lee Hwan says. "I have disturbing news. The young American, Kendrick Grant, has disappeared. We can find him nowhere on the compound." Lee stands there, his tall frame awkwardly tense as he awaits Kim's response.

"How? Did we not provide him with every convenience, fulfill even his smallest wishes?"

Lee looks downward and nods his agreement.

Kim scolds him. "I have carefully planned this oasis in the desert. The living arrangements are lavish, the salaries more than generous for my splendidly talented scientists. They have the choicest foods, the loveliest women to fill their leisure time. I have purchased their loyalty at a high price, but this arrogant American chooses to elude our elaborate security and leave us. He will regret his decision."

"Yes, Kim Yung." Lee cowers.

"When did Grant disappear? The mere thought that this gross oversight could occur is incomprehensible to me."

"He was last seen two days ago. We understood he was sick in his quarters yesterday. A check this morning revealed his absence."

"What must I do to gather trustworthy people around me? You have compounded your grievous error. He could be anywhere by now with information that could destroy our mission. Why must I bear the burden of your incompetence along with the inattention and deceit of our Arab companions?"

Lee Hwan does not reply directly. Instead he says, "I have called together the inner circle. They await your instructions."

Lee's words do not distract Kim. He sees the young man for the incompetent fool he is, standing shrouded in abject fear, emanating an aura of weakness and fright. He looks at Kim with fear overwhelming his spirit. Lee Hwan is weak and must be dealt with, but for the moment Kim has more pressing matters. He will allow Lee another day to ponder his shortcomings and to choke on his own dread. Hwan is uncertain of the depth or duration of the anger he has caused Kim to feel. Perhaps when the sun next rises, the master will entertain himself with Lee's punishment here in the *dojang* as is fitting.

"Take this message to the inner circle, Lee. They are to find Kendrick Grant wherever he has fled and bring him to me unharmed. He is valuable to our work. I alone will decide how he must be disciplined for his disloyalty."

The sniveling young man acknowledges Kim's words. He bows and turns to leave. But Kim has reached a decision.

"Lee Hwan, I will await you here at sunrise. Come dressed for combat. Live well today."

Lee visibly slumps and his shoulders sag. Through the entire day and night, his tortured mind will dwell on the intended outcome of the invitation.

Now it is time for Kim to go to Lotus and let her dispense her skilled delights.

CHAPTER 5

Dan Cooper

Our trip to Virginia is smooth and uneventful. The usual hassle at Dulles Airport seems less crowded and trying, and Ellen appears to be doing well so far. After sensing that she's caught me a couple of times looking at her with more than a casual degree of concern during the flight, I try hard to make my feelings a bit less obvious. Can't help hovering over her, but I know she'll be upset if I keep on doting. Have to put the whole Minerva caper, and her two lost weeks in the hospital, behind us somehow.

"There's my sweetie," I call out. Our daughter comes running.

Danielle hugs her Mom with a clear sign of relief. I give Rick a hearty handshake. Then I sweep my daughter into my arms and kiss her. Marvel once again at how alike these two women are—the two most important women in my life. It's been several months since we've seen Rick. Danielle came to Florida and spent hours each day at the hospital with Ellen. Things were pretty hectic then. Now the girls are back to spending time together on the phone daily. After the events of the past month, I'm more than glad to take a while to kick back and visit before I launch into what could turn into another frantic adventure.

Once we're out of the crowd in the terminal, my daughter steers us to her car. Before we drive off to pick up our rental vehicle, she turns to look at her mom then at me.

"Mom says you're up here on business, Dad," Danielle tells me. "Hope we can have a little of your time." I look at Ellen, and she's prompting me.

"Sure. Have to meet with Jud and Pat, my old partners, tomorrow afternoon, in Frederick, Maryland. We can do some catching up tonight. Then you and Mom can bend each other's ears at will while I tend to business and pop in and out."

"Well, I was going to wait to tell you this, but it's too good to keep." She puts her hand in Rick's and her face lights up. "You're going to be grandparents."

From her expression, I'm sure my mouth must be wide open. This is news we've both wanted, and now that it's finally happened, I'm positively knocked out.

Ellen grabs Danielle and excitedly asks, "When, honey?'

"The doctor confirmed yesterday that I'm about five weeks along. Looks like early November."

Well, that about takes care of picking the topic of the evening. Ellen and Danielle will be planning the nursery, the shower, a million details.

I turn to Rick and ask, "How does the prospective pop feel about all this?"

"Somewhere between happy and numb. We want a baby so much."

"Gonna finally have a hunting partner. Good for you, son." I shake his hand again. Then Danielle laughs and speaks up.

"I told him that if this is a girl, I get to fill her mind full of ballet, gymnastics, and music for a few years before she's old enough to lift a rifle. Hunting nut that he is, he'll probably be looking for a cut-down, kiddy-size gun to get her tromping in the woods with him. He gave up on me as a hunter. I prefer a warm fireside."

"We couldn't be happier, boy or girl," I tell her. "You'll have to be ready for your Mom to spoil either one. Of course, we can put jeans and clodhoppers on a boy, but a girl is a whole different matter .She hasn't bought a frilly dress for years now, so she's overdue."

Ellen just grins, knowing the truth behind my words. Then she says, rather tentatively, "There's another possibility, you know."

"I'm thinking, *let's see, boy, girl. She's stumped me.* Give her a blank stare and she laughs.

"Twins. Both families have twins in their past." She looks at our daughter and Danielle grins.

"Go for it, girl," I encourage.

I lean in close and whisper to Ellen, "You'll make a mighty sexy grandma."

* * * *

The guys are waiting the next day when I get to Pat's Irish bar in Maryland. The Slante is already buzzing with a late lunch crowd and a lineup of tipplers on the bar stools. The big Irishman reaches across the shamrock lined bar and grasps my hand so hard I wonder if he's left all my fingers intact. Jud Black is perched on a stool nursing a Murphy's Ale. He smiles that enigmatic grin of his that makes you wonder what's going on behind those puckish eyes. It's only been a few days since we were fighting the bad guys together, but when I thrust out my hand he says, "Don't hand me that," and clasps me in a bear hug.

A tall blonde, a strikingly attractive woman, watches the greetings and can't stifle a smile. I remember her from much earlier. She's not the sort of woman any red-blooded man could forget. She steps down from her bar stool and offers her hand.

"Celia, I was so sorry to hear about Kenny's illness. How's he doing?"

"Slowly improving, Dan," is her answer. "Though it could be days or weeks before we know what lasting effects this has on him."

Pat pulls the bar towel from his shoulder and tosses it to an employee.

"You're the man, Sean. I'll be over there in the corner with my friends."

"What can I pour for you, Dan?" Sean inquires.

"How about a draft—something domestic." I bite down on a big, salty pretzel.

Jud hears me say 'domestic' and makes a gagging sound as Pat crooks a finger for us all to follow him. He moves to a table in a back corner and we take our places.

Pat starts the conversation. He fills Jud and me in on what he knows so far.

I look into Celia's anxious eyes and tell her, "You know we're going to get to the bottom of whatever, or whoever, caused this."

She grins. "According to Pat, it has something to do with applying a certain part of the anatomy to a wall, I believe. Right, Pat?"

He blushes and nods.

"And it's who, Dan," she states without reservation. "Somebody did this on purpose or was negligent enough to let it happen. Either way, I want them nailed."

"You've got it, lady. What else do we know, guys?"

Pat jumps in. "Not much. Kenny went out west, flew to LA to take a new job. Came home within a month suffering from a rare disease he should never have gotten here in the good old US of A. What's more, it appears to be a man-made variety of dengue fever. That's pretty scary."

I look at Celia and she agrees. "We may be lucky with Kenny, but it doesn't bode well for the future if somebody has lab-developed a strong and deliverable strain of dengue. While I work on getting Kenny well, the long term work is shutting off the possibility of a full-fledged intentional dengue epidemic. That's where you fellows come in."

"Why are you so certain that's the plan?" Jud wants to know.

"The mere fact that the altered dengue virus exists is reason enough to fear the worst. I can't find any evidence that controlled lab research on dengue currently exists in this country. There is no reason anyone would be messing around with something this dangerous unsupervised if they didn't have ulterior motives. If they have an aggressive timetable, we could be up to our ears in rushing to root them out before they have the chance to strike."

"Well, I for one am ready to go to work, I announce. "Haven't dealt with a life-threatening challenge for—what, Jud?—at least a couple of days now?"

Jud lifts his bottle in a sort of salute and takes a long draw. He still bears the scars of our last outing. Long scratch marks course down his cheek. He's removed the temporary bandage and the marks look red and angry. That gets Celia Grant's attention.

"May I?" she asks, and reaches out to gently touch his damaged cheek. "How'd you get so banged up, Jud?" she inquires.

"Long story. Let's just say a tall blonde in a rage left her marks on me."

Celia rolls that around for a few seconds, touches her own gold locks and smiles a bit nervously. Then she pulls out a small pad and scribbles something. Tears off the top sheet and hands it to him.

"Here. Try this for the next seven days. Should help it heal faster."

"Thanks, doc."

"Celia to you."

Am I only imagining it or is there a new twinkle in Jud's eye. I know he's an incurable romantic, but this lady's at least a dozen years his senior.

We piece together the few facts available to us and ask Celia to see if she can remember anything else that may help. She shakes her head. Then she blurts out, "Wait. There is something he said. He was holding his bicep and groaning with the pain when I heard him mumble the same word two or three times. It sounded like 'Nan.' Didn't ring a bell to me. He's never mentioned a girl by that name."

"Hmmm. Nan. Could be a lead," I tell her.

* * * *

Celia Grant leaves the bar after Pat promises her we'll be in touch as soon as we've put together our plan. She's on her way back to the hospital and Kenny.

Pat says, "Search your memory banks for anything at all that could help us, Celia."

Jud, Pat and I bring each other up to date. Our story about our caper in Florida blows Pat away. Almost sounds like fun now that it's over, but we sure weren't laughing then. Too many close calls.

"Sounds like you could have used a big, angry leprechaun to sit on them," he laughs.

"Well, we've got one now," I assure him. "I can't wait to dive into this next case."

There seems to be a slow down in our conversation, some reason we're not concentrating on our plan of attack. Pat keeps looking at his watch as though he's stalling for a reason.

I look up to see another old friend from my Alltech days walking toward us.

"Jim Barnett! Where have you been, pal. Seems like ages." Jim is, without a doubt, the most knowledgeable computer security expert I've ever known.

Jim's a couple inches shorter than I am and goes about 170. He has slightly reddish hair and a bright smile.

He's a few years younger than Pat. Came to Alltech after a long career with the government and has always been a constant and trusted friend.

Pat says, "I invited him here to sit in on our talks about forming the new company, guys. Hope that's okay."

Jud and I both nod our approval.

CHAPTER 6

Pat O'Leary

It's like starting out fresh. I haven't felt this way since we took on the world with our software startup. Never thought I'd be this excited about going back to work!

Jim's already scanned the listings and located an office space here in Leesburg. It has five offices, a conference room and a reception area. Sort of an in-between spot not too far from any of our homes—except for Dan, of course. Needs some furnishing and a girl Friday, both of which we can leave up to Barnett if the guys buy my proposal.

"So how's Gramps today?" I ask Dan when he arrives.

"Hey, O'Leary," he says. "You may have a few pounds on me, but don't push your luck. I can still run circles around some younger guys I know." Hmmm, may have found a new way to get his goat.

Jim Barnett is already here. He leads us into the conference room. Dan scans the room and says, "Not bad, Jim. Not bad at all."

Jud shows up 'fashionably late' as usual.

"Now that you're gonna be a working slug for a change," I tell him, "guess we'll have to set your watch ahead, Black." His response is about what I would expect.

"Did an all-nighter programming binge, Pat. Crashed for a couple hours beauty rest so I could keep my youthful blush, old man."

I sneer at him. "Smart ass." He just laughs.

As I might expect, Jud is dressed in his customary black tee shirt and black jeans with those ever present boots. "Here's Johnny Cash," I pop at him. "Thinks black is his trademark as well as his name."

"Actually, my petite friend, I prefer grey as one of my songs says."

He's one deep dude. Probably one of the smartest guys I've ever run across. A computer whiz but not like any of the nerds that may come to mind. He can hold his own on any topic you pick. But Jud's real love is music. Has his own independent label, writes and performs. I catch his shows whenever I can. In fact, he's booked at the Slante for a gig in a few weeks. Dan and Ellen are big fans. They've been known to show up from Florida just to watch him perform. Hell of a singer and guitarist, this wiseacre.

"Here's the pitch," I start. "We need a home base, an HQ where clients can reach us. Jim did a good job of finding this place quickly. What do you think of it?"

Dan says, "It's about the right size and out of the confusion we'd have if we went closer into the city."

"Needs a pair of long legs out front," Jud answers in typical fashion.

Jim just looks at Jud and shakes his head.

"I want to propose something at the outset," I tell them. "Then we can get down to the business of tracking down Kenny's tormenters."

Jud answers, "You have the floor."

"Okay. We've all known Jim for a lot of years. I think we're agreed he's about as slick a computer security guy as we could find to join our firm. He's a little younger than you and me, Dan, and the kind of steady hand we can use to make a go of this venture as a business. I say we make him a full partner and let him be the anchor here at the office."

Jud opens his mouth to make some off-the-wall comment, probably about the word 'anchor.' I point a finger and cut him off.

"Sounds like the perfect arrangement to me if you agree," Dan replies.

Jim smiles. "Fine with me. Guess that would officially make me one of the crazies," he concludes.

Jud jumps in at this point. "Peachy! Even got a name. COBB Eye. With two B's. For Cooper, O'Leary, Black, and Barnett."

"So we're agreed?" I ask, and I get head nods all around.

Fantastic, I think. If we expect to get serious about this business, Barnett's skills are essential to our success. What he knows about computer security is downright scary, and he already knows our mode of operation. Jim spent a few months moonlighting at COB when we were just getting up a head of steam. When I used the term anchor, I meant it in the best sense of the word. He's perfect to provide the at home foundation for our activities while some of us traipse around getting into trouble.

"Then it's a done deal. Jim, you do what you feel is right about equipping the office and getting a pair of 'long legs', as Jud suggested. Might want to see she's quick witted, too, with this group to contend with. You can handle whatever's needed with the state to incorporate us and get county licenses and such."

Dan jumps in. "Just don't let Jud design the logo for the door. He'd probably put up a bloodshot eye."

That draws a middle finger salute from Jud.

"Let me make a suggestion for the spare room in back," Dan chimes in. "If we hope to be serious computer sleuths, we'll need our own high tech setup at the home office. Let's put together a computer room second to none. Equip it with the latest technology and all the special tools Black and Barnett need to weave their magic. We could call it Jud and Jim's sand box."

Jud starts to gesture, but Dan cuts him off. "You only get to salute me once a day, Black."

I tell them, "We did get a coffee pot as part of the deal. Everybody better have a cup. This could be a long session." The coffee is freshly brewed, hot and smells inviting. I pour and pass the pot around.

Dan hops to his feet and grabs a marker. Goes to the whiteboard and starts writing.

"Let's start with what we know." He's labeled three columns on the board 'Kenny', 'dengue', and 'source.' He taps the board and says, "Let's write down all we can remember about Kenny Grant, his habits, his quirks, his likes and hang-ups. Then we can set about gathering up all we can find on dengue fever. You know, where it occurs, how it can be transmitted, what it could mean to have a lab strain developed as far as its distribution. The matter of source—that is, exactly where he became infected—then becomes the long pole in the tent. We'll have to find out where Kenny's been for the past month and check out all the locations first hand."

Jud drains his coffee cup and pours a second. He lights a smoke and leans back. That grin tells me he's already in the zone.

"Think we let the engineer out of the cage again, folks!" he barks. "Let's brainstorm this sucker and see where it takes us."

For the next three hours we kick around every possible angle we can manufacture that may get us untracked toward solving the mystery of Kenny's illness. All of us remember facts about Kenny Grant that could be clues to his behavior in his new environment, wherever that may have been. We agree Celia Grant can probably help steer us if she can remember any other bits of information Kenny may have conveyed to her in their phone conversations. Jud quickly volunteers to meet with her. The discussion keeps coming back to where to physically start looking for leads. Until we learn exactly where Kenny's been working, we're stuck on block one as far as the source is concerned.

"Jud," Pat suggests, "in your discussions with Celia, press her for any indication of where his telephone calls to her originated. You know, phone records, references he may have made that could be clues to his whereabouts."

Jim looks at his watch and interrupts the discussion. "Hate to be the drag here, fellows, but it's past my lunchtime."

Dan adds, "Yeah. Better get some food in Jim and me before we turn green."

I realize we've been at it longer than I thought. Both Dan and Jim are diabetic. Dan's on pills and Jim is insulin dependent. They both need to observe a pretty strict regimen about meal times.

"We've made about all the progress we're going to without more information, anyway," I tell them. "Let's break and eat then we'll come back and plot our next moves. Any dining suggestions, Jim?"

"There's a place around the corner called The Kitchen. Nothing fancy but the food's good."

I smile. "They might as well get used to seeing this gnarly mob. Let's break away and try to wrap this up after lunch. Once Jud talks to Celia we can hit it again."

Dan offers, "I'll spend some time digging out whatever I can find on dengue and hemorrhagic fever. "I know we're operating in the blind here, but it can't hurt to gather more data on this virus. Besides, you've got me juiced now. I want to dive in head first."

When Jim and I cast skeptical looks, Jud comes to Dan's defense.

"Hey, Dan's learning. With the tricks I've taught him, he relates to a computer fairly well. We have plenty of research work to parcel out to all of us, partners."

* * * *

Forty five minutes later we're back at the office, stuffed and ready to continue with our skull session.

"Not too shoddy for little old Leesburg," I remark. "Have to remember Tuesday is pork chop day. And they serve Jenny's Surprise every day."

Dan smirks. "Oh, great. So what's that?"

"Don't know," I laugh. "It's a surprise."

"Looks like every day is pie day for Dan," Jud says. "Did you see the way he attacked that pie display? Thought he was going to crawl inside and eat his way out."

"Cut me some slack, Jud. I have to cheat now and then," Dan retorts.

Jud comes back with, "I heard you tell the waitress not to cut that chocolate pie into eight pieces because you could only eat one."

"Give me credit. I went light. Had soup and salad so I could sample dessert."

I can't let that pass. "But coconut *and* chocolate cream? Your blood sugar must be about 600 now. Lucky Ellen wasn't with us. She'd put a lump on your head."

Dan grins sheepishly. "She's little but she's strong."

We used to constantly kid Dan about having to be his conscience and keep him away from desserts. His answer was always something like '*every body deserves a treat now and then, even mine.*'

"What say we get back to business," I suggest. "Where were we?"

Dan replies, "Jud was to contact Celia and I'm assigned to do some research on dengue."

I add, "Jim can handle setting up the office, and he and I will get started on hiring somebody to do the office work."

Jud puts on his pouty face and I chide him. "Hell, you can't have *all* the good assignments, you horny toad. Just concentrate on Celia and report back."

That brings a lecherous grin from Jud.

I quickly amend my statement. "Or maybe we ought to rethink this. Have old straight arrow Dan do the talking to her."

"No," Jud says. "It's my solemn duty. I'll sacrifice and spend an evening with the grieving mother. She needs an understanding ear. In fact, I already left her a message when we went to lunch."

Jud gets up to visit the coffee pot and his cell phone rings. He answers with a very business-like "Jud Black here." Dan and I look at each other and I guess what Dan must be thinking. Normally, Jud's stock greeting would be a jaunty, 'Naked', or, more precisely, in his vernacular, 'Nekkid.'

Then I understand why. He's saying, "Yes, Mrs. Grant…Celia. How's Kenny?" He listens for a long time then answers. "Great. We need to talk. You name the time and place."

A short pause, then, "We've recapped all we know, but we really need more information. Maybe you and I can explore some possibilities. We'll sort of free wheel and see what you can remember."

Jud looks over at us and gives a high sign while he listens. Then he signs off with, "Fine. I'll be there," and flips his phone closed. The three of us wait for him to speak, but he walks to the coffee pot, pours a cup and returns to his seat without a word.

"So?" I ask and Dan and Jim lean forward to listen. A sly little smirk from Jud. He knows we're waiting and prolongs the suspense, slowly stirring his coffee.

"All right, chum, we all know there's nothing in that coffee. Quit baiting us and spit out what Celia said." I'm as impatient as the others to hear what Kenny's mother has told him.

"She says Kenny's looking better. Came around long enough to tell her the pain behind his eyes had disappeared."

"And?" I urge.

"I'm meeting her at her house this evening."

"That's it?"

"Well, Kenny dropped a couple of new bits of info. He went off to sleep shortly after his fever came down a bit, but first he managed to get out the words 'New Day' and 'nano.'"

Dan comes up out of his chair. "That could be the lead we need. New Day could be anything, maybe even the name of the company where he was working."

Jim volunteers, "I'll get on it and run down anything that's even close to New Day. If I can find an electronics company called New Day near LA, we may have the break we're looking for."

I'm a bit puzzled. "Nano," I repeat. "Maybe Kenny wasn't babbling about a girl named Nan after all. But what the hell does nano mean?"

Jud breaks out in a big smile. "How about nanotechnology? It's the science of the extremely small. A hot topic in the electronics world."

Except for a collective exhale all around the table, the room is suddenly very quiet.

CHAPTER 7

Jim Barnett

Good session we had today. It's great to be working with Pat, Jud, and Dan. COBB Eye, Huh? This could be a lot of fun—maybe dangerous, from the sound of the fix Kenny Grant is in. I'm looking forward to seeing Kenny again. We shared some good times and challenges when I worked with Kenny that summer at COB.

Well, time for me to hole up here in my den and chase down the one decent lead we have so far. I'll key in the words New Day—there. What will pop up? New Day Athletics—no. New Day Awareness? Surely not that one. New Day Church. Not hardly.

Bingo! This item says New Day Electronics.

Looks like they have offices in Los Angeles, California and Tampa, Florida. Appears to be a leading edge firm dabbling in some of the emerging technologies. Fits the mold so far. I'll dig out what I can then call Pat. Could be the best news we've had so far.

I grab the phone. "Pat. It's Jim. Did some data mining and came up with a few interesting tidbits about a company called New Day Electronics."

"New Day? Right on," Pat says.

"Yeah, that's right. Its home offices are in Los Angeles and they have a branch in Tampa, smack in the middle of Dan's home turf."

"What kind of work are they into?" he asks.

"Seems they operate research facilities in both places and do production as well. Produce integrated circuit boards for custom clients at the Tampa plant. Do process software and optics products out of the Los Angeles location."

"Maybe Celia Grant can tell Jud more about what Kenny's been working on and we can make a connection," Pat poses. "Then I think some of us need to check out both New Day facilities up close. We could contact them posing as potential clients and work our way in for first hand looks at their operations."

That sounds logical to me. I jot down 'LA and Tampa visits—pose as customers.'

"Sounds like a plan to me, Pat. I'll continue looking for more goodies on this outfit. Once I get into their system, we may learn all sorts of interesting facts about them. I'll call Jud to drop by my place so we can kick this around."

"Well, you know all the back doors, my friend. Keep plugging away. I'll ask Jud and Dan to get back with us tomorrow morning in Leesburg to add up what we've all uncovered by then."

"Say, Pat, do you know where Jud may be? I'd like to get his opinion on what I'm finding."

"He's going over to see Celia tonight. Keep working and I'll try to reach him. I'll suggest he drop by your place on the way."

"Thanks. I could really use his help."

Okay, time to get back to snooping. Now that Pat's on board I can dig deeper. New Day will never know I've had access to their system. Soon I'll know more about them than they know themselves. There's the back door. Now to burrow in.

Looks like this is a company that's been around for awhile. It was started by a guy named Jason Grimes in 1989. An electronics whiz with a couple of degrees and a lot of acquired money. Apparently got in on the ground floor of integrated circuit manufacturing and made his fortune. Appears he funneled some of his money into the real edge technologies including nanoelectronics, the science of exploring and rearranging matter at the scale of nanometers, a billionth of a meter.

All sorts of speculations are out there about what nano may do for, or to, society in the next few years. So far, though, the real breakthroughs people have expected haven't yet come about. I've read that there are experts who believe if we could master building things beginning at the molecular level, the implications for totally new materials are mind-boggling. Medical research could be advanced tremendously with new substances and radical new techniques for treatment.

Electronics in particular may be pushed to the extreme with super small components and computers with virtually unlimited capability.

There have also been a lot of doomsday predictions made about nanotech. Some say that in the hands of the wrong people, nano could rise to the level of one of the most potentially powerful forces known. Wow! I need somebody to bounce this off of. This has way too many possibilities for me to deal with alone. Maybe Jud's up to date on what's going on recently with nano. First I need to see what I can learn about New Day's interest in the science.

Seems like I've been at this for hours. Don't want to miss any tidbit of info that might put us on track chasing down the source of Grant's problem. Pat's right. If New Day was Kenny's employer, we need to get on the inside somehow and see for ourselves what's going on there.

I get a surprise interruption.

"Hey, Jim. Susie said you were hibernating back here. What's the story on this New Day outfit? Pat called."

Jud's found me in my den. He's already tapped my supply of beer and hands me a cool one.

"I needed a break," I tell him. Take the brew and settle back. I fill him in on the highlights of my back door search of New Day's system. Then I turn back to the keyboard.

"Digging out some helpful data, Jud. Take a look at my notes and downloads while I chase this financial report and give it a look. There's a rundown on the founder, a couple of his papers on nano, and some strong indications that the company is growing like gangbusters."

I continue with my sneak peek at the outfit's best kept secrets. Good thing I'm not a bona fide computer cracker. I could put New Day through some nervous fits with what I've seen so far. Jud's face tells me he's latched onto something in my notes that has an impact. Don't often see him frown, but his expression is pretty sour.

"Damn," Jud says, "this Grimes guy may have tapped some solid leads toward a breakthrough in nanotech! There are dozens of high tech companies out there making attempts to unlock nano's secrets, but his approach is as believable as any I've seen."

"Well, if I can believe what I'm reading here, Jason Grimes may not be the driving force behind New Day any longer, Jud. It looks to me like he may have been put out to pasture. There are new interests running the show, though I've gotta say somebody's been careful to cover up just who *they* may be."

Jud rubs his head and frowns even deeper. "Not good, pal. Grimes comes off as a good guy, maybe even a genuine patriot. But after he started chasing the nanotech game, there are indications that he became very close hold about all of his operations. Believe me, I've learned enough about this new technology that it scares me. People are mucking around with trying to redesign the universe one molecule at a time. Done in secret without legal or moral constraints, it could become a runaway science."

"Put that in terms I can grasp, Black."

"Let's assume for a minute that New Day is in the lead in perfecting nanotech. That could mean radically new materials constructed from the basic cell up. They could also be on the way to producing spore sized pollutants or even deadly biological agents that would be far more threatening and less detectable than nuclear power."

"Are you buying into these claims, Jud? That's pretty heavy."

"Hey, who knows what's about to come out of the next lab experiment. Most of the real scientific breakthroughs were preceded by years of frustration then a spark. If New Day is in the hands of people with less than honorable motives, we could all be in a peck of trouble."

"Wait a minute, Jud. You're painting a picture I don't like."

"We won't know, Jim, until we figure out what kind of freaks these guys may be. Could be we're dealing with people bent on using nano for the wrong reasons."

"You mean like terrorists?"

"You said it, Jim, not me."

CHAPTER 8

The sun rises like a great red lantern perched over the endless desert sky. The night winds have yet to calm, and heat rises in waves from the desert floor. Kim Yung sits outside and turns his face to the west in the direction of his beloved homeland, intent on the concentration that will precede the morning ritual *poomsae.* The winds punish his bare skin with the stinging, driven sand. He endures the needles of pain on his back, exults in the disciplines of patience and self-denial and lets his mind cross the sea.

Kim's journey in this land of fast living and loose morals has a profound purpose. Once his mission here is fulfilled, it will bring him home to the ultimate power he will achieve as Leader of the Korean people. The world will soon understand that Kim Yung holds their fate in his hands. Let the stinging sand pelt him, the sun sear his skin. It cannot harm Kim Yung, for he is invincible.

"Master, your *dojang* awaits you. Come in now, please."

The delicate Lotus beckons to him. She is a vision of loveliness with the light from inside framing her slender body beneath her garments. His nostrils sense the essence of her and flare with excitement.

"Precious Lotus Blossom, come and look at the fierce beauty of the desert. Feel the song of its power. When my work here is complete, we will return to our beloved homeland and enjoy the beauty of many dawns."

She sits by his side and they share a long moment of meditation as the sun lifts higher in the sky. Kim feels the destiny that beckons to him over that horizon. The peaceful shield of confidence sings through his body.

Lotus takes his hand and leads him through the private entry into the mountain fortress. She has laid out Kim's combat clothing, the red *dobok* emblazoned with the black mask of a medieval Javan warrior. It is Kim Yung's acknowledgement of the power in the *pentjak silat* martial arts he learned in Indonesia. What he has taken from that and the other disciplines—Korea's own *hwa rang do,* the Chinese *shaolin* and *kung fu*, the *karate* and *ninjitsu* of his own land's Japanese invaders, the many other disciplines of Korea, have conditioned his mind and body and made him a finely tuned warrior. Kim stands motionless, his mind in another place, while Lotus garbs him for what is soon to begin. Then she disappears and he commences to work through the intricate *poomsae* forms, preparing his body to become a fighting machine.

"Now witness the power of my art, Lotus. Stay and behold how swiftly retribution comes to those who fail in their mission."

Lotus retreats to a corner of the room to become a silent audience to the ritual. Kim performs the *poomsae* as she lingers in a quiet corner of the *dojang*. She will remain constantly near as he wishes, attentive to his needs and responsive to his wishes as always.

Lee Hwan dutifully reports as ordered, knowing well that his fate is in Kim's hands. He wears the white uniform assigned to the adversary for this day, the white of innocent prey that Kim seeks to stalk and conquer.

First, Lee must have one chance to atone.

"What of the American Kendrick Grant?" Kim asks. "You have found him and returned him to face my justice?"

Lee Hwan will not look directly into Kim Yung's eyes. That tells Kim that his failure persists.

"We have searched everywhere, Kim Yung, every corner of the citadel. Somehow he has fled the perimeter. He either lies parched in the desert or has escaped our search parties."

"Either way it is a serious blow to our important work here. This is an unforgivable breach of our carefully drawn security system."

Kim's words are calculated to raise Lee's level of concern for the match to follow. Lee Hwan hesitates, advances to the center of the mat slowly, unsure of his next move.

They address each other on the *dojang* mat, bow in the time-honored *kyung ryet* tradition of respect for one's opponent. Then Kim begins to circle the younger man slowly, deliberately keeping a distance and watching his growing panic. Lee begins to perceive the real purpose of Kim's invitation.

Kim Yung moves quicker than the eye can follow, spin kicks Lee's heaving chest and sends him backward into a heap. Lee lies stunned, as though he is considering whether to continue. But he must see the fire of anger in Kim's eyes and knows the choice is not his to make. He will be pressed until he responds. Lee rises from the mat, makes his stand, and the fright grows in his body.

Lee Hwan is not without skills, a fact that makes the promise of combat even more satisfying. He seeks to free his body of the force of Kim's first blow and takes a defensive position. There is determination, perhaps anger, in his eyes and Kim relishes the challenge.

Once again he attacks and sends Lee to the mat. The master's power is too much for him.

As Lee Hwan attempts once again to rise, Kim casts a momentary glance in the direction of Lotus. There is anticipation in her eyes. She knows, as Lee must surely suspect by now, that this will be no routine training session. Accordingly, Kim's honor dictates that he reveal the purpose of their meeting. They pause for refreshment and Kim announces his intent.

"Lee Hwan, my staff, under your supervision, has committed a lapse in attention for which someone must answer directly to me. If one person leaves the fold and breathes a hint of our mission, everything we have accomplished could be shattered. The one I have chosen to feel my wrath is—YOU, Lee Hwan. Prepare for full combat, young fool. Defend as if your life depends upon it—for it does!"

They return to center mat. Once more Kim launches his offensive. Lee Hwan, to his credit, counters and eludes the full force of the blows. But he appears unsure of his moves, wary of countering. The advantage is Kim's.

"Commendable, my friend. You have learned well the art of defense. But can you press an attack?"

Kim opens his arms and drops them to his sides, awaiting Lee's charge. When it comes, he evades, narrowly avoiding the impact of the younger man's slicing hand.

They spar, looking for openings, press the small opportunities they each offer to their adversary. Lee is youthful and quick, his eyes are keen and his youth is tempered with his diligent work at honing his own martial skills. A less than keen challenge for Kim's expertise, he thinks, but a welcome target for his controlled anger. Kim purposely exposes himself to Lee's charges to test his own defense. Lee is a practitioner of one of the lesser styles. He will be no match for Kim's moves.

At best his efforts inflict minor injury and serve to bring Kim to a deeper state of concentration. Gradually Kim Yung takes away his initiative, becomes the aggressor in a battle of increasing contact. Kim's blows produce the stinging slap of hand against flesh and Lee's resolve weakens. Kim executes a spinning knife chop behind Lee's neck and sweeps him to the mat.

For a fleeting moment Kim glances again in the direction of the silent Lotus. A strange look is in her eyes, not a fascination at his splendid moves, not even a thirst for the blood that will come soon enough. No, Kim sees a hint of discomfort, perhaps of the fear of what she knows the ultimate outcome must be. Why is she wavering in her blind loyalty to Kim's desires? Must he exact yet another measure of obedience from her to remind her he is master of this place and not to be doubted?

Lee Hwan senses an opening. He springs upright and strikes quickly. He delivers a chop to Kim's mouth then sends him reeling backward with a kick to his middle. Kim struggles for his wind; places the back of his hand to a split lip. The taste of his own blood enrages Kim. He rolls away from Lee's follow-up and springs to his feet, the sudden pain in his ribs both annoying and embarrassing Kim for having been distracted.

"You warned me to defend well, and now you have felt the power of my advance. Have I proven worthy of your pardon?" Lee stands confident of his ability and asking for a truce.

Kim answers his plea with a move Lee surely has never encountered, a lightning maneuver Kim learned studying under a wise Indonesian master of *silat.*

Hwan's face explodes in a bloody spray that covers his white uniform. He registers abject fear. The time has come to end his worthless existence and exact retribution for his shortcomings.

"There is your answer, Lee Hwan. No pardon, no truce. You belong to the tiger, and he is ready for the kill. It is the moment for *pil sung*, my ultimate victory."

His defenses are broken. As Kim rains blow after blow on his body, his eyes glaze over and Lee ceases to resist. Kim smiles broadly, the exquisite pleasure of delivering punishment heightened by the sound of his bones breaking under his force, the sight of Lee drooling life's fluids in a last gasp of humanity.

"You are finished," Kim announces and sends him to his knees with a powerful spin kick. Lee kneels and looks up, pleads through dim eyes, but Kim is unmoved. He executes a flying *garotte,* pins Lee's neck between his knees and thrusts toward the floor. Yung twists until he hears the snap of bone. Lee Hwan drops face down, motionless on the mat.

The girl emits an audible whimper. When Kim rises from the mat, Lotus remains motionless, withdrawn, as if she wishes to melt into the wall at her back.

Her face is expressionless, but she must know Kim has seen her uncertainty. One triumph has been earned, but a second is due the victor.

Kim Yung strides to where Lotus cowers and issues a sign of his displeasure with a sharp open-handed blow to the side of her head. She slumps prone and he pounces on her, ripping at her garments with a growing frenzy born both of disappointment in her and the desire she incites.

There, on the *dojang* mat now stained with Lee Hwan's blood, Kim takes Lotus Blossom.

CHAPTER 9

Jud Black

The guys probably wouldn't believe it, but old Jud cleans up pretty decent. No black garb or boots for me tonight. This is a class lady I'm going to see. Got my best duds on, the ones I use when I'm playing music exec or out on an infrequent quality date. The slacks and loafers, the cashmere blazer I can adapt to. Even thought about wearing a tie, but I decided that was over the edge. Opted for a silk shirt and ditched the tie idea. Don't know why it seems so important to make a good impression on Celia, but I've gotta go with my instincts.

"Hi, Jud." Celia Grant stands in the doorway looking every inch a woman. I like the way her blue silk blouse and navy slacks bring out the highlights in her hair and make it seem like burnished gold.

I caution, *Hold on, Jud, you're here on business.*

"Anything new on Kenny?" I ask her.

"He was resting when I left the hospital a while ago. I'll run by there as soon as we talk."

She's working me over with her eyes and clearly trying to avoid staring. Maybe this new Jud is a bit of a shock to her. I see the hint of an approving smile lift the corners of her lips. Makes me happy I went to the trouble to spruce up my act. Finally, she gives in and admits her surprise.

"I had to look twice to make sure it was you, Jud. Quite a turnaround. Impressive."

I'm not accustomed to such compliments—certainly not from a beautiful woman like Celia Grant. The best answer I can produce is a hesitant "Ummm hmm."

"Drink?" she asks.

"Maybe a brew."

She crooks a finger and leads me toward the den. Walks to a fridge behind the bar and shows me a tantalizing selection of imported suds. It's like a beer drinker's treasure trove.

"The brown ale will be fine," I answer and nearly drool.

Damn, her taste in brews almost rivals her classy looks. Nah!

She pours herself a glass of wine and steers me to a seat on the couch.

We talk about unimportant things, loosen up for awhile before we launch into talk about Kenny and why I'm really here. I get the impression she's still not quite sure about me, wants to work on her comfort level around me. Yeah, I'm probably a huge departure from the folks that move in her circles. After awhile I sense she's trying to move the conversation to more serious matters.

"Kenny used to remark to me that you were quite an inspiration to him when he was getting started. Said you had an unusual mind, whatever that meant. His favorite quote from Jud Black is 'Can't be done ain't in my phrase book.' He admires that attitude."

"Well, some people—like me, for instance—aren't smart enough to recognize the difference between difficult and impossible. A little brain power and a lot of perseverance can sometimes work magic."

"So you three are giving up retirement and going into this computer crimes business?"

"We're committed. It's a matter of thriving on a challenge. All three of us are getting itchy living the good life. We've added a fourth partner this time. Jim Barnett. He also knows and admires Kenny. They worked on some projects one summer while Jim was moonlighting with COB."

"But you're set for life, and this could be risky," Celia cautions.

"A little risk is the real spice of life. I like life as spicy as possible."

Don't know why but Celia looks down at her sky blue silk blouse standing open at the throat and works to make it a little less revealing.

"Can you bring me up to speed on your plans, Jud? How do I help you track down the low lifes that hurt my Kenny? I'm determined to nail these people and quickly. They could present a threat you can't even imagine."

"Maybe I appreciate the threat more than you think. Spent a little time reading about biological agents and what havoc they can wreak."

She straightens up and stares at me. "What got you interested in a gruesome subject like that?"

"Oh, I pride myself on knowing a bit about a lot of things, Doctor Grant."

She's finished her brew and steps back over to the cooler for another. Celia signals to me. I shake my head. I'm still working on my first brewsky.

"We're going to get along better if you drop the doctor title," she says and circles around from behind the bar. "I told you my name is Celia."

"Okay. To answer your question, I picked up a book that caught my interest a couple months ago. Read up on the history of chemical and biological warfare, all about the human experiments the Japanese Unit 731 carried out in the 1930's and 40's. Found out the old Soviet Union was playing around with agents like anthrax and plague for decades. Scares me witless what some terrorist element could do to the civilized world with toxins, bacteria and viruses."

"Then you know I'm not exaggerating when I say whoever spread the dengue virus to Kenny has to be found and squelched before they loose an epidemic on us that could bring the country to its knees. If this virus could be spread in its hemorrhagic fever state, the whole US population could be at risk."

"Lady, none of us will rest until we coop these guys up in a slammer. Jim's been doing some selective surfing, and he's come up with what we think could be a solid lead to where Kenny contracted dengue."

Celia sets down her glass, takes a seat next to me on the sofa, and digs in a purse for her cigarettes. I light her up and pull out my own smokes. She fishes an ashtray from an end table drawer. I had assumed, with her being a doctor and not seeing any ashtrays sitting out, that I'd have to hold off smoking in her house. Seems she's a surprise a minute. Now I can relax with a smoke and think about our problem.

"Do you have any idea where Kenny went to work? What he was doing at his new workplace?" I ask.

She perks up. "Why? Do you have a lead?"

"Not yet. It'll be baby steps at first until we find an opening and get a first hand view of an outfit named New Day Electronics."

"That's what he meant when he mumbled New Day? That's a company name?"

"We're not sure yet. But it's all we have at the moment. A company by that name has a plant in Los Angeles as well as one down in Tampa. We'll check out both of them and try to find a connection between Kenny and New Day."

"There is a second case of dengue in California," she says. "The victim died this morning."

"Any connection to Kenny?" I ask her.

"The patient's name was Richard Fetter. He walked into a hospital and went to the hemorrhagic state within two days. Kenny's speech was rambling by the time I found him at the airport, but I'd swear he spoke that name."

"Which makes it murder if they were both intentionally exposed."

She nods. "We have to hurry, Jud. What can I do to speed things up?"

"Just stay put, Celia, and let us keep in touch with you. Maybe Kenny will be able to tell you more as he improves. We already know much more about this outfit than they suspect, thanks to Jim's knowledge of hidden trap doors into computer systems."

"Hold on. You need to see these plants close up to do a real assessment, don't you?"

"That's what we'd like to do if we could put together a believable cover story to feed the New Day folks. Need a legitimate reason to be in Tampa and LA."

Celia thinks that over; nips at her wine.

"Maybe I can help, Jud. I have contacts all over government from our days in the diplomatic corps. There are some of them on Capitol Hill who owe me favors. Why don't I make a few calls? I should be able to get you an intro to New Day in a semi-official status."

"We'd be indebted, pretty lady."

"No, I owe more than I could ever repay for the way you've taken up the cause in Kenny's behalf. Tell me again what these folks sell."

"IC's, integrated circuits for electronic components made in their Tampa plant. And software and optical products, coatings and such, from their Los Angeles facility."

She wrinkles her brow and writes that down.

"I'll call you by tomorrow, Jud. Let you know when it's arranged."

Impressive, I think. Not *if* I can arrange it, but *when*.

"Sounds good to me, Celia. But let's be sure the people in LA won't connect us with the folks we send to Tampa. The sooner we could make our visits the better."

"Not to worry," she reassures me. "You'll hear from me before the end of the day tomorrow, Mr. Black."

She may be yanking my cord, but I correct her. "I don't see any Mr. Black in here."

"Sorry. Jud." She gives me a big smile and offers, "Think you could call me Cee?"

"Tell me, Cee, has Kenny done any work in miniaturization of electronics?"

"He's been deeply involved in that since his doctorate studies. Told me he'd helped make amazing advances in what he calls super small circuits and components. Said that's the main reason this new company offered him such a great benefits package to join them."

"Now this is important, Celia."

She perks up and brings her face closer, almost too close for comfort.

"What?"

"Did he ever use the term nano?"

"You mean what he blurted out wasn't about a girl named Nan? Let me think…nano…yes, he did use that term once to describe the tiny components they were experimenting with. The word was completely new to me. What does it mean?"

"It's an evolving science of reconstructing matter—materials, circuits, possibly even viruses—beginning at the molecular level. I think that's what New Day wanted him to do for them."

We review again every minute she's spent on the phone with her son since he left for LA. Dissect every word, every reference Kenny made to try to find leads to his condition. She tells me about their telephone contacts and tries to remember his statements verbatim in case we're overlooking something. There just isn't any substance there. It's mostly on the order of 'I'm doing fine, Mom. You'd be bored with the details, but it's exciting for me. Tell me what's new with you, Mom.'

"Nothing concrete about what his job entailed or about his surroundings?" I ask.

She shakes her head and looks frustrated.

"Wish I had more. Kenny never did talk to me much about his work. Maybe it's proprietary and he's just being cautious about disclosing company secrets."

"Not even a comment about his surroundings?" I press.

She gets up and walks across to the bar. Takes a seat on one of the stools and closes her eyes. I can tell she's straining to concentrate. Then her eyes pop open suddenly and a slight smile plays across her lips.

"A couple of words here and there…"

"Such as?" I walk toward her and find a pencil and note pad on the bar top.

"It's much hotter here than on the coast. No ocean breezes," he told me.

"Interesting. Anything else?"

"Told me they provide living arrangements for him. Plush quarters and the best foods. That's about all I can remember. Does any of this help, Jud?"

"I'll let you know. We'll put it all through a brainstorm session and sort out the possibilities."

"You're grinning," she says. "What's funny?"

"Nothing." I stare at her for a moment and cover a laugh.

"No. Tell me. What's that all about?" She looks herself over to see if she's all together.

"It's not you, lovely lady. Just a bit of nonsense we carry on most of the time between us guys. We don't call our sessions brainstorms. Refer to them as putting things through 'the bull shit grinder.' But we're good at it."

"I'd bet you have a lot of talents, Jud Black," she says and manages a little chuckle of her own.

There's no avoiding it. This is one drop-dead gorgeous woman. I know I should be working on her problem but, suddenly, all I can think about is how I'm sitting here with one of the most desirable women I've ever met. My head is filled with how her blonde curls fall to her shoulders, the depth and dazzling blue of those eyes, how perfectly edible she looks—beginning with a pair of perfect lips.

Feel myself drawing closer until I'm lost in her eyes and her full lips are only inches away. I'm not sure who makes the next move—only that it's a most enjoyable meeting. I'm kissing her and she's responding.

When we part I begin to sputter. "Cee, I…don't know what I was thinking."

"Don't apologize, Jud." She touches my cheek and I go warm all over. She's beaming at me, her face positively radiant.

We never quite get back on track with our conversation. Too many things are racing through my brain for me to make sense. But this is not the time and place for what I'm thinking. This lady is in the crisis of her life and I have my mind on thoughts that shouldn't be there. I need a while to sort it all out. Take her hand and kiss her lightly. Then I rise from the couch.

"May be best if we call it a night, Cee."

She nods and composes herself. Then she asks, "how can I help? What else can I tell you?"

"Maybe we can meet tomorrow for dinner," I suggest. "There has to be something we've missed."

"I'd like that, Jud. I plan to spend most of the day at the hospital. Why don't you stop by around six and we'll find some place quiet to eat and continue this…conversation."

As I leave her place my head is reeling with conflicting thoughts. Sure, I shouldn't pursue her this way. She's very vulnerable right now and I can't take advantage of her. But she pushes buttons for me that make it easy to convince myself it's all an innocent attraction. Sure, Jud.

CHAPTER 10

Dan Cooper

"Thanks, Carole. We'll close the conference room door. Things tend to get a little wild when we put our heads together on a problem. Stick your head in if there are any calls."

Our temporary receptionist gestures and turns her attention to the sign painter who arrived moments ago. He's from down the hall. Carole called him to come over and look at our requirements for a sign outside the building and one on the office door.

Pat, Jud and Jim are already milling around the coffee pot and pastry platter in the conference room. Jud's spinning some off-the-wall yarn that's cracked up Pat. He bellows, "You crazy ass, now I know what I've been missing. You're weird, man."

"Hey, Jim," I interject, "who did the hiring, you or Jud?"

"Why do you ask?" Jim fires back. "You approve?"

"Looks like a sterling choice to me. But five seven, red hair, with legs a mile long and an awesome set of pipes sounds more like our buddy Jud would pick 'em."

"Got a head on her shoulders, too, Dan," Jim replies. "Smart and quick. She should handle herself well while we're all out traipsing around chasing misdeeds and wrongdoers."

"I agree," says Pat. "She's a winner. Now, can we get down to the business at hand?" He tosses me the dry marker and says, "Your floor, Dan. Good luck."

I write on the whiteboard. Make the same three headings as before: Kenny, Dengue and Source.

"Let's begin where we left off. We've pretty much exhausted our storehouse of knowledge about Kenny. I put it down on a cheat sheet for each of you for ready reference in case it makes some light bulbs go on. We'll start with that."

They all pick up their sheets and do a quick scan.

"Okay, so we need to recap what we know about dengue fever," I say. "It's seldom been detected in victims in the continental US. Even then, most were recent returnees from areas where the day biting Aedes aegypti mosquitoes breed. The exceptions have been isolated cases in Texas, and there's a potential threat in the Southeastern US where mosquitoes and other insects are kept under control with widespread spraying."

"So what's its symptomatology, Dan?" Jud inquires. Pat looks at him as if to say 'where did you come up with that word?'

"Man, I learn quick. That means 'what it do and how do it do it?' What did you think I was doing with my time at Cee...uh, Celia's house?"

I grin, clear my throat and answer. "Dengue is a viral disease for which there is no specific treatment. Rest and plenty of liquids are the best counters to dengue. The symptoms are, most notably, high fever up to 105 degrees, severe headache, pain behind the eyes, and joint and muscle pain. Nausea and vomiting follow and sometimes an all-over body rash. Kenny has shown signs of all of these symptoms."

Jim interrupts. "And the blood test confirmed dengue infection, I understand."

"Tests showed that dengue was definitely the culprit," I reply. "Celia did them herself and completed the analysis. And they also revealed an important additional fact. She says this is a strain she's never seen before. She's convinced it's genetically altered—a laboratory developed mutation of the virus. That's the scary part of the equation."

Pat adds, "According to what I heard from her two days ago, they took emergency measures with Kenny and got ahead of the virus."

"Not entirely true, Pat," Jud corrects. "She's still worried sick about him progressing to the DHF stage."

"DHF?" Jim asks.

"Dengue hemorrhagic fever. Celia was petrified when I talked to her Tuesday night. If this virus reaches the DHF stage, the blood vessels can start to break down and cause internal bleeding. At that point the virus becomes a life-threatening bug. No cure exists. If DHF takes hold and advances too far, it can be lights out."

I'm writing on the board as we talk. Stand back and look at what we've come up with so far in the 'dengue' column.

"So can we move on to the source now?" I ask the group.

"One caution first," Jud says. "We're mad as hell about this happening to a good friend, but we should stop to think that it's much bigger than that. Celia stated in forceful terms that the manmade dengue strain could pose a tremendous threat to the general population. Let's assume she's right that somebody produced this monster virus for all the wrong reasons."

Pat throws in, "She posed the same scary threat scenario to me. Kind of jangles your nerves to think she could be right."

Jud says, "According to Celia there's already been one death in California this week from dengue. She thinks Kenny may have known the victim. If so, they could have been exposed at the same time."

"Damn," Pat spits. "We could be working against a short fuse time bomb if they find a doable way to deliver the virus and spread it around. Talk about a perfect terror tool!"

"Well put," I answer. "And all the more reason this baby here is the tough nut we have to crack as fast as we possibly can." I tap the marker on the word Source.

Pat gets the ball rolling. "He flew to Los Angeles last month. That has to be our starting point."

I write LA and give it an asterisk for emphasis.

Jim adds, "We have a reference point in the LA area. It's a company named New Day Electronics that has plants there and in Tampa. Jud and I did some hacking and found a number of interesting facts about New Day."

"Give us a dump," I urge.

Jim refers to his notes and begins. "The company's been a phenomenal performer in integrated circuit manufacture and some related activities. Genius named Jason Grimes formed the company in the late 80's. He branched out into a variety of the emerging technologies and showed particular interest in nanotech."

That piques our interest. I for one am suddenly becoming very interested in Mister Grimes and his company. Pat taps the table with an impatient rhythm and Jud adds an intriguing detail.

"Yeah," he says, "but the info well seems to dry up about the time Grimes plunged into studying the world of the teensy weensy. There's no direct mention of a nano lab at New Day or of his collecting up any of the leading figures that are dabbling in that science."

"In fact," Jim continues, "I got the feeling—although it was more implied than outright stated—that the founder may have been pushed aside by some new outside interests that came on the scene less than two years ago. Strictly my conclusion, but it's a strong gut impression."

"I'm writing," I say. "New Day, LA, Tampa. Integrated circuits. New controlling interests? This is riveting stuff, guys. I won't ask how you dug all this out."

"Good." Jim smiles. "You'd be dangerous if I told you."

"What else did you learn from Celia, Jud? Anything else of interest happen at her house?"

He hesitates long enough for me to prompt, "Anything you want to tell us, pal."

"Oh, yeah. Celia's place. Interesting. Let's see." He's baiting again.

"Bragging or yanking our chains?" Pat wants to know.

"She did drop a couple of very intriguing tidbits."

He pulls a sheet of paper from his pocket and I stand poised to write.

"Kenny mentioned nano sometime ago and told her he's helped make some real advances in miniaturization of electronic components."

"Could be a tie together," Jim suggests. I pen the words miniature and nano with the marker and add 'Kenny working.'

"He told her the new company made him a great offer. They also provided him with plush living arrangements and gourmet meals."

"Curious," I remark and add that to the board. What else?"

Jud jabs at the paper with his forefinger and says, "This one puzzles me. Kenny told her it was hot where he was working."

"LA can be hot and smoggy," Pat throws in.

"No. It was this part that stumped me. He said there were no ocean breezes. Doesn't sound like LA to me, folks."

CHAPTER 11

Dan Cooper

Our BS grinder is working at full speed. We kick around the details of our developing plan for the balance of the morning. Examine every note we've made to be sure we're not missing something.

Just before noon Jim points at the wall clock and tells us, "Time for a break, gents. Gotta get Dan a crack at the pie safe before the little hand catches up with the big hand."

Pat says, "Let's lock up the office and take Carole along. We can get to know her. See if she can cope with all four nut cases at once. Next to that, looking after the office should be a walk in the park for her."

"I vote for that," Jud says. "Celia Grant's supposed to get back to me with a critical input we need before we flesh out our plan. Says she thinks—no, she practically guarantees—she can get us into the two New Day Electronics plants."

"Then we'll take up where we left off after we eat," I agree. "Let's take Carole to lunch."

The four of us file out into the reception area. Must be wearing an odd assortment of expressions. Carole scans the group and asks, "WHAT?"

I offer her my arm. "We decided that taking you to lunch would be a lot more fun than looking at each other's ugly faces across the conference table. Lock up."

She's been busy trying to organize the office space and make it presentable. Carole starts to answer. Then she sweeps the quartet again with her eyes, smiles, and says, "Well, you're the boss…es."

"Actually,"` I tell her, "Jim's in charge here. The rest of us will tend to be in and out a lot. I mean, who knows where Jud's gonna be ten minutes from now?"

"Thank you very much," Jud replies. I'm glad he cleaned that one up.

We all take the opportunity over lunch to learn more about COBB's temporary girl Friday. Find she's not just another pretty…well, you know. She's quick on the uptake. Around this crowd of jokers, that could be a definite plus.

"What made you decide to take a chance on working at a brand new business, Carole?" I query.

"Sounded like a challenge," she replies. "I'm beginning to see it could be that and more." That brings a quartet of smiles.

"Any experience with private investigations?"

"I'm not exactly foreign to this line of work, Dan. My husband was a state trooper, and I worked in the county sheriff's office for a couple years. Even took a criminology course at the community college and firearms training at the county range."

Jim tells her, "Right away that gave you a leg up on the other resumes the temp agency sent over." Then he catches himself and quickly amends, "Sorry, Carole. You know what I mean."

She telegraphs a scowl that could blister when Jim makes the 'leg' comment, but when he sputters his recovery, Carole points at him. Reaches over and touches his hand then laughs out loud.

Pat wets his finger and makes a mark in midair to approve her response. "That's one."

"I understand you grew up here in Leesburg," Jud says.

"Been here all my life. Live about a mile away from the office. This is a perfect location for me, not to mention the generous offer if it turns into a full time position. What's the saying about an offer you can't refuse?"

Jim asks her, "What about family? You mentioned a trooper husband."

"There's just my son and me. We lost Tom last summer. Criminal ambushed him on a back road." Carole shows instant anger.

We all go silent. But she shakes off her pained expression and perks up.

"I have a beautiful son. He's the greatest kid that ever breathed. Kevin. He's five."

"You should bring him around to meet us," I suggest.

Carole does a slow scan around the table, and a mischievous little smile lights her face. "Maybe one at a time," she says.

This time Pat holds up two fingers on his left hand and makes another invisible mark in the air with his right.

Jim tells us, "I talked to her about setting up the office and being with us for six weeks minimum. Told her we'd talk about a permanent job if her temp stint works out for her and us."

"Well," she says, "So far this crowd is a very pleasant surprise."

"Not a shock?" Jud wants to know.

"Okay, that too. But then who likes dull?" Carole answers.

I look around the table as the waitress delivers our plates. Carole is focused on her meal, but the guys and I are flashing thumbs up signs at each other. Think we've found the lady we're looking for.

After lunch we settle into the conference room again. Before we can resume our discussion, though, Jud's cell phone rings He answers and listens intently. Nods, then scribbles down notes. From his expression what he's hearing must be important. We can't start without him, so I step out for a minute.

Carole has a visitor. The sign painter from down the hall is back again.

"Dan," she says, "Jim told me you wanted some signs painted. I've known Ralph for years. He's a great artistic designer. See what you think of this drawing he's done."

I take a quick look at his color pencil sketch and know immediately that he's captured our logo perfectly.

"Thanks for the rapid response," I tell him. "I'll drop this on my partners and we'll let you know today." Decide to hold this nice little surprise until our planning session is concluded.

When I return to the table, Jud is finishing his phone conversation.

"That was Cee…Celia Grant, folks. Woman has a mind devious enough to be a COBB partner. But she far outclasses this skaggly group."

"What's the word on Kenny?" Pat asks.

"No change, I'm afraid. But his Mom has some high-powered friends that could make our job a lot easier."

"Remember she moved in select circles when she was an ambassador's wife," I remind him, "and she has a world reputation in her own right."

Jud continues. "Apparently she can make our entry into the New Day facilities much simpler than we anticipated." He looks down at his jotted notes. "Seems we have two instant sponsors courtesy of Doctor Grant. Senator Crandall of California and Representative Feroukas of Florida are willing to set up visits for us next week at both locations. Volunteered to introduce us as people working on behalf of the government in a couple of unrelated time-sensitive programs."

"Great," says Jim. "Does that get us the dollar tour of both plants?"

"You got it, pal." Jud answers. "Two of us can get into the LA plant with Crandall's personal endorsement to look over their state-of-the-art optical surfacing materials production. They'll be told a limited access program is in need of a significant quantity of their product."

"What about Tampa?" I ask him.

"Feroukas will clear the way for two of us to get a complete look at the Tampa plant. They'll be told we're potential buyers of custom designed IC components for use in classified government hardware. The details he leaves up to us."

"Won't it seem suspicious to our hosts that two requests are coming to them at the same time?" I want to know.

"Not likely," Jud answers. "Crandall and Feroukas will keep the intros totally uncoupled. The plan is to give their New Day contacts fictitious project names—Cyclops for the optics materials and Galaxy as the destination project for the integrated circuits. They can even set up bogus ID's for us using our real names. Just need our go ahead."

"Awesome," Pat says. "She greased that in a hurry."

"Wonder how much she had to tell those two politicians?" I pose.

"Don't worry," is Jud's answer. "She says all they know is this could help avert a potentially dangerous threat to the country. They're willing to take the rest on faith for now."

"Persuasive woman," I say and shake my head.

Jud sits there with his pen poised. "Somebody flip a coin and tell us how we split up to do the visits. As soon as I give Celia the names and dates for each location, the arrangements will be set in motion."

"Let me take a shot at it," I suggest. "Why don't we send Jud and Jim to LA? They can bone up on optics and materials manufacturing. Pat and I will go to Tampa and talk electronic components. We'll ask for tours of both plants as early next week as they can be arranged."

Jim volunteers, "I'll give you the notes I took off the net on the optics products they make at the LA plant and the IC's they're doing in Tampa."

Head nods all around. Jud punches in Celia's number and gives her our instructions. "It's a go, gents. She'll get her politico buddies to press for early next week." Jud says something more into his phone then walks to the far end of the room with it. Seems to be having way too much fun making these serious plans.

Pat says, "Dan and I will talk about how we play the game in Tampa, Jim, while you and the guy over there with the big stupid grin wow them in LA."

As we prepare to call an end to our conflab and head off for separate skull sessions, I call out, "Hey, one more subject to cover before we scatter." I produce the painter's drawing.

"How does this grab you for signs on the door and the front lawn?"

The sketch shows a partially shucked ear of golden corn emerging from green leaves. The cob sits astride a bright blue eye, an orb almost menacing in its wide-open, penetrating stare. Atop the graphic are the curved letters COBB EYE.

Approval is swift and unanimous.

"Carole can get him started today," I tell them. "You realize once we hang out our shingle we're officially in business."

After an awkward moment of silence from everyone, Jud starts what turns out to be a hearty round of high fives. Then Jim makes a great suggestion.

"If we're gonna act like sure enough black world guys, we'd better bone up on the language and current contracting procedures. You three have been away from the business end for awhile and I don't deal a lot in classified proposals lately."

"Good point," I agree. "We wouldn't want to trip on our lips in front of savvy customers like these guys at New Day could be. What do you suggest, Jim?"

"We need somebody to brief us and get us up to speed on classified procurements. How about Al Erby at Alltech? He's been involved in some black world business proposals recently."

"My old lunch buddy," I reply. "Sounds like a plan to me. Besides, Al won't press us with embarrassing questions about what we're really doing."

"Okay," Jim offers. "I'll give him a call. Let me suggest you and I meet with him, Dan. That way we'll have one man on each team that's prepped on doing business in the classified realm."

"Just give me a time and place."

"I'll shoot for tomorrow lunch in Herndon if he can get away. That right for you?"

"Do it."

* * * *

For the second time this week I'm having a flashback. Jim, Al and I are sitting in a restaurant in Herndon. Seems just like a hundred other times we've shared lunch in our days at Alltech. Jim made a good choice. He's already filled Al in on our needs and told him only that it's for a sham we're pulling on a company we owe a payback. He understands we don't intend to follow through but are merely drawing out this particular outfit for information. Al's all right with that; in fact, he thinks it's a pretty cool gambit having been in the bidder's shoes way too many times.

We find our way to a corner of the eatery and I check out nearby tables for curious patrons. Seems about as isolated as we can expect. I begin my pitch.

"So, Al, I'm posing as a prime contractor to the government on a highly classified project. They'll be given the project name but little else. Jim will act out the part of the government rep handling the contract arrangements. Make us look smart, pal."

"You have to keep in mind," Al says, "the government is always in the driver's seat. If you're posing as government slobs, you only tell them what they absolutely have to know and hold back the rest. It's up to them to come with hat in hand begging for the business."

I look over at Jim with a big smirk. "So far, nothing has changed in the past six years. Should be fun playing these guys and watching them sweat."

Curiosity finally gets the best of Al. "I don't know what you guys are pulling, but I'd give a month's pay to watch you operate."

"Yeah, but then we'd have to shoot you," Jim chuckles.

Al laughs. "Message received. Where do we start?"

"Give us some buzz words that are in current use in the classified electronics world. Tell us the high points of the classified props you've worked recently. You know we've all been there, but we've all been debriefed for a long time. These guys will be looking for a pattern so we can't tip our hands as outsiders."

"Fair enough." Al launches into a dump of terms and conditions the prospective bidders would expect to see. He's typed out some notes and prompters since yesterday, too. He's come prepared, as I knew he would. This is prime info and it could save us from making fools of ourselves with New Day.

When Erby finishes re-blueing us on the niceties of classified procurement, I feel a lot more prepared to face the New Day crowd in Tampa. Jim expresses his thanks for the updates and we scoot along to get Al back to work.

Before we part with handshakes, I tell Al how good it was to see him again. Then I add a parting note without further explanation.

"If this gambit pays off, we'll be having a celebration. May even be able to tell you the whole story by then. In any case, you're a jewel for helping us out, Al."

"Any time, Dan."

CHAPTER 12

The men move with stealth through the desert night, their dark clothes leaving only the pinpoints of their eyes to reflect the scant light. A force of at least a dozen advances on the objective, a small adobe structure in which their leader stands silently. He follows their progress on his infrared glasses and approves of their performance.

"Well done, my friends. I heard no sound until you were near enough to strike my person. You are learning well the lessons of war."

The warriors assemble around Ali Hassan and give themselves congratulations for the success of the night's training session. Ali clicks on a flashlight and turns it upward to reflect on his face. In his hand he holds a flare gun. A smile plays across his lips as he instructs them.

"You are not yet finished. There is much time until the sunrise, and we must not waste it. The time is approaching when we will face our ultimate test. All must be ready for our glorious mission."

"You are to run in that direction." Ali points behind them into the emptiness of the desert. "You will move like the wind until I send a signal light. At that moment you will stop. Then I will come to you and see how far your speed has taken you."

One of the men steps forward and addresses him.

"The men are exhausted, Ali Hassan. We have trained hard today and our bodies cry out for rest and nourishment."

Hassan restrains himself, knowing they must learn that weakness neither garners victory nor marks the path to paradise. His stern stare is enough to send the foolish man back into his circle.

"Do not mistake lack of resolve for fatigue. You must go on beyond your limit of endurance. Our sworn pledge to *al-Qinaa'* demands you give your all."

"We have had no food or water for hours," another of the group complains. "How can we meet the test when our mouths are parched and our stomachs are empty?"

"Weakling!" Ali shouts and strikes him with the flashlight, extinguishing its glow. "I would remind you of the primitive conditions of your training camp in Africa. You have each survived severe trials, and you have been chosen as worthy of this sacred mission. It is time to be resolute, unflinching. Those who are not can return to the blistering heat of the camp in Chad."

Silence surrounds him. There are no further protests.

"Good. You will be true and loyal soldiers in the moment of ultimate victory over the American devils."

Ali steps outside the adobe hovel; looks at the dial on his watch. Its luminous glow is the only light in their surroundings.

"Now we will perform our sprint in total darkness. I have decided to lead the way to show the determination you must emulate. You may refresh yourselves first with water from the canister on the vehicle. A full stomach, however, would not serve you well for this test. Anyone who can not keep stride with me will feel my wrath."

* * * *

The training is completed for the night. Weary but satisfied with their efforts, the al-Qinaa' warriors have returned to the desert citadel. Kim Yung has summoned Ali in his usual manner, as if he is the master calling a servant. Ali resigns himself to meeting with Kim, but he will bow to no man, least of all a deceiving yellow infidel.

Kim Yung stands in his luxurious office, a place of decadent excess adorned with the tokens of his merit in martial arts. They are displayed, perhaps, to impress and intimidate, but Ali is unmoved. For all his presumed regal bearing, Kim is but a man who must depend on others to accomplish his work. This desert fortress is Ali's home as well as Kim's. Ali will not be made to feel inferior.

Kim Yung poses in his white linen suit and looks down his nose at Ali.

"Must you present yourself in such a condition, Ali Hassan? A man set upon by a pack of hungry pigs could look no worse. Your stench fills the room. I am ashamed for you."

"I do not apologize for my appearance, Kim Yung. While you lounged here in your comfortable quarters, I drilled the men unseen in the night of the desert. We will be prepared when the time comes to launch our attacks on the American devils. Will you be equally ready?"

"Your insolence bores me," Kim Yung spits, and the venom in his words stings.

Ali scowls and thinks *let him have his say. My time will come. He is an overeducated fool, one who believes his prized science will be the undoing of the Americans' dominance. I do not care to speculate what his army of scientists and machines may bring about. I know the power of the weapon we bring to our partnership. Whether he succeeds or not, al-Qinaa', The Mask, will see that a scourge is placed upon American soil that will convince the conceited fools. They will see the wisdom of leaving the Middle East for Muslims alone to shape. I pledge myself, and the lives of all my martyrs, to achieve that end.*

The swaggering Kim Yung continues. "Tell me how you were so inept as to let the American, Kendrick Grant, escape all your elaborate security mechanisms and reach the outside world. I have placed your people in charge of securing this refuge, and now I find that they are not to be trusted."

"One of my guards was caught unaware, but I have seen that he was made an example to the others. Even now he lies tethered in the desert pondering his shortcoming. The boiling sun will teach him a lesson he will long remember."

"Ali, you are a fool. The young scientist is a mortal danger to us every moment he remains free. What are you doing to find him?"

"My people assure me he has returned to his home on the east coast. I will dispatch some of my most dedicated men to return him if you desire."

"Do so immediately. I will expect a report each day he is gone. Your inattention has endangered our entire mission. I will not have your Arab incompetence threaten our work."

Kim's slur clearly annoys Ali, but he is careful not to let his anger spill over. There will be a time and place for that.

"Have you finished, Kim? My men await instruction at our daylight facility."

"Cancel the drill. We can not afford to take a chance on your men being seen in the open. Use the time to wash your filthy bodies and pretend you are civilized people. Then redouble your efforts to secure our fortress from within as well as from the outside."

Ali's fingers curl into a fist. He wants so to vent his anger on this little man who stands tall by belittling others.

"We must train and maintain our warriors' edge, Kim. The men and women I bring to your enterprise are focused and will accept only total domination of our adversaries. But you must allow me to keep them sharpened as a set of daggers aimed at the black heart of America."

"You have my order, Ali Hassan. Carry it out."

"*Stinking yellow savage,*" Ali Hassan mumbles as he leaves Kim's quarters. *"He fancies himself leader of Korea, perhaps dictator of the world. But he must deal with me and with our dark cloud of retribution that will envelop all who challenge us."*

CHAPTER 13

Jud Black

Jim and I are on our way to Los Angeles. How I hate flying! It's like a momentary lapse, a life suspension to me. Time wasted that goes to no good purpose. I'm trying to salvage some value from these long hours aloft by listening to my music.

Jim taps me on the arm, and I take off my headset and listen.

"I said 'you look mighty serious'. Keep wincing and making notes."

"Listening to some tracks I cut in my home studio, Jim. You know what a perfectionist I can be when it comes to my music. Got a cut on here for a movie track that needs some tweaking."

"Well, I don't want to screw up your concentration, Jud, but don't you think we should talk about what we do when we get to LA?"

"Good point." I put away my tunes and switch gears, ready to discuss how Jim and I bring off this scam in order to expose New Day.

"Where do we begin?" Jim asks.

I dig in my shirt pocket for the identification Celia's Senator friend has provided. "Says here I'm a lead engineer for some optics company with a sole source contract and a weird name. Excelorb. What the hell is that?"

"Don't knock it, Jud, just sound like an optics wienie who understands refractions, illuminations, light scale, and all that crap."

"Oh, that's no problem. I've given myself a crash course. If we were in fact in the market to buy optics surfacing materials for a government contract, I have an idea what to ask...about their properties and durability, I mean."

"Great. I'm supposed to be the government buyer from an undisclosed agency," Jim says. "I have a general grasp of what these products should cost Uncle Sam. As the feds usually do, I'll take a logical price and lop it in half, wave the flag and make the producer feel guilty about charging any more. After all, this Cyclops project is supposed to be a matter of top national security. New Day should feel honored to participate at a minimum profit."

"Right. Every man a patriot, yadada yadada. This is gonna be a toot, Jim, putting these guys on. Celia says their rep will meet us at LAX and take us to our hotel out of town. Guess they smell a big sale and want to sink a hook in us."

"Hey, Jud, it's a freebie. Let 'em jump through hoops. All we're here for is to rip this outfit open and find their dirty laundry. Remember, I worked with Kenny when I consulted to COB. He's a great guy. I want to hang whoever gave him the virus as much as you do."

"Have you studied the background info Celia gave us on the Senator?" I reach for my briefcase and fish for my own copy.

Jim answers, "Feel like I know him personally by now. New Day will be aware where the request for our visit came from, so we need to act like he's at least an acquaintance."

I nod and spend a few minutes reading the profile. Then I turn back to Jim and say, "Let's try an end run on them. You pick out one factory contact to work on and I'll do the same. The plan is to get them off premises and talking more than they should."

"Got it," he agrees. "We should be on the lookout for clues to penetrating their most protected data closets for a long peek at what they consider sacred. By the time we leave LA, my goal is to strip that outfit down to its skivvies and disassembleit. If they're clean, we'll move on. If they hurt Kenny, we'll harpoon them."

"Take it easy, Barnett. You'll run your sugar up. By the way, you brought all your paraphernalia, didn't you? Susie made me promise to keep you straight on this trip."

"All I need is a way to keep my insulin cooled. And it's more like I need to keep you in tow, cowboy. If they give us a female guide, I may have my hands full."

That brings back a wound that's too fresh to heal just yet. I look away from Jim and peer out the window, watching the clouds but seeing a face etched on my memory. When Dan and I hooked up to take down the mind benders down in Tampa, there was this girl. Strike that. There was this *woman*. She screwed up my head until

I found out we were on opposite sides of the law. Haven't quite gotten over her, though.

"Did I lose you, Jud?" I hear and snap out of my daydream.

"You were saying?" I quip.

"That you have a way of attaching yourself to the best looking woman in the room and, more often than not, charming her right out of her unmentionables."

"Moi? Bashful Black? I used to get gold stars in school for shy."

Jim says, "Just make sure info on New Day is at least one of the things you go probing for, my man."

I give him my best lecherous smile.

"Back to business, Jim. We have to insist on seeing both the manufacturing operation and the optics labs that back it up. I'll ask to talk to the owner, Jason Grimes, give him Senator Crandall's regards. Need to try to figure out if he's still the man in charge. If not, it could be important to pin down who's really running New Day."

"Damn, you're about as devious minded as I am, Jud. We've got this outfit skewered and on the spit already, and we don't even know if they have anything to hide."

"On a roll, baby. Let's go with this until a better prospect pops up. If Celia's right about the dengue virus and its possible uses, we don't have any time to waste."

"Speaking of Celia, Jud." Jim takes on this odd expression like he's not sure how far he should go with what he was about to say. It's pretty transparent.

"Don't. Not yet, Jim. Took her to dinner Tuesday night. Then we went by the hospital and sat and talked for a long time."

Jim says, "I'm not prying, I hope. You need to know that there's a noticeable change in you."

"How so, Jim?"

"You go off into lapses like you're in your own little world. Something has really got hold of you. If it's Celia, I can understand. She's pure class."

"Well, I'll admit she's not like anybody I've ever met. Actually, I spent time with her every day this week including a long visit to her place last night."

"Doesn't surprise me, pal."

"She's an amazing woman in a lot of ways, Jim. Makes it hard to think of her strictly as Kenny's mom. But that's the way it will have to stay while we're working on this problem."

"Sorry I intruded." Jim says and looks away.

CHAPTER 14

Jud Black

"Hi. I'm Jud Black. This is Jim Barnett."

We've rescued our bags from an LAX airport carousel. I've just hailed the man holding a card with big block letters MR BLACK/MR BARNETT.

He acknowledges my greeting, tips his hat and says, "I'm your driver. The car is outside."

A large black limousine sits at the curb. A thirtiesh-looking man in a gray suit, the picture of the brash young executive, emerges and thrusts out his hand.

"I'm Ted Meecham, Marketing Manager for New Day optics products. Our driver will take us to Torrance. We have a corporate rate at the Marriott there near our plant. Booked a couple of suites for you."

I glance at Jim quickly to see if he's reacting. Not a clue on his face. Normally, a contractor puke and a government slob like we're supposed to be wouldn't be put up in digs as elegant as a suite. The Senator must have laid it on thick to get us this kind of treatment. Normally, they would let us swing on our own and find our way to their place. New Day probably thinks they have a straight line to a sole source contractor and the congressional backing to sell their products; sure they have a first class inside track to a 'highly sensitive program' named Cyclops and a head start on a solid future reputation in optical coatings.

Jim and I have our best faces on, projecting proper decorum for a highly placed commercial guy and a government mid-level staffer with clout. I've made a quick trip to the mall and bought a couple of complete outfits on the condition they could tailor and deliver to me overnight. Must say I'm impressed by the way it worked out, and I'm not that easy to impress. Still, I see a note of pessimism in Meecham's eyes when he realizes I have a brow ring and ponytail to go with my tweed blazer, Egyptian cotton shirt and expensive loafers. Wait till he sees my seriously blue suit in the morning.

Get over it, Ted, I'm thinking to myself. *In your business you should be accustomed to slightly unconventional dudes. Test me and you'll find out exactly how off-center I can be.*

"Looking for a storm today?" I ask Ted.

He thinks for a moment then breaks into a broad grin. "No. This is your typical smoggy day in the City of Angels. We try to exhale a lot."

There's not a lot of chatter for a long while. He acts like I've stepped on it.

Just when I think I've put him off, though, the probes start.

"I understand the Cyclops program has a tight schedule. That you're looking to find a source quickly and expect rapid turnaround. Is that a reliable input?"

I fix him with a stare. "Later," I answer.

Now I have him wondering if he's breached some security no-no. It should keep him off guard. We need to go in with an advantage.

But Ted isn't finished with his examination. "We assumed you wanted to talk to our top scientists, so we've assembled our best talent for the meeting tomorrow. By the way, we didn't get a professional synopsis on you. These eggheads will be interested in your background. You know, matter of professional curiosity."

I stare him down again and don't say a word, but I'm thinking *I'm the customer, so you play the game on* my *terms. Probably have a team of people waiting to get their hands on a set of credentials and run off to check us out.*

Ted's becoming a little agitated. He looks at Jim, almost pleading for a way to get some edge. "I take it you've brought a detailed set of specifications for our product to meet. Think you'll find our optical coating material has some truly unique reflectivity and dispersion properties. It's a revolutionary development."

Jim is up to the task. He looks unimpressed and answers in a totally flat tone.

"Jud's the one you have to convince. I'm here to make certain the price is right and the delivery schedule is clear."

Thanks for the over to you, Jim. Good thing I spent some midnight oil framing this Cyclops ruse so I could withstand grilling like Ted is trying now.

Folks say I'm a quick study, and I suppose there's a kernel of truth in that. Did an intensive review of optics principles and built a fictitious program in my mind that would use New Day coatings to prime optical surfaces for reduced glare and extremely high reflectivity in combat situations. Think I'm ready for whatever these bad boys plan to throw at us.

At least for the time being, Mister Meecham's attempts have been thwarted.

"Should be an interesting session tomorrow, gents," he says. "Our driver will pick you up in the hotel lobby at nine AM. You'll be staying only a few minutes from our plant. We have a full day planned for you…subject, of course, to your wishes. Just let us know what you want to see."

I'm thinking. *The answer is we want to see* absolutely everything. *We want to peek into closets you didn't even know you had and turn New Day inside out.*

By now I'm looking forward to a challenging mind game with their technical folks they can't possibly win. Let the games begin, as they say.

The hotel suites are not shabby. A cut above what I would have expected, maybe a couple cuts. Then Jim draws me aside and issues a logical caution.

"Jud, we're assuming these guys are completely unaware of why we're really here. Just in case they're smarter than that, let's not get blindsided. Could be bugs in these rooms."

"You're right, of course. With the kind of high tech they're into, it might be routine to eavesdrop on their guests. Guard against industrial secret thieves, you know. Think we should ask for a change of rooms?"

"Let's do it. We can give them some concocted line. I'd feel a lot more comfortable knowing some guy isn't recording our conversations."

After switches digs Jim and I spend the evening reviewing our plans for tomorrow, how we're going to put these guys on the defensive and do our own probing for facts. I'm suspicious by nature, and what I've seen in our computer search just doesn't smell right. There are too many disconnects. Where does Jason Grimes fit into New Day's plans as of today? Has he been shoved to the sidelines? How can they promise such wonderfully improved properties for their coatings unless they're dabbling in nanotech science at some level? Why would they hire Kenny and what possible connection could this have to his contracting a deadly virus?

* * * *

The limo and driver are at the hotel promptly at nine AM. As we crawl through the morning traffic, I note it's another smoggy day. We pull up in front of the New Day building about thirty minutes later.

The array of talent they've gathered to throw at us reeks of edge technology. They run in a mix of old line optics experts to young bulls with probably more brilliant ideas than New Day has the dollars to finance. Other people may be intimidated by such a show of force. But Jim and I are strictly winging it so let them fire away. They have a product to sell, so let's see them sell it. If my memory serves me I was on their side of the fence not so long ago groveling for government business.

Ted Meecham gets the proceedings started. "Doctor Zellman, our optics materials lead engineer here at Department L, will give you an overview of the product we believe will interest you for your program," he says.

One of the older guys organizes himself, proceeds to the front of the room and clears his throat. He's clearly overwhelmed by his own brilliance. Even his throaty rattle has an officious air of authority.

"I will assume you are well founded in the principles of optics so I will go light on the tutorial comments." He smiles.

That's probably about as amusing as Zellman will get. Despite his words I prepare for the 'me PhD, you dummy' routine.

I can tell Jim knows what's running around in my head. I feign a yawn. He gives me a slight head nod that signals me to be patient and let them hang themselves. I'll need a lot of prompting if the day continues the way it's started. Puffed up blowhards aren't my favorite people.

For the next thirty minutes or so, Zellman takes a complete trip through the world of state-of-the-art optics. He talks about refractions and magnifications, instructs on the properties of light absorption and dispersion, extols on the wonderful breakthroughs by New Day in the areas of light diffraction and interference. So much for avoiding tutorials.

It's time for a test.

"Some of the improvements you're touting, Doctor Zellman, sound less than credible unless you're working in the nanotech world. Are you building your optical coatings from the molecular level up?"

The seemingly unflappable Zellman is suddenly more than a little 'flapped.' He peers around the table at his associates and collects himself, shuffling his slides as he attempts to continue. Think I've struck a bulls-eye with my dart.

"We have done some investigations into the nanotechnology world," he admits nervously. "But our processes do not depend on that unproven field of science. You will find that we have significantly improved the characteristics of our materials without resorting to designing materials from the molecular level."

I don't buy that explanation for one minute. He's hiding something and it's more obvious than he imagines. Decide I'll just let him run with it and pull the noose tight around his own neck.

We endure another half an hour or so of dissertations by Zellman's associates. They amount to no more than an elaborately contrived sales pitch that says 'come on, Uncle Sam, but my optical coatings, make me famous. We are so good. Trust us.' I keep my mouth shut and let them talk, not knowing how much of their horse manure is sticking.

Finally I interrupt. "I think I have a good picture of your product. Let's take a look at the manufacturing plant."

"Do you have written specifications for us to discuss filling?" one of the young scientists asks.

"We'll get to that. First I want to see the plant." Something in the reactions around the table makes me think I've rearranged their intended schedule.

Jim and I make the excuse we need a quick health break, and they direct us to the men's room. Just in case, we flush a couple johns and turn on a hand dryer to cover our conversation. Then we share our amusement at how hard these guys are working to smoke us with their experts.

"We may not be in the right pew yet, Jim, but I'd skewer these guys, anyway. If they had nothing to do with Kenny's problem, I'd enjoy smacking them strictly for their conceit and self-importance. Makes you gag, doesn't it? If they did hurt Kenny…well, they'll deserve whatever we dish out."

"I singled out that young PhD Lowry as my target. I'll work him for as much info as I can get on the side during our walking tours. Who's your pick?"

"Haven't settled on one yet, Jim," I reply. "It's like a duck shoot at a carnival."

We rejoin the group and do a tour of the clean room where the coating materials are produced. No small time operation, this New Day. They have clearly sunk big bucks into building a first class factory for producing next generation materials. I'm a lot more impressed by the sight of the plant than any amount of prattling on they could have done back there in the conference room.

"Now let's stop in at your labs," I suggest. "Take a look at your spectroscopes, your polarizers, the TEMs."

Doctor Zellman jumps on that last item in a hurry. "Transmission electron microscopes? I stated that we are not actively pursuing the nano level of light properties, Mister Black."

"Understand. But we need to know the capabilities of New Day to continue progress in turning out new coating materials for future programs. The labs, please?"

"First let's take a break for lunch." Zellman suggests. "We've set up in the executive dining room," he says. "We'll alert the lab and do our tour there after the meal."

And an impressive meal it is. All the accoutrements are there. Fine linen and china, uniformed wait staff, great food, a panoramic view of the California landscape. Some of the strap hangers disappear from the group, and I notice that Ted Meecham is no longer here. Zellman apologizes and explains that Ted has been called away on urgent business.

Shortly after we begin the meal, a tall, striking young Oriental woman takes her place at the table. No introduction is made, and she confines her conversation to two of the younger technical types at the far end of the table. She's a major distraction for me, though. I can't help watching her movements, admiring her lines, thinking that severely cut business suit does a poor job of hiding one classy woman. Twice our eyes meet and she manages a coy smile that does little to calm my pulse rate.

After lunch, and with noticeable reluctance, we are escorted through their lab area. It's quite obvious why they were holding back. I see some of the tools that would permit them to work at the nano level, though they've vehemently denied that's their intent. They have two transmission electron microscopes, both of which they've tried to disguise. But I've seen TEMs. Their profile is hard to mask. Those babies operate in the super capable range that would permit them to view chemical structures down to the nanometer level. That would enable New Day to design totally new materials from the bottom up, substances never before offered to the market. Coatings with amazing properties such as they've described to us. And I could see Kenny using his expertise to good purpose in an environment like this.

If I were running New Day and had their expertise, I'd be touting it at every turn. So why are they hiding their nano capability? Maybe it's because they're doing things with nanotech they would rather no one knew about.

As soon as we begin the lab tour, Zellman calls over the new member of our group. She's introduced as Miss Su Lin Kim, an assistant to Ted Meecham, with the explanation that Ted has been called away temporarily. Miss Kim also happens to be a technical expert. I take one look at this Oriental beauty and cast a smile in Jim's direction. That's all the communication we need. He immediately understands that I've picked my target for information gathering.

CHAPTER 15

Jud Black

The afternoon is more instructional to us, not in product technical terms but in the matter of what New Day's capabilities may be. Considering that's what Jim and I are actually here for, things are progressing fairly well. I also take a shot at scoping out the company founder's status.

"Miss Kim," I ask, "the Senator specifically asked us to personally deliver his warmest regards to Mr. Grimes."

She reacts entirely too defensively. "Unfortunately, he is not available at the moment."

"Perhaps tomorrow?" I persist. "Senator Crandall was very complimentary of Jason Grimes' reputation and patriotism. We were both looking forward to meeting him. We still have the business arrangements to talk about here, and I've given our general specifications to your people to review this evening."

Again, a too obvious hesitation as she considers her reply.

"I will check, but I am afraid his schedule may not permit it."

The words have a way of dripping from her lips like honey. Her every motion, each spoken word, sends a tingle down my back. Yeah, I know. Sound like a horny teenager, don't I? But she is a dynamite package. Right now Su Lin is a breath of loveliness among a clutch of ugly toads, but she would stand out in a room full of raving beauties. Watch it, Jud. Don't lose sight of the business at hand.

As we walk across the parking lot back to the main building, I notice a transport van with a logo showing it's from Henderson, Nevada. Boxes are being loaded into the van. That reminds me I have a side interest on this trip.

"Su Lin, how long does it take to get to Las Vegas from here?"

She's a bit taken aback by my off-the-wall question, but she collects herself and says, "It's probably four or five hours by car but a quick hop by air. Why do you ask? Planning a side trip?"

"Never been to Sin City. Thought this may be a good opportunity for a short stopover."

"Ever been to LA, or is this your first visit here, too?"

"I'm not exactly a world traveler, Su Lin. Actually, I hate to fly. Might try going over to Vegas, though. Take a day or two to see some sights."

"And LA? You know we have quite a lot to see here."

"With the right guide, that would be interesting. Might save Vegas for later."

"How about me? As your guide, I mean." She turns those almond eyes up at me and I go defenseless.

"Okay," I manage. "Where do I call for you?"

"Let's make it simple. I'll come by your hotel at, what, six o'clock? That should give us time to see a few points of interest."

Right now I'm thinking there's only one point of interest I want to explore and she's walking beside me, looking mighty fine.

My mind turns back to the events of the week just past. Things are moving well in my new relationship with Celia Grant—better than well. But I'm nowhere near an exclusive commitment. That's something that has always scared me. Besides, who knows what I may learn from Su Lin about New Day in unguarded moments. And there's no harm in finding a little diversion.

* * * *

Jim and I compare notes once we're back in the hotel. He agrees that there is much more going on inside New Day than they're letting on. Grimes, or whoever's in charge there now, has sunk some serious capital into cutting edge machinery and smart guys. I tell him I believe Kenny could well have been lured there by the promise of boundary breaking work, but I'm still puzzled by his reference to the absence of ocean breezes where he was working. We conclude that somehow we have to unlock data repositories we haven't yet found.

"Got an in with that engineer Lowry," Jim reports. "Frankly, I suspect he may be a little 'light in the loafers', you know, partial to guys. That's a complication

I'll deal with if necessary. Convinced him I'm a connoisseur of the subtleties of fine seafood. Lowry tells me there's a great gourmet seafood place near Malibu I have to try. They know him there, so he can get the three of us in on short notice. Could be a chance to pump him for some inside info on New Day."

"Good shot, Jim. But give him my regrets. You'll have to defend yourself. I have a date I wouldn't miss for the best seafood dinner in North America."

"Susie Wong?"

"That's Su Lin, pal, and if I'm on my game, she could be the delicacy of the evening for old Jud. Don't wait up."

* * * *

I'm waiting in the lobby when this vision sweeps in. Not a doubt in my mind that every male eye is homed in on her in that lemon yellow dress, her smile lighting up the room. She sees me and walks to where I'm sitting with a fluid gait that sets my head spinning. I'd go to meet her, but I'm enjoying the view too much from here to move.

"Kim Excursions at your service," she trills and gives me a wink. "Would you like the standard tour or the deluxe package?"

"Think I'm already looking at the super special package. I'm in your hands," I answer and take her arm.

We walk to the front entrance and she points to a red, top-down Mercedes convertible. Circles around and takes the driver's seat. I crawl in beside her on the unbelievably soft white leather seat. Barely have time to buckle in when she jump starts from the curb and roars out into traffic. Makes me feel like a victim of whiplash. I understand why her hair is carefully wound tightly atop her head. This woman is a speedster behind the wheel. We're creating our own windstorm whizzing down the freeway while she makes small talk.

"LA has about anything you could ever want, Jud. We run the gamut from movie stars to beach bums, from hillside castles to slums. We can do weird or ritzy, even the sand and surf scene if you're so inclined. What's your pleasure?"

"You're in charge, Su Lin. Just take me away for a few hours and show me what you do for entertainment."

We hit some of the high spots. Run up through Beverly Hills over into Hollywood and along the boulevard. Travel some of the streets I've often heard about but never seen. Stop in a night spot to sample the early action and take a couple of turns on the dance floor.

"It's way too early for the real scene to get underway in here," Su says over the music. "This place starts rocking about ten or eleven o'clock and swings all night."

If it generates more swing than her curvy hips are showing me now, I may not be cut out for the dance scene.

"How about some dinner, Su? Got some place in mind or do we start cruising?"

"I know the perfect spot," she answers. "Absolutely authentic Korean food in a spot with a view of the sunset you couldn't conjure up in your best dreams."

She takes my hand in hers and leads me back to the car.

At dinner in a cozy little out of the way Korean restaurant we sample all the delicacies of the Land of the Morning Calm accompanied by her commentary on how the dishes are prepared and how they are to be savored. Her conversation is punctuated with subtle little probes about my background, where I live, how I got into this business. She even hazards a query about the Cyclops program without naming it. I do a lot of skirting of issues and answering in terms that will be hard for anyone to check.

I'm beginning to get into the spirit of this excursion, hoping it will last for as long as possible. In fact, I'd like nothing better than to have Su Lin's pretty face be my first sight when the morning light peeks through.

We walk along in the gentle Pacific breezes on the shoreline after dinner, and Su Lin stops at an overlook above the ocean. She stands with her back to me and leans against my chest, warm and soft through her dress. A sudden shiver goes through her. She remarks, "The breeze off the water is a bit on the chilly side tonight."

I respond by wrapping her in my arms and pulling her closer to me.

"Ahhh. That's much better, Jud."

"I was thinking, Su Lin. You ever been to Vegas? Maybe we could motor over there and spend a day. Maybe even a couple days."

"Not enjoying LA?" she teases and moves my arm a little lower around her hips. She leans back against me and I feel my mouth go dry.

"Very much," I answer. I bury my face in her hair. The scent of her perfume and the sea mist evoke some pretty tantalizing thoughts. As close as she's pressing against me, I don't doubt she can tell what those thoughts are doing to me.

She turns and faces me, her thigh planted hard against my middle. I would estimate she's at least five eight, slender and oh, so shapely. In fact, some of the more prominent points of her shape are nestled quite comfortably near.

Su Lin turns her face up to mine and inches it nearer. I'm no dummy. It's time old Jud took the initiative. Her lips are firm but pliant and they invite me to linger. In fact, they part and invite me in. I give this lady about a ninety nine point eight in the smooch department.

When we break long enough to breathe, Su Lin trains her incredible dark eyes on mine and says, "I was going to suggest going back to the disco, but perhaps you can think of something more stimulating than that."

"Can't thpeak right now, Thu Lin. My tongueth hard."

"I have a fix for that. My place is only a mile or so away."

"Lead on, foxy lady. Your fondest wish is my desire. Or I desire to fondle your wishes. Oh, hell, woman—I want you like crazy, and it's way too public here."

We turn to leave and a sudden shower drifts in from the ocean. She takes off running for the car, pulling me behind her. She runs up the convertible top and drives onto the freeway. The short distance to her cozy condo seems more like twenty miles given the condition she's got me in. I rest one hand on her right thigh. Every time she shifts gears it sends a shiver up my arm.

As soon as we're inside she says, "Pick a wine from the rack and pour us a glass," and disappears. I find the kitchen and hear water running. Sounds like a shower. Reminds me I've been out in the rain, so I do a quick check in the powder room. Judge myself about as presentable as I'm gonna get.

Minutes later Su appears in the living room wearing a filmy something that does little to cover her curves. She's let her glistening black hair down so it falls around her shoulders. Like I needed any further enticement. By now I'm about to explode.

I hand her a glass of wine. She takes a sip then drains it in a single pull. Sets down the glass, turns away and walks to the doorway to her bedroom.

I follow her in and close the door.

CHAPTER 16

Jud Black

Bright light is coming from somewhere. I open one eye and a beam of sunlight streaming through the curtains blinds me. Must be morning already, I think. Look around and try to orient myself. No sound, strange bed, somebody's perfume on my pillow.

Yes. It was definitely a night to remember. Su Lin was everything I imagined and more. But where is she now? The way we clung together in the wee hours I'd swear we'd be tangled for round two—or is it three? Then I hear her voice from across the room and close my eyes.

"No, he's tough to break. Adept at fending off my questions. And I found nothing in his pockets that would give us a clue, except that he's carrying a Virginia driver's license with an address in someplace called Boyce. His clothes have labels from a store in Fairfax."

I lie as still as possible and strain to catch every word. She was an incredible partner, but now the bitch is setting me up with somebody. Helping them run a check on me, from the sound of it.

"Maybe he's legitimate," she says. "Could really be who he says he is, just a customer with a big streak of curiosity." There's an almost hopeful note in her voice. I'm conceited enough to believe it means last night was special for her, too.

"Let's see how it goes today," she says. "If we get a contract, maybe all our worries were misplaced."

A long pause then Su Lin speaks again. "He left here pretty late. Said you may have to push back the meeting to more like eleven o'clock. I kept him out and worked him over for information, but he's a tough nut."

She worked me over, that's for sure. But not like she's implying. She also doesn't know it yet, but I'm not through with this vixen yet. If Su Lin gets closer than an arm's length, she's going to get a big surprise.

I hear her hang up and set the phone down. Wait for her to crawl back into the warm bed. No such luck. She's off to the kitchen banging pots and pans around.

"Don't you think it's time to wake up?" I hear after awhile.

I open an eye just a sliver and see that she's wearing that same flimsy garment that set me off earlier. In the morning light it leaves even less to the imagination than it did last evening.

"I said it's time to rise and shine, lover boy. Got places to go and things to do this morning." She walks nearer and leans down to see if I'm breathing.

Before she knows what's happening, I pull her onto the bed with me and whisper, "Don't need to go anywhere to have what I want this morning."

She resists momentarily but her will weakens when I begin to kiss her lips then move to other inviting places.

"Maybe you're right," she whispers, and curls up in my arms. "I changed the meeting time to eleven. We have all morning."

* * * *

Maybe an hour later I stir and plant a light kiss on Su's cheek. She makes a little whimper and returns to her even breathing. Well, she's earned her rest. I slip away and return to my hotel by taxi. Jim is anxiously pacing the floor when I arrive.

"Jeez, man, I thought the gypsies had run off with you. Where in merry hell have you been? We have a meeting at New Day at nine and it's already after eight."

"Relax, Jim, we have plenty of time. Su rescheduled the meeting to eleven o'clock."

"Su, huh? Should I ask?"

I hold both hands over my head to signal touchdown. That answers his question.

"Dan told me he'd taken to calling you Studley. Guess he's right about you."

"Let it lay, Jim. Let's just say I came out ahead in this exchange. She didn't get any information out of me."

"But what did you learn?" he asks.

"For one thing, she was reporting to somebody when she didn't know I was listening. They may not be buying our story, Jim."

"Not much we can do at this point," he says, "other than to play it out the way we planned. Maybe we have what we came for, anyway."

"Really? How was your night, Jim?"

"You wouldn't believe it, Jud. Remember I said I had my doubts about young mister Lowry. The place we went for dinner turned out to be a gay hangout. The food was great until I figured out some guy in the kitchen had probably been handling more than my lobster and scallops back there. I was the only straight guy in the place. Knew I was in trouble when the little son of a bitch looked me in the eye and started to stroke my hand. If he'd called me Sweetie, I would have mopped the floor with the fruit."

Now I'm curious. "How did you get out of that joint without some sizable lumps? More important, do you think he picked up on anything that might give us trouble?"

"No. I just told him, 'What you have in mind isn't my cup 'o noodles, Mary Jane. Let's call it even and split now.' He was more than willing to write it off as a failed sortie to avoid a mouth full of knuckles."

"Whoa, pal. The question is what did *you* learn from *him?*"

"Enough to get me into places on their data system we hadn't been yet. Made it an early evening and came back here. Spent most of the night on my trusty laptop, riding the internet range."

"And?"

"Picked up some very interesting facts," Jim tells me. "The New Day headquarters personnel files were extremely enlightening. There's a resume on file on Doctor Kendrick Grant. Says he was assigned to Department P as of four weeks ago."

"Bingo! That alone makes our trip out here worthwhile. Now I know I'm gonna gnaw on this outfit till it coughs up what happened to Kenny."

Jim grins. "Thought you'd like that little nugget. It's only the beginning. There are four more resumes with strong nanotech credentials. Two are people in Department T and two in Department P." He hands me his notes listing the four names.

"Wait," I say. "Zellman was introduced to us as Department L's lead optics engineer. Doesn't take a genius to figure that means Los Angeles. Department T could be Tampa logically. But where might Department P be located? Let's throw them a sinker today. I'll ask about these two dudes, Adams and Eastman, and we'll clue in Dan and Pat to check on the other two at the Tampa plant. If they're not into nanotech, why all the obviously high priced nano talent?"

"Any other jewels you unearthed, mister master snoop?" I ask him.

"Just one. Do you realize you were out with a dame whose name could have been Pyongyang Patty?"

"Wait. That's in *North* Korea, Barnett. What are you telling me?"

"I'm saying that Su Lin Kim is actually Kim Moon Su, a card-carrying North Korean Communist. She's been in the US for three years, but they didn't cover her tracks quite well enough to escape some determined digging."

"Wonder what that means? Is she a plant by the commies or what?"

"Think about it, Jud. She holds down a solid job with New Day, and she didn't show up until our questions got a bit dicey for them to answer. It's kind of like they called in the heavies to check us out. Wouldn't it be a fright if North Korea was pulling the strings at New Day?'

"You mean I didn't get that date on my charm alone? What have we put our big feet into, friend?"

"Hey, Jud, I know we kid around a lot, but we both know how serious this situation looks."

"Got that right, pal. For all the foolishness we carry on, the way this thing is unfolding scares the shit out of me."

"Whole setup has a putrid odor, doesn't it? Think it's time we brought Dan and Pat up to speed?"

I grab my cell phone and dial Dan's number.

* * * *

"Howzit, Dan? You guys catch anything yet?"

"Hey, Jud, give us time. We just got to Tampa a few minutes ago. Have a meeting with the New Day people this afternoon. What's the word from LA?"

I tell him, "We had a productive meeting with their reps at the plant yesterday."

Dan sounds a bit puzzled. "What does that mean?"

"Well, Dan, it was more productive for us than it was for them. They still think they're selling us high priced materials for a covert program. We gathered some information and enough doubts to convince me they have a lot to hide.

New Day could be our bad guys, though we haven't made a connection to Kenny's illness yet."

"How's Jim?" he asks. "You guys need anything?"

"Oh, we're both fine. Jim did get caught up in something pretty weird. Almost had to fight his way out of a gay bar. I'll let him tell you about it later." I can hear Dan snickering on the other end of the line. Jim mumbles something at me that insults my ancestry.

"What about you, Jud. I can't believe you've been in fruit and nut city for more than a day without putting your nose somewhere it didn't belong."

"Oh, ye of little faith," I chide. "When did I ever do that?"

"You don't have time for me to tick off the list, pal."

I assume my best indignant tone and report, "Why, I spent a quiet evening with a charming young lady of the Oriental persuasion learning about the cultural points of this fine city."

"Wanta put Jim on the line?" Dan inquires.

Jim takes the phone and says, "Yeah, Dan." He turns up the volume and punches 'speaker'.

"Just wanted to get the straight story. Did you take Jud to a bath house or was this a take out order from one of those 'escort services'?"

Jim replies, "I'm sworn to uphold the integrity of my illustrious partner. If he says he was soaking up culture, who am I to dispute his word?"

"Then what I want to know, Jim, is did either of you learn anything of substance that may help us here in Tampa?"

"The day certainly wasn't wasted," is Jim's answer. "I rooted out enough to get into some dark corners of New Day's privileged communications. Guess whose resume I located in their data files?"

"Kenny?" Dan guesses and nearly shouts his excitement.

"Right on," Jim confirms. "Shows he was in Department P of New Day, wherever that is. And two more nano whizzes work in Department T, which we believe is in Tampa. Might want to watch for two men named Teasdale and Wiggins. They're a couple of PhD's."

"Here's Jud." Jim hands the phone back to me.

"Jim's been busy," Dan says. "Anything else?"

"Well, their founder, Jason Grimes, is nowhere to be seen. Could be he's not even in charge any longer. Worse than that, there's a possibility the North Koreans could be calling the shots. And both of us strongly suspect New Day is into nano science, but instead of touting it, they're making a concerted effort to hide that fact."

Now Dan is flustered. "Koreans? What in hell? That's a real curve ball. What's your plan for today, Jud?"

"In fact," I continue, "that's part of the story about the Oriental lady. Turns out she's North Korean and she was pumping me."

"Yeah, well, what's new about that?" Dan cracks.

"No, I mean she was prodding me for information. I'm not sure they believed our cover story, so you guys watch yourselves."

Dan acknowledges my warning. "Okay. I'll let Jim tell me about the gay bar later. Anything else to report?"

"Jim and I toured their manufacturing plant and the labs and today we get down to talking about whether they can meet the government's needs and how fast. We gave them some tough specs to fill, demands they can't possibly meet unless they're seriously into nano materials production. Then we'll check in with you before we move on. Think we may make a quick stop in Vegas to pull some handles on our way back."

"Okay, Jud. Keep us in the loop. You have my cell number and home phone. We expect to be in Tampa through Thursday then fly home."

CHAPTER 17

Dan Cooper

We stop by my house in Trinity to pick up my car. Everything looks normal. Then I drive us to a downtown hotel where we'll set up for appearances. Fact is, Pat's never seen my house in Trinity. He likes what he sees during the few minutes we're there. We grab a quick snack before moving on—sandwiches and some frosty fresh Florida orange juice. I tell him we'll probably split our time between here and town. But the New Day folks will expect to be able to contact us at the hotel. Besides, the last thing I want them to know about me is that I'm a local.

They send a limo for us at the hotel shortly after noon and drive us to their plant near the waterfront. Pat's taking everything in like a kid in a candy store.

"Pat, I told you this is the place to retire. It's treating Ellen and me great, anyway. If we can't talk you and Judy away from Maryland, at least take some time and come down here to visit us."

"It is a beautiful place, Dan. Think I could get used to the weather and scenery."

Our limo arrives at the New Day facility and we're escorted into a large conference room with about ten other people. I scan the room looking for clues and similarities to what Jud has described over the phone. It's not hard to pick out one obvious match. One of the men at the table is definitely Oriental, and from his features, his high cheek bones and such, I speculate he could well be Korean.

Don't jump to conclusions, Cooper, I caution myself. .

"Welcome, gentlemen," says our host, Fred Michaels, head of the Sales Department. He makes a quick round of introductions and launches into their pitch. "Doctor Palmer will give you a corporate overview then we can discuss your requirements and how New Day can fill them."

By the time Palmer is five minutes into his presentation I'm having a hard time staying tuned in. This is a standard integrated circuit board operation I assume, so why the big rush to impress us? I hear Representative Feroukas mentioned and nod acknowledgement of our sponsor. Hell, I really could care less about the politician that paid off a favor to get us in here. What I want to know is what does this place have to do, if anything, with the threat of a serious epidemic? We don't have a lot of time to play games with these people.

Mercifully, the presentations are kept relatively short and it's our turn to state the purpose of our trip. Pat nods and I walk to the lectern.

My opening statement is, "Ladies and gentlemen, I won't burden you with the agonizing details of our requirements. We've brought along a set of notional specs the government has drawn up for the Galaxy project. You'll see they demand the latest technology. Pat and I are looking for a reliable source that can meet these parameters with a delivery time of six weeks or sooner."

I proceed to knock their socks off by distributing copies of the spec sheets that would clearly force them into delivering nano size design or shutting off the discussions now. A low murmur runs through the group. We've set some tough gates for them to meet. More important, they don't know it's all a huge scam aimed at exposing their possible complicity in a threat to national security. By the time they discover why we're actually in Tampa we'll have them nailed. We know Kenny contracted his illness while he was at some New Day location, so they're going to answer to us.

Before our audience can recover from their initial shock over the specs, Pat hangs a second jolt on them.

"We expected that Doctors Teasdale and Wiggins would be at our discussions today. Will they be joining us?"

They don't suspect it's a test. Those are the two names Jim has dug out of New Day personnel data files as nanotech experts working at Department T. That's Tampa in my mind.

The color drains from Doctor Palmer's face as I watch. He looks like a trapped raccoon searching for a way to skitter away and hide.

"Uh…they are no longer with the company."

"Oh?" Pat says. "Can I ask where they've gone?"

"Somewhere out on the west coast. This is a highly competitive field and their talents were much in demand," Palmer replies.

I try to look satisfied with his answer, but I recognize it as pure baloney. How could two scientists with their strong nanotech credentials have been lured away so recently that their resumes were still in the system? And how can New Day produce the IC's we're asking for if their super stars, including Kenny Grant, have left?

I'm having a hard time containing my amusement as I watch the pained expressions and foot shuffling around the conference table. Pat's probably as amused as I am, but he's concealing it well. People are pointing to items in our spec sheets and buzzing among themselves in guarded whispers.

"May I suggest," Palmer injects, "that you give us overnight to examine this data? You realize these are stringent requirements, of course."

I glance over at Pat and think to myself, *No shit, Sherlock. Let's see you wiggle off that big raggedy hook.*

But I just offer a smile and reassure him. "We look forward to your answer. Nine AM tomorrow okay for you?"

"That will be fine," he manages. He's still reeling. We've put him in a pinch. "We can do a walkthrough of the clean room and lab then, too."

On our way out we stop by the receptionist's station to drop off our temporary visitor badges. "Thank you, miss. We'll be back tomorrow."

Nosy soul that I am, I'm scanning everything in sight for clues. I see a special delivery package on the counter top addressed to New Day Electronics, Primm, Nevada, a town I've never heard of.

CHAPTER 18

Dan Cooper

According to Jim and Jud, we can now be certain that Kenny was on the New Day payroll. We have to find a way to attach ourselves to this company like leeches and suck dry their information pools. Where could Kenny have gone from LA to his eventual work site, Department P? Philadelphia? Phoenix? Portland?

Pat and I home in on the hotel bar as soon as we are dropped off. It's been a long day. Time to kick back with a cool one and add up our gains for the day. Maybe one night here at the hotel won't be so bad. Then I'll take Pat to my house and show him what Florida living is all about. Sit by the pool with a Murphy's and soak up some vitamin C.

Pat laughs. "You see how flustered those guys were this afternoon?"

"Think we pushed too hard?" I pose. "I was watching them squirm. What puzzled me, though, was why they didn't call it off when they saw our specs. Where's the expertise to deliver when they claim no great interest in nanotech?"

"Did it occur to you that they may still have a handle on those two I asked about?" Pat suggests. "Maybe they have them stowed away at this Department P where Kenny's been hanging his hat."

"Possibility," he says.

"Source is the big unknown, Pat. There has to be a lead to the source location we haven't put our finger on yet. If we can find it, maybe we can run down this virus in time to head off an outbreak."

He takes a pull on his brew and shows a sober expression. "Don't know about you, Dan, but it scared the crap out of me when Jim mentioned North Koreans mucking around at the New Day headquarters. And that one Korean looking dude here didn't say a word, but I got the impression he was sizing us up, trying to figure out our game."

"He was an odd duck, all right."

I reach for a handful of peanuts just as an eerie feeling freezes me. I look around the bar to see if anybody is watching our conversation. Have the odd sensation we're not alone. A young Oriental chap has taken a seat at the end of the bar nearest our table. He has one of those rigs that are in mode these days for hands-free conversations over a cell phone. At least that's what it looks like. Could just as well be a sensitive pickup to listen in on our conversation.

I lean across the table and say very softly to Pat, "Look at the guy with the headset sitting at the bar. Think he can hear us?"

"I don't know, but watch this," the Irishman says.

He walks in the direction of the bartender. Takes a hard, sidelong look at the guy on the bar stool and says something to him. I can't hear what it is. Pat puts a squeeze on the man's drinking arm with his big paw that brings pain to the guy's eyes. Reaches for the phone on the chap's belt and rips it away. Next thing I know Pat's dragging the dude off the bar stool and shoving him toward the door.

When he comes back and sits down at our table I ask, "What was that all about, Pat?"

He holds up a small device that on closer inspection isn't a cell phone at all. "Bastard had a listening device trained on us," he says, and frowns. "Asked him if he wanted to walk out of the bar or ride out on my foot. He chose to leave quietly."

"Maybe these guys we were talking to today aren't as dense as I thought," I tell him. "They could be breathing down our necks."

Pat turns the little amplifier over and over in his palm and studies it. "I spent a tour in service in Korea, Dan. That guy was definitely Korean—probably from North of the tracks, the way things have been going so far. If those commie bastards have their hands on a new virus strain, it could be big trouble. I don't like them being on the same continent with me."

* * * *

After our experience in the bar, we agree a sweep of our rooms for listening bugs is advisable. No pickups found. We continue our talk in my room. Call for room service and dig in for a skull session. Pick apart what we've gathered from Jim and Jud as well as our impressions of the visit to New Day. We agree that things are definitely picking up. Plot ahead for ways to draw out our hosts and get them to show their hand.

"Dan, we asked Celia Grant to check her phone records for the origination point for Kenny's calls to her. She said she was waiting on her monthly bill to show up this week. Let's give her a call. We have to pin down the virus source."

I nod and fetch my phone. Dial Celia's number.

She's already found the answer to my question. Every one of his calls came from area code 702. That code has a familiar sound. I thank her and tell her what we've learned about the suspect company. She's encouraged that we have pinned down New Day as Kenny's employer. I tell her to hang in and let us run it to ground. I'll be in touch real soon.

Before I finish, she drops a new bombshell.

Hanging up the phone, I turn to Pat and say, "See if there's a phone directory in that drawer."

He produces a phone book and I tell him, "Look for the area code map in the front. Tell me what's included in area code 702."

Pat scans the map of the US and puts a finger on the state of Nevada. "That's the area code for Las Vegas and all of Clark County. The rest of Nevada is a different code."

I pound my fist on the table "Thought it sounded familiar. Ellen and I spent a few days there last fall. Our source is somewhere near Vegas."

"From the way your face lit up, Dan, she must have passed along some other news, too. What was it?"

"Celia said Kenny's temperature lowered some and the rash isn't developing as they anticipated. He's really tapped out, mostly sleeping, while they pump him full of things to help him recover. But he did speak a couple of words to Celia while he was lucid. Said the word 'sphinx' and then something that sounded like 'prim.' The words meant nothing to her, though."

"Odd." Pat thinks about that. "What do you make of it, Dan?"

"I saw an out going package at New Day, Pat. It was addressed to Primm, Nevada. Maybe that's where Department P is located."

"Okay. It's worth checking. But sphinx? What in blue blazes could that be?"

"Don't know. Let's bounce this off the guys in California and see what they come up with." I'm already punching in Jud's number.

When Jud answers, my first words to him are a caution. "Pal, Pat just ran a Korean snoop out of the hotel bar. He was trying to listen in on our private conversation. You guys better watch your backs."

"I'm already painfully aware how vulnerable we may be, Dan," he tells me. "I spent Tuesday night in the clutches of one of his countrywomen. Scary, ain't it?"

"Depends on what you mean by 'in the clutches', Jud."

"Well..."

"Time to discuss that later," I tell him. "How did the session in LA go today?"

"Well. It was a bit tense to tell the truth," Jud answers. "The engineer that was sweet on Jim kept giving him the eye. I told him if he slugged the guy I'd have to kick his ass. We were almost home free so we didn't need a scene. The Korean chick spent most of the afternoon with her hand on various parts of my anatomy."

"I meant on other than the extracurricular level." I laugh. "Anything of value?"

"Not really, Dan. We left them talking to themselves. By now they're probably tied in knots trying to figure out how to bid the Cyclops work up without tipping their nanotech expertise. They don't understand they could bid it at a loss and still be wasting their time—'cause there ain't no Cyclops program, pal."

"Okay, new subject, Jud. What does the word sphinx mean to you?" I wait while some side conversation goes on that I can't quite make out.

"Jim says it's a code word for a technique he's used to penetrate particularly secure computer systems."

"How would Kenny know the term?"

A long pause follows then Jud answers.

"Sure. Jim says he showed Kenny how to use Sphinx when he was working at COB."

"Okay. Put Jim on speaker with us and listen carefully."

"I'm listening," Jim says.

"I think you two should make that trip over to Las Vegas. Now it's for business. Find a place called Primm. Somewhere in that vicinity we believe is where New Day has a facility they're probably carefully hiding. The source of the virus could be at that site."

"Say no more," Jud fires back. "We agreed to spend one day on the beach here then we'll drive up to Vegas. Soon as we finish kicking sand here we'll be bound for the desert. Looks like I'll be doing more than playing the slots my first time there."

CHAPTER 19

Dan Cooper

The second day of our meetings with New Day in Tampa will be of minimum value. Merely a matter of keeping up the front till we can melt away. Pat and I have all we came for. The ball is in Jud and Jim's court now. We need to wind up our business here and leave town while we're still ahead of the game.

The morning session begins calmly enough. Palmer and his cohorts have an endless list of questions about the tough specs we've laid on them, the nature of the Galaxy program, and, by implication, where we may be willing to relax our requirements. Eventually I get enough of their whining and their poorly veiled attempts to wheedle more program information out of us.

We both dodge their probes and take a hard line. Insist on seeing the production plant and looking at the labs before we close our discussions. Neither tour produces anything out of the ordinary. The clean room production is well managed and up to the standards we would expect. The on-site lab is a modern and well-organized operation, but it doesn't smack of state-of-the-art. A carbon copy of what a dozen firms could show us in the way of a microchip design and testing platform.

When we return to the conference table, the questions begin anew. I take another fifteen minutes or so of their onslaught then hold up my hand and wave it in frustration.

"Gentlemen, we're going in circles. You have our specifications. They stand as is. We're not at liberty to disclose any more about Galaxy than we've already told you. The question now is whether you can deliver."

The room is suddenly quiet and all eyes turn toward Palmer. "It's a tough requirement to fill, but we're confident New Day can deliver."

He just slipped a noose around his neck with that statement. Now I have no doubt New Day is nano capable and hiding it from us, but not very well. Are they going to get a huge shock when their proposal is rejected out of hand. By the time that news comes back we should be well on our way to hurting somebody in this outfit far worse than they could imagine.

"Thank you, Doctor Palmer. You have the written instructions for submitting your bid through our trusted agent. We will expect to hear from you within a week. As the instructions dictate, if New Day is selected your first delivery will be expected six weeks from the date of contract award. Thank you for your attention and your hospitality."

* * * *

We return to the hotel, gather up our belongings and make a beeline for the Suncoast Parkway. Then we head north to Pasco County.

Both of us are on the lookout for other cars in the traffic flow. These New Day cats have been hanging some strange behavior on us and the guys in California. No time for me to be exposed as a local. I do a couple of zigzags and side steps on the way north. Each time we check our surroundings and see nothing suspicious behind us. My license tag says Sunshine State so it could be any rental car on the lot, not one registered in Pasco County.

"Looks like we're clear, Dano," Pat says and wriggles out of his coat and tie. "All in all, I'd say that went pretty well." He turns and lays the coat on the back seat and goes into relaxed mode.

"I'd give a day's pay to see the expression on Palmer's face when they get their rejection," I say and laugh.

"Watch it, Cooper. You forget we waved a tidy chunk of business in their faces. Now that you're one of those stinking rich guys we used to complain about, don't forget how we used to grub for government jobs. Have a little compassion, man."

"I might feel sorry for them, Pat, if I didn't believe New Day is mixed up in something totally rotten."

We both fall silent for awhile then I gloat a bit. "Have to admit we were pretty slick the way we bid at COB Software. Won more than our share of the runoffs. Can't remember whose idea COB was in the first place, but it sure paid us handsomely."

Pat's about to doze off but that gets his attention. He opens his eyes and mumbles, "Jud put the idea on the table. But don't remind him. His head's big enough."

"Gotta tell you," I say, "it's great to be back working with you clutch of wise guys.

"Wonder who's gonna handle the bid New Day makes?" Pat speculates.

"That address we gave them is probably some dead end mailbox set up by one of the Senator's friends," I answer.

Pat points out, "It served its purpose, though. Got them to commit to delivering a product they can't possibly make unless they're hiding a nanometer scale design and production house somewhere besides Tampa. Primm, maybe?"

"Think we ought to reinforce the troops in the desert, Pat? Double up on these slippery operators?"

"Let's wait and see what the guys report from Nevada. I'm for unwinding at your place tonight, Dan, and heading back to Virginia tomorrow as planned."

The trip to Trinity is relatively quick. We've beaten the rush hour, such as it is. I take the opportunity to point out to Pat how little traffic we have compared to the metro area. Tell him it means a lot less time behind the wheel and more leisure to soak up Florida's beauty.

"My neighbors would appreciate an authentic Irish bar, O'Leary, if you insist on working that line of business. Still leaves us plenty of time to enjoy the Bay area. I'm already pushing on Jim. Told him he and Susie could float any size fishing boat they choose down here. We'll even find a good spot for bass fishing if that's what they want."

"Given enough time and snake oil, you'll have the whole population of the D.C. area down here. Maybe you ought to take up real estate as a sideline."

"No. Just looking for a few special friends to share America's paradise with us."

We pull into the driveway at my house. Once inside I go directly to the refrigerator and hand Pat a Murphy's.

"I know you're a discerning brew quaffer, so here's my best shot."

"No complaints here," he says and pops the top on the long neck.

The doorbell rings. It's Dino Curci from next door. He and his wife Patty are our closest friends here in Florida.

"Come in and have a brew, Dino. Want you to meet somebody."

He steps in and hands me two small packages. "Ellen asked us to watch out for deliveries on your front porch. UPS dropped these off."

I take a quick look and quip, "Ellen accuses me of trying to buy the accumulated published wisdom of the Western world. I tell her it's my solemn duty as a writer to soak up all the knowledge I can."

Pat comes in from the family room. "Oh. jeez," he says. "He's on his soap box again." Sticks out his hand and introduces himself. "Pat O'Leary, Cooper's sometimes business partner."

"Dino Curci." He turns to me and asks," How's Ellen, Dan?"

"She's doing great, Dino."

"Will you guys be in town long?" he asks.

"No, we're heading back on a morning flight to Virginia. Ellen and I will probably spend a week or two with Danielle and Rick."

We take a while to unwind in the family room. Feels great after the circus Pat and I have been through the past two days in Tampa. It's hell having to weigh every word you say with a bunch of vultures breathing down your neck. What a relief to be able to relax with two good friends. I can feel my blood pressure going down already.

Later, Dino excuses himself and Pat and I hit the patio. We sit and soak up the quiet of a balmy Florida evening. Makes me appreciate how quiet and peaceful Trinity can be after dark.

"Not bad, Cooper," Pat says. "Last day of March and it's in the seventies out here. Maybe I will talk Judy into a swing down here as soon as we clean up this mess we've stepped into."

I tap my bottle against his in a sort of toast. "I'm gonna hold you to that promise, pal."

* * * *

Pat and I take an early morning flight home. We go our separate ways at Dulles Airport and I drive on to Danielle's house below Fredericksburg.

"Good trip?" Ellen wants to know.

"Actually, we accomplished exactly what we wanted—that is, between us and the guys on the west coast."

"I won't ask what that means," she says. "Got a few days for us now?"

"Except for seeing Pat at the Leesburg office for awhile this afternoon, I'm ready to enjoy being with my two best girls. What's on the agenda?"

"Thought you could cook for everybody tonight. How does that sound?"

I look at Danielle and tell her, "In case you don't remember Mom's code that means 'where are you taking us for dinner out.' I like the sound of that place on Caroline Street Danielle was telling us about. I'll make a reservation. Meet the three of you there at seven."

With that settled I catch up on the news on the baby front. The girls have already planned for us to be in Virginia for an extended stay when the baby arrives. Ellen insists on being here for Danielle and I can tell that's perfectly fine with the prospective mother. After all, when has she *not* been there for her daughter? I think Danielle feels like I do these days, too. We're so lucky to have her Mom back to normal to light up our lives.

When we have a few moments alone Ellen confides that she was worried about why all four of us guys took off in such a hurry. "Made me think something urgent had come up. You sure everything's all right?"

I feel just a bit guilty glossing over the far-reaching implications of what we may be involved in, but there's no need for her to fret over it. If we continue to make progress like we did this week, we could have these bad boys wrapped up and salted away soon. No need to raise the specters of nano terror plots and virus pandemics. Scares the crap out of me, so I can imagine how Ellen would react. She's been through enough.

CHAPTER 20

Pat O'Leary

I make it to Leesburg a few minutes after one. Carole is sitting in the reception area alone.

"Hi, Carole. Dan not here yet?"

She says, "Just me and a visitor for you in the conference room."

I walk past her and look in at a gleaming new cherry conference table and a red-headed youngster. She's right behind me.

"Kevin," she says, and the boy looks up from a coloring book Carole has placed on a big white mat to protect the new table. "this is Mister O'Leary."

The little fellow stands up and greets me with his hand stuck out for a handshake. "Pleased to meet you, Mister O'Leary," he says then jumps back up into his chair to color.

"He's a charming young man, Carole. Think I could find a treat for him if it's okay."

She nods and goes to answer the door.

We're having a great visit and he's telling me what colors to use where on his picture when I hear Dan outside.

"He's in the conference room," Carole says. "Has a client in there, but he said come on in."

Dan peeks in to find Kevin and me hard at work on the serious task of coloring Easter bunnies and baskets of eggs. I'm telling Kevin, "Well, Mister Wilson, I think we can handle your case. Just where was it you last saw them?"

Dan asks, "Got a new customer, Mister O'Leary?"

"Yes, and not a minute to waste. This is Mister Wilson. We're looking for a fast-moving bunch of suckers that are trying to elude him. He says his Mom told him he could have a treat if us detectives could find out who ran off with them. Believe I've located the loot." With that Pat produces a big grape lollipop to Kevin's wide-eyed amusement.

"Thank you, Mister O'Leary."

"You must belong to that lovely lady, sir," Dan says to the boy and nods toward a smiling Carole in the doorway.

"Yes sir, that's my Mom. I'm Kevin and I'm five years old." He puts out his hand.

"Very pleased to meet you, Kevin. My name is Mister Cooper. Can I borrow Mister O'Leary for a while now that he's solved your case for you?"

"Yes sir," he says and goes to his mother. She takes him out into the reception area.

"Beautiful little fellow. Can't wait to have a grandchild to dote on," I tell Pat. "Heard from the guys yet?"

I look at my watch. "Let's see. Should be mid-morning in Los Angeles. Let's see if they're alone and what they've rooted out so far." I dial the new phone on the conference table and put it on speaker so we can both listen.

"Nekkid!" comes Jud Black's answer.

I ask him, "How'd you know it was us, wild man?"

"Who else would call me from a 703 number? Are you in Leesburg?"

"Jud," Dan says, "You wouldn't believe what Carole's done to this place in the past few days. Don't know what kind of budget Jim gave her, but this is class."

"I'll ask him. He's right here," Jud says.

"No matter. I like the results. What's the story on your end?"

"We decided to chill out and take in the Malibu scene since it was nearby. All work and no play…you know."

"Nobody ever accused you of being a dull boy, Jud."

"Anyway," he says, "we're on our way driving to Vegas. Jim prefers it and you know me and flying. Left about an hour ago."

I prompt, "Before we forget, give us a telephone number where you're staying, too, in case we need it."

Jim comes on line. "We're staying at the Venetian. Here's the number."

"How did your day on the beach go?" I ask.

"Think I got eye strain. You wouldn't believe what walks around out there. I thought for awhile Jud was going into overload."

"Clean break from the New Day crowd?"

"Not a peep. Guess they believed our act. They're probably up to their humps in stacks of paper trying to grab the Cyclops work. But Jud and I got all we needed. We know New Day is the right target, that they're doing nano work and hired Kenny Grant. We also have a strong idea there's a New Day facility somewhere near Primm, Nevada and that Kenny was calling his mom from there or from Las Vegas. Here, talk to Jud. I'm trying to drive on the Interstate with these California idiots."

When I get Jud on the phone I prod. "Want to tell me about the escapades you hinted at from the first day?"

"Oh, you mean the gay bar and the Korean hatchet woman. Well, I'll leave the first story to Jim. He can tell it much better than I can. As for my adventure, there was this long-legged, gorgeous gal that worked me over in ways that amazed even me, pumped me for information I wouldn't give her, and reported back to somebody when she didn't think I was listening. It was terrible, Pat, but I survived."

"Yeah, well, Dan's listening in and I think he believes about as much of your sad story as I do. Sounds to me like you got yourself laid as usual and probably screwed over this gal's mind in the bargain."

Pronounced silence from the other end.

I prod, "So what's the plan now, guys?"

"Jim's already found Primm on the local map," Jud says. It's between Vegas and the California state line down Interstate 15 about 40 miles. We'll look for a chopper service that will take us on a daytime flight over the Primm area so we can scout it out. Give the pilot some sort of story about looking for Indian mounds or gold mines or something. Who knows, maybe we can spot something interesting out there and follow up."

"You want us to fly out, too?" Dan asks.

"We'll call for help if we need it. Just sit tight and wait to hear from us. Any news from Tampa?"

Dan breaks in again. "They gave us some sort of lame story about the two nano scientists having left for parts unknown. But they also said they expected to bid on the Galaxy job. It definitely takes nanotech design to do that work."

Jud comes back with, "Same kind of crap they fed us. Couldn't explain where Fetter and Drehlin had gone. Those were the other two nano freaks Jim sniffed out from personnel files."

"Well, we located one of them," Dan says. "Had a death from dengue fever out in California a few days ago. His name was Richard Fetter. Celia wrote out his last name on a card and showed it to Kenny. He answered 'Richard'. They could have been exposed at the same place."

"Sounds like they're gathering the talent all in one location, maybe at Primm, huh? This is getting more interesting by the minute."

Jim's obviously been following our conversation. He remarks, "I did some more surfing. Seems there are at least three more prominent nanotech gurus mysteriously no longer working at a couple of the national labs. Could be New Day's coaxed them to join the team as well."

"Let's keep the pressure on, guys. Have to move fast and hope they don't get suspicious before we make our move. And keep Jud away from the show girls in Vegas, Jim."

Jud rescues his phone and gives me a big Bronx cheer. Then he says, "Seriously, Pat, if there's something out there in the desert we'll find it. Let me call Celia and alert her we may need an assault team and a biohazards crew ready to move."

"Good idea, Jud. With her contacts that shouldn't be too hard. And tell her to thank her pals on the Hill for all their help so far. Appears to me we still have the advantage if we move fast."

I hang up and turn to Dan. "Think you could entertain Kevin for a few minutes? We owe it to Carole to let her know the kind of people we could be dealing with. Don't want her caught off guard if they connect any of us with this office. Kevin doesn't need to hear this."

Dan goes out and asks Carole if he can take Kevin down the street for ice cream. She agrees and I sit down for a serious discussion with her.

"Carole, it's only fair to tell you we're into chasing some shady characters that could turn on us. We don't think they know who we really are, but I suspect they have the resources to find out. If they connect us to COBB Eye, you could have some unwelcome visitors to Leesburg."

Feel queasy about hanging this on her. After all, she's only temporary and we may have put her in harm's way.

She smiles and says, "Do your job and don't worry about this place. I have a licensed handgun and I know how to use it. That little beauty stays right with me till you snare these bad actors. Anybody lays a hand on Kevin or gets out of line on your private property, I'll blow them away."

No idle threat in her words, just a statement of fact. Don't know how we got so lucky, but I'd say the home office is in capable hands.

Chapter 21

"You have ignored my instructions, Ali Hassan. What am I to do to impress upon you that my word is the law here?" Kim Yung glares at the Arab and bores a hole through him with eyes as cold as a blizzard.

Ali stares back as if the words are a mystery to him.

"What can you possibly mean, Kim Yung? What directions have you given that were not followed to the letter?"

"You have resumed training your assault forces during the day when they could be observed by outsiders. Do you not consider the security of our desert fortress?" Kim's anger begins to rise.

Ali answers, "I have explained that the men and women of *al-Qinaa'*, The Mask, thrive on the pleasure derived from seeing how effective their strikes will be against the American infidels. I must be permitted to do what I think is necessary to keep them ready for the moment of *jihad*."

"Do not tell me what I must do, Ali. I alone will set the rules for as long as you and your people remain our guests. Why do you suppose this place is called the *song*, the citadel? I have entrusted the safety of our entire force to your complement of assassins. Your inattention to my orders endangers us all."

Kim looks away and busies himself with papers on his desk. His dismissive attitude grates on the man standing before him.

"When I came here to provide the biological materials you needed, Kim Yung, it was my understanding that we would carry out this plan as brothers, not as overlord and servant. My people are essential to achieving your goals. Do not lecture me, lest the teacher become the student."

"A threat? Do not sink to that level. I ask only that you respect the need to have unquestioning cooperation if we are to succeed. We must not draw attention to our remote location if we expect to remain safe from the eyes of the Americans."

A soft rap at the door.

"Yes?"

"It is Lotus, *sah bum nim.*"

"Yes, *chagun* kkot. Enter," Kim answers.

Lotus has arrived at an opportune moment. The two men are having difficulty containing their anger. She has come to summon Kim to his midday exercise and has given him time to control his rage.

"Master," she says, "I have made preparations for your afternoon *poomsae.* Will you come to the *dojang* now?"

"Yes, precious flower. Wait for me there while we finish our business." She casts her eyes at Hassan, and sees the tension that hangs in the air between the men. Lotus is not only beautiful but perceptive as well. She surely must recognize the almost tangible aura of animosity in the room, a conflict that has been building and is near the boiling point.

She acknowledges Kim's instruction and withdraws. As soon as she has left, Kim turns again to Ali and continues.

"The subject is closed. There will be no more outdoor daylight exercises." He prepares to answer but Kim dismisses his protest, waving an arm.

"Since Lee Hwan met with his unfortunate accident, you, Ali, are responsible for the recovery of Kendrick Grant to the citadel. Tell me now of your success in locating the deserter and returning him to our fold."

Ali's frown tells Kim all he needs to know. The Arab has failed.

A dark grin starts at the corners of Kim's mouth. Ali fancies himself as menacing as the venomous *mamushi* serpent, but he is no match for Kim in body or mind. Kim Yung is as the tiger, the *horangi,* and he can crush Ali at will.

Hassan continues. "My emissary, Abdul, has found the young escapee where we supposed he would be. He has fled back to Virginia to his mother. We have no way of gaining access to him to bring him back."

"Explain. I do not accept this excuse."

"He is isolated, Kim Yung, secured in a hospital ward where diseases of unknown origin or consequence are contained. My man can not enter that space."

"Then your path is clear, Ali. Your agent must risk his life to see that Kendrick Grant is restored to the fold."

"What are you saying?"

"You must convey to your man that this is part of his mission. He wishes to carry out *jihad,* to be a martyr. This is his opportunity."

Ali's expression transforms into a deep scowl. He is struggling with a decision. But Kim will not let him retreat from his commitment. Ali assured him that the members of al-Qinaa' would gladly accept that they may be martyred before their plan concluded. They would go gladly forth to find their reward in paradise. Very well, Kim is ready to test their will.

"But you said this young scientist was essential to your design, Kim. You have told me he must be returned alive."

"That is unchanged, Ali. Grant must be returned unharmed. Your man will achieve paradise and my valuable scientist will be back in the citadel where he belongs. With his help we have progressed near to our goal. I will not forfeit his knowledge now."

"I understand. We will make it impossible for Grant's protectors to refuse. He will be returned safely to you."

"Yes, Ali. But we do not know if he remains too ill to speak to others of our work. The sooner we act the better."

"Then I will send the order to retrieve Grant at all cost. Any who stand in the way will be cut down. I will dispatch your message and two of my best people to assist Abdul in carrying out the mission."

Kim nods assent and motions for Ali to leave the office. He has taken enough time with his inane excuses.

Returning to his leather chair, Kim sits and begins to reflect. When he came to this country as a student, Kim could only hope to play a role in reuniting his Korea. Now that goal is near at hand. He will destroy anyone who stands in his way. He has been more than patient, attended the finest universities to learn skills in electronics and biology. The realization that the two worlds could be merged into an overwhelming force has driven him to the brink of success.

The annoying Arab does not comprehend his true role in this undertaking. He and his people are convenient tools to arrive at the end goal. How they share the outcomes will be Kim's decision alone to make.

"Do not challenge me, Ali," Kim admonishes. "*Al-Qinaa'* has been a reliable source for the biological agents with which we are building our weapons. You provide the trained guards to secure our desert fortress and keep us from prying eyes. When the time comes, and that is sooner than anyone other than I can realize, your people will be our messengers of destruction. But you must conform to my edicts."

"Kim Yung, my warriors' skills will enable you to distribute the 'cloud of death'. If not by concealment, then they will happily offer themselves to martyrdom in personal attacks to achieve our purposes. The *Sulafi* will succeed, but you must not offend them."

Kim stares at Ali and thinks how he is deceiving him. The fanatic fools, in particular the deluded Ali Hassan, will believe he will aid their cause in the Middle East. Kim does not care what happens to them or their Muslim brethren.

"I must go now to my ritual in the *dojang,*" Kim announces. "Lotus awaits me. Leave me now and heed my commands."

Lotus patiently awaits Kim Yung's arrival. "Master, I have laid out your *dobok.* The black always seems to heighten your passion for excelling and adds grace to your moves."

She offers the uniform and assists him in removing his business attire. Her hands move over his body, fingers flutter across Kim's muscles. Now he can transform both his body and spirit into the true nature of Kim Yung, warrior of the people, conqueror of all who would doubt. He stands as she winds the belt about his waist and places the sandals on his feet for the ceremony of humility and obedience to honored ancestors.

Then Kim prepares for the *poomsae* under the adoring eyes of Lotus, his delicate *chagun kkot,* and feels the surge of power in his body.

Soon the Communist fools in the north will know his wrath. He is Kim Yung, deliverer of his people. He embodies the future of a nation.

CHAPTER 22

Ali Hassan leaves Kim's office and returns to his own sparse quarters.

"Pompous yellow ass! He deludes himself. If not for his promise I would kill him now. Kim says he can force the Americans to leave our Arab lands."

He contents himself for the moment to vent his anger in words. The one person at this desert compound who he can trust listens patiently. She listens without questioning, knows that though Ali is filled with rage, he is intent on concealing that fact from others.

His sister Jamila lets his words linger then calmly replies.

"Your patience will be rewarded, my brother. The Mask will prevail over all who seek to divert the *jihad.* Even Kim Yung will feel our vengeance when the time is ripe."

"Allahu akbar," she declares and raises one arm high. "God is great. We glorify his name."

Jamila. Even her very name means beautiful. She is short of stature but a powerfully strong woman in so many ways. Her dark eyes and raven hair, her beaming smile all remind Ali of their dear mother who was violated and killed by the Russian soldiers when they invaded Afghanistan. Jamila understands as no one else can what Ali burns to achieve. Others have boasted of their willingness to give their all for the Arab people and the holy war. Ali Hassan will carry out that promise and dwell in paradise. Others praise fools who have gone before, fools like bin Laden and Al-Zawahiri who fancied themselves instruments of the people. But those false prophets are weak and fall short. Ali understands the mind of America, knows that it must fall from within.

"Our *Sulafi* brothers have carefully built our base in America, Jamila. One cell, one *medrasa* at a time, we have grown into a force that will not be defeated. With *al-Qinaa'* serving as the sword of retribution, we will triumph."

"Al-Qinaa'," Jamila salutes. Ali's sister sees the joy of his passion and assents.

"Tell me, Jamila, what have you learned of our mister Grant?"

"Abdul reports he is watching closely for his first opportunity to steal the deserter away from his protectors and return him here as you wish, brother."

"Kim Yung has issued the order to retrieve Grant to resume his pivotal role in our attack plan. I am sending help to Abdul to perform this task."

"What of my report as to Grant's associates?" she asks. "How did Kim Yung react to that?"

"I withheld it, Jamila. As the treacherous Korean has done with us, we shall conceal from him all that it is not essential for him to know."

"Then what shall *we* do to terminate the efforts of those who would seek to learn the cause of Kendrick Grant's illness?"

"Sister, we know that he has ties to his former employers and that one of them met with his mother at the hospital. Our informers at the Los Angeles and Tampa sites are certain his friends have tried to penetrate New Day. That is information we will use to our own advantage."

"But will we silence them as well?" she asks.

"No, we will track their movements and act only when we believe they present an immediate danger."

She nods agreement but Ali can feel her uncertainty. As she turns to leave, he questions her.

"Why do you doubt my decision?"

"Ali, as I told you, two of the young scientist's friends may now be in Las Vegas. Su Lin Kim, who is Kim Yung's agent in Los Angeles, has befriended me. You met her on her visits here. She has a loose tongue. Su called and told me that one of Grant's friends attached himself to her. He pictures himself a virile man. Did not know he was in the grasp of a determined and resourceful woman. But she did not break him. He spoke to her of coming to Las Vegas to visit. They will be much too near our citadel. Should we not divert them?"

"Let me ponder that. For now, I want you to alert our entire number, all of the Mask not detailed to stand guard over the citadel, that we will commence training at dusk."

Jamila hesitates and searches his eyes for more.

"Tell me the rest, brother. I know your expressions, your unspoken concerns. How may I lighten the burden?"

Once again she has kept his temper from spilling out when it could have diverted him from their goal. She deserves to hear what he is thinking.

"Kim Yung has made a promise to us. He vows that his weapons of doom will panic the Americans; that the ultimatum to follow will ensure they leave the Middle East for good. His promise alone keeps him alive."

"And we are content for the moment to help bring that about, are we not?" she asks.

"I have known Kim Yung much longer than you have, sister. He and I were classmates long before I brought you over from Afghanistan. At our New England campus I could not imagine the impact our acquaintance would have on the world. He was another of those far eastern intellects I learned to despise for their smug confidence. He had exceptional knowledge of electronics and the physical sciences, a fact that only heightened my suspicion of him. When we discussed our biological studies, I learned that he had quickly adapted to a totally different discipline and mastered it as well. Such a mind is capable of feats most normal men would shudder at undertaking."

"But he has promised to rid our homeland of the Americans."

"Yes, Jamila. Still, he is *maskhuteh*—much hated. One day I will send him to *dshehenna*, to hell where the devil lives."

"And for now, my brother?"

"Kim Yung ranted on to me about his own homeland and how it must be cleansed of its despotic leaders, reunited for the sake of all Koreans. He seemed to think a higher power had anointed him to be his countrymen's savior. For months at school I listened and kept my own feelings to myself. Then I saw the possibilities that an alliance with him might offer."

"Yes," Jamila says, "And so far the benefits have been to both the Koreans and the Mask."

"When I first broached my plans for *al-Qinaa'* and told him recruitment had begun, he registered interest immediately. Many nights we sat until late into the evening mapping a plan that could bring both of us deserved renown among our own peoples and break the backs of the American imperialists. But even then I believed it was only a far off dream."

"Remember that the *Q'uran* teaches patience in the extreme."

"I know the teachings well. It is Kim Yung's deceit that worries me. I have, since the outset, recognized that he is a manipulator of people, a user of one's talents for the good that accrues only to him. How do we know he will not betray us?"

"I can not answer that, Ali."

"Then I will consider the weight of that doubt. For now, we will concern ourselves with matters of the present. Prepare our band for a rigorous session in the hills tonight."

"Yes, brother."

* * * *

The members of the dedicated al-Qinaa' band are assembled. They have trekked into the barren hills several miles away from the citadel. Only those on guard duty and the men sent to retrieve Kendrick Grant are excused from this demonstration. Their strength has grown steadily these past months. The word reached people of like minds, immigrants from Afghanistan and those in the homeland willing to travel here and cross the US border into California. Ali and his followers offer each of them an important role in taking down the hated Americans. Twenty three faithful warriors now stand in the desert dusk awaiting Ali Hassan's instructions.

Jamila looks at her brother intently, perhaps still wondering about the meaning of their earlier conversation. He studies her face, the dark mystery of this woman child, her intense eyes. His decision is made. She will receive her special assignment tonight.

"Loyal followers of the Mask, our moment of victory draws ever nearer. Soon we will announce ourselves to the world. The shock waves will rock this land from coast to coast. They will know of our resolve, our commitment to rescue ourselves and others from the persecution of the infidel American dogs. Our forebears will be glorified and the non-believers will writhe crushed by our force."

Their faces brighten and a chant begins: "*al-Qinaa'! al-Qinaa'! Death to the infidels!*"

"Tonight we test our stealth and endurance, brothers and sisters. I have designated that place as a protected target." Ali sweeps his arm in the direction of a small earthen hut in the midst of the arid hills. "This night a team of five attackers has been dispatched to find our location and overwhelm it. Three defenders wait inside. We will observe the skill of our companions as they carry out their assault. They will succeed for they are the *melek el mot*, angels of death."

Whispers ripple through the group and there is a tide of excitement.

Ali explains, "Light sensors and explosive devices guard the objective. If any on the team are careless, they will meet with the fate of the impure."

There is a look of both uncertainty and anticipation on the faces of the warriors. To a person they are anxious to see the test commence, knowing that each of them will face the same or equal test soon. Ali has laid out the objectives of this trial on three occasions pointing toward this night. Now they will each in turn finally prove their merit to be called *al-Qinaa'*.

Jamila looks at him and he senses her disbelief that he would put her, his own blood, at risk. She should know by now that all loyalists are equal in Ali's eyes and she is not permitted a special preference. The strict code demands no less from each member.

All observe total silence while the exercise unfolds. In the moonlit night they can observe subtle signs of movement on the landscape. There is no way of knowing whether those inside the shelter can detect the same motions. Long minutes pass and only occasional fleeting blurs, an instant of reflected light or dimly perceived activity betray the clandestine movement of the skilled warriors. Splendid! They are the *khanjar*, the dagger Ali will drive into the American heart.

In a hushed tone he issues a reminder to the assembled group.

"The rules establish that the trial is a success if all five penetrate the inner space. Failure occurs and the test concludes upon the first shot from a defender or when a sensor explodes."

He waits, his mouth dry, heart racing, anxious to declare attainment of the objective.

They rivet their attention to the small structure and await response by the defenders. But none comes, no sound of automatic gunfire, no signal of recognition. The assassin team is performing brilliantly. All praise to their skill.

A cloud passes from the face of the moon and the attackers are outlined in profile to those observing from a distance. They are within seconds of achieving a resounding victory. Then a loud explosion rocks one corner of the roof and a dark figure is catapulted into the air, tossed to the desert floor.

Ali rises and sounds the horn to signal an end to the test. *"Silahlari jeer kojyn*, put the rifles down," he orders.

All rush to observe the result of the detonation. For one the outcome is final.

"Observe closely the harvest of haste and inattention. We regret the loss of our companion for what she could have contributed to our final success. But we value her effort and rejoice that she is in paradise with the martyrs."

A graphic lesson has been learned. No measure of error is to go unanswered.

Jamila looks down at the ravaged body of her sister in arms and a shudder passes through her small body. She looks at Ali, a question in her eyes. Could this be her fate before the mission is complete?

"Jamila. Stand aside. I would have a word with you."

Ali and Jamila separate themselves from the group as they recover the martyr's body for burial. He draws his sister aside to the row of trucks and poses a question.

"Do you have one person in whom you can place special trust to accompany you on an important mission?"

"Leila is dedicated and capable. I would choose her."

"Then notify her and prepare yourselves to drive to the city tomorrow. The troublemakers in Las Vegas must be diverted from their queries. Bring them back to me to be questioned. If that is not possible, you must dispose of them. Do you understand?"

"Perfectly, Ali. We will not fail."

"Baraskallah. May the blessings of Allah be with you."

CHAPTER 23

Jud Black

Jim and I are sitting on the freeway in a rental car. We picked it up at the LA airport after dumping our New Day escort. They insisted on seeing us to the plane, but we blew off their offer and hightailed it to the rental counter. Stowed our bags and set out north of town.

That was yesterday. Now we're humming eastward after talking to Dan and Pat by phone. They want us to go over to Las Vegas and snoop out this Primm connection.

"Glad you convinced me to take a day off and unwind, Jim. I was beginning to get spooked about the whole LA area. Kept looking over my shoulder watching for fruits and mad Koreans chasing after us."

"Yeah, once we turned loose and took a breather, California didn't look half bad, Jud. Have to say your suggesting a day at Malibu was one of your better ideas."

"Liked the scenery, huh?" I make a gesture with both hands like I'm propping up a huge pair of boobs. Jim just smirks.

"Don't know about that. Susie told me I'd be struck blind if I dwelled on such things.

But the extra day to clear our heads was great. Now I'm ready to plunge into the rattlesnakes' den in the Nevada desert."

"What do you think we'll run into over there, Jim?"

"I'll be better able to answer that as soon as I figure out a way to penetrate their system and do some data mining," he says.

I lift a map from the seat and open it. "Looks to be about 270, maybe two hundred eighty miles over to Las Vegas. We'll get a chance to see the town of Primm on the way. It's about forty miles this side of Vegas."

Jim takes his eyes off the road and looks over at me with a big smile. "Bet those guys back at New Day are putting on the full press to figure out just what the hell our game is. After the weird hoops the folks in LA put us through and what the guys reported from Tampa, we could have a pack of angry wolves breathing down our necks."

"Let 'em sweat, Jimbo. Both visits were worthwhile. We're gonna nail these gibroneys." I sink back into the soft leather seat and prepare myself for a long ride. "Holler when you want to switch drivers, pal."

In a matter of a couple minutes I'm oblivious to the freeway traffic and the morning heat. Let Jim cope with that for awhile. I'll be fresh to spell him when he's ready.

It's not the restful nap I'd anticipated, though. Some pretty weird visions parade through my head. Kind of like a bad dream with side benefits.

I seem to be sitting in a room full of odd looking people and all of them are giving me a steady grilling. Their efforts don't intimidate me—it's the fact that one of them is a stunning Korean babe and she's sitting next to me with her hand on my leg. Makes it a bit testy to keep my story straight. I strain to listen to their questions and hear about every third or fourth word. Make up my answers as I go along. They're so fascinated by their own voices that I'm getting away with it, though.

Then I lose my concentration completely. Somehow optic coating materials and nanotech labs don't seem so important any more. When that cutie brushes her tongue across those pouty lips and says, "Hi, I'm Su. Let's go to my place," *I stand and address the room.* "Some other time, guys. Just mail us your cost estimate."

I look over at Jim. He's in the middle of fighting off three or four bare-chested guys with leather bikers' jackets. They all have this odd expression like they're on a hunt and he's the quarry. Well, he's on his own. I have serious business to attend to.

Just as I take Su by the hand to leave, my dream is interrupted.

"Wake up, Jud. Snap out of it." Jim's tugging at me. "I'd swear you were reliving your interlude with Miss Pyongyang." He chuckles but keeps his eyes glued to the road.

"Idiot!" he calls out. "Did you see that dumb ass? Good thing my brakes work."

"Wha...? Oh, I was about to get it on, dude. Didn't you have something better to do than wake me?"

Jim doesn't answer. He pulls off at the next exit and turns to me. "Okay, I fought these freeway cowboys through town. Now it's your turn. Don't get us lost in the desert." He steps out on the driver's side and walks around the car. I shrug and scoot over to take the wheel.

Before Jim can get in on the passenger side, something screams by and nearly runs him over. My first thought is the bad guys have tracked us down. I'm out of the car checking on him in an eye blink. Don't know which one pisses me off the most, being chased by some Korean hit man or seeing Jim come within inches of being run over.

"Come out of there, dipstick," I bellow and head for the black SUV.

I'm ready to pound the driver into the ground, but before I can yank the door open, a figure comes hurtling out. At least he's not one of Su's countrymen.

"You cut me off!"

My momentary relief goes away in a flash when the man reaches into his jacket and produces a nasty looking knife.

"Whoa, neighbor. No harm intended. Just settle down and let's talk," I offer.

"Screw you, buddy. Probably a damned tourist. Think I'll cut you a little at a time to watch you squirm."

This is going from bad to scary in a hurry. I'm facing a raving mad crazy. No room for logic here. Just make a move and hope he's slow on the uptake. I'm about to dive at him and hope when an arm curls around his neck and he falls backward. The knife flies out of his hand and I dive for it.

The guy splutters and chokes. I hear, "Don't say a word, Wyatt Earp. You'll be lucky if I don't break your face."

Jim is standing over him with one fist cocked. How he circled around the SUV and hit him from behind I don't know, but it was one hell of a maneuver. Very likely saved me from a couple of extra body holes I couldn't live with.

"Put that shiv in the car," Jim says. "He doesn't need to be running around with it." Jim picks him up by the neck and pins him against his vehicle.

I drop the knife in the glove compartment of the car then walk over and remove the keys from his SUV. Heave them as far as I can. "Maybe you can cool off while you hunt for them," I flip at the flustered man. We leave him there talking to himself.

When we've merged back into traffic I ask, "You okay, Jim?"

"Didn't touch me," he answers. "But it wasn't because he didn't try. Guy was boozed up or on something. Little guy like him doesn't need a temper like that.

And he for sure doesn't need to be carrying a weapon." He grins and says, "Maybe we can put it to better use in the desert."

We're well along beyond town on I-15 when I ask Jim, "Just what is this Sphinx thing, anyway?"

He thinks for a long minute then gives me what sounds like a guarded reply.

"It's a series of steps in a technique to penetrate hard-to-access data systems. Takes advantage of one of the lesser known back door entry points to break down some pretty tough security measures. I only know Sphinx because I worked with government info nets. Studied both defensive techniques and penetration methods so we could block intrusions. Kenny and I used Sphinx effectively several times in the past."

"So you think we can get into New Day's knickers with these routines?"

"I'd bet that's what Kenny was trying to tell his mother. All I need is a connection to the network somehow and I'm off and running."

"Think I'm gonna like Vegas," I tell him.

CHAPTER 24

"How does Kenny look this morning, Doctor Samuels?"

"Your son is a lucky young man, Celia. Kenny can thank your quick action for his survival. I think I'll move him to a private room today. We know now that his condition isn't contagious and he's much improved."

For the first time in more than two weeks, Celia Grant feels the pain lifting. It's been pure hell watching her son suffer, not knowing whether he would survive this vicious dengue attack. She prides herself on being able to hold her emotions in check when she's faced with an emergency, but the mother in Celia takes over when Samuels speaks those encouraging words. She literally falls into one of his office chairs and buries her face in her hands. Celia bawls like a baby; lets it all out.

"Celia," he says, "the best therapy of all will be for him to see you today. But you'll have to show him a happy face."

"I know. Give me a few minutes then we'll go to him."

She walks toward the powder room outside isolation to recover her composure. Frank Kane, the plainclothes policeman on duty at the isolation ward entrance, sees she's upset and inquires, "Everything okay in there, Doctor Grant?"

"This could be a great day, Frank. Kenny may be moving to a private room."

"That could be a big change for me," he says. I'll call for backup until we figure out how to handle this."

Seeing Frank reminds her the troubles are far from over. The nature of Kenny's illness alerted them that he could be in continuing danger from whoever exposed him to the dengue virus. They've stationed a plainclothes policeman at the door as an extra precaution. There hasn't been any suspicious activity, but that doesn't mean Kenny is out of the woods yet.

All the waiting and agonizing is swept away in an instant when Celia enters the isolation ward, approaches Kenny's bed, and sees his beaming face. She bites her lip and works hard to keep herself together for his sake.

He motions for his mother to come closer. She leans over him and he says "Thanks, Mom. You saved my hide."

Those words are the first ones he's spoken to her—other than disjointed feverish bits—since she brought him to the hospital. They're like music to her. She kisses him and says a prayerful silent thank you; turns away for a moment and brushes her wet cheek.

"You had us worried, Kenny, but you'll get your glow back, son."

"What was it, Mom?"

"No reason for you to worry about that now. Just lie there and rest."

"Tell me."

He's still feverish. No telling how much he could even comprehend at this point. But he's talking. Celia just wants to hear him.

"It was dengue fever, son, but the staff here built up your strength before it took hold and brought you through. Everything will be great now."

He looks up at her and moves his head side to side on the pillow. "Never be right." He's trying hard to tell her more but he can't seem to make the words come.

"That can wait, Kenny. Get your strength back then you can tell me all about it."

He points toward the ice bucket on the bedside table. Celia looks over at the nurse who nods and gives him ice chips to wet his mouth.

"Labs," he manages. Celia can see it's getting harder and harder for him but he has her stubborn streak.

"Nano labs…Bio…Chimera."

His words send a shock through her. He's confirming her worst suspicions. She'd had a queasy feeling ever since she peered through that microscope at his blood sample. No wonder the structure looked odd—it *must* be a dengue virus that was laboratory-modified on purpose to make it more virulent and aggressive. Kenny could have progressed to the hemorrhaging stage and been beyond help if they hadn't acted rapidly.

But the scariest part of all is that he said chimera. In biology a chimera is an organism made up of two or more different genetic components. Celia rolls over in her mind the implications of that word coupled with nanotechnology. If someone has been able to build a single combined molecule with pieces of two biological agents—it's almost too horrible to imagine. What if Kenny has been exposed to a chimera containing dengue and another deadly agent? A chill comes over her.

Kenny is tugging at her hand. "You called Pat?" he wants to know.

"Just as you asked, Kenny. He's already working the problem. Your old friends from COB are all descending on New Day for answers."

"Primm. Sphinx." Kenny is fading fast now. His temperature seems to be on the rise. Celia needs to leave so he can rest.

"I know, Kenny. Jim Barnett has already joined them on the search. I'm in touch with Jud Black. He's in Las Vegas now along with Jim."

"So sleepy," Kenny mumbles. She checks his forehead and finds he's burning up.

"You're sedated, son. Just relax and let it work."

That seems to relieve his anxiety. He relaxes and momentarily nods off. It's time she let him have some quiet and a chance to recharge his batteries. Celia watches over him for awhile then kisses his cheek and turns to leave. There will be plenty of time later after he's moved.

"Mom?" he calls out weakly.

"Yes, Kenny."

"Koreans. Arabs. Ummm." He's reached the limit of his energy reserve. His lids close and he goes off to sleep.

Celia Grant walks out of the ward numb down to her fingertips. If Kenny's right, someone at New Day is putting together biological agents with altered characteristics for who knows what insane purpose. They could be mixing multiple agents into a single delivery dose. What if they really are terrorists planning to deliver a double punch, say dengue and smallpox together? It could bring mass panic and death.

Now Celia realizes what disturbed her about the blood test they performed on Kenny. She knew the strain of dengue differed from any she'd ever seen. But there was another anomaly there she couldn't quite grasp. Celia needs a high power microscope to look at another blood sample. Somewhere in the DC area there has to be an electron microscope. If there are multiple agents loose in Kenny's blood stream, she has to know now!

She leaves Kenny resting and draws Doctor Samuels aside. "Let me issue a caution. Maybe you shouldn't move Kenny just yet."

"You'll have to explain why, Celia," he says.

"He may be infected with more than one disease. Although we wouldn't be dealing with a contagious disease in dengue, there may be another problem lurking. I need a fresh blood sample to scan under the nearest available scanning microscope."

"We'll draw one now and you can scan it over at Johns Hopkins. Celia, I hope you're wrong."

"So do I, Sam. Oh god, so do I."

CHAPTER 25

Celia is only away from the ward for a few minutes. When she returns, Frank Kane, the policeman, isn't at his normal post. She finds that odd. He did say, though, that he had to call his backup about Kenny's changing rooms.

"It's Doctor Grant," she tells the nurse on the house phone. There is a long pause.

Finally, the door release trips and Celia enters the ward. A large shock is waiting for her. Some of the people standing inside shouldn't be there. Frank Kane stares at her with a helpless look of frustration, and she immediately sees why. A slender, dark man in green hospital scrubs has Frank firmly in his grasp with one hand circled around Frank's neck. In the other hand the stranger, who has a scraggly black beard, is holding an ugly weapon that's nearly buried in Frank's ear.

"Welcome, Doctor Grant. You will make a splendid bonus catch," the dark man says.

She scans quickly to her right. The other intruder, also dressed as a hospital orderly, is only a few steps away. He's also holding a weapon and he's aiming it directly at her. Kenny had mumbled something about Koreans and Arabs. These two certainly fit the second category.

"Karim will accept your purse now, madam, and you may turn to face the wall," Scraggly Beard tells her.

She hands the leering young man her handbag. His partner's tone tells her she has absolutely no option but to do as she's told. Karim folds her hands behind her and wraps something around them, drawing it painfully tight. For a fleeting moment Celia debates with herself about raising a protest, but the man's rough manner tells her that's not a good idea. The scum even takes the opportunity to grab her breast and squeeze it. At that moment Celia would give anything to have her hands free to scratch the weasel blind. He spins her around to face the bearded man who is obviously calling the moves.

"Now," Scraggly Beard says, "we will all leave the ward quietly and calmly. You, mister policeman, will assist Doctor Grant the younger to the wheelchair and I will wheel him out. Be assured that we are on a holy mission. Karim and I will be more than happy to end your lives if you resist in any way."

"You could hurt Kenny," Celia protests. "He hasn't fully recovered."

Karim, the one who tied her up, steps forward. He strikes her with the back of his hand across her cheek. The stinging blow sends her staggering on unsteady feet.

"Silence!" he barks.

The talkative one assures them again that they would kill in an instant if anyone calls out for help. He informs the head nurse that the first to go if they sound an alarm will be the doctor followed by "both of the Grants." They leave the ward, all six of them moving somberly into the corridor. Doctor Samuels and Celia are in front followed by the younger of the two Arabs with gun in hand concealed by a towel. Her son, in robe and sandals but only half awake, is in a wheelchair with Frank walking at his side. The bearded man pushes the chair and keeps his weapon at the ready dangling behind the chair's back. Celia has no doubt the two men will shoot them and anyone else who gets in their way at the slightest provocation.

Down the hall and up the elevator they go. The group emerges into the main lobby and proceeds toward a side hospital entrance. Celia sees a large white van with hospital markings waiting outside. Scraggly Beard coaxes everyone toward the van and steers Kenny toward a third stranger by its open door. Celia's heart is racing now. All the time she senses that Frank is looking for an opening, calculating his options. Dangerous thoughts are running through her head—thoughts that, if acted upon, could get her killed.

As Scraggly Beard leans over to set the wheelchair's brake, Celia sees her chance. She steps forward and spins toward the younger Arab, swings her leg up forcefully and catches him squarely in the crotch with her high heel. His eyes water; he expels a long breath and drops to both knees.

A commotion breaks out behind her, but Celia is too engrossed to see what's happening. People are running around and someone shouts. But all she wants to do is be sure she's disabled Karim, who is no longer grinning at her. He clutches his middle and groans. She kicks the gun away from his reach.

A sharp crack and a thud sound. She whirls around to see the bearded man fall to the pavement and drop his weapon. Frank hovers over him. As Scraggly Beard attempts to rise, Frank dives for the weapon on the sidewalk, snatches it away and shoots him in the stomach. Then Frank turns to focus on the van, but the driver pulls Karim into the vehicle and roars off with tires squealing. The van slams against a parked car, bounces off and speeds away.

The sidewalk is swarming with people, some gawking, some trying to help. One woman looks at the bleeding Arab and screams. One startled driver swerves to miss the van and runs off the pavement onto a grassy slope with his horn blaring.

Hospital security arrives and takes charge. The wounded bearded man is taken into custody by Frank and rushed inside for treatment.

"Kenny, are you all right?" Celia pleads.

He grins and says, "Great move, Mom." Then he laughs and she sits down on the sidewalk and lets out all her tension in a wave of tears. The heel on her pump is broken, so she takes off both shoes, tosses them aside and breaks into uncontrolled laughter.

Minutes later they are back at the isolation ward as a precaution until Celia can check the blood sample for other possible germs. Kenny is resting under sedation and Frank is sitting in the anteroom with her.

"How in hell did you pull that off, Doctor Grant?" Frank asks and chuckles.

"Instinct, I guess. Knew you might take advantage of a diversion if I could create one. When my husband was a diplomat, I was often in touchy situations in foreign countries. He insisted I take self-defense training. That came in handy today."

"I'll say. Hit him where it hurts. Bet that Karim fellow is wondering right now if he'll ever have any little Arabs."

"My oath says *First do no harm.* It doesn't say I can't level somebody when he's about to hurt my only child."

"Thanks, lady. I'm impressed."

"Now if you'll excuse me, Frank, I have a date with a big microscope."

Frank registers a puzzled look as Celia hurries off to pick up the blood sample from Doctor Samuels.

CHAPTER 26

Dan Cooper

Pat calls to tell me about Kenny and Celia Grant's close call at the hospital. That puts a whole new spin on things. I'm beginning to wonder just how secure my wife and daughter will be here in Fredericksburg. Celia has told Pat there are covert FBI details assigned to keep a watch on our wives. The girls won't even know they're being protected. The feds are convinced the loose Arabs are a definite threat. But the New Day crowd is no doubt resourceful. Walking into the hospital like they did—they're capable of anything. I'll have to trust that the agents know their business.

I had hoped to spend more time here before we went running off again. But it sounds like Jud and Jim will need help in Las Vegas. Guess I'll have to cut the visit short and convince Ellen to stay in Virginia a bit longer while I go to Las Vegas. Pat's already booked our flight west.

I take my son-in-law aside. "Rick, I'm going to tell you something you won't like, but it can't be helped."

I can see the apprehension in his eyes. He probably wonders what new mess I've gotten embroiled in this time. I'm sure Danielle has told him about the Minerva's Net caper and how close that came to taking Ellen from us.

"Thought you had retired and left all this high tension stuff behind, Dan," he says.

"I'm struggling with just how much I can say here, Rick. Believe me, if I could back away from this I would. It's a matter of the gravest importance to our future and, in fact, to the country's future. That probably sounds melodramatic but, unfortunately, it's true. Pat and I have to fly out west for a few days, maybe a week."

"You know Mom's welcome here," he assures me.

"I know, but that's not all. There could be some pretty shady characters looking for me back here. They've already surfaced in Fairfax and tried to kidnap a friend of mine, but the police have them. Others could be running around."

"Oh, no! What can I do?"

"They've called in surveillance. In case the bad guys track me to Danielle and come looking here, there will be a protective detail waiting to nab them. The girls don't need to know. I'm sorry to put you through this, Rick. But believe me, it's too important for me to let go now."

"I'll trust you on this, Dan. But what if harm comes to Danielle or the baby…"

"You know how important Danielle and her Mom are to me. I would never do anything that may expose them to harm. We're performing an important service for the government and they've assured us our families will be guarded around the clock.. We should have this whole mess wrapped up quickly, and we could avoid the worst…well, let's just leave it at that."

One of the hardest things I've ever done in my life is to leave Ellen behind under this cloud. There is barely time to say our goodbyes before I rush away to Dulles to meet Pat for our flight.

"Ellen," I tell her, "it seems I'm always asking you to trust me on something and to have patience just one more time. And you're without a doubt the most patient person in the world. I'm asking again. Pat and I need to fly out west for a week or so. This is important—critically important to a lot of people. Wait here and visit while I'm gone. Please?"

"That's all you're going to tell me?"

"Honey, I would tell you more if I could. You know I've had to keep some things from you about my classified work in the Air Force. You always understood there was no choice."

"But you're a civilian now, Dan. The only silly civilian I have, you big galoot. Are you sure this is necessary?"

"More than you can imagine, baby. Give me a week."

Her brown eyes cloud up, and it's clear she's read my own concern over what I'm facing. But Ellen is a real trooper.

"Well, I don't like the sound of this, but I see you're determined to do whatever it is you guys are wound up in. Be careful, Dan—and call me."

"I will, sweetheart."

An agonizing vision keeps coming back to me all the way to the airport and across the country. I see Ellen in that hospital back in Florida just two weeks ago fighting for her life and it gives me the cold sweats. The best I can hope for is that Ellen will continue to survive my penchant for sticking both feet into the middle of the nearest trouble spot.

Sadly there is no good alternative. The quicker all four of us COBB guys turn to and help root out the terrorists' den, the sooner we can all rest easy.

CHAPTER 27

Jud Black

Jim tells me he had a good reason for driving to Las Vegas. Says he picked up a couple toys in LA that the airline may object to. I guess he'll explain that when he's ready. When we reach Primm, Nevada forty miles from the Strip we stop for a quick meal.

"Hey, Jud, they have those things in the hotels, too," Jim says. I've already lost a roll of quarters in the slot machines and we're not even in Vegas yet.

"Figured I'd better take my chances while I could, Barnett. You'll probably put me to work as soon as we check in."

"Surprise! Thought I'd give you this evening to relax and chill out after your trying episode with Miss North Korea. Want you fresh and clear-headed when we get down to business."

We swing by McCarran Airport to gather up airline schedules. Plan on a couple nights here at most then we'll head home—unless we make a big find out in the desert..

"I take it you know where we're headed," I offer when we leave the airport.

"Relax. Got you covered, Jud. You're gonna like this place."

We zip along going west on Tropicana Boulevard. I'm stunned by the sights of Sin City. Never saw anything like it. Nothing but sand in every direction and then all of a sudden the damnedest oasis you could ever imagine.

"Booked us something special," Jim says as we motor toward the strip.

"Uh-huh." I'm too absorbed by what I'm ogling out there to pay attention. It's one visual shock after another.

We drive by the Hard Rock with its huge guitar marquee. Rocker and blues man that I am, that place will definitely be a stop on whatever tour of the city we manage to work into our schedule. We get a straight-on shot of the Excalibur rising like a medieval castle out of the desert. Then Jim rounds the corner by the MGM lion and starts up the Strip.

"Looks like a war of the hotels, Jim. You build your wildest dream and I'll top you. A foot race to see who can be the biggest and most eye-catching. You know, I've heard a lot of stories about this town, but you can't really grasp what it's about till you see it for yourself."

"Get a load of that, pal," Jim says. "That's the New York New York. Has its own Statue of Liberty, Brooklyn Bridge and Coney Island roller coaster."

"I know we have serious business here, buddy," I tell him. "but this is too good to miss. I can't wait to play tourist."

"Let's treat ourselves," he agrees. "We'll check in and make the circuit. Then we can find one of those helicopter services and take a chopper ride out over the Primm area."

"Great idea, Jim. We'll give Primm a look see from the air and plot our approach. Who knows what we may find out in the hills. Did you see how many miles of open country we drove through back there?"

Jim smiles. "I was thinking that if these bad guys want to hide an operation," he says, "there's lots of room in that stretch of desert."

I'm already absorbed in staring and enjoying this feast for the orbs. There's the Bellagio and its much ballyhooed dancing fountains. That definitely goes on our schedule. And the Paris with a version of the Eiffel Tower perched over it. Caesar's Palace showing the new front I've read about. Impressive. Have to admit these hotels with their giant showrooms bring to mind this humble guitar picker stepping out onto the big stage. Dreams of my shot at playing for a crowd in a glittery room and holding them with my tunes.

"Damn, Jim, this is one long string of eye candy. It's bright, brassy, phony and totally fascinating."

"Hang tight a minute," he says and grins. "You haven't seen the best yet. Ever seen pictures of Venice, Italy?"

"With the boats and canals and all those old buildings topped by statues?"

"That's the place. Take a look up ahead."

Jim turns in at the most impressive hotel on the Strip. It stands out from its surroundings. Gondolas glide through waterways in front as statues of Roman figures keep watch. Tall clock tower and bridges, the look of an Italian postcard. Looks like somebody built a private world and plopped it right down in the middle of a busy city on its own preserve.

"Incredible!" is the best I can come up with. "What is this place?"

"It's the Venetian," Jim says, "and we have a couple of suites booked."

"As my favorite Little Orphan Annie, might say, 'Gloriosky, James, I think I wet my pants."

"Time to make like the beautiful people, Jud."

"Wow! Speaking of which—do you see what's milling around out there?"

"Jim laughs and says, "Keep it together, pal. They're everywhere."

I take my eyes off the scenery, architectural *and* female, long enough to get checked in. There is a message waiting at the front desk for us.

Jim looks at the call slip and says, "Pat. I let him know where we'd be bunking in. His message asks if we took a mule train over here. Wants us to call as soon as possible."

On our way to our rooms—excuse me, our suites—we walk past the casino. I start to veer off and Jim nudges me toward the elevators.

"Later, Black. It'll keep till we ring Pat and find out what's on his mind. Sounded urgent."

I turn to make a wisecrack and collide with somebody. She reels and I reach out to catch her. Meet a pair of deep, dark eyes so intense they send a tingle down my neck. Looks to be Hispanic or maybe Indian.

"I'm sorry," I say and help her stay upright. "Clumsy of me. Are you okay?"

She beams up at me and those eyes do a number on my hormones.

"No harm," she says and slides away toward the lobby. For once I've been outmaneuvered before I even have a chance to make my play.

"Did you see those…uh…eyes and things, Jim?"

"Steady, man," he laughs. He's watching my stare follow her as she melts into the crowd.

"This town's full of them."

We walk onto the elevator and I punch 12, the floor on my room key folder. As the doors close I have this sudden urge to check my pockets. Search my pants for keys, billfold, credit cards. Everything seems to be there. Then I pat my shirt pocket and find something missing. The small pad where I've been jotting down notes is gone.

"Damn," I spit. Jim casts a puzzled look at me.

"My note pad's not here. Must have dropped it in the taxi or the lobby."

"Anything important in it?" he asks.

"Depends on your definition of important," I answer. "I usually scribble down lyrics as they come to mind. A songwriter's mind kicks in at odd times and weird places. Hate to lose any ideas that may not come to me again."

"Oh," he says and checks his key card. "I'm in Suite 1212. Heard the clerk say yours is 1216. That'll be handy."

Just then it hits me. "Bad news, Jim. There was something else in that book. I wrote down some bits and pieces that could be important."

"Like what?"

"Just disjointed words. Primm. Sphinx. Dengue. Don't remember how much I wrote but it likely gave some details about dengue fever and nanotechnology. You know, things to jog my memory about angles on what we're chasing. Probably jotted down a few words about our experiences in LA, too."

"Hope you didn't mention the fruity engineer or the Korean babe," Jim cracks.

"The more I think about it, my notes wouldn't mean much to anybody but the dudes we're trying to track down. We don't want them to see that book and figure out how much we may already know about them."

"Oh, no, Jud. The girl. Could she…?"

"Hell, she could have given me an all-over massage. I was so absorbed taking stock of the rest of her I had no idea what she was doing with her hands except for one big thrill. When she stumbled and grabbed my upper leg to stop her fall my brain sort of short circuited."

"No fixing it now," he says. "She's long gone. We'll have to hope the driver found your book in the taxi. If the girl did take it, she could be a common thief and won't even know what she's lifted." The elevator stops at our floor and he says, "Stop by my place and we'll tell them to hold your bags downstairs for a few minutes. We'll call Pat."

Quite a place, I think to myself when we step into 1212. Not exactly my place back home I call Nekkid Hideout. I can take a little pampering for a few days. Big bedroom and elegant bath then a few steps down to a sitting room with a view. This is a view! Looks out on the volcano fountain across the street at the Mirage. Bet that's quite a sight after dark. Brings to mind lyrics for a song. I reach for my note pad and curse my inattention that I let it get away in light fingers.

Well, what's done is done. Time to attend to business.

"Before we forget it, let's trade key cards, Jud." We'd taken the extra precaution of having two keys cut for each suite in case we needed access to each other's digs. No telling what could unfold here in the big town. Jim holds out his extra key and I swap with him.

He grabs the phone and puts it on speaker then calls Pat. Motions for me to have a seat and listen. "Jim here," he says. "Got your message."

"About time," Pat's voice bellows at us. "I was going bonkers trying to reach you guys."

"We both had our cells turned off and just checked in here at the Venetian. What's up?" I ask.

"The buzzards are out and we're targeted as the road kill," Pat says. "Couple of bad actors tried to kidnap Kenny and Celia right out of the hospital. She and a policeman assigned by her Senator friend outsmarted them."

"Jeez," I fire back. "Are they okay?"

Pat laughs. "Yeah. Celia did a job on one of them. Speared him in the middle with a high heel. He was a hurtin' puppy."

"Ouch," Jim squeals.

"The cop blasted one of the dudes. Not sure whether the guy survived the drilling. The other two got away."

"Got away?" Jim blurts out. "If they're on the loose and have connected any of us with Kenny…I have to check on Susie."

"Hang on, Jim. Protective details are hovering over Susie, Ellen and Judy till this caper is over. All our wives are in capable hands."

Jud chimes in. "Looks like all the real action is back on the east coast."

"Maybe not for long. Listen up, you two." Pat's voice takes on a serious note. "These bums are playing by some pretty nasty rules. They walked right into the intensive care unit packing automatic weapons under their orderlies' uniforms. Talk about a big set of cohones!"

"Which means what?" Jim asks. "Does it change what we're here to do?"

"No," is Pat's answer. "We still need to find out what New Day has going out at Primm. But we may have to work a lot faster, and you guys will have to watch your backs. I'd be willing to bet they've connected us to the Grants by this time."

That strikes a chord. I ask, "So what or who do we watch out for? There are about a million folks swarming all over this place. All shapes and sizes. Do we avoid Koreans or what?"

"Maybe." Pat pauses then adds, "But these bad boys were Arabs."

Jim looks at me with a pained expression and the hair on my neck bristles. We both go very quiet.

"You guys quit breathing or something?" Pat throws at us. "Sounds like mighty dead air on your end."

I try to recover and say, "I heard your remark about little Arabs. Hoped it was just you generalizing."

Jim speaks up. "Think we may have already run into the enemy, Pat." He relates how I nearly bowled over this smoky-looking chick downstairs and found the tables turned when she copped a feel. Tells them about my missing notes.

"This girl—what did she look like?"

Jim takes a deep breath. "Arab, Pat. Now that I think about it, she looked very Arab."

It gives me a queasy feeling. I wonder who I may run into next. If she'd been wielding a knife she could have gutted me on the spot.

"Look," says Pat. "Let me gather up Dan and fly out there. Vegas is where we're going to find our answers. Maybe strength in numbers is what we need. They can't put us *all* out of commission."

Jim gulps and says, "I'm not sure I like the thought of them nailing *any* of us."

"Hang tight guys. We'll book into a different hotel and be in touch. Keep your cells turned on in case we need to ring you. And Jud...if you bump into another babe, deck her *then* check for weapons."

"No," Jim says, "I'll deck her for him. He'd forget what he was looking for." Then he adds, "Wanta guess what his reaction was to that?"

"Probably involved a middle finger," Pat responds.

Well, let them have their fun, I think. I've been giving them my horny kid routine for so long they're beginning to believe it. It's part of my act just like my guitar strumming. The girls go for old bashful Jud. I can't argue with success. As a friend of mine used to say, I've had my face slapped a lot, but I've also spent some interesting evenings. Old Jud's not about to let any woman outthink him.

"Watch your step," Pat cautions. "Kenny told his mother there were weird things going on in the hills near Primm."

"How so?" I ask.

"Nanotech labs and biological agents," he says.

"Nuff said," Jim answers. "I bought some protection in LA. We may need it."

After the call I ask Jim, "What was that crack about protection? What kind of toys did you pick up back in LA?"

"Made a quick stop to retrieve some items I ordered from a friend before we came out," he says. "Telephone bugs, listening equipment, that sort of thing. And this." Jim takes a small gun from the side pocket of his laptop case. "Now you know why I wanted to drive over."

I go to my suite and look up the Las Vegas helicopter tours. Place a couple of calls. Ask about a private tour for two people and inquire how much latitude we have on the pattern they'll fly. The second guy I reach sounds intrigued by the chance to do something different. He says we can do just about whatever we want as long as he knows ahead of time. I tell him we want to swing out over the desert toward Primm and the state line then double back to see the strip lit up at night. We work out some details and he quotes me a price. Most any fee he would have asked for would have been okay, but he doesn't know that. I agree and he tells me we're all set as long as we come by within the hour and pre-pay.

"Jim," I announce when I call his room, "I'm ready for the fifty cent tour of the Strip. The chopper's lined up for later. Swing by. We'll leave the car here and grab a cab. I'll fill you in."

At the chopper trailer down the Strip we make it clear to the pilot that we want to make a sweep around the whole Primm area and do some loitering over the hills. He looks a bit perplexed over our interest in that desolate section.

"Real estate," Jim tells him.

That seems to answer his curiosity. The way the Vegas area is booming, I expect he's become accustomed to real estate speculators. He shrugs his shoulders and says he can provide the flight. Quotes a new price and adds onto his earlier quote. I'm in no mood to dicker over cost so we agree and pay him. He gives us a confirmation.

"You know there's a line of hills out there called the McCullough Range", he says. "It's rugged terrain."

"Is that a problem?" Jim wants to know.

"Not for me. It'll be some tossing around for you guys, though."

I look at Jim. Maybe he's thinking what I am. Couldn't be a better place to tuck away a covert operation New Day wants to keep away from prying eyes. Anyway, we don't have much of a choice at this point. Have to get a line on these characters somehow.

"How low can you get over those hills?" Jim asks, almost as if he's afraid to hear the answer.

"Fellows, if you can stand the jarring, I can put you so close you'll be able to count the coyote droppings." I have this strange feeling he's looking forward to seeing the reactions of two first-timers.

"Fine by me," Jim manages without much conviction. He's not fooling me. He's as spooked as I am, but a close look is exactly what we need. If the ride is as rocky as the pilot has advertised, we'll both have to cross our legs and grit our teeth.

With the flight arranged and a takeoff time of five o'clock, I look at my watch. Tell Jim, "We have a couple of hours before the chopper lifts off. What say we do some cab hopping and check out a few of these monster hotels?"

"Okay by me, Jud. Where do you want to start?"

"How about that pyramid hotel, the Luxor?"

"Whatever. Then I'd like to see the Eiffel Tower and the Bellagio fountains. Understand they're both real spectacles." He steers me in the direction of the nearest hotel to search for a taxi.

It's a quick tour but totally mind-boggling. We pull up outside the Luxor and I take a long gaze up the side of that massive building. This is probably as close as I'll ever come to appreciating the size of a real pyramid. Then we walk into the Luxor and I'd swear we had just landed on the banks of the Nile. The statuary inside that hotel is overwhelming. I'm trying my best to keep from looking like the country boy spirited away to the big city, but the whole Egyptian thing is more than I expected. Just for kicks I lure Jim onto the inclinators to prove that not all elevators go straight up and down. It's a creepy experience.

I drop a few coins in the casino slots. The machines are hungry today. They make this kind of hum and clunk sound like "whir...thank you very much, whir...thank you very much." Maybe later, I'm thinking.

We hop another taxi and work our way down the Strip to the glitzy Mandalay Bay. Take in the view of the gold front and the lobby with its overhead mobiles. Quite a place. Then it's off to the Paris Hotel.

Jim and I get our tickets and catch the elevator up to the tower. This may be a scaled down replica of the real thing but it's plenty tall for me. Turns out it's one of the better places along the Strip to get a good view of town from south of the airport to the hills in the west. Still plenty of sunlight left and I'm absorbed by the spectacular sights. I've always had just a bit of fear of heights. Could be one of the reasons I don't like airplanes. But with those big steel girders on all sides boxing us in, I actually feel almost comfortable up here.

Jim tugs at my arm. "The Bellagio fountains are starting up, Jud. Look at that."

The music plays and the fountains dance in rhythm. We're too far away to hear the classical music I'm told they feature, so I watch and add my own melody to the waving sprays. Imagine a blues beat, one of my own tunes driving their patterns. If Dan was here, engineer that he is, he'd probably be explaining how it's all rigged underneath and timed to the score. Guess his engineer noodle can't help working in that mode. For me it's all about the beauty of plumes of water several stories high moving to the beat in my head.

I'm so riveted to the sight that I jump when a hand touches my elbow. Turn toward the contact and stare into those same dark eyes that mystified me back in the Venetian casino. My first impulse is to go into defensive mode.

She smiles and says, "Didn't mean to alarm you. I had to be certain it was you. I have something that belongs to you."

"Oh?" This should be interesting. *Watch her moves, Black.* Then I see Jim standing close behind her and decide she wouldn't try anything with him here. We're all three trapped on this platform with no way down but an elevator that comes and goes every few minutes. Besides, we've already tried and convicted her of theft and here she is contacting me.

"A little book," she says. "You must have dropped it when we ran into each other."

Okay, I'm game. Let's hear her story.

"I looked back," she says, "and saw it lying on the floor. By the time I fought my way through the crowd back to it you were gone."

That sounds credible enough, I think. *I'll test her.*

"Hope you weren't shocked by what was in that little black book."

Without hesitation she answers, "I only looked inside the front cover to see if there was a name or phone number where I could reach you. Anything else in there was your business and not mine. But it could be important to you. I'm glad I ran into you again."

I'm watching her eyes. Except that they are still a most intriguing pair I see no hint of what's behind them. Maybe she's telling me the truth. Even if she's one of the New Day rogues I can certainly handle myself. There's an Oriental chick back in LA that can attest I'm no easy pickings. Either way a little time with this honey could prove interesting.

"Would like to have it back," I tell her. "I'm a song writer and it has some of my new lyrics."

"Tell me where I can get it to you." She bats those lashes at me. *Careful,* I caution, *Pat said be wary of strangers.* That book certainly doesn't need to be floating around, no matter whose side she may be on. And I'm still not convinced she's leveling with me.

"Will you be in town tomorrow?" I ask. "I have something planned the rest of today that I can't cancel."

"Just tell me where and when you want it," she purrs.

The words *right here* and *right now* come to mind.

"Meet me for lunch tomorrow?" I propose.

"I know just the place." She describes a little sidewalk cafe just off the Strip. It sounds safe and very public. Says we can have a leisurely lunch and visit for a while. We agree on noon.

Almost as an afterthought she says, "Now that we seem to have a date of sorts, maybe I should ask your name."

"Jud. Jud Black. And you are…?"

"Jamila. Jamila Hassan."

CHAPTER 28

Jud Black

"You're not really gonna meet that girl, are you, Jud?"

"Hey, Jim, we agreed we don't want the New Day guys getting access to my notes. What if you're right about her and she's after us. It can't hurt to meet her out in the open in a very public place. I mean, I *am* a big boy."

"I keep thinking," Jim tells me, "That it was either one hell of a coincidence she ran into us again or she's been following us. Nobody's saying you can't take care of yourself, but how can we know how much backup she has, how many helpers could show up and do you harm or cart you off somewhere? Sounds mighty risky to me."

"Trust me, pal. If this gal is looking to sock it to old Jud, I may have a surprise or two for her. She won't know I'm on to her. I might pick up some important info. Besides, she could be squaring with me. And if you're wrong—well, a little diversion won't spoil our plans while we wait for Pat and Dan to arrive."

"That's your hormones talking, pal. The town's teeming with women."

"Give me a break, Jim. I'll keep my eyes open."

"Well, I still have overnight to talk you out of it," Jim says. He looks at his watch. "Right now it's time to grab our chopper ride."

The pilot gives us a short orientation to the hop we're about to take. He warns us again that low-level flying over the mountain ridges could be more than we're bargaining for. Jim insists that's the whole point of the flight. Says we're checking out real estate possibilities and need to hover over both Primm and the mountains. The pilot asks us to sign a responsibility waiver in case we're injured. Don't know how Jim feels about that, but it makes me nervous as hell.

Then the helicopter revs up and we're airborne. We're lifting off to the west.

I watch the city slip away as our bird climbs out for the hills. When the desert looms ahead it's like stepping back in time—just miles of open space and no visible signs of people. But I soon realize the desert is by no means barren as I expected. Cactus and a whole variety of other plants dot the landscape and there are actually patches of green. Still I feel like I'm looking at the world's longest beach without a shore.

"How hot do you think it is down there?" I ask our driver.

"Oh, we aren't in the hot weather season yet. Probably not even 90 in the sun. It'll be well over a hundred when the hot days arrive this summer. Want to try a little walk today?"

As soon as he starts to drop altitude I resolve to keep any future questions to myself. "No thanks. I like it up here just fine." That gets a chuckle from Jim.

"Quite a sight, huh?" the pilot says. He smiles and does a little maneuver that brings us over the highway. "That's I-15 down there. Notice most of the structures are clustered near the highway. It runs southwest from town across the California state line. Death Valley is on our right a few miles north."

Jim questions, "Are there any loners out there away from the Interstate?"

"Sure. Some hardy souls like the peace and solitude of the desert. If you look close enough you'll see roads snaking out through the sand. And there's lots of animal life—some of which you don't want to meet on foot."

That brings some pretty weird pictures to mind. "I'd rather not meet them on foot or other wise, if it's all the same to you," Jim barks.

"That's the town of Primm down there. I'll circle around and let you get a good look. Actually has some local hotels and casinos. They catch a few of the headline entertainers between Vegas engagements. Not all the amenities of the Strip but the locals and the Californians like it. Fewer tourists to contend with."

He veers over and gives us a good view of the California side and flies back to Primm. The town stands out like a green oasis in the midst of a lot of open country. I look at Jim. He's taking a closer view through his binoculars and writing notes. We make several passes back and forth over Primm until Jim says, "Okay, now swing through the mountains."

"You got it. Hang on, guys."

Jim asks, "Where could I find a Primm telephone book?" The pilot does a double take at his off-the-wall question.

"You can check the book in our office when we get back. Looking for something in particular?"

"Just curious," Jim says. Jim is never 'just curious'. His convoluted mind is hatching something he'll tell me about in his own good time.

The pilot tells us, "You fellows said you wanted some time over the McCullough at low level. I have plenty of fuel to give us a few minutes loiter time. Show me a spot and I'll try to get low. Then we'll take a look at the lights along the Strip and head home."

"Give it a go," I tell him.

Jim nudges me as we fly toward the hills. Shows me a note he's made. It says 'Primm phone number for New Day'. He taps his pen on another entry that reads 'Sphinx'. He's told me that Kenny's reference to Sphinx has to do with a series of actions the two of them used previously to penetrate computer systems. Jim learned it working with government computer security measures. Turns out it's an elegant process for passing firewalls and sniffing out a back door into a computer network.

"Listen up." The pilot's voice has a note of urgency that gets my attention. "Be sure you're buckled in securely. You may need to use those straps on the wall to steady yourself if the wind currents are heavy. If it gets too rough for you, shout out for me to break and I'll pull up and out."

I yank my seat belt so tight I'm barely breathing. Take a death grip on the strap and ring. Not a second too soon. The wind currents through these hills are a bitch and we hit some pretty scary updrafts. I can't shout 'break' or anything else. Too busy chewing the inside of my cheek and hauling my butt back in the seat every time we lurch.

"Jeez!" Jim shrieks. "You weren't kii-i-iding."

The chopper labors and rocks till it feels like riding one of those mechanical bulls. If I had any fillings they'd all be rattling.

Then suddenly everything goes calm and peaceful.

"Found a crease in the turbulence, fellows. Don't know how long it'll last. Show me where you want to home in for a closer peek." He's enjoying this ride a lot more than he should.

Both of us have been searching the ground for roads and signs of life. My eyes have been darting every which way tying to focus on anything that would take my mind off the jitterbug our bird is doing in the sky. Jim's giving the landscape a gander through his binoculars.

"Over there," he says and points. "Follow that road."

The helicopter pilot swoops in and tracks along maybe two hundred feet up and off to the side of the rocky road. He follows a vehicle winding down the road for a mile or more. Just as we pull up and get tossed in our seats again I see the vehicle stop.

I twist around and point at the object. Jim says, "Got it." He trains his glasses on the stopped vehicle and tells me, "White van with a sign on the side that reads New Day, Primm, Nevada. Write this down, Jud." I grab his note paper and write. It's a telephone number.

I nudge the pilot and ask, "How about another pass over that road?"

He brings the chopper around and dips down. No sign of the van. It's like the thing vanished right into the hillside.

I tap the pilot on the shoulder. "Thanks. Now let's have some calm air and city lights."

He jerks a thumb in the air and climbs out over the ridge.

CHAPTER 29

Jud Black

Once we're back on the ground and I'm beginning to get my balance on good old mother earth, we duck into the chopper service shelter with the pilot.

"Sorry about the bump and grind over the desert, fellows. The air currents were worse than expected." He opens a desk drawer, sets out a bottle and finds three paper cups. The way his hand is shaking when he pours, I get a whole new set of goose bumps. SOB almost ran us into the ground out there. My shot goes down quickly.

"You wanted to see a telephone book," he tells Jim.

"That's okay," Jim answers. "Don't need it. Thanks for the ride and the drink."

"Once in a lifetime experience—if I'm lucky," I add. "Was quite a view over the Strip. Whose spotlight was that again?"

"The Luxor," he says. "You can see that light for miles. Have a great time in Vegas, guys." He stashes the bottle when new customers walk in and turns his attention to them.

In the taxi on the way back to the Venetian Jim tells me, "Good start, huh, Jud? We may have found the snakes' den in the mountains. The whole tour was a real eye-opener."

"Just deposit me at the nearest bar, Jim. I need a couple more stiff belts to settle me down. I want a long sit down in a seat that isn't moving around."

Jim laughs. "I know the feeling. But it was worth the hassle. Now we need a visit to New Day's office in Primm and a closer look at where that mountain road leads."

"What was the deal with the telephone book?" I ask.

"Oh, I need a way to get into their computer network. All it should take is to lock onto their phone line and burrow in from there. The telephone number on that van gave me all I need. Unless they have a mighty strong firewall the Sphinx routines will get me deep inside their data banks." Jim's on a roll and anxious to get to work with his laptop.

I backtrack. "So bar time can wait. I'll hang out in your digs while you do your magic."

Once Jim is into his search he's like me on a programming binge. Between the mumbled 'ah-has' and 'sumbitches', he's tapping data reservoirs and writing pages of notes.

"This is priceless, Jud. Their security isn't all that bad at the Primm office I've been able to navigate their data with ease. Their whole operation is really wormy. Kenny probably got into their shorts and found out more than he could handle. My guess is he cut and ran—somehow survived the desert—and got out of McCarran Field before New Day could throw up an airport blanket."

"Sounds logical to me. It would explain his condition when he showed up at Dulles. Celia said he was strung out, dehydrated and looked like he'd rolled on the beach somewhere."

Jim says, "I'd bet that when Kenny recovers, he and I can put together a convincing case against New Day."

"Can you give me a dump, Jim, on what you're finding in those files?"

"Sure. Appears whatever they have in the town of Primm is just a front. The real action is up in those mountains past the dead end road." He checks over his notes. "Their files refer to a place called 'the citadel'."

"Any clues about what's going on up there?"

"Yeah, I picked up some info on that. It's scary stuff, Jud. They're transporting materials to the mountain for use in labs somewhere inside those hills."

"Labs? Nanotech operations?"

"Can't tell. I do know it involves hazardous materials—biohazards."

"I'm almost afraid to ask, Jim. Can you tell what they're doing with these nasty agents?"

"Not till we get direct access to the Primm office's computers. There's a firewall I'll need to get around by using one of their machines that's connected to the mountain site. Sphinx will do the rest."

"So what's your guess about this operation so far, Jim?"

"Terror, pal. I believe these guys are terrorists right here in the midst of our own country preparing to pull off surprise attacks."

I jump up out of my seat. "What leads you to that conclusion?"

"References in the data to 'dispersing agents' and 'destination sites'. I read that as target locations where the bio agents will be released."

"But who exactly are these people?"

"We'll need an after hours trip to Primm to answer that question, Jud."

"Great work," I tell him. "As soon as Pat and Dan get here, we need to read them in. This Arab thing is disturbing. Considering their radical types, they could deliver some nasty surprises. Think what one suicide bomber in a Las Vegas hotel could do to a crowd of tourists."

"This whole mess may be even bigger than we thought, Jud."

"Right. The chances are that breaking up New Day's operation is well beyond what the four of us can pull off. We're gonna need the pros on this one. Celia can sic her high-powered friends on them and overrun this—what is it, citadel?"

Jim takes on a very troubled look. He slumps back in his chair and lets out a long breath. "Considering the ballsy attack at the hospital, I'd say they're in a panic over what Kenny might reveal. That and their failure to capture him could prompt them to strike sooner than planned. We could be sitting on a bomb with a lit fuse."

"Is there any indication as to what that strike might be, Jim?"

"If these are terrorist fanatics they would consider any type of attack fair game. Mass gassing, starting epidemics, one crazy in the seats at a concert with an audience of thousands. Maybe all the above."

He continues to probe but seems to be frustrated that some of his targets won't open.

"Assuming you're right about Jamila, Jim, maybe I can pump her for leads," I suggest.

"Still makes me jittery thinking about that lunch date you made with her, buddy. I'll follow you and hang back to cover your tracks. If she pulls anything or has friends show up, I'm gonna be on her like white on rice."

"Does that mean using your new toy, Jim?"

He thinks for a second. "Oh, the gun? If necessary. They'll play hell taking you."

"Fair enough, but give me some room. If she's tainted I want to trap her, but if she's on the up and up, well…."

CHAPTER 30

The Arab stands facing Kim Yung in his office far below the desert. Kim knows before he speaks that Ali will lie.

"Report your progress, Ali Hassan."

"I dispatched my men as you wished, Kim. Three of them went to the hospital and took young Grant from his ward. His mother and another person were also there. They too were taken as prisoners by my men."

"This is good. And they are on their way to the citadel?"

"No, Kim Yung. My people were attacked by a force that overpowered them. Two were barely able to escape. One was disabled and clings to his life in the hands of their police."

"Fool!"

Kim strikes him. The blow is calculated to bring sharp pain. Ali and his people are yet of use to Kim, but he must learn to do his job as instructed. He falls heavily and lies stunned. Ali has said that to place one's foot atop any of his people is a grievous insult. Kim Yung raises his foot but reconsiders and steps away. The Oriental's eyes burn with rage. He lifts the Arab by the hand and Ali scowls at him.

"Kim, it was not possible to face the overwhelming odds and ensure Grant's safety. Abdul went to the hospital prepared to die but not if it meant Grant would escape. Abdul was seriously injured in his heroic attempt to carry out your orders."

"Nevertheless, you have failed me, Ali. What shall I do with you? Perhaps I must summon Lotus to teach you a lesson. She has learned well the demands of discipline. Her mastery of the *hwa rang do* martial arts is exceptional. She can break bones with a simple twist of her strong hands."

Kim turns away as if he is purposely testing Ali's ability to restrain himself. Hassan would be disgraced to be subjected to the discipline of a woman. Perhaps his anger is so great that he will attempt to strike back at Kim and they will have the issue settled for good. Instead Ali holds out one empty palm.

"Wait!" Ali says. "My man will tell their police nothing. He would die first."

"Small consolation," Kim snaps. "They already know that Kenny Grant has been targeted and will throw a protective net around him. If he recovers he will lead them here. We must strike before they find our citadel."

"Perhaps there is another way," Hassan counters.

"Tell me," Kim demands.

"You are aware of the visit made by two men to the New Day plant in Los Angeles. They professed to be buyers for a government contract."

"I am fully aware of their visit. One of our operatives issued a warning that they may be imposters. But how did you learn of this?"

"Your agent Su Lin Kim and my sister Jamila are friends. Su Lin called her. They had a laugh over her experience with one of the men, a Jud Black. Su said both men were on their way to Las Vegas and asked if one of our *al-Qinaa'* could track them. She believes they are industrial spies from a competitor firm at worst, but I want to be assured."

Kim Yung makes a mental note for later. Su Lin Kim—or Kim Moon Su as he knows her—will be summoned here and reminded that she answers to him alone. Kim will tolerate no idle talk or making of decisions without his approval. She will regret her loose tongue and lack of adherence to his instructions. Why should he permit such slipshod behavior by subordinates? They can follow him to greatness or fall by the wayside from their own shortcomings. Lee Hwan tried Kim's patience and he paid the full price.

"Ali, why are you dwelling on these men?"

"Because one of my people in Virginia has reported that Jud Black and Jim Barnett are friends of Kenny Grant. They are a danger to us, but we can put them to good use."

"And when did you plan to tell me all this," he asks Ali. "Perhaps there is other information you withhold at your own peril. What have you not revealed about your men's failure at the hospital?"

"I spoke the truth as always, Kim. They were overpowered by a large number of policemen."

He looks Kim in the eye and lies to him. But Kim is not deceived. Ali's days are numbered.

"So what do you propose we do about these two who are lurking so close to the citadel?"

"We can capture them and bring them here. Grant's silence can be bought for the promise of their safety. Americans are insanely loyal. They miss the lesson that all are expendable to achieve one's ultimate goals. We understand sacrifices must be made for our *jihad.*"

"You believe this enough to risk our mission?"

"Grant will not reveal our location or anything he knows about our plans if we threaten to kill his friends."

"Which leaves us where, Ali? That would seem to be what the Americans refer to as a Mexican standoff."

"Ah, Kim, but then we will arrange to assassinate Grant and any who are in his presence. If I order it as a sacred mission, my men will martyr themselves. Grant will die. Once it is done, the other two will perish in our hands."

"No! You will not harm Grant. He must be returned to me."

Ali stares at him in disbelief; he goes silent then speaks with resolve.

"Then we will do so, Kim. Any who obstruct our path will be killed. Grant will be returned."

"These are grandiose promises, Ali. If you can deliver on them, I will be inclined to consider it atonement for having twice failed me. Bring these two persons to me so I may see the fear in their eyes."

"It will be done, Kim Yung. Even now two of my most trusted warriors are in the city. They await my order to bring Black and Barnett to our fortress."

"I will not forgive another failure," Kim warns him.

He answers, "Jamila and Laila will succeed."

CHAPTER 31

Jud Black

Jim answers his room phone.

"Hey, Mom," I throw at him. "Little Juddy's ready to wander into the lair of the big bad Jamila."

"Joke if you want," he replies. "The way things are unfolding, we should take no chances. Let this babe take one false step and I'll be all over her."

"Just yanking your cord, Jim. Thanks for covering my back. If I get lucky, though, give me some room to operate."

"It's exactly eleven thirty two," he says. "Let me finish up here and I'll be on your tail in ten minutes down in the lobby. That gives you plenty of time to meet your lunch date. By the way, Pat called. Said he and Dan are arriving late this afternoon and they're staying at the Mirage. They'll ring us later."

I take my time and linger in the Venetian's lobby till I see Jim coming. Then I proceed out onto the street and walk the few blocks to the sidewalk café. It's straight up noon when I find Jamila seated at one of the tables. She's wearing a breezy sun dress and looking all cheerful and scrumptious. I take a quick scan around the café and see nothing unusual but I'm still on guard. No sign of Jim, either. He's doing a good job of concealing himself.

"Hi, Jamila. You're looking gorgeous. Beautiful day, too, huh?" Las Vegas has reached that best of all times, something often referred to as the elbow season.

I've been told April is a great time in this town. It's past cold weather and not yet uncomfortably hot.

She beams and those eyes draw me in again. This is some woman I've met by chance. A least I'm hoping it was a random meeting and not a planned trap by New Day. Guess I'm not quite as suspicious as Jim on that count. Anyway, the bad dudes already tried once to work me over with Su Lin, but that turned out not bad at all.

"Hi Jud. Perfect day I'd say. Enjoying Vegas?" I'd swear she was shifting in that seat to give me a free shot of her cleavage.

"Oh, yeah. This town is like Disneyland on speed. Valhalla in the desert."

"Ever been to Disneyland or LA?" she asks and seems rather intent on my response.

"Squinted at LA one time through the smog. I like it here better."

"Recently?" she queries. "LA, I mean."

She's a bit overanxious. Wonder why? I'll play along.

"Spent a couple days there last week."

"Business?"

"Nah. Just sightseeing. Maybe we can take in some sights here together, Jamila. Do you know the town?"

She changes the subject abruptly. "I brought your book." Digs out my scribble pad and hands it to me.

"What did you think of my lyrics?" That seems to catch her off guard.

"I didn't...well, yes, I did peek inside the cover looking for a name or phone number. Read one set of lyrics. You have talent."

I'm thinking, '*and you saw what else?'* But her eyes give me no clue.

We have a great time over lunch. She's not my idea of the normally reserved Middle Eastern woman. She tells me she's native born of immigrant parents from Afghanistan. Her father is a professor of Arab studies at Berkeley and her surname is Hassan. Jamila has a quick wit and a good sense of humor. Try as I might to paint this gorgeous woman as one of the enemy, I'm hard put to believe it.

I periodically do a visual sweep for signs of danger around us. Beginning to believe Jim's concerns are overblown. She seems to be traveling alone. There also is no sign of Jim hovering over us. He's good at this snoop routine. Even I can't pick him out of the crowd.

We linger over a couple of rounds of drinks. I'm sticking to cold beer and she's ordering something I've never heard of before. It's a frosty concoction. We polish off our lunch and share a dessert she advertises as a special treat. It is.

She says, "You wanted to sightsee. I get over here pretty often so I know most of the places in town that are worth seeing. My schedule is open for the rest of the day. How about you?"

"Great," I answer. "Where do we begin?"

"Let us begin down the street at Harrah's," she suggests. "Are you a gambler?"

"Not much of one. That doesn't keep me from trying, though."

"Maybe you're not playing the right game, Jud. Tried the blackjack tables?"

I admit I haven't made that plunge. As we walk up the street and into Harrah's she takes my hand and steers me toward the game tables.

"You watch and I'll show you some tricks."

Our first stop is a ten dollar blackjack table where I stake her and she begins to build her chip stack. Have to admit, though, that her lessons are lost on me. It's almost like she knows what cards are going to fall next. I've heard stories about players that could read the deck but thought the casinos had pretty much covered that possibility. She's almost too good at the game to be merely lucky.

We're at that table for maybe an hour and she's tapped the house for at least several hundred bucks. "Don't you want to get in the game?" she asks me.

"Think I'm safer watching. You're doing fine and I'm enjoying."

She gathers up her chips and says, "Let's find a quiet corner. I'll throw out some suggestions for points of interest and you can tell me where we can go next. You've already been to the Paris and seen the Bellagio fountains. I can show you some other interesting things."

I'll bet you can, I'm saying to myself. She bats those smoky eyes at me. *The view's pretty damned good right here.*

Don't know what she's putting away in those tall glasses but she orders three rounds. I stick to cool brews. Wonder how much more of the hard stuff she can slug down. Or maybe she's a devout Muslim and those drinks are non-alcoholic. Eventually I beg off for a pit stop and head for the men's room. When I turn the corner I peer back at our table and catch a glimpse of her picking up my bottle. I was beginning to feel comfortable with her but now an alarm goes off. Watch from behind a pillar while she does something to my beer and gives it a hearty shake.

Jim's repeated cautions hit me now with full force. This broad's getting ready to mess with my head! Probably slipped me a dose of sleepy time or worse. I wonder if Jim's on my tail watching her moves and saying, *What did I tell you, Jud?*

I snatch my cell phone and punch in Jim's number. His cell rings four times then I hear a slow, measured, "Hel-lo..."

"Hallelujah! I thought you…" I stop in mid-sentence when the voice continues, "The person at this number is not available." You may leave a message after the tone."

"Damn," I blurt out. If he's tailing me, the phone should be in his pocket. Why isn't he answering? And I don't even know the hotel number. Did I really spot him in the Venetian lobby? Am I strung out here all alone?

CHAPTER 32

Jud Black

Jamila's sitting there all perky and innocent when I return. "Want to go up to the Stratosphere? Best view in town. No girders in the way like at the Eiffel Tower. Maybe you want to try the ride up there that lets you hang your feet out into midair nine hundred feet above the street and then drops you. It's a thrill."

"Sure," I answer. "But I'll give the ride a pass." I reach for my brew and her eyes follow it to my mouth. Make like I'm taking a swallow for effect.

Jamila smiles and says, "Finish your beer and I'll be right back. Have to cash in our chips." She downs the last of her drink and stands up. Not even a waiver. Either this gal has a steel gut or those concoctions actually are the Vegas version of Shirley Temples.

When she disappears I sniff my beer. Hold it up to the light. Nothing unusual about the smell or appearance, but I'm not risking it. I look to be sure she's left and pour the rest of my brew into an empty glass at the next table. As soon as I see her coming back I tip up my bottle. Pretend to drain it.

Now I have to wing it. She no doubt knows how long the knock-out dose, if it was one, will take to affect me.

"Jud, before we go up the street, I need to stop by my room and pick up something. It's upstairs."

Be there, Jim. I look around. Beginning to be a little nervous that he hasn't given me a sign he's watching. If Jamila has anything besides fun on her mind, the trip to her room could be her way of trapping me.

We go to her room on the eighth floor and she invites me in. I do a quick sweep of the room and follow her carefully. No surprises yet.

I watch as she rummages through her bag then disappears into the bathroom. Maybe I'm a bit hyper. Her moving my beer bottle may not have meant anything. Maybe she's just luring me to her place hoping for some extracurricular activity.

She comes out of the bathroom and walks directly to me.

"Let's stop stalling around, Jud," she purrs. "You don't want to go to that tower up the street. I can take you much higher right here."

Jamila drapes herself against me and offers me her lips. She starts doing that magic with her wandering fingers. Hell, I'm no dummy. But I need to give her one more test. I start to kiss her then pull away and blink my eyes several times. Is it my imagination that her inviting mouth is turning up into a crooked little sneer? I begin to wobble and she reaches to steady me. No shock or surprise in her eyes. It's almost like she's waiting for me to black out.

"Last time we did this," she says, "I was the one reeling. Sit down over here." She steers me to a couch. "Relax. Jamila will take care of you."

She releases me and I sag. I hear her giggle and say, "Sweet dreams, Mister Black."

That's my cue. She's sure the knockout dosage she slipped me has taken hold. I slump face forward on the couch and, instead of showing alarm, she carefully swings my feet onto the sofa. Checks my reflexes then allows herself a hearty laugh.

Jamila leaves me lying on my face on the sofa and walks across the room. I hear her speaking softly. She must be on the phone.

"He's out, Hamid. Come quickly. We'll walk him out to the car and make it look like he's drunk. The *al-Qinaa'* will be delivering two visitors to the citadel today."

That's all I need. Her I can handle, but if there are others, I have to get out of here pronto.

She walks back and stands over me. "Too bad for you, Jud Black. Thought you were in for a fun afternoon, didn't you? This is the unluckiest day you'll ever have."

The way I'm lying all I can see is her foot. When she turns away from me I'm on her in an instant. Hate to hurt a woman, but this one is about to truss and deliver me to the bad guys.

I grab her around the neck. She's lightning fast; spins toward me holding something in her right hand. I sidestep on instinct and plow her one directly on her pretty little nose. Hear a crunch and blood spurts all over both of us. Jamila slumps to the floor and drops the menacing looking knife she was about to slice me with. I pick it up and run toward the door.

Hear somebody in the hall and a key card in the door. An ugly, swarthy dude with big arms puts one foot inside the room. I slam the knife up into his stomach and twist. Withdraw it and get set to stick him again. He stares at me for a split second then his eyes roll back. I yank him into the room and head for the stairs. Find a button on the side of the knife case and retract the switchblade.

I emerge into the parking lot behind the hotel and get my bearings. Run across the rear lots toward the Venetian. I'm puzzling over why Jim didn't break into her room and pull my fat out of the fire. Did he lose me completely back there at the café? Maybe even before? Wait! She told her helper they would deliver *two* visitors to the citadel. I dig out Jim's spare key card and run full tilt to find him.

Huff and puff from the elevator to Suite 1212. I have this sinking feeling I'm not going to like what I find. Pound on the door and slide the key into the slot at the same time. No response from inside.

"Jim! Where the hell are you?"

The place is empty. I walk to the sitting room and plop onto the sofa. Have to think this through. What do I do now?

My first instinct is to call our partners and bring them on board. I reach for my cell phone and try first Pat then Dan. Get 'not available' messages from both. I figure they must still be in the air with their phones turned off. Well, without a clue where to look for Jim all I can do is wait here for him to show up and look around for clues.

I try to settle down; get to the business of thinking this knotty problem through. I check the bedroom. Nothing missing that I can identify. Looks like all the chest drawers are organized and undisturbed. His empty bags sit against the wall and his shoes are neatly lined up. If Jim has left he has only the clothes on his back.

Maybe that's a good sign. He could be somewhere trying to track me down. Could return and walk through that door any second.

I don't recall seeing his laptop in the sitting room. Spin around and look toward the desk. No computer on top and no case anywhere to be seen. This is not good. He wouldn't carry his machine with him if he was providing cover for me.

Come on Black. Ring Jim's number. He'll tell you he lost the string on you and to stay put. It'll be okay.

When I call a muffled ring comes back to me from the sofa. I pick up a cushion and find Jim's cell phone and his sheets of notes. Damn. That blows the theory that he's just 'out for a walk'. More like he was surprised by somebody and used the best hiding place available.

I rummage in the chest and find the gun and ammo under his shirts. The bugs and listening gear are in the otherwise empty luggage. Gather it all up for later. Then I see something lying on the floor. Stoop down and pick up the good luck charm from Susie that he carries everywhere he goes. He never left the room on his own and this is his way of alerting me. It wasn't Jim I caught a glimpse of in the lobby. Maybe Jamila was right. I would have been the second guest at their hideaway.

There's a small refrigerator sitting next to the desk. It's the unit Jim asked the hotel to provide to keep his insulin cool. Everything appears to be there and that's the worst news of all. Without his medicine Jim could be in serious trouble.

By now my mind is warped. My thoughts are meeting themselves coming back. Short of knocking down the door in that desert fortress there's not much I can do on my own.

The room phone rings. I lunge for it and hope I'll hear Jim's voice. Instead it's Dan.

"I was calling Jim," he says. "You guys both in there? Pat and I are in town heading for our hotel now."

"This is Jim's room but I have some rotten news, Dan. Somebody's snatched him."

"Say that again?"

"Jim's gone. I think the enemy has him. They came damned close to taking me along, too, but I slipped them."

"What? Jim missing? Get out of there, Jud. Meet us in the lobby of the Mirage Hotel. We'll sort it out."

CHAPTER 33

Dan Cooper

"You heard?" The way Pat's looking at me I must have gone pale at Jud's news.

"All I picked up was Jim's missing. What else did Jud tell you?"

"That they not only snatched Jim but almost got him, too. Pat, these folks are hot after us. Looks like time to call in the cavalry."

"Let's see what Jud says when we see him. Then a call to Celia Grant may be in order." He looks out the taxi window, clearly upset at the turn of events.

We turn in our bags out front to the bellhop and go to look for Jud in the lobby. He's not here. I steer Pat to the front desk. We may as well get checked in while we're waiting.

Get our room keys and peer around again for our pal. He comes huffing across the lobby carrying a piece of luggage. Jud is usual pretty unflappable, but whatever misadventure he and Jim have experienced has him plenty shook.

"This is bad, guys!"

He starts to say something else when Pat cautions, "Save it till we get upstairs, Jud. Take a deep breath."

Once we're in Dan's room Jud unloads.

"Scum buckets ran off with him. I know it. I'm gonna blow somebody away." He opens his bag and lifts out a pistol.

"Whoa! Where'd you come by that thing, buddy?" Pat and I both know that Jud has no love for guns. He keeps one for emergency protection, but that's because he lives so far out in the country. Seems out of character to see him with a gun of any kind.

"Jim got it in LA from a friend."

"I see you stuffed some clothes in that bag," I say. "Good idea. I wouldn't recommend you go back to your room." Then I do a double take. "What's all that other stuff you're carrying?"

Jud picks up the largest item and shows it to me. "It's a listening device with headphones—the whole bit. He picked up a variety of bugs in case we needed them. Did you ever know Jim to go anywhere not prepared?"

"Okay, bring us up to speed," Pat says. "I ordered up a supply of suds, guys. This could be a long session. Let's get to it."

Jud relates their experiences in LA in detail. Tells us what they saw and their suspicions that New Day isn't playing above board. We have a good laugh over Jim's experience with the young gay engineer hitting on him and Jud nearly being harpooned by the Korean chick. Then Jud relates their trip in the helicopter and what happened with the Arab woman at Harrah's. I put it all together with what we saw in Tampa.

"No doubt in my mind we've found the enemy. Digging them out of that mountain stronghold may be a bit more difficult." Pat and Jud nod their agreement.

Jud reaches into the side pocket of his bag and pulls out a flat metal object. Holds it up and presses on one side. A nasty looking blade springs out.

"Was it something I said?" Pat quips.

Jud smirks. "Bitch tried to cut me with this. It's razor sharp. She damn near stuck me before I could deck her."

"You hit a woman, Studley?" I laugh.

"Flattened her little butt, Dan. I don't take kindly to knife wielders regardless of gender."

"What's that on the blade?" I ask. "Looks like dried blood. Maybe you'd better check again for missing skin, pal."

"Not mine," Jud says. "Had to use it on a big, ugly guy named Hamid who came to help Jamila haul me away. By now he's either dead or a mighty hurting puppy."

Pat reaches out with a handkerchief in his hand. Takes the knife, secures the blade, wraps it in the handkerchief and carefully puts it in his back pocket. It's not large, rather flat and compact, but, according to Jud, that's a nasty blade.

"When our help gets here, they may want to check this thing for DNA."

Jud shrugs. "I could use a brew, guys. Where's that beer?"

Our conversation is interrupted by a knock on the door and a voice calls out, "Room service."

Jud's still feeling jumpy. He fingers the handgun and I shake my head.

"Put it down, pal," I tell him. "That's either the beer or my bags."

But Jud holds onto the gun at his side until we see the deliveryman is a bright faced all-American youngster.

Later over a round of brews we debate our next move. We can call on Celia for help but that will take time. With Jim missing and minus his medicine, time is a luxury we don't have a lot of. There has to be something we can do on our own.

"Look," I propose. "We'll ask Celia Grant to mount an offensive. They should be able to get an attack force out here and break open that mountain hideaway. But it'll take longer than we like. Let's grab some gear and a vehicle that'll maneuver in the desert. We'll go mineral prospecting in the McCullough Range."

"Could be a good cover," Pat agrees. "Could also get us killed."

"It beats sitting here wondering what's happening to Jim," Jud says.

"Okay. Time to call Celia." I pick up the phone and Jud and Pat pull chairs over.

She's a bit surprised to hear from us. I quickly get across to her that crunch time is upon us. Give her a rundown on the happenings and tell her we need to call in some favors those influential friends of hers may owe her.

"Not a problem," she answers. "Kenny is doing much better now. I worried that he may have another bug running around in his system but nothing shows up in a microscopic analysis. He's been able to tell Crandall and Feroukas some of what he knows about the place outside Las Vegas. They're prepared to send the help we need."

"Tell them Jim's been snatched and we're going out there to find him."

"Snatched?" she asks.

"Yeah. They took him right out of his hotel room. Maybe we can sniff out a way to penetrate their hangout in the desert. Your pals can assemble their assault team, Celia, and contact us on one of these three numbers." I give her the numbers for all three cell phones.

"That's too risky," she cautions. "We don't know what bio agents they could release against you. Hold off and let the professionals do their work. We have to bring along decontamination gear and chemical biological experts."

"All well and good, Celia, but we can't wait. That's our compadre out there."

"I'll speed it up all I can, Dan. Please wait till we get there."

"No way. Jim would do the same for us. You know how to reach us. And bring along a good supply of insulin. Jim could be hurting." I read her the data off one of the empty vials Jud has brought over from Jim's cooler.

I agree to find a place to buy prospecting gear and Jud will find us a rugged vehicle for desert traipsing.

"Our only problem is locating duds that will make us look believable as prospectors." I pick up the phone book. "Let's see who might have super size coveralls for the Irishman. Then we can all go roll in the dirt so we look the part." Jud laughs but Pat doesn't see the humor in my jibe.

It's not easy this late in the day, but I scare up a place that will outfit us with tools and one where we can pick up the kind of clothes we need. Pat writes down his sizes and hurries off to unpack and prepare for the desert.

CHAPTER 34

Pat O'Leary

I feel like I'm in fast forward. That was a long flight from Virginia and we hit the ground running. Jim kidnapped! What a rotten thing to face. Have to get our act together and start fighting back at these characters. Koreans and Arabs. Odd put together.

They obviously have Jud and Jim targeted. Maybe Dan and I will be a surprise they didn't count on. Don't know what we can learn out in the desert, but I'm sure ready to give it a go. Now I have two good reasons to kick somebody's ass—first Kenny now Jim.

Let's see, Room 814. Door's open. Guess the fellow already got up here with my bags. Must have a fiver here somewhere for him. Funny. I don't see him.

What's this? "Just who the hell are you, ugly?"

"You will please to come in and close the door. Now!"

Well, he's the one with the gun. Guess that gives him the edge for now. All I want is one chance at that swarthy looking dude. Then I see there are two of them. The other is a woman.

"Welcome. One false move and Hamid will end your day." The woman speaks with authority.

"I don't argue with people on the hammer end of a barrel. On the other hand, Hamid, if you'd like to try me one on one…No guts, huh?"

"Hamid is a patient man, the small, dark woman says. "He will tolerate your insults. We shall see how smart your mouth is when we introduce you to our friends."

I'm thinking that one through while she circles around behind me. "Same offer. Bring them on one at a time," I tell her. Start to turn in her direction but Hamid waves the gun at me.

"Do not move," he barks.

I feel a sharp sting in my left arm. "Ow! What was that? You little bi…"

Have this overwhelming urge to backhand the woman. I flex my arm to give her a good whack but she steps away from me.

"Enough of your insults, O'Leary. In a few moments you will be flying. Then you will join your friend Mister Barnett."

"Barnett? Never heard of him." The words come out slurred and my tongue feels like a fuzzy dish rag. Whatever was in that needle is damn fast.

"Good, Hamid," she says. "Kim…hostages…others…to the couch."

I'm picking up bits and pieces of their chatter but it means nothing.

"What…with…hotel employee?"

"Leave him…closet…miles away."

It's all a jumble. Then I quit trying to listen and give in to a warm fuzziness that drops around me, numbs my arms and legs and gives me a sensation of floating. I try to resist Hamid's tugging, double my fist and swing at him. Turns out to be more of a wave than a punch. I hear him laugh and he shoves me onto the couch. Then it's one last swirl and lights out for me.

* * * *

My head is pounding. I haven't felt this crappy since I had that bout with the flu. Can't get sick now. With my mouth covered I can't even upchuck without choking.

Where am I? Moving…sense of hurtling along tossing from side to side, darkness on all sides. I lift my head and wish I hadn't when it feels like it could explode. The pain makes me squeeze both eyes tight shut. I reopen one and wince at a thin shaft of bright light.

My hands are bound behind me and my feet feel like they're taped together. I try to protest, call out the foulest names I can dredge up, but my mouth is taped shut. Somebody's done a good job of securing my hands at the wrists, but my fingers are free. All the twisting and squirming I can do won't change the fact that I'm trussed up and out of options.

With nothing to do but collect myself, I concentrate on hearing what's going on around me. Hear two, maybe three voices. I seem to be in a windowless vehicle of some sort and the voices are coming from the other side of a wall. The closed space they've stuffed me into is stifling and hot. My breath comes hard and I'm drowning in my own sweat. Have to clear my head and think this through if I expect to get out of this fix.

I scan my surroundings. Not sure yet just what I'm looking for, but my mind is slowly beginning to function again. Maybe this is one time I can feel fortunate to be such a big guy. Probably only had enough of a dose in that needle for a normal size fellow. And the jostling around would have thrown a smaller fellow all over this vehicle.

This whole computer sleuthing thing is getting more complex than I ever imagined. Oh, I never thought it would be a free ride. But terrorists? We're in a foot race and these bad guys are more resourceful than I gave them credit for being.

By twisting on my side I can see enough of my wrist to figure out they've used some kind of tape to bind me. Maybe there's something sharp I can snag the tape on and work my way free.

Then a totally illogical thought hits me. That switchblade I took from Jud was sharp but thin. If I'm lucky they were in too big a hurry to check my pockets well. Just manage to work my fingertips into my back pocket and feel around. Fumble with the handkerchief and feel something solid. It's still there!

Carefully I slide the switchblade from its wrapping with the ends of my fingers and lift it from my pants pocket. With great effort I roll onto one side and hit the release button on the knife. Confirm that the blade is out by gingerly snagging my trouser seat with the blade's tip. Now to find a way to use it.

The way the vehicle is tossing and bumping, I have a hard time positioning myself. Hit one hard bump and almost lose my grip on the knife, but I hold on like my life depends on it. The effects of the drug are beginning to wear off now and I can start to get my thoughts organized. I find a position where I can use hold the knife upright and jam it, point out, between a block of wood and the wheel well. Shove my butt up against the block and lean hard. *See, Jud,* I think, *this big old backside's good for more than just sitting on.*

It's gonna be a long, tedious process sawing through this tape. Just hope I have enough time to get my hands free before we reach where we're going. Ouch! That damn thing is sharp. Good thing Jud dodged it when the Arab babe swung or he could have been filleted.

As I concentrate on cutting the tape the voices drone on. Once I have the cutting rhythm I begin to tune in. There are definitely two voices. One I recognize as the woman who gave me the needle. The other must be the hairy guy she called Hamid.

"We will soon be there," she says. "My brother will be happy to see the surprise we bring him. Leila and Javad will be at the citadel by now with Mister Barnett. All in all, a fruitful day."

"I want the other one, Jamila." He coughs and groans. "He cut me deeply. I owe him a strong lesson. Perhaps I will rip out his brow ring with my teeth and swallow his eyeballs."

"We will have aid for you soon enough, Hamid. And I, too, owe Jud Black a debt he will not enjoy me paying off. I will retrieve that knife and put it to good use on him. Perhaps I will make sport of carving him from the belly down."

They both have a hearty laugh and I want to heave. A pair of blood-thirsty rogues. Give me half a chance and I'll change their tune.

If I could just break free...

CHAPTER 35

Pat O'Leary

I'm watching the little window opening on the front wall. Don't want to be caught in the act before I get these bindings sawed through.

The chatter up front has suddenly died down. I make sure I'm lying still and slumped against the vehicle's side wall. A shaft of intense light hits the dark around me. Force myself not to look, but I can sense that I'm being watched. Whoever dumped me in here must have the sliding window open taking a check on me.

The female voice again. "He's still out, Hamid. Another ten minutes to the citadel. The sun is just going down. We did it, my friend. All glory to *al-Qinaa'*."

"My wound is painful," the man says. "I still bleed where that other American stabbed me with your knife."

"Bear it a little longer, Hamid. They will attend to you at the citadel."

I hear the soft thump of the window sliding shut and warily open my eyes. It's dark back here again, but I've learned a couple of important facts. There is still daylight outside and we're within minutes of reaching our destination. That means I have to act fast before there are more than two of them to deal with at their hideaway. Resume my sawing motion but make a slip. The blade is like a razor. It slices my skin. I want to call out, but bite my lip. Feel the bindings on my wrists begin to give. I strain hard to pull my hands apart and the restraints give way.

Okay, folks. Now give me a couple of minutes and I'll spoil your celebration.

Pulling the tape away from my arms, I break free and retrieve the knife. Go to work on the tape wound tight around my ankles. It's a short task now that I can direct my efforts. I note that one hand is bloody where the knife cut me. Hurts like hell but I'm about to transform from punching bag to ass kicker. What's a little blood when payback time is coming?

Now my feet are free and I grab one edge of the tape over my mouth. Steel myself and rip. Yowee! I won't have to shave around my chops for a week. But it's a whole new ball game!

No time to waste. We'll soon be on their turf so I have to be fast. I make enough noise to get their attention but not enough ruckus for them to see I'm fully awake. Then I lie very still and wait.

A swishing sound I now recognize as the opening of the window and the sensation of light streaming in. My eyes are barely open.

"Sounds as if our prisoner is restless, Hamid. Maybe he needs a booster shot. I'll let you do the honors this time."

"It will be my pleasure, Jamila," the ugly one grunts. I feel the van pull to a stop. No doubt the woman is still watching me so I'll keep my eyes closed.

He called her Jamila! This is the same woman that lured Jud to her room and almost impaled him on the knife I'm now holding behind me.

There is a pause. I picture the woman preparing the dose for me and giving it to Hamid. Then the driver's side door slams shut. Hamid is on his way. I gauge the distance between myself and the rear doors of the van. Rehearse my next move in my mind and prepare to give him a surprise he won't forget. I hear him rattle the handle, count to three and spring toward the door with both legs extended.

"Watch out!" Jamila shouts through the window behind me.

But she's too late. I kick the doors open and send the big guy sprawling on his back. He tries to collect himself and raise the gun he's holding, but I knock it away, dive for it and fire one shot smack between his eyes. The force jerks his head back and he lies motionless.

Realizing the girl is probably heading for me by now, I roll over and aim toward the van. To my surprise the tires squeal and the van speeds away.

As the vehicle disappears up the road I have a large economy size sinking feeling.

Okay, O'Leary. Now that you've done your Rambo impersonation where does that leave you? Alone somewhere in the desert with a dead Arab for company and a whole pack of bad guys minutes from descending on you.

I look up at the sky and see the sun is not nearly as intense as I imagined. Must be getting close to twilight. If I can find cover and conceal myself until dark, there's an even chance I may elude whoever they send out looking for me. When I went through Army survival training I never dreamed I would be using it right here in the good old US of A to save my hide!

CHAPTER 36

Dan Cooper

"We're being outmaneuvered, Jud says. "These Arabs are everywhere."

"Don't know about that, Jud, but it appears they have Jim and Pat in tow. Now it's up to us to turn this thing around. Fun time is over. Now it's them or us, and I intend to come out on top."

"Time to kick butt, old buddy," Jud echoes.

It's been a couple of hours since we discovered Pat was missing from his room. Found his door open and the bellhop tied up in the closet. He confirmed that two people that looked like Middle Easterners had jumped him when he tried to deliver Pat's bags. Said they knocked him around and dumped him in the closet. There was a guy and a woman. They gave the bellhop a love tap with a gun butt and that's the last he remembered until we came storming into the room.

With Celia and her buddies still getting organized for their assault on the desert fortress, Jud and I decide to carry on with our plan to do our own snooping around Primm and the hills beyond. We're hell bent on finding these guys and breaking Jim and Pat loose. First we swing by a rental car office to check out a Jeep with a canvas top for the desert trek. Then we shop at an out of the way store for prospecting gear and Army surplus clothing.

The guy at the tool store stares at us like we're two throwbacks—and crazies at that—when we talk about searching for minerals in the open country. Couldn't be that big a shock to him, though. Every kind of wacko in the universe must pass through Las Vegas. If we want to throw away money on his stuff, who's he to argue?

The jungle gear we find at the surplus store makes us resemble a couple of Army troops out on patrol. Even find jungle boots to fit. We're hopeful Pat will turn up unharmed somewhere along our path so we buy him boots and the biggest size fatigues the store has and throw them into the Jeep. By the time we change and muss ourselves up, do some facial disguise and make up as sunburned old coots, even our best friends wouldn't recognize us. I turn west on I-15 and kick the accelerator.

"Well, kiss my…" Jud blurts out in the middle of swapping his shirt for a fatigue top.

"What is it?"

"Look what I found," he says.

I glance over and he's holding up a small round object.

"Remember I said this Jamila was mighty frisky with her hands? In fact that was one of the better points that got my attention. Wasn't used to a good looking babe like her copping a feel every time she got near me. That could be habit forming."

"So? What's your point, Jud?"

"She planted this bug on me. Could have done it any time while I was distracted. Maybe even the first time she bumped into me. No wonder they were tracking me so close and knew I had gone over to the Mirage."

I take the bug in my left hand and sail it as far off the elevated road as possible.

"That should keep them busy."

"Guess they hung around waiting to get one of us alone somewhere and it happened to be Pat," I tell him. "You slipped their grasp so they took him instead."

"How dumb can a guy be?" Jud stares off into the distance and I can tell he's kicking himself for letting his hormones divert his attention.

"Hey. Drop it, pal. Sooner or later they were bound to find us. Let's think about what we do to screw up their party."

* * * *

After some off-road driving to eat a little dust and add to our disguise I pull into the parking lot of a general store on the edge of Primm near the Interstate. Thumb through a dog-eared telephone book that's dangling on a cord. New Day Electronics is listed at an address on Prairie Street. I ask for directions from the store clerk and find that's just a couple of blocks off the main thoroughfare of Primm.

"Been out in the hills long?" the clerk asks. He sort of takes me by surprise. Then I can't help smiling. Maybe our impromptu coverup isn't so bad after all.

"Longer'n I'd like. Pretty slim pickins' out there," I reply. "But we got a line on a good digging spot. Wish us luck."

The store attendant grins skeptically and says, "Yeah. You'll need it." He's shaking his head when I turn to leave.

Right, I think, *just two crazy coots chasing a rainbow and digging worthless holes. Wonder how many of those unfortunates he's seen?*

"Okay, Jud, we have a line on the New Day office and a sack of sandwiches to tide us over. Let's scout out their place and plan a nighttime visit."

He grins and starts jiggling his fingers. "Great. Can't wait to get a crack at their data. I needled Jim until he explained the Sphinx sequence to me. Think I can break open their data banks. Maybe we can pinpoint where to look in the hills for this 'citadel'."

We cruise the back streets of Primm and pass by the New Day office three times before sunset. On the last trip I see a man locking up and driving away in a white van.

"Probably the same vehicle we saw from the air," Jud says, "when that insane pilot was shaking up my insides. Let's give it a go, Dan—crash their office and burrow into their system."

"Patience, pal. We have all night. Don't want to get caught if he returns for something."

We park around the corner and chow down on sandwiches and snacks. Jud wants a cool brew but I convince him the sodas I bought at the store and stashed in our cooler will have to suffice. Need a clear head for what we're about to undertake.

It's hot out here even in the shadows cast by the buildings. Occurs to me that we could be in for a real ordeal if we hit the desert during daylight. Even after dark it could still be stuffy hot. But there's not much of an alternative now. Our two pals are missing and they'll count on us to spring them loose. If Jud and I were in the clutches of the bad boys, Jim and Pat would be busting their humps to set us loose.

"Maybe we should find a place to bunk in between stints in the sun, Jud. What say we find a local motel and dump our excess gear. That'll give us a place to escape when the sun gets to be too much for us. No need to suffer around the clock until reinforcements arrive."

"Good thought," he answers. We drive around awhile and find a rather nondescript motel outside town. I wander into the office like a Mohave survivor and ask, "Got a room, neighbor?"

The look I get from the desk clerk tells me our disguise work and bumping around in the sand must have done the trick. He's not at all sure he wants a character like me in his establishment. This certainly is not a five star and it's too good for the likes of me? That's encouraging.

"How many people?" he asks.

"Two."

"Twenty seven bucks a night with tax. Two single beds, air conditioned, telephone and TV. Cash up front," he croaks and holds out his hand.

"Done. Three nights."

"Got a name for the register?" he inquires as if it's entirely optional.

"Craig," I answer. J. Craig, Esquire."

He laughs and hands me a key with a ring and a small metal tag that reads '4'. "Only got one key to that room, Mister Esquire. Okay?" What if I said no? Still wouldn't get me the Presidential Suite with two keys, would it?

We stow our extra clothes and some of our gear in the room. I give the place a good going over and decide I'll be due for a nice long stay in some luxury hotel after this stint. This is not quite a dump but certainly not in the AAA guide. I check the bathroom. Yeah, it's a dump, after all. Bathroom faucet leaks, tub is stained, and the window air conditioner rattles and works hard to keep pace with the outside heat. The room has a really grungy look about it; kind of gives the impression it's a shady spot amid the cactus and sand. Come to think of it I guess that's all it is. Has a stale odor about it, too, but it's a place to cool off and snooze.

"Is this the worst you could find, Dan?" Jud quips. "Maybe we should take our chances sleeping out in the open."

"Hey, Jud, get on my case after you've been under that hot sun for a day. That floppy fatigue hat won't keep the sun from boiling your brains. By tomorrow evening this place will be like coming home to Paris Hilton."

"And you say I always have women on the brain! For shame, Dan."

"The *hotel*, wise ass. The *hotel.*"

He points at me and laughs.

Just when I get uptight, old Jud knows how to bring me around. "Thanks, Jud. To get me through the next few days I'm gonna need your warped sense of humor, you mental case."

Jud nods his head.

He disappears into the bathroom. I issue a caution.

"Don't clean up your act too much in there. Remember we're supposed to be seedy prospectors. Calls for a layer or two of desert grime."

He calls back. "I'm almost afraid to turn on the water in here. If it comes out brown, maybe I'll just pour the tub full and roll around in it till I'm covered with slime. That seedy enough for you?" Then he backs out of the bathroom holding his nose and heads for the door.

"Something stinks in there! On second thought think I'll just whiz on a cactus."

CHAPTER 37

Dan Cooper

We drive down the block from the New Day office and Jud circles around back on foot. We spend about a half hour making sure there's no sign of activity in the front or the rear. After awhile I see Jud come sauntering up the sidewalk with his loping gait whistling softly. He comes up alongside the Jeep and beams a big grin.

"Found an easy way in the back, Dan. Ready to rumble?"

I try to restrain myself but have this great urge to laugh.

"Remember the last time you led me on an after dark expedition? We were breaking into that mad Minerva's Net doctor's townhouse. I damn near broke my ass flopping over that 'easy' fence you scaled."

"Oh, this is much better," he says. "Beat their alarm system and jimmied the back door. Piece of cake. Let's get at it."

I follow him in the back door and he immediately goes in search of the nearest computer. My target is their filing cabinets for tidbits of info on what's going on out there in the McCullough Range. Jud stops on the way and extracts a bug from his pocket. Installs it in the telephone on the desk nearest the computer.

"Let's beat them at their own game, Dan. Who knows what we may pick up by listening in? Jim went to a lot of trouble to gather up this equipment. It's only fair we use it to help pull his cookies out of the fire." I nod agreement.

There are several filing cabinets that I eagerly attack. Most of the juicy stuff is no doubt buried in those data files Jud's about to crack open. Doesn't keep me from surfing for whatever may pop out of the unlocked drawers of these files. I'm well into the second drawer of the first cabinet when Jud blurts out.

"Hot damn, he was right. Sphinx works like a charm! Glad I talked him into showing me how to use it."

"Sounds like you're into their drawers more than I am, buddy," I fire back.

"Big time, Dan. Give me awhile and I'll pick them clean." He goes back to work with his fingers dancing over the computer keys.

Meanwhile I'm extracting bits and pieces from the files. There are bills of lading from the New Day offices in both Tampa and Los Angeles. Items shipped through Primm and moved on to the hideaway include electronic components, chemicals, lab equipment, a whole variety of things that could support nanoelectronics operations and maybe even biological agents handling. In fact, there are three or four invoices for shipments of what I take to be protective gear—masks, gloves, goggles, something listed as 'airtight lab suits'. I'm taking snaps with my small digital camera to get this all documented.

The records show this office has three employees—two guys and one female. I jot down their home addresses and phone numbers. Stick the note in my pocket for future reference. See two sets of keys hanging on wall hooks. Must be backup sets for two vans like the one we spotted in the desert.

After awhile I glance over and see that Jud has settled back in his seat and is staring at the screen. His expression stops me cold. Behind that pancake makeup he's wearing to simulate a deep tan, I'd bet all the color has drained from his face. He's frozen in place.

"What is it, Jud?"

"Come over here, pal. Take a gander at this screen. I'm into their most private files."

I peer at the computer and see a jumble of numbers with accompanying text that doesn't register right away. Stare at Jud and he's looking a hole through me.

"Don't you see, Dan? Those are the casualty predictions for their planned bio attack in Las Vegas. The big numbers you see are the projections for deaths their terrorist plot will cause. And look at the top line." He scrolls back.

Now it's my turn to pale. The heading says 'Dengue/Anthrax at Venetian Hotel'.

"The place Jim and I were staying," Jud says. "It's target central for one of their planned bio outbreaks. Nearest I can tell they plan to spread the agents throughout the hotel. Those are the numbers of deaths they expect to cause."

"It says dengue and anthrax. Do they really intend to use both agents at once?"

He gives me a smirk then returns to the screen. What's this?" he blurts out. Jud's staring at the screen with a puzzled look.

"New input?" I ask.

"Chimera," he says. "What is a chimera?. Thought it was some sort of monster."

I search my memory. "You're right on one count, Jud. In Greek mythology a chimera is a fire-breathing female monster made up of parts of a lion, a goat and a serpent."

"Ugh. Not the kind of woman you'd want to wake up with, is it?"

"But here's the bad part, Jud. The same term is used in modern science to describe an organism with two or more parts combined by grafting or genetic engineering."

"Whoa. Sounds serious." He looks disgusted.

"Think about the possibilities, Jud, especially for terrorist attacks. One of the biggest promises of nanotech is the hope it will lead to rebuilding matter from the molecule up. Combine that concept with biological agents. What if these devious bastards could combine dengue and some other agent into a single dose killer spray or gas? Maybe spread it through hotel air conditioning systems? It would be a perfect terror tool. Multiple epidemics simultaneously. Panic and mass death."

He looks at me and his face drops. "They're building chimeras, Dan, combinations of multiple agents. In the case of the Venetian the combo is those two. Stop and think about it. The attack causes symptoms of dengue fever. While the doctors and emergency workers are scurrying around trying to fend off dengue before it becomes hemorrhagic fever, the anthrax is taking hold. By the time they recognize a two-threat scenario, the anthrax has progressed too far to beat. The outcome is ugly."

"And they've built some sort of elaborate underground infrastructure in the desert to pull off a single terrorist act?" I'm puzzled.

"No way, Dan. That place must be the lab platform that got them to the point of being ready to launch. Now these guys have simultaneous actions planned across the country," Jud says. "The chimera varies, but the obvious agent that first appears in all circumstances is dengue fever. There are plans laid out for separate, concurrent attacks in Las Vegas, Chicago, New York, and Atlanta. There are other equally deadly agents—things like smallpox and plague—used in combination with the dengue virus at the other sites. On day one it will appear a dengue fever epidemic has broken out in four large metropolitan areas."

"Damn, this is a real horror story," I gasp.

"And well-planned," Jud replies. "There will be no evidence of infestation by the mosquitoes that would normally cause the dengue. While the medical personnel work to combat the apparent problem, the more deadly agents will be taking a firm hold on their victims. Some of those bio agents are contagious so they'll spread as the victims travel. By the time the medics sort out what's going on they'll be staring at a whole shopping list of killer diseases taking victims all over the country."

"You're scaring me, Jud. The last time we hooked up to solve a crime, it involved individual, carefully selected victims. This time we're looking at wholesale, random slaughter of Americans in multiple places."

"That's right, Danny boy. These bums are playing for keeps. They intend to bring down the country with a mass pandemic. And the plans were buried deep in their archives, so deep only the most elegant techniques could access them through elaborate security guards."

"So who exactly are we dealing with here?"

"Our worst nightmare, Jud. Two of our rogue enemies joining forces to do maximum harm. Korean and Arab fanatics."

"Not a likely combo."

"I know. But that's what I'm reading. Seems the Koreans are in charge. Head guy may be somebody named Kim. That's not much of a lead. Hell, I understand half the population of North and South Korea have the surname Kim."

"You said Arabs, too?"

Jud gives me a pained look. "Like I said, the Koreans are running the show on the nano research and the Arabs—most likely Saudis or Afghans—must be the source for the dirty bugs. Saw more than one reference to something called *al-Qinaa'*."

He backs out of the New Day system and does an internet search. Calls up some reference page and gives it a scan then laughs out loud.

"What was that for?" I ask.

"Found a translation for *al-Qinaa'*. Roughly it means the mask."

"Hell, Jud, that doesn't sound very threatening. If these guys are out to wreak havoc, I'd think they'd choose a name with more punch."

"Do you know what al-Qaida means?" he asks.

"No," I answer.

The translation of al-Qaida is roughly "the foundation" or "the base." That doesn't sound very intimidating either, does it? But look what the bastards did to us on September 11th."

"You made your point," I tell him.

"Hope you're getting this all down for the Feds, Jud."

"I'm putting it on CD and that printer is cranking out paper copies. If the Feds have any remaining reservations about our suspicions, this should tip the scales."

"Great work. Bone-chilling results but great sleuthing. If I wasn't on your side you'd scare the crap out of me."

"Hold your congratulations until we get our pals out of that place in the hills. By the way, did you find references to the citadel in those file cabinets?"

"Lots of stuff, Jud. It seems to be a secret they jealously guard. How the hell are we going to get inside that mountain?"

"We'll find a way. Whoever set up these heavily guarded computer files is a stickler for details. There's a layout of a large structure that has to be the underground. Damn thing must be four or five hundred feet on a side. I printed a copy in case we need an idea about the physical arrangement. Only shows one entrance, though, and a series of room layouts. Looks like a lot of people could be living in there."

"The map will be a big help to the pros when they hit that place."

"We need to get the information to Celia and check on her progress with the Feds. Now that our hand has been exposed in Vegas and they've got Jim and Pat, the pressure will be on to accelerate the attacks. There's no time to waste."

Chapter 38

Dan Cooper

We spend most of the evening hours before midnight harvesting the most damaging kinds of information from New Day's documents and data files. Jud has them nailed with the facts he's downloading. I've added some disturbing details about shipments into the mountain site and the staffing out there. Seems we're dealing with a force somewhat larger than we had imagined. If I've put my facts together correctly, there could be maybe seventy to eighty residents of that facility in the McCullough Range. That also tells us it could be a large, well-guarded underground complex that will be hard to penetrate.

As we're riding back to our motel room, Jud insists we stop and pick up some six-packs. I relent. There's not much more we can do tonight beyond getting the information to Celia and her friends. He also springs for a large can of detergent spray and some plug-in air cleaners with a fresh air fragrance. I'm all for that given the stench of our room.

"Haven't told you everything, Dan," Jud says as he takes a pull on his second brew and sounds a loud belch.

"Is that the best you have to offer?" I throw back at him.

"Seriously, there's more. When I said I'd penetrated the most guarded files I meant it. Appears they are the personal notes of the head guy. His name is Kim Yung. He seems to have a penchant for logging even minor details. Guess he figures they're well hidden in his data banks away from prying eyes. He didn't count on Sphinx and a couple of data mining idiots like Jim and me."

"I'm all ears," I say and take another hit on my brewsky. Feels good to be out of the heat draining a cool one and sitting next to the window air unit. It's noisy but working.

"This Kim fellow is so sure his words are safe that he tends to drone on with some pretty wild diatribes. Comes off as an isolated, paranoid loner with no one he can trust to share his innermost thoughts. Probably so hung up on his computer he's given it a female name and kisses it good night. Anyway, he admits to having snuffed one of his own staff for 'gross incompetence' in his words. Some guy named Lee Hwan. Has a lot to say, too, about an Ali Hassan who appears to be next on his hit list."

"Real nut case. Jud, we have to put this guy out of circulation permanently."

He nods his head. "Now for the worst part."

"You mean it gets worse? I find that hard to believe."

"For us it does, pal. Our cover is blown."

I think about that for a second. His words have all kinds of bad implications.

"Kim has connected the two visits to Tampa and LA. There's no indication in the files that he knows about COBB and the fact we're all working together to pay back for Kenny, but that shouldn't take too long to figure out."

"Which means our families and Carole at the office are vulnerable. We have to build a fire under Celia's friends and get the swat team out here now!"

"Cool down, Dan. Remember Celia promised the folks at home protection. We need to add Carole to that list. But there's nothing more we can do for them back there. The key is to press hard and bring these crooks to their knees in their own lair."

"You're right, of course. Let's give Celia a call. It's wee hours back there so she'll be at home."

Jud nods and reaches for his cell phone.

"Better hope we can get through on this thing. Can't have anybody eavesdropping on a landline conversation."

We wait impatiently while Celia Grant's phone rings six, seven times. Beginning to wonder where she could be this time of night. Surely Kenny's condition hasn't taken a nose dive.

"Cee?" Jud asks. "Uh...Celia, it's Jud Black." He casts a sheepish grin at me.

He pauses and holds the phone away from his ear. She must be blistering him.

"Yeah. Your clock is right. Should be four AM your time. Sorry, but we have some news that wouldn't keep. Maybe I should give you a few minutes to wake up and call back."

Again a pause and a little grin from Jud. Wish I could hear both ends of this conversation.

"First of all, how's Kenny?" he asks. He listens then turns to me and says, "Kenny's doing great. He has news for us, too."

"Listen," he continues, "Dan and I are in Nevada, Celia. We're in the rattiest motel you could ever imagine. In a few hours we'll be on our way out into the desert."

That obviously opens the flood gates. He listens and starts to interrupt two or three times but can't break in. His shoulders drop and he hands the phone to me.

"She wants to speak to you, Dan." He covers the phone with his hand and says, "Calm her down."

"Dan here."

She's primed for me. "Dan, you don't want to go charging in after these characters on your own. We expect to leave here by Wednesday with a force big enough to take down that place safely and contain anything that might leak out. It would be extremely dangerous—no, downright foolish—for you to go in unprotected."

"They have Jim and Pat, Celia," I argue.

"What?"

"Sent some of their Arab thugs into Vegas and snatched Jim then corralled Pat when he and I showed up in town. We intend to go in after them."

"No! Wait for us, Dan."

"We'll be careful. But we may be able to pave the way and make it easier for the attack force. These are our best pals, Celia. Can't just sit and wait."

"Listen carefully," she says. "And don't repeat a word of this to Jud. I haven't sorted it out yet but I'm more than a little fond of that big lug. Don't think I like the thought of either one of you hurtling into that mountain headquarters with mayhem on your mind. Let the professionals handle this. Promise me you'll wait."

"Best I can do is reassure you we're not suicide prone," I tell her. "This is something we have to do, so just hurry with the reinforcements."

"But…," she begins, and I cut her off.

"Celia, this is important. Jud has been able to crack their data system. We found the Primm New Day office and burrowed in on one of their computers after dark. They know who we are. This could get dicey for us and for the folks at home."

"Don't worry about them. They're well covered as I promised," she reassures me.

"Better add the COBB office in Leesburg to the surveillance list. Carole could get some unwelcome visitors once they figure out that's our place of business."

"I'll arrange it. Now you and Jud just sit tight and wait for us to get there. Kenny will want to talk to you, too."

"See if you can speed up the troops, Celia. We'll be somewhere in the desert by the time you land in Vegas."

"Don't do it, Dan," she scolds.

"Here's Jud." I ignore her pleading and hand the phone over.

He carries the phone outside and talks for a long while. Comes back in with this stupid grin on his face like he's got a secret and isn't sharing. Then he realizes I'm waiting to hear what else she may have told him about the assault plans. Jud looks at his watch and does a quick calculation.

"If we're gonna hit the road early we'd better grab some sleep. I gave Celia our local phone number and the room number. Told her to ask for J. Craig. She promised she'd be calling us here by eight AM her time. That means five o'clock here. You hit the rack. I have work to do on my laptop. Told her I'd send her some email attachments with the gist of our findings from the New Day files. She'll gather up Kenny and the task force head as soon as she has my messages. Plans to put Kenny on the phone with us to do a dump."

"As much as I dislike taking the chance on phone landlines, guess we have little choice at this point. I'll turn in unless you need help getting the info out to her. I'm setting the alarm for four thirty. Try to get some sleep, buddy."

"Crash, Dan. I'll be fine."

CHAPTER 39

Dan Cooper

Morning comes way too soon. When the alarm trips and the radio clicks on, I wake up with a terrible taste and a fierce hunger. The taste I can brush away but my stomach will have to wait. Potato chips and peanut butter crackers won't be much of a breakfast.

As much as I hate to do it, after a few minutes I shake Jud awake for our expected call. He's a bit reluctant to roll out of bed. Opens one eye and grunts.

"Did you get the word to Celia?" I ask. He manages to sit on the side of his bed.

"She knows most everything we do now. The pros can sift through our data and refine their attack plans. Couldn't send the layouts, but I described them the best I could."

"Okay. I'll scrounge some coffee from the desk clerk while you get yourself together. By my watch it's ten minutes till Celia calls."

When I return with two paper cups of strong coffee Jud is poised and ready. He even looks fifty percent awake.

The phone rings and I answer. "Yes, Cee. It's Dan."

"We're on a secure line," Celia says, "using a new technology that lets us talk secure without you having a special instrument. Anybody between us will hear garble, so don't hold back."

I'm relaying her words the best I can to Jud.

"Wonders of science!" he blurts.

"Tell Jud his update was a big help. I have two of the folks here who will be leading the charge. Also have somebody you haven't met but he sends his thanks for your work so far. Says he's glad we talked him into sponsoring your visit."

I look over at Jud and mouth the name Crandall.

"There's another someone that would like to say hello," she says. The next voice I hear is familiar and, at this stage, very welcome.

"Hi, guys. It's Kenny. Hope I didn't get you into too much trouble."

"I'm just glad you're okay. We're on them, Kenny."

"Hang tough, pal," Jud calls out.

"My fever broke. I avoided DHF, thanks to Mom's quick thinking. Wish Fetter had come with me as I asked. I feel really weak but that will pass with time and nourishment."

"What can you tell us about the bad boys," I ask.

"A lot. Let me lay it out for you," Kenny says. "I read your notes. Glad Jud knew how to use Sphinx. Looks like you have them pegged but I can confirm your findings. It's at least as bad as you paint it. They're planning a series of attacks carried out by Ali Hassan's suicidal fanatics. The goal is to issue an ultimatum for a signed hands-off treaty that covers the whole Middle East. It also calls for a huge cash payment to Kim Yung from every major power to save them from further attacks. He expects to use it to carry out his plan for taking over as Leader in Korea."

"They're not reds?"

"Just the opposite, Dan. He wants to overthrow the North Korean dictator and be the big cheese. This guy Kim is a raving, power-hungry lunatic. As much as I hate to say it, we'd be better off with the Communists in charge."

"How'd you come by this information? From what Jud tells me the guy is a paranoid loner. Can't imagine him telling you any of this."

"Sphinx, Dan. I was queasy about what I was seeing so I penetrated their files—read mad ramblings by Yung that made me sick. That's when I decided to make my break."

I'm relaying bits of the conversation to Jud. Damn shame we don't have a speaker phone.

"Tell us," Jud asks, "can you get us in there?"

Kenny hears him and answers, "Both Mom and the colonel are against you trying to penetrate before they get there. I agree. Those guys can turn some nasties loose on you that will make dengue look like a common cold."

"Okay, you've delivered your speech as directed," I tell him. "Now answer the question. The way in."

There is a noticeable delay then a strange voice comes on line.

"You are ordered to hold off!" I grimace and give a shrug in Jud's direction. He makes an obscene gesture.

"I don't know who you are," I say, "but my question wasn't for you. We appreciate what you're doing but this is our fight to pick. We're going in. Now hand the phone to my young friend and let's hear what he has to say."

Dead silence for even longer. Then Kenny speaks.

"I'm still getting some big scowls, but I know from experience you're determined guys. I'd rather give you an even chance of surviving."

"So? The back way?"

"There is one. It's off a store room near one of the labs. Few people know about it—possibly only Kim Yung. I found it by accident. First locate the front entrance where the mountain road disappears into the mountainside. Work your way to the back side of that hill. Keep in mind Ali Hassan's people patrol there. About a quarter mile beyond the front entrance is a deep gorge with twin Joshua trees on its upper rim toward the citadel. Make the descent down over the edge by the trees for about twenty feet. There is a ledge down there directly below those trees and a cave opening obscured by scrub brush. If you go in and follow the cave to its end, you'll see a metal door. I left it unlocked. If they've secured it you're on your own from there. Good luck."

"Thanks, pal. Can you tell us what to expect inside?"

"I estimate Ali has thirty guards deployed around the facility minus the ones he's sent here and after you. They're trained killers and they'll give no quarter. Shoot first and sort them out later."

"Good advice. How were you exposed?"

"It was an accident, Dan. Lee Hwan saw Richard Fetter and me in a restricted room and went into panic mode. He knocked over a vial of something and ran like hell. Fetter was splashed. Hwan closed the door behind him. By then we had both been exposed to the dengue virus. I'd previously stumbled onto the hidden door. We made our way out and spent all night working our way to the Interstate and catching a ride to Vegas. We took a charter hop to Phoenix. Fetter insisted on going to LA but I caught a flight from Phoenix to Dulles."

"Well, you sound good now," I tell him.

"Still have some aches and dizziness, but it's ninety percent better than a few days ago. There were times I would have welcomed death for relief."

Jud takes the phone. "Thanks for the rundown, Kenny…and welcome back." Then he adds, "And to the rest of you, y'all come now, ya hyeah? We'll have the party in progress."

"Damn it, listen to me," insists the voice so loud that I hear him too, but Jud hangs up.

I do a dump to Jud. We speculate about who the kibitzer with all the demands could be. Then we decide it could have been the President for all we care. He's outnumbered two to one.

"Didn't know what a hard-headed pair he was dealing with, huh, Dan?"

"I'm not waiting on anybody, Jud. We're breaking Jim and Pat out of that rat hole, and the sooner the better."

"Right on, pal."

CHAPTER 40

Jim Barnett

What is this place? How did I get here? I remember a knock at the door and a female voice saying, "Housekeeping." Stashed my notes and phone as a precaution and went to answer the door. The woman in the maid's uniform looked genuine enough kind of young and attractive for the job—but I didn't give it a second thought when she disappeared into the bathroom. Never thought about not seeing a cleaning cart outside my door.

Came as a total surprise when she slipped up behind me and I felt a sharp pain in my head. Now I know what it feels like to be sapped. My guess is she followed that with an injection because I've been either out or half-conscious ever since. I do remember this guy that's sitting on one side of me—looks Arab or something. He seems to be behind a steering wheel and I'm wedged between him and the woman. She's grinning at me.

"You are awake. I am Laila. Welcome to the citadel, Mister Barnett."

Our vehicle slows and stops. I hear some chatter then the fog takes over and I'm slipping away again. Some time later I come around in a small room with high walls and not much light.

Where am I, the United Nations? The guy is definitely Oriental and he's huge. No sign of the other two, but there's an Arab and a second Oriental in the room. They're leading me by the arms to a small table and chair.

"Who are you? What do you want with me?"

"Patience, James. All in good time. For now I will ask the questions. My large friend is Mister Kang. You may call me Kim," the shorter Oriental says.

"Yeah. I may call you grinning possum, maybe ferret face. Call off your goons and disappear. You're a bad dream."

Kang nods and a sadistic little smile turns up the corners of his mouth. He plows me one in the chops. I come close to blacking out again.

"Perhaps you will come to understand your situation, Mister Barnett," Kim hisses. "You are our guest and we need some answers from you. This can happen quickly, in which case you will be cared for and made comfortable. Or we will take a path you will not enjoy. Mister Kang knows subtle ways of persuasion with painful results."

I scan around the room. It's a fairly bare enclosure except for some minimum furnishings. There are two small bunks, one above the other, suspended from one wall by chains, a table and chair, a basin and toilet bowl. On the table I see a clay pitcher and a metal cup. A rug covers the middle of the floor. Beyond that, very little. Curiously there are wall outlets but no light switches and no light bulbs. I can see a single window high up on the far wall and a beam of bright light is focused on the concrete wall above my head. On that surface is a large framed sheet of paper filled with what could be Arabic characters and I notice other similar symbols that have been scrawled on the partitions. To my right is the only exit from my temporary home; it's a metal door with a small window. Appears to be an opening with a side and a shelf jutting into the room. As my brain begins to work again, I have this trapped sensation. Always did have a tendency toward claustrophobia, but I can't let it show. These mongrels want something from me, and I don't need to give them another way of wringing it out of me.

Stay cool, Jim. Keep your wits, babe. It's one on three but you can do this.

"That's it," Kim says. "Take it all in. You are deep inside our fortress where your friends can not find you. We have as much time as it takes. I am a patient man."

"And I'm a man with a sore head and an empty stomach. Not in a talking mood."

Now that I've had a few minutes to take stock, the effects of my rough treatment are adding up. That wench hit me harder than I thought. I feel the top of my head and there's a large lump. Have no idea what time of day it is, but I must be well overdue for an insulin dose. Stress can send my blood sugar rocketing up. I'd describe this as pretty stressful. I rub my face with both hands and try to focus on my next move.

The smaller Oriental dude finally speaks up. "You must be wondering what we've done with this," he says with some satisfaction. He's holding an insulin pen. "We brought along a few doses from your room. If you cooperate we will provide more as you need it."

"Look, Charlie Chan, I don't know what your game is, but you're getting nothing from me till I have a shot and something to eat."

Kim speaks slowly. "You are an insolent fool, Barnett! I will grant your wish to show good faith. We would prefer not to make this an ordeal for you, but do not underestimate Mister Kang's skills. He can make you wish you had cooperated."

Kang stands there with a grim stare and flexes his fingers. Something tells me I don't want a demonstration of his skills.

Kim nods to the Arab who knocks on the door and a food tray appears through the window. He carries it to the table. Kim hands me the single insulin dose and signals to his companions. Then the gruesome trio turns to leave. As a parting shot, Kim croons out a warning. "Two hours. You have two hours to decide how we shall proceed, James Barnett. Enjoy your meal and choose wisely. We merely want to know who you really are and why you are intimidating New Day."

They troop out of the room and the door clangs shut with a metallic sound. I'm thinking this Kim character is probably as fruity as the young engineer in LA that put the rush on me. But I'd guess those other two are ready to apply whatever means of persuasion it takes to get me talking.

I give myself a shot and try to collect my wits for what will follow. I sample the food. Not bad eats given my Spartan accommodations. This room is quite a comedown from the digs they dragged me out of back there in Vegas. I try to calm down and take my time with the meal. The wheels are turning frantically in my head. There has to be a way out of this sorry situation.

For the first time since I came around I think about Jud and wonder where he could be. Did they snatch both of us right off the streets of sin city? Hell, he could be in the next cell taking the same kind of abuse. Considering Jud's smart mouth I can picture him wising off and getting himself smacked around. Hope he's cautious enough to avoid that. Kang would no doubt revel in giving him a free lesson in discipline.

As much as I want to close my eyes and wish this place away, I'm too stoked to do more than pace the small room and plot my options. What do they want me to say? I can't let them connect me with Kenny. By now I'm convinced he was in this place and made his escape through the desert somehow. When he's recovered enough to be helpful, he could hand us their heads. Surely the guys are on top of the situation and have called out the cavalry. If Jud is here, too, they'll be in a hurry to storm this fortress—or whatever it is—and kick some butt. I just have to stand firm and hold out on them.

CHAPTER 41

Jim Barnett

I fish in my pocket for my lucky charm. Have a nervous habit of stroking the token Susie gave me whenever I'm under stress. When I find my pocket empty my first thought is that they took away anything I might use before they threw me in here. Then I remember I dropped it on the floor back at the Venetian. Funny how fast the brain can work in emergencies. I must have instinctively flipped that coin on the carpet as I was crumping after the Arab broad swatted me. With a bit of luck Jud found it and concluded I was collared by somebody. If he's free, he will be after them and so will Pat and Dan. I'll take that for now as my best hope.

*   *   *   *

What did Kim say? He gave me two hours. Without a watch it's hard to gauge how much time has passed. The bright light is still streaming in from the tiny window. Daylight. What day? Still Sunday? Maybe Monday? Who knows? I could have been out for hours. Hell, even days for that matter. The closed in feeling is crowding me again. Better get up and walk.

I work hard to get my story straight before Kim returns.

Noise in the hallway. Oh, crap. They're back.

"Greetings, Mister Barnett," the ferret slurps in that oily voice. "You are in better spirits, I trust?"

"Not until you let me out of here. I have nothing to tell you."

"Oh, I believe you do. Tell us why you went to Los Angeles and pretended to be someone you are not. What did you hope to gain?"

Well, let's see if the story I trumped up on the fly will stand up. Got little to lose by trying.

"Appears you've figured out that was a ruse so I won't deny it. Senator Crandall owed me a favor. More precisely, he needed to keep me quiet about a little incident I witnessed. Something not good for his career. So he agreed to help me get into the New Day plant."

"Not convincing. Do you wish to persist in this fable?"

"You can believe it or not. That's your choice. All I can do is give it to you straight. To use a rather inelegant term, I'm an industrial spy for a high tech company that wanted to scope out New Day's progress in the field of nanotechnology."

"Interesting. Continue." Can't tell whether he's buying this or just reeling out the rope before he makes a noose.

"I signed up my traveling companion to help and we got a good first hand look at the New Day plant," I continue. "That persuaded us they were no threat to our client for the time being. Doesn't seem to be enough reason to lock me up here."

"And you want me to believe you will merely walk away, give your report and forget about New Day?" His tone is one of surprise but there's a large hint of doubt.

"Something like that. Did a job and I'll draw my pay for it."

"Then why did you come to Las Vegas?" he fires at me with a sudden threatening tone that catches me off balance. I try to avoid reacting and take a deep breath before calmly replying.

"My friend insisted we swing by since we were this close. He'd never been to the Strip. It was innocent enough until all hell broke loose and your guys nabbed me. What the hell were you trying to prove sending your goons after me?"

Kang bristles but Kim remains calm.

"Must I remind you I expect only answers from you…not questions?" I can already see the Arab and Kang both chomping to lay some hard licks on me for emphasis.

"Look, I just want away from here. Took a swipe at your New Day pals and did what I came for. No foul, no harm as we say in the grand old sport of basketball. Now how about cutting me loose so we can part friends?"

He doesn't answer. Motions to both of his goons and they retreat from the room.

"Wait here, Mister Barnett," Kim says and steps out.

"Like I really have a choice," I mumble to myself when the door closes. *"Thought I'd take a little stroll with the desert critters."*

A couple of minutes pass and the door reopens. Kim glides into the room with his sickening grin. I stand up and step backward to avoid any contact with him, not sure what he may have in mind. He's entirely too polished and calm, and his speech is soft and oily. After the encounter with the LA engineer and his gay friends, I'm taking no chances.

Kim tells me, "You will be our guest overnight. We will provide basic comforts but you are not absolved of suspicion yet."

Well, at least I've bought a temporary reprieve from Kang's bone breaking.

He continues. "You will be given another two doses of insulin should you need them. Do not try my patience further with your tall tales."

Without warning Kim takes one quick pace forward, whirls and demolishes the wooden chair with a spin kick. I watch the explosion of splinters and instantly change my mind about this guy. It's obvious he could break me into pocket-size sections if he was so inclined. Guess he prefers to have others do his dirty work.

I try hard to avoid showing any fear. Can't let him see he's shook me.

"Now look what you've done. What kind of host makes his guest eat standing up?"

He's not amused. "We shall see if your keep your smart mouth after I have talked with your friend."

"Jud Black doesn't know what I got him into. He's totally innocent of spying. Let him go, Kim, if you expect to get any information out of me.""

"Oh, it isn't Mister Black we have." He grins. "Mister O'Leary is our other guest."

With that he gives me one last possum grin, wheels about and slides from the room.

"Damn! Not Pat," I croak and pound the wall with my fist.

CHAPTER 42

Jim Barnett

This is a lonesome feeling. I'm cooped up in a room that's getting smaller by the minute. Running out of options. I lie in my bunk staring into the pitch black darkness of my prison. Even the light through the window has disappeared.

So far I haven't found a way to get myself out of here. The heavy metal door is too much to take on without tools of any sort. Seems from the noise there's a well traveled hallway out there, anyway. The little window way up on the outside wall is far beyond my reach. Only a spider could make it up there without help.

I could use the chains holding up the top bunk if I could hook one end around the window frame and boost myself. Yeah, like I could get either chain loose from their wall brackets. If my shaky story doesn't hold up, I'm afraid I could be at Kang's mercy. And if they really do have Pat, we're both in the soup unless we can find our way out of here somehow.

Damn! It just hit me. If they picked up Pat they could be aware by now that the Tampa visit was connected to our little soiree in Los Angeles. The cheese is getting binding, as my friend Dan would say.

A rattle in the door lock. Not already. They didn't even give me the night to get myself together. First Kim and Kang tried threats and smacked me around, then they floated a test balloon, sounded conciliatory, maybe even beginning to believe my concocted tale. Wonder what round three will bring?

Two people enter the room almost without making a sound. I pretend to be sleeping. Maybe this is only a precautionary bed check, though they surely know escape is rather remote. I glimpse a small electric lantern held above me as if confirming I'm still present.

"He is asleep, Lotus Blossom. Shall we rouse him?"

"Yes, master."

The first voice definitely has the smooth delivery of Kim, but the other one is soft and vary feminine. I debate briefly then curiosity gets the best of me. I slowly open my eyes halfway.

"Ah, Mister Barnett. So you are awake. Welcome again to your home away from home. I trust you are comfortable?"

I peer up at the Oriental man of small but powerful stature. He exudes charm, yet I feel distinctly insecure in his presence even without Kang. At least I knew Kang was here to play the heavy. This guy seems, in an eerie sort of way, far more dangerous. His demonstration earlier with the chair convinced me he's an explosion waiting to happen if I provoke him.

"Give us some light, Lotus," he says and my other visitor slides noiselessly away. I hear that pleasant female voice again.

"I am plugging in the lamp, *sah bum nimh.*" A click sounds and a welcome glow penetrates the room's somber darkness.

"I have decided you will have the company of lamplight for as many nights as you choose to remain here," Kim says. "You will find me amenable as long as you cooperate."

"Gee, thanks. How about a steak and a bottle of Scotch?"

His voice is even and calm as he says, "Do not test me."

I take a closer look at Kim. He's made a change since his last visit. Dressed in a white, long-waisted, belted smock and white trousers that look like a martial arts uniform. But this outfit is more tailored and casts the lamp light with the luster of fine cloth. There is no mistaking that he has a powerful, muscled build. I flash back to the kung fu movies of Bruce Lee and for a moment I can imagine this man scaling that wall to the little window with ease. His very posture is intimidating. He has to be the chief bad ass around here.

"Why the late night visit?" I ask and consciously soft pedal my instinct to be curt.

"That's more like it, James Barnett. We know much about you. I only ask your cooperation to fill in the gaps."

I look him dead on and think to myself, *Yeah, pal, you know bupkus about old Jim, and I'm not about to tell you anything.*

He goes silent while a strikingly attractive young woman steps from behind him and leads me to a seat at the table. Somehow they've managed to replace the broken chair with two seats while I slept. The woman fascinates me. I can't recall seeing anyone move with as much fluid grace as this lovely female.

"Now we will talk and you will tell me how you came to be in Las Vegas," he says and sits in the other chair. The woman stands slightly to one side and behind him.

"So you know all about me," I venture. "But all I know is your name is Kim."

"Fair enough," he replies. "I am Kim Yung and this is my citadel. You are some miles from the city in a place well hidden from prying eyes."

Well, that comes as no great surprise. And it tells me I was right about Kim being the ring leader of this desert band. Sure, I'll talk. Maybe I can pump him for info..

"No, Mister Barnett, I will be the inquisitor. You will listen and answer my questions honestly if you value your health. There will be no mind games."

What is this guy, a mind reader? Could be a long night, Jim.

"Now that we understand the ground rules, I will ask again why you came here from Los Angeles."

"Recreation, Kim. Strictly time out from work. I told you already why we were in LA. No excuse for being an industrial snoop. It's how I make a living."

"A good story, but we both know that is not the truth." His eyes bore holes into me. They are about the most intense pair of eyes anybody's ever trained on me.

"Wish I could give you what you want, but all I can do is tell it straight." Before the words are out of my mouth I know he's not buying my line. This is one tough cookie and I'm sinking fast.

"You are acquainted with one of New Day's employees—one Kendrick Grant—are you not?"

I'm determined now not to give an inch. He's not getting under my skin.

Kim speaks to his companion without moving. "Lotus, I require your skills. Show our guest that we will have his honest answer no matter how long it takes."

I watch the slender little nymph circle from behind him and reach out toward me. What's this delicate girl going to do to me—bite my nose?

"Perhaps a wrist," Kim says.

I feel her velvet hands slide across my palm. Without warning she bends my hand back at the wrist until the pain shoots all the way up my arm. Those delicate hands turn as strong as steel in an instant. Her expression doesn't change. God, it hurts!

"Enough, Lotus." He instructs.

She releases her hold and steps away. I cradle my wrist gingerly and marvel at her strength.

"Please do not force me to have Lotus hurt you. This is not necessary. Answer my question."

"Never heard of this Kenwick or whoever."

"I do not believe you."

"Believe what you choose, Kim. He's not a friend of mine."

"We shall see whether that is true after I speak with your friend, Mister O'Leary."

I grit my teeth and refuse to show emotion. *Do they really have Pat here somewhere? Can I contact him. Maybe he's in the next room.*

"Nevertheless, I want you to remain in good health for now. Here are the insulin doses I promised." He hands me a cooler case. I find two insulin pens inside.

"I will see you again within a few hours, Mister Barnett. I will ask again for your purpose in traveling to our city. Then I expect an admission of your friendship with Mister Grant. You have brought me to the end of my patience. Think carefully about the consequences if you choose to remain obstinate."

Kim waits for Lotus to precede him then they leave and close the door. The clank echoes through the room and forcefully reminds me I'm trapped here until Kim learns all I have to tell. I have to hang tough and make his job as difficult as possible.

My heart is thumping so hard it's uncomfortable. I make my way back to the bunk and sit on its edge. Lean too heavily on my wrist and wince with the pain. Think about lying down but I'm too hyper to sleep. I try to stare across the room. Want to focus on anything that will distract my racing brain. As hard as I try there are only the bare walls and the low hum of an overhead transom pumping in cold air.

Not able to sleep and unable to divert my thoughts from my obvious dilemma, I grasp at the one slim hope that has formed in my confused thoughts. There are two interior walls that don't lead to the open hallway. My eyes fall on the tin cup sitting on my table. Pick it up and go to the partition nearest the head of my bunk. Begin tapping it against the concrete in a monotonous rhythm. I pause periodically to listen for sounds on the other side; place the open end of the cup against the wall as a magnifier and plaster my ear against the cup's bottom. Nothing.

"Pat. Hey, man. O'Leary. Are you there?

I repeat the sequence over and over without result. Frustrated, I walk to the far end of the room and test the other partition. Tap, tap, tap. Softly at first then harder.

"Pat. It's Jim. Give me a sign if you're there."

A faint tapping then a steadier beat from beyond the wall. Now my heart goes into overdrive.

I dig into my memory banks and dredge up a nearly forgotten sequence of da-dits. With Pat's Army background we can use Morse code to talk if I can recall the patterns.

"Let's see. J—I-M. That's the right order of taps and pauses. Now answer Pat."

Same rhythmic beat as before. Come on, O'Leary. If it's you, tap out a message.

I'm so revved up by the initial response that I call out louder than I should.

"PAT. MORSE CODE, PAT. ANSWER."

That brings a louder series of sounds from across the partition. Sounds like he's whacking it with some heavy object. Just as I'm about to begin celebrating, I hear a cascade of language I don't understand.

Put my ear against the cup and the cup to the wall and strain to make out the words. It's no use. Might as well be Greek or Arabic. I look over at the framed paper on my wall with its ornate characters. Hits me so hard it nearly makes me sick. Of course! Dual bunks and Arab symbols. Part of the force in this fortress is made up of Arabs. I must be in a hastily prepared cell fashioned from the quarters of two of the Arab guards.

"Pat. Pat." The noise outside my door startles me. Then a symphony of cups banging against the door, the clinking of metal against metal in some sort of Middle Eastern rhythm. Sounds like half the guard force pounding on the door ribbing me.

The din is deafening. All I can think to do is pound on my side of the door and answer their taunts.

"Get bent, you bunch of scabs!" I take out my frustrations till that little tin cup is bent and battered, but it doesn't change the fact I'm trapped—surrounded by a pack of hungry rats. I dive for the bunk and hold both hands tightly over my ears.

This time, Barnett, you've stepped in the johnny hole with both feet.

CHAPTER 43

Pat O'Leary

That sun is murder! At least I've found a place to hide that shades me from its blistering heat. Damn, I'm thirsty and I hurt all over.

The hole I'm skulking in is dry and full of grit that rubs my skin like sand paper. The skeletons of some sort of scrub bushes are draped over top of me, and every time I move their limbs and thorns rake at me. I wonder how any place this dry could smell so musty. Then I realize It's me. I'm soaked in my own sweat, rapidly losing what moisture my body has left.

My mind drifts back to the Army survival school when I was taught how to get along on my own until the rescue team arrives. One of the lessons I learned was to avoid dwelling on things I couldn't change and think about staying busy. I close my eyes and concentrate. There's Judy ragging my ass about staying out of the boiling sun and telling me that some nondescript home repair job needs completing. But no matter how much I work at distracting myself, she keeps appearing with a cold brew in her hand and I can feel the bottle against my cheek, the cool liquid pouring down my throat.

Extreme thirst is a punishing thing. I begin to see threatening sights all around me. Can't be sure how much I see is real and what part may be mirages brought on by my extreme dryness. People appear out of nowhere and rush to my hiding place, weapons at the ready. Then they fade into the sunlight. I see coyotes skulking nearby sniffing the air for my scent, sidewinders slipping nearer to the brush-filled depression where I've found shelter. Feel something on my skin and look down at the biggest scorpion I've ever seen perched on my elbow. When I jerk violently to shake it loose I realize it's only in my mind. My vision blurs and I want to call out. I reach down next to my foot and pick up some sort of small branch. Jam it between my teeth and clamp down to keep from screaming.

That gives me an idea. We were taught that plants could contain life-giving moisture in the desert. It's worth a try. I find the switchblade and cut away a chunk from the trunk of one bush. Work at trying to suck out whatever it holds. But, beyond a foul, bitter taste, that turns out to be a lost cause—not a drop of moisture. Either I get out of this hole soon and find water or I'll have to surrender to somebody just to survive.

Hold it together, Pat. Let your training kick in. You can make it.

I shut my eyes and think about being in an easy chair back at home with the air conditioning at full tilt. Feels good until a noise nearby brings me around. When I sneak a look there's a large shock waiting.

Two tanned and bearded men with automatic rifles are climbing the sand dune no more than thirty feet from where I'm lying. I hunker down as far as possible in my shelter that's beginning to feel like a lot less cover than I need. Extract the terrible tasting branch from my mouth and laugh when I see the deep tooth marks I've made. I finger the switchblade knife and pick up a rock. Not much protection against their guns but I'll go down fighting.

One of the men is pointing in my direction and babbling something in a foreign tongue. Could be Arabic. Can't understand a word. Has he found my hiding place?

"English, Khalid" the other one says. "Practice your English. As Ali says, we must learn to fit in if we're to dupe the stupid Americans." He has a nasty cackle.

Thank you, scum bag. Keep talking. Let me know what you're thinking. Give me an edge.

"There is only a deep gorge on that side, Khalid. Search over there." He points to my right and I let out a long sigh of relief. They start to walk across my field of vision slightly downhill from my foxhole.

Then they both stop suddenly. I hear something. The roar of an engine.

"Halt! Stop there now!" one guard screams out. He raises his rifle and points it menacingly at someone I can't quite see from my vantage point. I'm not about to move and draw their attention.

What I hear next could be another one of my illusions. It's probably a voice conjured up from wishful thinking and dizzy dehydration.

"Little on the warm side out here, huh?" the voice says. I try to process what I'm hearing and balance it against what I want to believe, but it's almost too good to be true.

"Hey, man. Which way to the nearest gas station?" the voice continues. No doubt about it now. Jud Black is out there. Somehow I have to let him know where I am.

"You must leave," says the Arab who takes the lead. "Do your digging elsewhere." He waves his rifle as if to say 'shoo'. He and his companion stand their ground and the engine revs up again. My heart sinks when I think about Jud leaving before I can signal him.

I shift around, taking care not to disturb any of my cover, until I can see who they're talking to. There are two men sitting in a canvas-top jeep looking like a couple of relics from the past. Except for their motorized mule they could be two grisly prospectors from the eighteen hundreds, hard bitten, dirty, burned and haggard looking. Despite all their efforts to camouflage their appearance, I'd know those two hides in a tanning yard. It's Jud and Dan!

"Bit hot, huh, sahib?" Jud flips at him.

"Kalid," the armed man corrects. "This is private property. You must leave," the guard repeats. "Turn around and go back."

"We'd like to oblige," Jud says. "Seems we have a little problem. Our horsey here has pulled up lame. Needs a motor doctor. What do you guys know about engines?"

"Do not jest. You must leave now. If your auto will not take you, begin walking."

Dan steps out of the Jeep and raises the hood. I nearly laugh out loud. For all his smarts about other things, Dan knows next to nothing about cars. He's always said they're only good for getting you from point A to point B. That's another way of saying he's mechanically naïve and, further, he doesn't care.

Jud walks in the direction of the two Arabs and offers his canteen. "How about a drink. That sun is brutal."

The one who called himself Khalid shrugs. Seems he's figured out they're not going anywhere even if they could. He approaches the Jeep and shoves Dan aside. Says, "Stand away." Then he sets down the rifle and says, "I will have a look. Guard them." The other one stares at him and nods.

That's all the opening Jud needs. He whips out a small handgun he's concealing behind the canteen and fires a single shot that strikes the rifle holder in the chest. He flinches, hangs motionless in midair, then slumps to the ground firing a burst from his automatic weapon. Jud hits the ground and rolls. Dan grabs Khalid with both hands as the man attempts to straighten up and shoves him into the engine compartment. Swings the hood down on him. Khalid shrieks. Dan holds the hood with both hands and I can almost feel the Arab roasting on that hot engine, trying to scream but managing only gurgles and whimpers.

Jud walks over to the Jeep. "He's well done, pal. You can take him off the griddle." Dan yanks the fried guard out onto the sand. Jud looks at the man writhing in agony and applies the coup de gras, a bullet through the ear.

"Seemed like the only humane thing to do, Dan. Put him out of his misery."

Dan stares at Jud holding the handgun and frowns. "Thought you had an aversion to guns."

Jud shrugs and hands him the pistol, but Dan returns it.

The action has taken place so quickly I lie there for a moment in complete shock. Have to get through my addled brain that this isn't just a sun-crazed fantasy. My pals have given me a way out of my life-threatening predicament. I find a way to move my stiff legs from my cramped position in the hole and push away the limbs over my head. Stand upright and, to my surprise, I don't fall on my keister.

I raise one arm and croak through parched lips, "Bring that taxi over here."

They both stop and stare at me in disbelief. Dan comes running toward me with Jud close behind. Dan bear hugs me and pants, "How the bloody hell…?"

"It's about damned time you guys showed up. Got a cold brew in your pocket?"

CHAPTER 44

Pat O'Leary

"Now I know how a desert jackrabbit must feel," I tell the guys. "Between fighting off scorpions and sidewinders and keeping an eye peeled for Arabs, I had less fun than I wanted in that burrow back there. There are some wild dogs out here, too. Thought I was gonna have to grapple with them to keep from being dog food."

"Must have been coyotes," Dan says.

"Whatever. All I had was a pocket knife and they looked rabid."

We have little time for a reunion after I shake them out of their shoes by materializing out here in the desert. There will be plenty of time for celebration later. Right now we have to avoid being stopped again and get to somewhere we can do a group head scratching session.

"What do we do with these two?" Jud points to the two dead Arab guards lying nearby. "We can't have their buddies finding them before we break in."

I say, "That rabbit warren of a dry hole I was using served me well. I made it through the night and most of a day without being found. Let's dump them there and cover it. The sun is about to go down. If we're lucky, nobody will find them till morning."

I feel nearly back to normal after draining a canteen and bitching about it not being Murphy's Ale. Dan tries to convince me to go slow on the liquid intake. Guess this big old body is too dry for me to listen. I gobble down one of their stale leftover sandwiches like it was a gourmet meal, gulp down another long slug of water and belch heartily.

Dan laughs. "Sounds like something Jud would say, O'Leary. That's one of his more cultured utterances."

"Oh, shut up, Cooper," Jud snaps. "Let's get these bodies stowed."

When the dirty work is done we decide to cool it for a few hours. I'm drained and my pals are no rosy cheeked kids, either. Jud's driving. We motor away through the dark without lights, hoping the sound of the jeep doesn't draw more unfriendlies.

* * * *

"How'd you end up in a dive like this?" I ask and toss away another empty. Unwrap another burger and dig in.

"Cool digs, huh?" Dan flips back.

"Only thing cool here is the suds and it ain't no bargain." I grunt.

"See, Jud," Dan says, "I told you all he needed was a couple beers and he'd be right back to his lovable old self—bitching and complaining. That's a big improvement for a guy that was about to pose for one of those skull and crossbones billboards."

"Stuff it, Jud. Why did we come back to the Taj Mahal?"

"Well—first off," Jud says, "the guy in the office thinks we're a couple of broken down prospectors fresh in off the dunes. Probably thinks this is the best we've seen in weeks."

"Yeah, he gave me the twice over when I asked for a room."

Dan chimes in with, "Probably thought *'where are all these reprobates coming from?'*. Don't blow our cover, Pat. We only need a sleeping spot till Celia and the forces get here. Looks like day after tomorrow now."

"What you guys got in mind till then?" I ask.

Dan offers, "Maybe another day in the sandbox. See if we can find the back entrance Kenny told us about. Do a little reconnoitering of our own before the storm troopers arrive."

I think about that. Considering that Jim could be at the mercy of those bad asses, I don't see how we can sit here and count our toes for two days. Jud is nodding his agreement.

"Okay by me," I tell them. "Might as well tempt fate again. That seems to be our strong suit these days. Right now, though, this puppy's ragged out. Gonna take some brews and chow and go to my pit. Need to rewind. Wake me up tomorrow morning."

*   *   *   *

Bright and much earlier than they bargained for I'm back at Dan's room banging on the door.

"Reveille, sunshine! Shake it and move."

A sleepy eyed Dan answers my call and looks at his watch. Mumbles something. "Too early," is about all I understand.

"Come on, Cooper. I'm the one that groveled in the desert all night and half the day. It's time for biscuits and gravy, fried eggs and a rasher of bacon—whatever the hell a rasher is. Shake a leg while I go get Jud started."

He grumbles and staggers off for the john. I look across the room.

"Surprise, surprise," Jud says. Wiseacre is already dressed in his surplus duds and beaming at me through his painted-on suntan. "Ready for a stroll in the sand?" he flips at me.

"First we're gonna grab some breakfast, Jud. Dan's still groggy. Tell him we'll be in that coffee shop on the corner. I'll get us a place to sit and order as much coffee as the waitress can carry, buddy."

Ten minutes later Dan and Jud join me. Not much to getting ready when you want to retain that fried in the desert look. If the Arabs snatch us again, well just stink them to death.

Over food in a back corner we get down to cases.

"From the top, guys," I begin. "What's our plan?"

"Whatever it takes to pry Jim out of that underground," Jud replies.

"What if there are dudes out there that see us first?"

"Doing okay so far. We're ahead two to zip." Jud's feeling his oats.

"I've been down this path before. Things can turn sour in a hurry when you're up against folks armed like those people. You saw what they were packing—enough power to make quick work of three slow senior citizens like us."

"Speak for yourself," Jud quips.

"All right, two old farts and a brash kid."

Dan jumps in. "Kenny said there was a back way in, Pat. That's what Jud and I were looking for when we were jumped by the guards. If we can get in down there we may be able to bring Jim back. Who knows what they might put him through if we wait too long."

"You're right. We have to try. He'd do the same for us."

"Jud and I broke into the New Day office in Primm," Dan says. "Found out volumes about what's going on in the mountain. Those guys are bona fide terrorists about to come down hard on us. They have biological agents of the worst order stockpiled in there."

"Settled," I say. "Won't be the first time we hung our butts out in the wind. Let's stoke up, pick up a poke of traveling grub and get at it."

CHAPTER 45

Jim Barnett

Light is pouring through that pitiful little hole high up in the wall. I open my eyes and peer across the small room. The Arab plaque reflects the sparse light and reminds me I'd rather be waking up somewhere else—anywhere else.

After I woke up in the middle of the night and gave myself an insulin shot my nerves started to calm and my heart returned to a more normal pace. Must have conked out for a good long snooze because I feel renewed. But I can't take a lot of comfort in that considering the Korean guy is due back—in his words 'after a few hours'. Got some soul searching to do while it's daylight outside. How much do I tell him and where do I draw the line. More important is the question of how much time I can buy for the guys to track me down and help me ditch this hell hole.

A gnawing hunger and a growling stomach bring me upright in the bunk. I sit for a minute then scan over toward the door. Guess the breakfast service hasn't arrived since there's nothing on that shelf inside the door. Lousy hosts.

I'm in the process of dousing my face with tepid tap water from the basin when there is activity in the hallway. Voices and moving around. The door swings open.

"Good morning, Mister Barnett. You had a restful night?"

It's the lovely but deadly little woman who nearly broke my wrist last night, the one Kim called Lotus. The sight of her makes me instinctively cradle my wrist and turn my back to her.

When I face her again she seems to be checking to assure no one else is listening at the window. "Please. I mean you no harm," she says barely above a whisper. Lotus holds out her hand with a tray of food and moves toward me, gliding in a fluid motion that intrigues me but doesn't diminish my fear of her incredible strength.

"Hold it, sister. Last time I felt those fingers you damn near broke off my hand."

She raises one finger to her lips and speaks very softly. Walks over to the table and sets down my meal, turns on the lamp, then retreats to a safe distance.

"Eat. Then we will talk."

She doesn't have to ring the breakfast bell but once. I'm famished. Set about devouring the chow which isn't half bad. Occurs to me it must have been specially prepared. Surely the Arab guards don't eat this well every morning. She stands aside and watches me silently.

"What could we possibly have to talk about?" I ask when I've cleaned my plate and settled back with my coffee.

"I can help you, James Barnett. I come as a friend." Her smile looks genuine enough but I'm still wary.

"Like you helped me to a sprain last night? How does a little woman like you generate such power?"

She beams at me. I can't help but be taken by her delicate beauty. Her words sound sincere, but my mind says it's a trap, some ruse to get me spilling my guts.

"Kim has taught me the skills of the *hwa rang do*. I know the martial arts and work hard to hone my skills. I am truly regretful for my action. There was no choice with Kim watching. I had to follow his orders."

"Glad it wasn't my neck you took a fancy to. I wouldn't be sitting here with a full stomach this morning."

She frowns then the corners of her mouth turn up as she catches my stab at humor. Her musical giggle is a delight. More in keeping with her childish appearance than was her display of joint mangling that almost cost me a limb. Despite my concerted effort to dislike this young woman I'm taken by her charm.

"You are amusing, James."

"Jim. My friends call me Jim." As soon as I say it the words strike me as inane, maybe even naïve. Here's this little slip of a thing who could snuff me out in an instant if she was so inclined and I'm making friends with her? Sounds like something Jud might pull and get away with but not old heavy handed Jim. Still, she's likable and sounds sincere.

"Listen carefully, Jim." She reaches out and I let her take my hand. Her fingers are smooth and soft, her hand oh so warm. Doesn't feel at all like the deadly weapon I know it to be. I begin to relax and she softly strokes my sore wrist.

"I want your help as well, Jim. We can make our way out of the citadel and away from these hills. I can show you the way, but you must see that I am not harmed when we reach your people. I have done nothing against them. My knowledge of the citadel and what is happening here will aid you in bringing down Kim Yung and his followers."

"Why should I believe you, Lotus? This could be an elaborate trap by your friend Kim to open me up and get me blabbing. I have nothing to tell that weasel."

"No. He is not my friend. If it were in my power I would kill him myself. He is a monster, a maniac mad with his quest for power. He abuses me in ways you can not imagine. I detest him."

Suddenly she stops speaking and turns her head toward the door. She's obviously concerned about her outburst being overheard. Then she takes a step backward and opens her robe.

I'm stunned by the perfection of her slender body. This is truly a beautiful woman in the bloom of her youth.

She turns slowly and shows me her back. Ugly bruises mar the olive skin and a prominent red welt rises angrily on one buttock. She holds out her arm and shows me an impression, one that looks newly made, on her upper arm. It looks suspiciously like a set of tooth marks.

"He is an animal who treats me like chattel. The marks do not last because Kim has been careful not to permanently mar what he calls 'my perfection'. I am his *chagun kkot,* his little flower. He adores yet punishes me, professes his love but heaps abuse on my person."

"I'm sorry, Lotus."

"Those are only the visible wounds. Mentally he has made me a wisened old woman—and a very sad one. I am no more than his harlot, his possession to be dominated. Help me, Jim."

She retrieves her robe and covers herself. Sits in the chair across the table from me and continues. "Now you see why I must make good my departure from his side. You can help see that I am not blamed for his crimes, explain that I was held here against my will, a prisoner with no choice but to obey."

I'm not going for her pitch, but I'll play along. Given that I don't have any other options for un-assing this place, throwing in with Lotus sounds like the best and only choice for saving my butt.

"Okay, Lotus. What's your plan?" I'm still not committing, Let's see how far she goes.

"Kim Yung plans to return to question you. I know that he is busy today making preparations. His visit will likely not take place until late in the afternoon."

"Preparations for what, Lotus?"

She goes quiet and peers up at the window with its little shaft of light streaming in. She lifts the table lamp. Light floods her face revealing her flawless skin. She touches her remarkably smooth cheek and ponders her answer.

"Kim is convinced that Kenny Grant's escape and your visits to the New Day sites mean he must act quickly. He is planning attacks that will bring horrible consequences to the American people. Then he will issue an ultimatum to your country and the world. He will threaten massive destruction of their populations unless his terms are met."

"His terms being what?" I ask in shock.

"I do not know. His goal is to take control of Korea then blackmail the world to bow to his will. Kim has powerful tools at his call. His scientists have developed and combined deadly organisms and he holds the keys to amazing power through molecular restructuring."

"Biological warfare and nanotechnology," I confirm in flat tones.

"Yes. You know of these things?"

"Too well, Lotus.

"I fear, Jim, that he will launch these attacks within days now that his intentions may have been exposed. Kendrick Grant worked here and knows enough to be a great danger. Kim will send his Arab helpers to the cities he has targeted and we will witness disease and panic you can not imagine."

"Let's get started," I prompt. "What do you want me to do?"

She doesn't answer. Instead she once again sheds the robe and stands totally nude for a moment holding something in one hand. She looks up at the window, begins to circle the room like a pacing jaguar. Lotus crouches and springs at the wall; digs her toes against the surface and scales upward literally defying gravity. I see it but I don't believe it.

Lotus clutches the window ledge with one arm and raises herself up. She uses her free hand to do something to the window I can't make out. Then she completes her astounding feat by backing hand over hand down what appears to be a nylon rope.

I stand there dumbfounded while the lovely little nymph dons her robe and calmly turns in my direction. "There. The rope is fastened and you will find the window open for your escape. Use the rope to let yourself down on the outside. You will find a ditch running along the building. Take it to your right to the corner of the building. Look for me at the entrance just beyond that corner. We are underground. It is not daylight you see through the window but intense security floodlights. They merely turn them off at night so the guards can sleep and they activate ground sensors. Stay low in the ditch and move cautiously."

"Sounds like a large chance I'll be seen. There must be guards in the nearby rooms."

"Their windows are as high up as this one is so they do not have a good view of the building exterior. The guard station is not always manned and they tend to be sloppy in observing. After all, how many times would they expect someone to escape from the guard quarters? Try not to make noise that will attract attention."

"How will I join up with you and find my way out?"

"Below the window bear to your right. Look around the corner for the first exit door. Only Kim uses that door from the *dojang* but I have a key. I will be standing outside the *dojang* waiting for you."

For the first time since I woke up in my cell I have a glimmer of hope. My situation has gone from hopeless to frantically optimistic. Hope this gal isn't smoking. me. I may need to fight her off to get away. I have to shake this place and find Pat, Dan and Jud. We have serious work to do. From what Lotus says there's not a lot of time to stop this mad devil Kim Yung.

"As soon as I leave with your breakfast tray I will create a distraction in the hallway. Climb quickly and be away."

I watch her leave and grasp the rope. Say a prayer that I can remember my rope climbing technique and get to that window.

CHAPTER 46

"So, Ali Hassan. Once again you have fallen short of my expectations."

"What can you mean?" Ali replies and glowers back at Kim Yung.

"Your mission was to bring two meddlers to me from the city. I see only James Barnett and another broken promise."

"Surely you will derive valuable information from this Barnett. The other one eluded us in the desert but we will find him. He will be in the hands of my guards before the day is over."

Kim knows the Arab is jealous of his power and his own inability to rise to Kim's level. No matter. The plan must be launched quickly. Kim can feel the peril closing in on them. Within days he will issue the order and Ali's sorry group will fulfill their task as messengers of death. Then he will rid himself of Ali and all of his followers.

"So you are telling me that another of your infallible warriors, a member of your much touted *al-Qinaa'*, has failed his mission? Why do I even tolerate the inept actions of such a weakling force? Must I instill my own brand of discipline in them?"

Ali's anger is rising and Kim seems to exult in the Arab's powerless frustration.

"Your words are unfair, Kim Yung." His eyes reveal his fear.

"Then bring the one responsible for this travesty to me and let me hear first hand how the American duped your trained fighter and disappeared. I will decide the slacker's fate."

Ali is torn with uncertainty. He stares at Kim and tries to manufacture an acceptable answer. He is at the Oriental's mercy.

"Uhhh…the one responsible, Kim, is yet in the desert pursuing this O'Leary. Sh…he will not rest until he has the prisoner in his grasp. You will see."

"Enough for now. I will expect success by nightfall or someone will pay dearly. You shall have no more excuses!"

Ali's look of concern disappears for the moment and he searches for a way to divert Kim's attention. This man fancies himself capable of matching wits with Kim, but he is no challenge. The Korean has bested men with intellects far superior to Ali's. If it were not for the sport of belittling him and seeing his internal agony, Kim reflects that he would end his miserable existence with a single thrust.

"Our plan is unstoppable, Kim. We will allow no one, certainly not these meddlers, to stop our quest to humble the whole of America. Al-Qinaa' has made a pledge and it will be kept."

"Idle talk unless you begin to show me results. Your mistakes have cost us one of our brightest scientists then failed to return him when he was within your grasp. If he has revealed the location of the citadel, we must know it and revise our schedule. Now a new threat, perhaps as a direct result of Grant's escape, has appeared, and you can not carry out the simplest order to bring two meddlers to me."

"Both of which will be remedied in time," Ali answers. "My agent is still near to Kenny Grant and will secure him or die with him. Either way, your secrets will remain unspoken."

"No!" Kim screams. "I want Grant returned unharmed. He is essential to achieve my long term goals. I will be Leader! I *will* succeed in spite of your mistakes. When the world of nanotechnology is my own personal possession I will bring the American dogs to their knees and take my rightful position as Leader of a unified Korea. Then the world will know my power and pay me homage."

"The prisoner we have brought you, Kim—you have spoken with him?"

Ali knows the answer. The moment Kim entered the guard quarters his people were relaying to him news of Kim's arrival.

"Mister Barnett is clever, Hassan. He is in denial even though we hold his life in our hands. Swears he is only an industrial spy and that the other man is blameless."

"Perhaps you would permit me to interrogate him, Kim. I can assure you his information will be given once I apply my methods of persuasion."

Kim wonders if Ali notices the smile that plays at the corners of his mouth. If the threat of Kang could not extract the truth from Barnett, how does Ali hope to succeed? But if he has ways that will not render the prisoner useless….

"Very well, Ali. Take your turn with him. I want him to tell us why he and the other one are here and how much he knows about New Day and this place. If you go too far and gravely damage our best link to our adversaries, my wrath will be on you directly."

"Do not fear, Kim. He will not die, but he will know agonies he never dreamed the living could endure. I will break him."

"Then you have four hours until I return to his cell for my answers. Use the time well, Ali."

Kim motions for him to depart and summons his beautiful assistant. Lotus arrives, her silent feet gliding noiselessly across the floor. She bows.

"Yes, *sah bum nimh?* What is your pleasure?"

"I will go to the *dojang* now, precious flower. There is time for a spirited *poomsae* then perhaps more delightful pleasures. We will return to our visitor after that."

"As you wish, master." She leaves to prepare his uniform.

Kim considers his decision a wise one. Ali does not know he has already dispatched someone he can trust to return Kendrick Grant. The scientist's talents can not be lost to Kim. Only Yung realizes exactly how important Grant is. For all his life, Kim has worked to perfect his body and mind. Now this evil contamination grows inside him and must be stopped. Kendrick Grant and his fellow worker are so close to making that possible. All other achievements will pale in comparison with unlocking the power that can grant cell healing and—dare Kim hope—extension of life.

By the time Ali's tardy henchmen act, Grant could be recovered and telling all he knows about the desert labs. Kim knows he can rely upon his own agent to return him here before that happens. She will not fail.

Her mission must be carried out immediately. She awaits Kim's orders. Where is the telephone?

CHAPTER 47

Once again he has been insulted and demeaned by Kim Yung. Ali is being treated as an inferior, an ignorant underling. But Ali, too, has trained diligently in the universities of the very people they will soon crush under a cloud of death. Then Kim will know his anger as well.

Ali Hassan hurries off to alert his sister Jamila. She will leave the citadel where Kim can not touch her until there is time to work out the problem of how O'Leary escaped. If necessary Ali will accuse one of the *al-Qinaa'* and let Kim punish him instead. Ali is dedicated to carrying out the *jihad*, but he can not offer up his beloved sister to Kim's wrath. For now Jamila must remain unseen and attempt to recover the prisoner she lost. Even if the big American is brought in dead from exposure in the desert, he will at least no longer be a threat to the citadel.

Jamila is in Ali's room waiting for word of his meeting with Kim Yung. Only Ali knows she has returned. He assures that no one else is near and gives his instructions.

"Sister, you must leave now. I will summon Laila and have her go to meet you at the desert training site. She will accompany you to search for, as you call him, the big American. By this time he will be wandering in the heat of the day, parched and dry in the sun, and should be no challenge for you. If he resists, kill him then bring him back for Kim to see. A carcass will be just as convincing to the yellow one."

"Ali, my brother, I am ashamed of my failure. If I do not find him, this will be my last mission. I will offer up my earthly body to the desert jackals as my atonement."

Her words pain Ali's ears, but there is no recourse now. If he takes her to Kim he will no doubt exact a penalty of swift death upon her. If he would destroy his own lackey, Lee Hwan, for a mistake, Jamila's life will be of no consequence to him. Perhaps he would snuff out her light merely to prove that he is Ali's superior.

"Your dedication will drive you," Ali tells her. "You will find the fugitive."

She smiles and raises one arm. "I am heartened by your confidence, Ali. We will succeed. "Al-Qinaa'!" She clenches her fist in a salute.

"Jamila," he says with finality, "if Allah wills, you will bring him to us. If not, go and forget me and this place. Save yourself. Do not return here."

She departs with resolve.

Now to complete two important tasks. First Ali must give Karim the order to sacrifice himself to rescue Kendrick Grant. This time there will be no half-measures. He must be prepared to die as a martyr for the cause. He must hold others at bay while his helpers escape with Grant. Karim will make their statement with force when he sends the American police to oblivion and himself to paradise. Grant will be returned long enough to complete the attack plan and carry it out. Then he and all of the Oriental infidels will perish when Ali takes control.

His order will be given quickly. Then he has an appointment to loosen this James Barnett's tongue.

CHAPTER 48

Dan Cooper

We've found our way back to the spot where the two guards pounced on us. I take a quick check to see if their bodies have been discovered. Still there. The desert heat and the scavengers have devastated their bodies. We cover our faces against the stench and the flies. Dig down with our 'prospecting' equipment and leave the guards planted deeper.

Then I point off in the direction where I thought I saw Joshua trees yesterday. Sure enough there are twin trees. I get out of the jeep and peer over the edge at the sheer drop of probably close to a hundred feet. Shake my head and whistle.

"Not the place to make a misstep, guys." I step right to the edge and a small trickle of rocks showers down the cliff side. Shuffle back quickly before I lose my balance.

"Could be tricky getting down there. Should be a ledge about twenty feet below the top according to Kenny. Park the vehicle in that depression and we'll cover it with brush. Then we can tie a rope to one of the trees and let ourselves down one at a time."

Jud affixes the rope and looks up to ask, "Who's gonna be the guinea pig?"

I shrug and say, "I'll give it a go. Hope you tied that rope like you meant to be first, Jud." He just grins and says, "Happy sailing, good buddy."

Give the tether a stiff yank and it holds. Walk to the edge and feel the ground crumbling beneath my feet sending another stream of pebbles down the side.

Well, I either step off or get left standing in midair over a sheer drop. Can't guarantee I didn't let out a helpless squeak when I swung out. When my feet bump against the rock face of that gorge it feels good to have something solid under my boots.

I slide down the rope as quickly as I can without hurrying and losing my grip. For a non-outdoorsy type, I'm amazed how easy it seems. Not that I'd want to make a habit of it. The ledge is there as advertised. Must be three to four feet wide front to back and about ten feet across.

"You okay?" comes Jud's voice from above.

"Feel like a mountain goat. The ledge is here and it's decent footing. I see some sort of opening. Let me get this rope loose and I'll give you a report."

I sweep away some scrub brush and see two sizeable rocks on either side of a depression in the side of the hill. A closer look tells me it's an opening in the rock wall. I unhook my emergency light from my belt and turn it on. There's a tunnel ahead.

"Think I've found it, folks," I call out. "A tunnel. Could be the back way in. By the way, Jud, better tie ropes to both trees before the porky one climbs down. Feel sorry for the beating those two trees are gonna take."

As expected, I hear Pat answer, "Kiss my what?"

I stand out of the way in the tunnel entrance and watch for the next daring fool to step off that cliff. Jud shinnies down like a monkey on the rope and plants both feet firmly on the ledge. He grins and says, "That was a rush." Yanks his rope end and Pat reels it in from above.

A minute or so later I watch a steady shower of rocks and dust cascade over the hillside like an avalanche in miniature. That's followed by two gunboat boots thudding to a halt outside the tunnel entrance.

"It's been a long time and a lot of pounds since my Army days," Pat says. "You goofballs sure get me into some weird situations." Pat loosens not one but two ropes and casts them away. He steps into the tunnel behind Jud and me.

"Well, if the desert critters don't eat us, we're on our way," I announce.

Jud gives me a big smirk and says, "Had to say it, didn't you?"

CHAPTER 49

Jim Barnett

That window is a long way above my head. God, I feel terrible! My blood sugar must be off the scale and I have only one dose of insulin left. Better take it and rest a bit before I tackle that rope climb. Couldn't even take advantage of Lotus distracting everybody in the hall. Tried to scale up and near broke my butt when I fell.

Well, it's been thirty minutes since the shot. I still feeling crappy but have no choice now. Somehow I have to scramble up that wall and get out. Just hope I can do it without rousing any of those hyenas that were cackling at me. What did she say...right...around the corner...exit door.

Sure could use a boost. Where's old Barney Plummer when I need him? That guy had million dollar muscles and a fifty cent head. Used to boost me half way to the ceiling and make the rope climb easy in gym. Well, Barney, guess I'm on my own this time.

Walk the wall, Jim. Foot over foot. Halfway there. Grunt and dig deep.

Okay, I'm up. The window's open as Lotus said. I'll reach through and hold the outside wall long enough to reel this rope up onto the ledge. Hang in, Barnett. It's either this or face that grinning lump Kang and his pain games again.

Didn't realize how wrung out I was. Had to make it quick and leave the rope lying on the windowsill. A dangling rope would have been a dead giveaway.

Came freaking close to blacking out when I climbed over the sill, let go and dropped. Good thing I was close enough to the ground to fall without breaking anything. Now I'll just sprawl here for a while and get a second wind....

Okay, Lotus. You better be waiting or my ass is grass. Those spotlights are boring in on me like I was out there on the sand dunes. Hope I can stay low enough to keep out of sight. Must be guards watching from up there somewhere. They may have already spotted me.

There she is. Curiously there are no spotlights on that side. She said Kim uses that exit from whatever she called it—a *dojang?* Better stay down, anyway, in case there are eyes anywhere. She sees me. Good.

"I feared for you, Jim," she whispers when I reach her. "What took you so long?"

"Need some of your magic, Lotus. Took me a couple tries to walk that rope."

She smiles broadly. It's an incredibly beautiful smile. Then she reassures me. "Well, the hard part is behind you now. Follow me."

I look around. Darker on this side of the building. Open space, though, soaring up maybe a hundred feet to a solid overhead. A thin beam of light through the only opening up there.

We work our way along the outside wall of the building. The rock wall looms closer and closer. A solid cliff of rock on our left closes in to leave no more than two feet of space between it and the building. She turns sideway and reaches for my hand. Feel like I'm walking into a pitch black corridor with no idea what's at the other end.

She must sense my reluctance. Maybe it's because I'm pulling back on her hand about as hard as she's yanking me forward. In her soft, melodic voice she urges me on.

"Trust me, Jim."

"Don't like tight places," I try to say without faltering. This is getting creepy. The wall is closing in. Space can't be much more than a foot wide now. Knew I didn't like tight squeezes, but now I'm convinced it's an unhealthy case of claustrophobia. I have this mental picture of somebody discovering a skeleton wedged in here years from now—and it's mine!

I'm about to wig out when I hear Lotus say, very calmly, "This is it, Jim." She pulls my hand and I'm facing a large opening in the rock wall directly in front of me. There's only a faint hint of light but I can feel air moving. Step toward her voice and seem to be in a room of some sort.

Lotus can't hold back a tittering laugh. "It frightened me, Jim, the first time. This is the way Kim Yung enters and leaves the citadel. We are now in a tunnel under the desert."

I can hear her moving around and get the feeling she's searching the rock wall for something.

"Ah," she says. "Now we can have light." Suddenly my eyes are met by an intense beam..

"Kim keeps a battery-powered light in here. We're far enough away from the guards to avoid raising an alarm. He treasures the secret of this exit."

I peer around in all directions. The emergency lantern casts strange shadows around us, but I much prefer it to the gooey blackness we slithered through in that crawl space. This opening is, I estimate, a small room maybe eight feet square with an overhead of rock and timbers barely high enough for me to stand upright. Ahead of us an opening leads off in a single direction.

"The laboratories are on the nearest side of the building," Lotus says. "This is an old mining tunnel Kim discovered and put to his own use. Those who shored it up and made it safe for him can no longer tell of its existence. He..."

"Killed them?" I manage to choke out.

"As he does with anyone who is a threat to him. I expect he will eliminate all in the citadel who pose any danger to his dominance once the deadly attacks on your people are carried out. Kim Yung will tolerate no sharing of his power. Despite his promises to me, I know he will take my life when he ascends to power."

We begin to pick our way through the tunnel with only the light Lotus carries to show the way. All along the tunnel I hear skitters and rustles, sounds of things I'd prefer to believe were not living, but I know we're not alone in this dungeon.

There is a damp, musky feel to the tunnel. I touch one wall surface and feel a surprising dampness given that somewhere above us must be an arid surface of sand dunes. Several times I step over or around animal waste and the ravaged carcasses of desert vermin. The odors of waste and rotting flesh fill my nose, and I resist the urge to retch.

"The path is not too long, but it is difficult at times," Lotus says as we begin to climb. The ground shifts beneath me, and I labor to follow her. A shower of pebbles rains down behind every step I take. The sound of the stones tumbling is magnified and echoed by the tunnel walls.

"Is this place safe, Lotus?" Strikes me we could easily start a chain of events that would bury us down here.

She reaches back and makes contact with her fingertips. "The structure is sturdy, Jim. The three workmen Kim dispatched to the bowels of this place did their job well." She points to one side of the burrow. I see a skeleton standing in a wall recess with its bony arm pointing as if to warn intruders. Guess Kim left three permanent guards in here.

Yeah, and he really rewarded them for their efforts, didn't he? I think. Well, at least that tells me who we're dealing with. Come crunch time we'd better not show him any quarter or Kim will see we regret it.

CHAPTER 50

Jim Barnett

After some time we arrive in a second hollowed out area the size of a large room. Lotus sits by one wall and I follow her lead.

"Must be near the exit by now," I pose.

"The path you see to your right connects to the main tunnel. At one end it leads to a store room door near the labs known only to Kim Yung and to me. At the far end it exits into a ravine wall behind the citadel where we will emerge into the desert."

"Then let's get at it," I tell her and start to rise. Lotus places a hand on my arm and whispers, "We will rest briefly then continue. Soon we will be free." Her tone is calm and confident.

"Lotus, I hate to be the wuss here. It's beyond my control, this blood sugar thing. Really drags me down sometimes. Hope you understand."

"You are doing well, Jim. The tunnel will be no danger for us, but we must be alert when we reach the surface. Ali Hassan surely has his guard patrols out."

That gives me an opening to see how much more she can tell me about this operation. Could be valuable to the guys when Celia Grant and her buddies get here.

"What's the story behind this odd partnership, Lotus. I mean, since when have your people and the Arabs been known to take the same side on anything?"

"It is a marriage of convenience only," she answers. "Kim Yung is consumed by two goals. First he must survive an affliction that threatens his very life. Then he aspires to bend the entire world to his will by blackmailing the major powers with annihilation."

"Sounds ambitious. How the hell does he plan to pull that off?"

Lotus frowns deeply and hesitates. She looks up at the tiny beam of light from overhead then back over at me, pointing toward the sunlight.

"As the light filters its rays through the most insignificant of portals so Kim Yung has found the way to change the structure of our world from one tiny cell outward."

"Nanotechnology," I say and she nods.

"You know of this science?"

"Enough to appreciate the potential it holds and the threat it poses in the wrong hands, Lotus."

"Then you know that new substances and combinations of matter can be constructed such as the world has never before known. That is the basis of the ultimatum he will soon issue."

"How is it you know all this?" I ask her.

"Kim Yung is a conceited and jealous man. He shares his secrets with no one—except me. A boastful man such as he must have someone in whom he can confide his delusions of power. He believes I am so dedicated I will not betray his trust. And I could have been had he not ruined it all with his mental and physical abuse.

"Sounds a bit naïve, though. I can't believe he would spill his guts to you, Lotus."

"He is unaware of many of the secrets he has revealed." She reaches down with the light and shows me an ugly bruise and broken skin at her ankle.

"What the devil is that?"

"Kim lusts for me. He always begins his lovemaking gently but soon becomes a beast. His favorite way to dominate me is to restrain my ankle with a chain and padlocked leather sleeve so I may not leave his bed until he is satisfied. At times he sleeps and awakens to continue his assault."

"I'm sorry, Lotus. No one deserves to be treated that way."

She waves off my comment and continues.

"This is also his most foolish mistake. I listen while he sleeps. His mind never rests. Even while he slumbers he mumbles and reviews his master plan, boasts of his genius. I lie chained by his side and learn many facts. Now I share most of his darkest secrets. Something in his eyes tells me he suspects how much I know.

That is why I am certain he will kill me once his plan has been executed for he will see me as a continuing threat."

"But exactly how does he expect to pull this off, Lotus?"

"There are laboratories in the citadel that have made astounding advances in this field you call nanotechnology. They have achieved the melding of biological agents bonded onto single molecules of substance. Terrible scourges such as anthrax and dengue fever in a single application."

She's confirming precisely what I suspected could be the real threat. Makes my skin crawl.

"The combined agents..." she begins.

"Yes, what's called a chimera," I interject.

"Yes, the...chimera has been reproduced in the form of spores. These deadly agents will be released in at least four major cities to create panic among the American populace. One such site is Las Vegas where Ali's henchmen will release the spores into the ventilation systems of hotels that have already been selected. Kim is using the Arabs for this task because, if anything goes wrong, say accidental breathing of the spores by the messengers, he considers the *al-Qinaa'* radicals expendable."

"Then what?"

"Then, when the full realization of what is happening sinks in, Kim will announce that he alone is responsible for the outbreaks of disease and death. He will demand that all governments pay him tribute in huge sums of money and goods to stop further attacks."

"And what do this Ali and his followers get out of this?"

"They believe Kim will demand that all westerners leave the Middle East. Ali is wrong. Kim will turn on *al-Qinaa'* as he has on everyone else he has used in the past."

"Sounds like this Kim is rotten to the core."

"Ah," she says. "But that is only phase one of his plan. Doctor Grant and Kim's lead biologist, Doctor Warren, are working on the ultimate weapon, though I think Grant believes it is only for honest widespread medical use."

"Something more powerful than disease and pandemic? What is it, the next generation nuclear device?"

"Much more subtle and vastly more powerful, Jim. With the help of tiny control devices and micromedicines, both developed through nanotech, Kim's scientists will be able to direct doses of tailored cures to human body cells. They will be able to select, repair and regenerate individual human cells."

"Near as I can tell, Lotus, scientists are working around the clock to reach that point with nanotech. By all reports, they're still a decade away from any real success."

"Ah, but Kim Yung has assembled the finest minds available and is on the verge of triumph. Doctor Kendrick Grant is one of his most valuable resources. Kim Yung is infected with cancer that will be reversible because of the work in the citadel labs. Tiny controlled delivery vehicles equipped with tailored doses of immunizing proteins will be inserted into his body. They will seek out the diseased cells and restore them to health."

"That's a noble undertaking, Lotus. It could overcome diseases we now consider incurable, even slow down aging and prolong life."

"Not so noble at all, Jim. Kim Yung's goal is to achieve for his use only the ultimate weapon against all other humans—immortality."

Chapter 51

Dan Cooper

"Glad two of us had flashlights," I tell Pat and Jud. "Mine's fizzled out. If Jud's batteries die we're gonna be wandering in the blind."

"Don't make his head swell," Pat quips. "Strictly by chance he shoved that thing in his fatigues before we scaled down here."

"Hey, give me a break," Jud protests. "I've slipped two pretty determined wenches. Both of them were hell bent on wrapping me up and delivering me to somebody. Guess that was just by chance, too, huh?"

"I will have to admit," says Pat. "You have more than your share of an admirable quality, Jud. Got a lot of DL."

"What's that," Jud wants to know, "Dynamite looks, dashing lovability?"

"Try dumb-ass luck, pal," Pat retorts.

"Come on, guys," I plead. "This is serious stuff here. We have bad guys on all sides of us and who knows what furry beasts ready to jump us in this tunnel. Quit picking at each other and keep an eye out."

"Loosen up, Dan," Jud fires back. "You and I have been through some tight scrapes together. No time to let the odds spook us."

We're groping our way slowly through the mine shaft lighting our way with a flashlight beam that's unsteady at best. Something strikes me as odd about the overhead. I nudge Jud and say, "Turn that light up here, buddy. I want a closer look at the ceiling supports."

"Man, those are no mine timbers," Jud exclaims. "That's structural ironworks. Somebody's done major work to keep this access open."

I nod. "Looks like the best way in for a surprise attack. I hope Kenny's laid out this route for the troops Celia's bringing."

Pat says, "That's their job to worry about. Ours is to concentrate on snatching Jim out of these guys' grasp. Once we're out of here with him they can do whatever they want with this whole damned mountain."

"I agree. Let's pick up the pace and get out of this spooky tunnel. I've had about all of the dust and cobwebs I want for one day."

Jud stays on the point and I'm close behind with the Irishman bringing up the rear. We must be a couple hundred feet down the tunnel by now and the incline is getting steeper.

Pat blurts out, "What's that god awful smell? If there's such a thing as a desert yeti, I think we just ran into him."

I agree. The stench is sickening.

"Hold it," Jud says. "Hear that. Sounds like…oh, shit!" He stands frozen in front of me and I listen. Sounds like a panting animal directly in our path. Jud plays the beam out ahead and I see two red eyes reflecting his light.

"Too short to be a man," Jud says, "and I don't think snakes stand that tall or have eyes near that big."

"Coyote," Pat whispers, "sounds like more than one of them."

The light beam starts to waver and I think, *oh, no! we're about to be left in the dark facing a pack of wild coyotes and us with nowhere to turn.*

From over my shoulder comes Pat's whispered prompt. "Hug the left wall and give me an opening.

We both press hard against the rocks and Pat hurls something past us that's bright and burning. The most awful chorus of shrieks breaks out and three shaggy beasts scatter and run away.

"What the hell was that trick, O'Leary?" I call out.

"Those fatigues you brought me were okay but the cap was too small. It barely kept the spider webs off my head. I put it to better use; set it off with my lighter. Figured those prairie dogs would shy away from fire."

"Quick thinking, Pat," Jud says. "But after this I'm keeping my gun at the ready. I may have to shoot them if they come back."

I pat the gun in my own holster. Glad the guy in the surplus store had a working firearm under the counter. Paid him a dear price to bypass registration. O'Leary grabbed the rifle one of the guards was carrying, but we're still woefully under-equipped against the manpower these dudes can throw against us.

I take a deep breath to slow down my pulse. "Guess that takes care of the need for a rest stop, fellows. The way Jud shrieked I think I already soiled my jumpers."

We start to walk again, all of us listening carefully for any signs our visitors may return.

"Thought your light was failing for a second there, Jud." I say. "It seems to be okay now."

"Hell, that was my hand shaking, Dan. Those critters had big teeth and I would have been their first meal."

"Yeah, but you and I are skin and bones compared to the Irishman. They'd probably pass us by and go right to the real feast."

"Real comedian, that Dan," Pat pants from behind me. "Shut up and keep walking, Cooper."

The pace slows considerably. It's a climb now and we're already being more cautious where we step. Could be we haven't seen all of this tunnel's wildlife yet. On top of that, a disturbing thought has occurred to me.

"Hey, guys…I hate to bring this up, but we're coming from the only way out of this black hole. Those coyotes have to come through us to get outside. Sooner or later, we have to meet up with them again."

My words are answered by another round of high-pitched yelps up ahead. Then everything goes still…too still.

We all halt and freeze for maybe half a minute, every one of us quiet and intent on any new sound from down the tunnel. Then I hear a shuffling sound. Maybe footsteps or paws scratching through the loose rock.

Nobody moves but Jud lifts his pistol and aims.

A distant light glows in the tunnel and moves toward us.

Jud calls out, "Stop right there. You're in my sights." He's dropped his flashlight and is about to shoot in the blind.

"Jeez, Jud, cool it. It's just me out for a walk."

I can't see their expressions, but I can imagine my partners are as shocked and happy as I am.

"Jim," I answer, "You sure know how to make an entrance."

Jim and another person are coming toward us. That appears to be a female with him waving a battery pack lantern. This should be some story.

We do the best we can, given the cramped space, to have our little reunion here in the tunnel of horrors. Jim looks mighty relieved when the light catches his face. He does the honors.

"Folks, this is Lotus. She saved my hide from a pack of rough characters back there—as well as a bunch of wild animals. She could be our key to kicking some butt—knows this place inside out. Lotus, this is Jud, Dan and Pat."

"Quickly. Let us continue through the tunnel. There is no time to waste," she tells us. "The guards will be alerted and looking for us by now."

I offer a different plan. "How about you three guys head back to the big outside world and let Lotus show me the way in."

"Too risky," she says. "We must leave now."

"Listen," I argue. "There are people on the way to storm this fort. I need to gather all the info I can and pass it on to them."

"What is it you want, Dan?" She sounds unsure and more than a little perturbed.

"I want to get an idea of the way in and the inside layout, anything that will give the feds an edge for a tough underground assault."

She thinks for a moment then says, "There is a map that shows everything they should need. I will retrieve it from Kim Yung's office. You will go with me to the entrance but not inside the citadel. I have free rein of the area, but the guards would shoot you on sight."

My impulse is to look at Jim to see how her words register on him.

"Trust her, Dan. She's the best friend we have right now. Lotus wants Kim's head on a stick as much as we do."

"Okay, I'm with you, Lotus. Guys, we'll see you, as they say, under the big desert moon."

They turn to leave. Lotus catches Jim's arm and says, "Here. You may need this." She hands him a small container.

"Thanks, Lotus. With this kind of stress, I may need another dose soon. You're a jewel, pretty lady." He bends and kisses her cheek.

Pat, Jud and Jim hurry off in the other direction as Lotus and I continue toward the underground building.

She cautions, "We will reach a closed door at the end of the tunnel. Let me go in alone. If I am seen any time after entering the store room on the other side of that door, I can explain my presence and pass unchallenged. Everyone in the citadel knows I am Kim Yung's closest confidante. They would not dare confront me."

In the excitement of finding Jim I had let a very important fact slip my mind. "Lotus, we ran onto a pack of wild coyotes. They must still be in the tunnel somewhere between us and the building."

She nods to show she heard me but shows no other reaction at all. We move through the tunnel and start down a grade toward what appears to be the tunnel's end. Then I realize why Lotus isn't worried about the animals. Three carcasses lie at the entrance to a side tunnel—our canine adversaries Pat gave the fire treatment.

"They were not difficult to stop. I am a *hwa rang do* master," she says softly. I don't know what that means, but she must be quick on her feet and pack a hell of a wallop. These bad boys are all very much stopped.

"This is the door." She points toward a smooth area on the rock wall and reaches overhead to retrieve something. Produces a key and runs her hand over the wall until she finds the spot she's looking for. Inserts the key and turns to hand me the emergency lamp. "Turn it off and wait here for me. Be patient. I will return."

I sit huddled by that door in the darkness with the fluorescent face of my watch the only light in the tunnel. Ten minutes pass...fifteen. Finally the temptation is too great. I fumble around until I find the key in the lock and push. Here goes, Cooper. For better or worse, you're inside!

CHAPTER 52

Dan Cooper

Almost from the second I slip through that doorway I wonder if this time my curiosity will get me killed. There is enough artificial light to see that I've stepped into some sort of store room. There are muffled voices near—entirely too near. I'm no language expert, but it sounds like Arabic. Cooper, old boy, you've stuck your foot in the stink hole this time.

I crouch as low as possible and work my way behind a stack of crates. Hug the floor and hope I haven't been seen. The patter continues and comes closer. A light goes on overhead. I double check to confirm that my sidearm is still there on my hip. The holster is full, though the handgun probably won't get me out of a scrape with a crowd. Unfortunately, it sounds like there could be three or four of these guys.

Slide the gun out of the holster very carefully and clutch it. If they discover me and start shooting, I intend to take at least a couple with me. The room is cold, unusually chill. Could be a clue that whatever they're storing in here needs low temperature to remain stable. That means I could be smack in the middle of a room full of biological agents with no protection.

Another voice. This one is also muffled and deeper and the words are English. "Over here. Put that cylinder in this cradle. No! Right here. Stupid heathens."

One of the men replies sharply. "Infidel!" They sound like a real congenial lot.

I can just see enough between boxes and crates to make out the latest arrival in the room. He's wearing a protective suit and looking out through the visor of some kind of headgear. From the way they all seem to rustle when they move, I conclude bumbling old Dan Cooper is the only one who's skulking about in this room full of nasties without wearing proper coverups. Well, too late to worry about that now.

Just don't touch anything, Cooper, I prompt, *and keep your breathing shallow.*

Somebody comes within a foot of my hiding place. I stop breathing altogether. More words in that foreign tongue and a clang of metal almost directly over my head.

"Careful. Treat it gently, you dolt!" snaps the deep voice. I do my level best to hug the floor.

The overhead light goes off and I lie still for another minute or so until I'm convinced the room has emptied out. Cautiously I raise my head and stare into the murky darkness while my eyes adjust. No one in sight and the voices are gone. I turn on the lantern and keep it low to the floor. Cast just enough of a glow to check the cylinder near my head. There are cradles in every direction with similar containers nestled in them. Can't tell what's in any of them but the biohazard markings are clear enough to tell me I need away from here fast. If there's the slightest leak in any of these canisters, I could be in a world of hurts.

Retracing my path into the room I find the back door well concealed behind acoustic tiles. I manage to open it just enough to slide through into the tunnel and put the door between me and those deadly containers. Flop on the rocky floor and take my first normal breath since more than ten minutes ago. Check my glowing watch and see that Lotus has been gone for at least half an hour. After what I've seen I want to break for the tunnel entrance and get away from this place.

Cool down, Cooper. What other option do you have? Got to trust her and wait.

No telling how long I'm sitting in front of that door. After the cold of the store room the stifling heat of the tunnel presses in on me. In minutes I'm uncomfortably warm, sweaty and drowsy. The fast pace of the past couple of days is finally catching up with me. I feel so relieved to be out of that store room I begin to relax, close my eyes and actually doze off. The next thing I remember is a voice whispering in my ear.

"Dan, wake up. It's time to leave."

I flick on the lamp stowed between my knees. Lotus is hovering over me with a look of urgency. She's tugging at my right arm. Lotus is holding a helmet with a visor and wearing a silvery suit. She's pointing down. I look down and realize that I still have the gun gripped tightly in my left hand. I look up at Lotus. Probably have a stupid expression on my face having her find me sleeping when there's so much going on. Shove the gun back into its holster and get my feet under me.

"Why the gun?" she asks with an almost amused look.

"Why not?" I answer. "Evens the odds."

"Dan, did you go through that door? Have you been in the lab store room?"

No need now to deny it. "Had to check it out. No harm done. Nobody saw me."

"You could have died in there."

"I know. Place was swarming with bad guys," I say kind of sheepishly.

"Never mind them. There are bio agents in that room—anthrax, typhoid, smallpox—terrible things that could kill you quickly or bring you a lingering death. I worried about going through that place on my way in without a protective suit. There could be leaks in those canisters."

Well, that tears it. Now I'll be imagining all kinds of symptoms. Bad enough I've ignored my pills and forgot about eating on schedule what with all the excitement. My blood sugar problem is nowhere near as critical as Jim's, but Ellen would be all over me about my sloppiness these past couple of days.

I swallow hard and answer, "Have to hope I got lucky. Let me know if I start to turn purple."

My manufactured laugh isn't convincing to either one of us.

Lotus climbs out of her chemical suit. She's changed into a sleek, form-fitting jumpsuit underneath and her dark hair is wound atop her head. I take a long look at her in the glow of the lantern and think what a louse this Kim Yung must be to heap abuse on such a lovely girl. That alone makes me want to nail the bastard.

"Wait," she says and reaches for the zipper on her jump suit. Pulls it down halfway and reaches inside.

"The map," she explains, showing me a folded packet then stowing it back in place. "It shows the entire layout of the citadel, all the rooms and corridors. Even marks the locations of monitor sensors and alarm devices."

"Great work, Lotus. Let's crawl out of this hole and see that the feds get that baby. They should be here in a few hours to take this place down."

CHAPTER 53

"Open the door. I have business with the prisoner." Ali Hassan strides in.

Now, Ali thinks, we will see how well this James Barnett resists. He will feel pain he never imagined. The information Kim Yung wants must be obtained to quiet Kim's unjustified criticism. No matter how much Ali may despise that man, he is serving al-Qinaa's purpose. Once the bio attacks are leveled and Kim's ultimatum is issued for all infidels to cease their meddling in Middle Eastern affairs, Ali will settle the score with Kim. Until then he must continue to play the obedient follower of a man he loathes.

"That's it. Let me in and do not disturb us. What...where? The prisoner is gone!"

"Do not look at me that way. You were to guard him. Sound the alarm."

They can find no signs of how he could have left. The only exits are the door and a window too high up for him to reach. There is no way...unless...

"Did Barnett have any visitors other than Kim Yung?"

"Kim's woman Lotus paid a visit some time ago, Ali. She brought him a meal and left with his tray after he ate. He was still in the room when I looked."

"Fools! I am surrounded by fools. Why do you not understand what must be done? We have the destiny of the Americans in our grasp and you fail me. If I didn't need your help to carry out the attacks, I would dispose of you now!"

"I beg your patience, Ali Hassan. There is no way I could have prevented his leaving. It is as if he melted through the solid walls and fled. My guards would have seen him if he had entered the hallway. How can you blame me?"

"No error is blameless. *Al-Qinaa'* does not tolerate such weakness."

Ali hurries back to his room to assess the harm that has been done. The guards will swarm the compound and patrol the desert until they find Barnett. Karim has his orders to offer up his life to ensure Kendrick Grant is retaken and brought to the citadel. Jamila is tracking the one who slipped her hold and will drag him back however she chooses. In case Lotus had anything to do with the prisoner's escape, Ali must inform Kim and set him on her. *Allah aid me*, he ponders, *I only want to punish the infidels yet my own people are falling short of their duties.*

CHAPTER 54

Kenny Grant finally believes he will live. What a nightmare he's been through. Last thing he remembered clearly until two days ago was his mother bringing him to the hospital with a raging fever and pain in his head that felt like somebody was slicing his eyeballs.

The doctors must have this dengue whipped. Kenny reflects that he feels like taking on the world today. But he can't do it from the basement of this hospital. Where's the doctor and where is his mother? She wouldn't leave him alone if she could help it.

Here's the call button. Kenny tries it to see who will respond.

"Yes, Mister Grant? What is it? Are you awake now?"

"Nurse, I have to get out of here. It's been a long, unpleasant dream, but you folks did wonders for me. I have business to attend to. Find my clothes."

She touches his brow and smiles. "You look worlds better. Let me call the doctor. You can tell him what you want."

Before he can get on her case further she's gone. Kenny scans around the room. The machines are gone and so is his fever. Completely. Time he got up and started moving. Those walls without windows spook him. He wants to go somewhere he can see sunshine and feel human again.

A voice comes from the doorway.

"Well, I see you decided to come around and greet the bright new day."

It's Doctor Samuels. He checks Kenny's pulse and nods for the nurse to take his blood pressure.

"How would I know what the day looks like, doctor? Seems I've been shut off from the outside world."

"I explained to you that we have you in our most protected area. You obviously were too sedated to understand. Someone's already tried to kidnap you." He's busy checking reflexes and looking at Kenny's pupils.

"Nurse says your temperature is normal. Your other signs are good, too. How do you feel?"

"Like I was kicked and scratched all the way from Las Vegas to here. But the world looks clear for the first time since I got back. Where's Mom?"

"She'll be gone for a short while. You had us worried, Kenny...sorry...Doctor Grant. I went over this with you after your fever broke, but you were still having trouble taking it all in. Your mom brought you directly here from the airport and got the ball rolling to treat you. It's fortunate for you she did. Took us three weeks to get you to this stage."

"I hope that's my one and only scrape with dengue, Doctor Samuels. Never felt so lousy in my life. If I'd been a horse, I would have whinnied for you to shoot me."

"You're the son of an extraordinary doctor and a scientist yourself. I think I can give it to you straight. A delay of even a day in getting your treatment started could have been fatal to you. We've whipped it, though."

"Oh, yeah. Dengue...the labs."

"What?"

"Later, doctor. When can I get out of this hospital basement? I've spent more than my share of time underground."

"It's for your protection. There are some bad people looking for you."

That brings back murky images to Kenny of being in a wheelchair and a lot of people running around. His mother was there. She kicked somebody hard.

"Where's Mom? What do you mean she'll be gone for a short while?"

Doctor Samuels gives him a long stare and seems to be struggling with what to tell him. Kenny knows dengue isn't contagious. What could be the matter with Mom that she's not here with him?

"I'm waiting."

He finally decides to speak.

"Doctor Grant is fine. She's left temporarily for somewhere she said you would recognize. A place called Primm."

It takes a moment or two for the word to sink in. Then Kenny comes straight up out of bed and kicks away the covers. His head goes all aflutter. The doctor puts his hand on Kenny's shoulder and cautions, "You're too weak for sudden moves like that. Take it slow and easy."

"I can't just lie here when she's heading into serious danger. How long has she been gone?"

The doctor's calm manner helps to reassure Grant, but Kenny wonders if his Mom really understands what she faces out there in the desert.

"How long, doctor?"

"She stopped by last night," Samuels says. "Said to tell you she would be okay. Has a whole team of experts with her, medical and law enforcement. She wouldn't tell me any more."

"Who told her about Primm?"

"Why, you did. We've been getting bits and words from you while you were fighting the fever. Let's see—you mentioned Primm and something called Sphinx. I was to tell you Pat and the others are working with her. She said you also told her about a fortress and a back way into it. I didn't understand that part at all."

Kenny stares at Samuels. He understands perfectly. He vaguely remembers telling Dan about the Joshua trees and the tunnel. That was two days ago before Kenny conked out again while his body finally rested. Wonder how much more Mom's found out? If Pat O'Leary is chasing this, she must be alert to just how dangerous that fortress in the desert can be for her. Jim Barnett will know what Kenny meant about Sphinx if they are still in contact with him. Damn. He could be helping, not lying here like a wet dish rag.

"How soon can you have me on my feet, Doctor Samuels? I need to be up and with Mom and help her."

"Can't let you go anywhere until we confirm your blood is free of the dengue virus, Kenny. It'll take us a while to get you back to normal even then. You need to restore your energy."

"Great. Let's start with a big, juicy steak and a banana split."

"Trust me. You're my patient, so you'll have to take things at the pace I set for you."

"How long?" Kenny insists.

"Five days, a week, could be longer. Don't jeopardize your health now—not after all you've been through." He hesitates then asks, "Can you tell me how you came in contact with dengue fever? Do you know?"

"Oh, I know exactly how it happened. From the sound of things I can't tell you yet, though. All I can say is it didn't involve mosquitoes."

Doctor Samuels lets out a long sigh and mutters under his breath. "That's why you said the labs. She was right. This was a laboratory-developed strain. And you had a friend who was exposed?"

Kenny just stares at him. He's already said too much.

"Listen. You of all people know your mother is about the most together person either of us will ever meet. She wouldn't go running off into serious danger, as you frame it, unless she has all possibilities covered. She did let it slip that somebody named Crandall was providing armed help, whatever that means."

"It means volumes to me. I call him Uncle Gerry. I need a telephone."

"Nurse." She nods and plugs in a phone by Kenny's bed.

"Operator, I need Senator Gerard Crandall's office. That's right, US Senator Crandall. Give me his office on Capitol Hill."

Chapter 55

"I came as soon as I could, Kenny," Senator Crandall says when he comes puffing into the room. He motions to the policeman to close the door, hurries over and wraps Kenny in his arms. "Seems like ages since I saw you, but I've followed your career closely."

"Gerry…Senator, I want your help."

"Gerry's fine, Kenny. You've always been like a nephew to me."

"How much do you know so far, Gerry?"

"More than I'd like. Your bout with the virus has tipped us to a terrorist plot we have to stop without delay. Celia is on her way to Nevada with a task force of elite troops and decontamination experts to pry open their mountain hideout and take them down."

"That's about what I expected." Kenny says. "Mom took the initiative. God, it could be pure agony lying here wondering where Mom is every minute and whether the New Day people know she's on their tails. If Kim Yung catches wind of what she's doing, he's capable of anything. I have to help her somehow. That whole mountain could go up in a cloud of biological smoke that would kill everybody within miles—take out Las Vegas and, if the winds are right, who knows how far downwind."

"You need to slow down, Kenny. We can't have you taking a relapse."

"Look, Gerry, I have information about that place your people could use. Get me out of here. Take me somewhere I can be in touch with them."

"I don't know, Kenny. Are you up to it?"

"That's my mother out there with her neck on the block, Gerry. Wheel me out of here and let's get going."

Doctor Samuels gives a dozen reasons why Kenny's leaving the hospital is unwise. He soon sees his logical arguments don't mean a thing to the patient, though. Kenny is going. He comes back with an Oriental woman pushing a wheelchair. She's tall and attractive and she's careful not to rush Grant.

"Thank you, miss. Get me out into the fresh air, Betty."

"Su Lin," she corrects and smiles broadly.

* * * *

"We'll be all right, Frank," Gerry says to the man outside the room. Kenny does a double take. Somehow it seems he should know Frank. Then Gerry turns and explains. "He's a plainclothes policeman, Kenny. They've been watching you ever since you came to the hospital."

"Are you sure you're okay, Senator?" the man asks.

"Take a break, Frank. You've earned it. Kenny will be with me."

They find the elevator and get on as two other passengers enter. One is wearing a doctor's white coat. He smiles and nods. He's followed by a rather portly man wearing orderly scrubs. There is a familiarity about his face, too, Kenny thinks, but it escapes him.

"Where are we headed?" Kenny asks Gerry. The Senator looks over at their female escort and shakes his head. Okay, it will wait.

The five of them ride in silence to the main floor. When the elevator stops Gerry points and says, "My car is in the parking garage out back."

The Korean lady—Su Lin, did she say—pushes the chair along and they fall in line behind Gerry. As they approach the walkway to the garage Kenny has the uneasy feeling someone is hovering close by. He twists around and glances over his shoulder. Both of the men who were on the elevator are only a few paces behind. Maybe he's getting paranoid over the past few weeks' events, but it worries Kenny that both of them have a middle-eastern look about them. Still can't place the second man's face, though. They find Senator Crandall's car and he motions for the lady to wheel Kenny up to the rear door. Both of the men behind them suddenly catch up and draw alongside the wheelchair.

Then everything disassembles.

The pudgy man in the scrubs takes Gerry by the arm and says, "You will drive us where I tell you." Kenny recognizes the accent as Arabic from his contacts with the mountain citadel guards.

"The hell you say, buster," Gerry answers. "I'm a US Senator. You can't order me around. I'll have your ass for this."

The Arab smiles and says, "And I am your captor who will shoot you dead if you do not remain quiet, mister Senator."

It comes back to Kenny in a flood. He was in that fuzzy blur of action outside the hospital. "Karim!" Kenny shouts.

Karim laughs and raises the scrub top to show why he looks so heavy. He's wearing a belt full of explosives. That ends Gerry's debate with him.

The man in the doctor's coat grabs Su Lin's arm roughly and spits out, "Place him in the car now." She starts to say something then thinks better of it and helps Kenny into the rear seat.

Karim snaps at his friend. "Leave the chair, Ahmed. Get in the back with Grant and the woman." Gerry is already in the driver's seat waiting for instructions.

"You realize this won't work," Gerry says. "They'll be on you before we're two blocks away."

Karim backhands him hard across the mouth. Kenny wants at this grinning ferret, but there's little he can do in his present condition. Gerry gets the message and begins to drive.

"Turn right and take the Beltway," Karim barks.

The Korean looking woman sits very quietly, no panic on her face, only a blank look of disbelief. She's sandwiched between Kenny and the phony doctor. Kenny sits directly behind Gerry who is looking back at him in the rear view mirror. If he's trying to tell Kenny something it's not clear at the moment. Grant is too busy thinking *how many times do I have to go through this drill?* The whole scene with Arabs, Mom and somebody she called Frank flashes past in full color. It wasn't a dream after all.

Now it appears these persistent kidnappers have finally succeeded, though why they want him is a mystery.

"What do we do with this woman?" the phony 'doc' asks.

"She is of no use to us, Ahmed. As soon as we reach a convenient spot, you will shoot her and dump her on the road."

Su Lin visibly recoils at his words. She turns to Ahmed and says, "Kim Yung…"

He slaps her and shouts, "Silence, bitch!" She slumps and emits a whimper.

"Wait," says Karim. "Repeat what you said, woman."

"I am Su Lin Kim. I was sent here by Kim Yung, your leader."

He laughs.

"Kim is not my leader. I await instructions from Ali. Then we will decide what happens to these two miserable Americans."

She goes silent. This is getting very confusing. Kenny wonders who he should root for here—anybody?

In a matter of moments there is a muffled pop. Ahmed moans softly and goes rigid. By the time Kenny realizes the phony doctor is not breathing, the woman places a long pistol with a silencer in Karim's left ear and there is another pop. He keels over and his head hits the dashboard.

Gerry brakes, but she says, "No! Keep driving. I will tell you when to stop." He does a double take then picks up his speed.

"I don't know who you are, lady, but we owe you our lives."

"A debt you will soon pay, Senator. You are an unexpected bonus catch. Now you are my prisoners."

CHAPTER 56

Things are tense in Senator Gerry Crandall's car. He's following Su Lin's instructions. Doubles back on the Beltway and drives west on the Dulles Access Road. Kenny shares the back seat with a crazy woman and a dead man and Gerry has another body loaded with explosives on the front seat with him.

As they zip along the access road Su is telling them, in a smug sort of way, that they will soon be Kim Yung's guests at his citadel in the desert. "A charter flight will be waiting at the airport," she says. "Kim will be most happy to see you, Doctor Grant." Gerry casts a puzzled frown at Kenny in the mirror.

"He's no friend of mine, Gerry. Runs the place I was trying to get away from."

Gerry raises his eyebrows and a smile plays across his lips. Kenny guesses what he's thinking. Uncle Gerry and he go way back in the unspoken communication department.

That's right, Kenny signals silently, *the place Mom and the troops are about to open like an expired can of worms.*

"And all your efforts have been wasted," Su crows. "Tell me, did you send Jud Black to Los Angeles? Is that fool one of your misguided friends?"

There is a hefty amount of sarcasm in her words. Given Jud's reputation it sets Kenny to thinking. Could he...surely not. But then, with Jud you never know.

"Who? Doesn't sound like one of my friends. Sure you don't mean Jed Slack? He's a little guy about five feet five with red hair."

She's not impressed with Kenny's attempt at humor.

"We will know soon enough. All of the meddlers will be rounded up waiting for your arrival. There is work to be done. Kim has high expectations for you in his new world order."

Grant tries hard not to show the disgust he feels for that pompous ass and everything he's trying to do out there in the desert. Took Kenny awhile to see through his sleek exterior and recognize him for the bastard he is. He's betting on the feds to take the little animal down before he and Gerry get anywhere near the mountain. If Kim cuts loose his viruses and bacteria before they can stop him, Kenny doesn't even want to think about the results.

The road begins to look familiar. They're almost to the airport now. All Kenny can do is ride this out and wait for an opening.

"Here," Su snaps. "Take the Greenway exit."

Now he's stumped. If they have a flight waiting, why would they bypass Dulles Airport and head off into the Virginia countryside? A few minutes later he understands when she orders Gerry to turn off the Greenway and they head south toward Leesburg Airport. Of course. She has a small aircraft waiting to confuse anyone tracking her.

Gerry parks on the tarmac and Su points off to one side. The airport is almost dark now, but Kenny can see the outline of an airplane.

"That is our aircraft, Senator. Walk quietly and calmly and do not force me to shoot you."

She takes Kenny's arm and helps him out of the back seat. "You must walk on your own."

"What if I can't make it," he asks her.

"You will make it," she says and it sounds like a threat.

As they approach the small jet aircraft Su signals the pilot. He opens the side door. Gerry looks undecided, but Su waves her gun and urges him forward. Kenny is beginning to feel dizzy and sags. She jams a hand under his arm to prop him up. He feels like he's about to pass out. He and Su Lin come to a dead stop maybe thirty feet from the plane.

"I can't do this," he pleads.

"Then I will kill you here. Kim will be disappointed."

That makes Kenny's legs suddenly feel a great deal stronger. He starts to walk.

Seconds later something flies past him in a blur and Su falls to the tarmac. Her gun clatters across the concrete. A man has her in his grasp and he's pummeling her with both fists. She fights and scratches, chops at him and shouts.

Kenny picks up the gun and brandishes it but hesitates to shoot. After the earlier experience this could be two more baddies fighting over rights to claim the Senator and him.

The man gets an arm free and sends a fist directly at her chops. When he stands up Su is lying motionless.

Gerry stammers in obvious confusion. "Okay, so who's taking us prisoner now?" he mutters, sounding resigned to his fate.

"Nobody, Senator. It's Frank Kane."

A spark of recognition in Gerry's eyes. The man comes closer and Gerry looks bewildered. "Frank. How in the world did you…"

"Been tracking you since the hospital, Senator. I had this bad feeling I shouldn't let you two leave without me. Chased up the stairs after your elevator and caught sight of you going outside. When those two guys made a move on you I had to hang back. Saw enough of the explosives belt to know I could kill us all if I rushed him."

"So you were behind us all the way here?" Kenny asks.

"I nearly lost you in traffic a couple times. This was the first decent chance I had to take down that wench. Man, I thought I was tangled up with a pit full of mongoose the way she was biting and scratching." He takes the handgun from me and bends down to cuff Su Lin.

"Let's find out where this buggy is headed," Frank says and disappears into the aircraft dragging a groggy and whipped Su Lin. Gerry and I wait outside for maybe five minutes. Finally he returns with a big smile.

"What did you find out, Frank?" Gerry asks him.

"Gentlemen, how would you like an all expenses paid trip to Las Vegas?"

Kenny only knows he wants to be as far away from that place as possible. Then he remembers where Mom has gone. "Let's do it," he says.

Gerry begs off. Says his absence could provoke some thorny questions before he's ready to answer them. He thinks it best he go back to town and let the situation in the desert play out in its own time.

"Kenny," he says and hugs him, "say hi to Celia for me. Tell her I said she's still one in a million. Stay well. I'll be in touch from the command post."

* * * *

The pilot is leery about making this trip after what he witnessed out there on the tarmac. Frank establishes right away that Steve, the pilot, had no inkling what he was tied up in. To him this was just another prepaid charter on short notice.

Frank talks him into lifting off with the explanation that the man he saw briefly was an important government official. He will be doing the country a huge favor by taking them to Nevada. Now Frank has to resell him when he looks at Su Lin bound and gagged in one of the rear seats in the Learjet.

"I don't usually carry live baggage," he protests. "What the hell are you guys into here, anyway? This could be a kidnapping for all I know."

"Calm down, Steve," Frank answers. "See this gun? She was probably going to silence you with it once you got her to Vegas. Chances are I saved your life."

"Show me that badge again, Frank," Steve says.

Kane flips open his wallet and shows Steve a Fairfax County Police badge. "I'm on official business and you're directly aiding in a national security matter. She shot two people in that car that just left. Just fly, pal."

By the time they are half way across the country Kenny has filled Frank in on most of what he knows about the desert fortress and the Korean and Arab terrorists that are hanging out there. What he doesn't tell him is the very significant part about the plot itself. To think about the powers of nanotechnology and biological warfare and what they could do is almost too much for Kenny. He decides to spare Frank the headache.

The airplane is well stocked with food and beverage for the long flight. They keep a wary eye on Su Lin who's undoubtedly hurling the nastiest Korean insults she knows. Mostly they just sound like 'mmm-phhh blurbbb'. Frank says that gag stays in place until they turn her over. She has a full set of teeth and he has the marks to prove it.

CHAPTER 57

"Yes, Major. I'm right here. What is it?"

The assault team leader is motioning to Celia Grant, but it's difficult to hear him over the noise in the C-17 transport. There must be thirty people sitting around checking their gear and chattering away. The full load of people and equipment is flying somewhere over the middle of the country. Major Thomas motions for Celia to come up front.

"I'm in touch with the command post, Doctor Grant," he says when they are standing next to the radioman. "They have some news about your son." Celia doesn't like his expression.

"Has he relapsed? Oh, I knew I shouldn't have left him." She holds onto the doorway and listens.

"Your son called the Senator and insisted he had to be involved. His fever's broken. He wanted to be part of our operation."

She breathes a long sigh of relief. It's been three weeks of pure hell watching Kenny suffer, seeing him linger without knowing whether they had done enough in time. But why is the Major frowning?

"And what else?" she asks.

"There is a problem, Doctor. On the way to the CP they were diverted by persons unknown. Our people think they're on their way to Dulles Airport. A local policeman is in pursuit in an unmarked car."

"Policeman? Did they have a name?" Thomas seems to think that's an odd question. "It's important, Major," Celia says.

"CP, this is Sand Bird. Say name of party in pursuit." A few seconds of silence follow then there is a reply.

"Kane. Frank Kane. Fairfax County cop."

"That's reassuring news. Frank and I have already been through this once. He's a good man. Kenny really must be valuable to these terrorist monsters for them to make two tries to grab him. I swear if they hurt him I'll never stop till every one of them is dead or behind bars."

"Thought you should know," Major Thomas says.

"Thank you."

A thousand things are running through Celia's head, but her medical training, as always, starts to take over. This is no time to give in to emotion. She has to leave it up to Frank to get Kenny and Gerry out of this fix. Her task for now is to keep her mind on the work at hand, see that the decontamination team is prepared for what they have to do out there in the desert.

She rounds up the members of her team and gets them into one corner of the passenger compartment where she can be heard. There are six people charged with ensuring all necessary measures are taken before and during the assault to guard against release of any biological agents.

"Let's go over our precautions once more," Celia tells them. "When the assault starts, three of us will be in a forward element hitting the front entrance and three from the rear entry. Each element will have one of Major Thomas's sharpshooters as our escort and protective firepower."

The two men in jungle fatigues smile confidently.

"It's our job to follow up the initial attacks and find and secure the bio agents quickly. "If we or other members of the force inhale any of those pathogens...well, you are all well aware what quick-acting anthrax, smallpox, who knows what else could do. Ladies and gents, this is something we're not accustomed to, but our military friends are experts. Listen to your guides and heed their instructions."

A hand goes up. Mary Parker has a question. Celia nods.

"When will we put on our decon suits?"

"Good question, Mary. As uncomfortable as it may be, those suits go on before the Major gives the 'go' signal for the attacks. It could be very hot out there even at night, but unless we do our job properly, the whole mission fails. So it's suits on, main assault, decon teams in. Everyone understand?" She gets head wags all around.

"All right then. Anything to add?" Celia turns to the two armed guides. Hawkins speaks up.

"Could be hectic in there, folks. Once the shooting starts, your life may depend on heeding our orders. Listen up. Those suits you'll be wearing and the surrounding noise could make it hard to hear us. Keep an eye on us for signals."

"That's it for now," Celia tells them. "We'll cover last minute details on the way to the desert."

Her eyes sweep the group. There is apprehension on the faces of medical people not accustomed to being thrust into this kind of action. But, to a person, they look determined.

* * * *

The long ride is particularly grating on Celia when she thinks about what could be happening back in Virginia. Everything was looking so much better with Kenny recovering and their lives about to return to normal. Now he's in the hands of terrorists and she's a thousand miles away. She slides down in her seat and listens to the drone of the engines as they cut through the night sky on their way to an uncertain outcome.

Kenny's been her whole life since Mark was taken from them. There's so much of his Dad in Kenny. He's the bright, handsome, well-mannered son any mother wishes for, and his career is just now blossoming. Why did he have to get tangled up with that crowd of homicidal fanatics at New Day?

Celia scans the interior of the big aircraft and thinks how illogical it is for her to be on her way to crash a mountain fort. She never bargained for something like this. There is no way she can back out now, not with the threat these people pose to the country's future; in fact, the whole world's future for that matter. If they don't pull this off, things could very quickly go to hell in a pushcart.

A little rest wouldn't hurt if she could stop the whirling in her brain long enough to take a short nap. Ummmm. That's better. This is odd. Is she dreaming? Why is Jud Black grinning at her in that enigmatic fashion of his?

Jud. Where are you? We've lost contact. You and your partners just seemed to drop out of sight. What's that? Kicking butt in the desert? Surely you didn't take on the terrorists on your own?

I have a strange feeling about you, Jud. There could be something long term in the wind for you and me. You're like no one I ever met. I know it sounds far fetched, but I could go for you. When this insanity all plays out, I hope you're there so I can see if this is real.

Haven't seen a man in a long time I could feel this way about. Don't let those monsters hurt you. Uhhhh.

"Are you all right, Celia?" She wakes with a start. Mary is nudging her arm and looking at her with concern.

"Wha…? Oh, yes. I'm fine, Mary."

"You were thrashing around and mumbling."

"Guess I'm not meant to sleep on this plane."

Celia feels a flush come over her.

CHAPTER 58

Dan Cooper

Lotus and I are well on our way to the tunnel entrance when I hear voices up ahead. One of them is saying, "Take care, Laila." Then there's a jumble of Arabic.

"Stop," Lotus prompts in a whisper and grabs my arm. "I know that voice. It's Jamila Hassan. She said 'We have found the fugitive'."

I come to a halt and look around for Lotus behind me. Not a sign of her. She just vanishes.

Before I can look for her the voices come closer and the same one shouts, "Hands up."

A beam of light shines in my eyes. Can't see who has trapped me but there's nowhere to go. The odds are against me with Lotus suddenly gone absent. I drop my light and thrust both hands high in the air. "Okay. Don't do anything rash."

The light plays over me and down to my feet. For the first time I can see two people outlined in the dimness of the tunnel. They're jabbering at each other. Both of them sound like women. The one in the lead is pointing the business end of an automatic weapon at me as a convincer.

Still no sign of Lotus.

"Are you alone?" the first woman asks.

"All by my lonesome," I lie. "Digging for samples in this old tunnel. What's your story, deary?"

"Not likely," she spits at me. She's not buying my appearance and 'old prospector' act.

"Turn around."

I do an about face and continue to peer into the darkness hoping to find Lotus hasn't abandoned me. How could she have left without so much as a sound? There just isn't anybody there. Crunch time for Danny boy.

"Laila," she says roughly and I feel something being wound around my wrists.

"There, Jamila, that should hold him," says her companion.

One of them jabs what feels like a rifle barrel between my shoulder blades then steps back and says, "Turn around slowly and start walking."

I'm facing the tunnel entrance now. Move out and slide by the women who are both grim faced. The rifle point nudges me and I stumble ahead on the loose rocks of the tunnel floor.

"You will tell me who you are and why you are here. Speak!" says the one called Jamila.

"Told you. I'm digging for minerals. Just found this place yesterday."

"Fool! I will deal with you outside. You will confess or die."

Almost before I have time to think about the scary implications of what I've stepped into, I hear a loud snap and a moan. Automatic fire rings out and echoes through the tunnel. Then a scream and another crunch like bone breaking. I turn half way around slowly to avoid setting off Jamila and her serious looking firearm. I see her flashlight lying at my feet and peer ahead into the blackness. No motion, no sound.

"What happened?" I call out and hear a most welcome voice reply.

"They had an accident, Dan. Pick up the light." She frees my hands.

I retrieve the flashlight and sweep it over two prone figures crumpled in front of me. Then I raise the light to the face of a smiling Lotus holding one of their weapons in her hand.

"*Hwa rang do*, Dan," she says. "My training."

She rescues my fallen lantern and I slide Jamila's weapon from under her. Both of the women are staring at me through open, blank eyes. Their necks are tilted at awkward angles and a trickle of blood shows at Laila's mouth.

"No time to spare," Lotus prompts. "I will take her radio. Hurry. We must join your friends."

Once we emerge from the tunnel I feel almost safe again. Hell, with this dynamo of a fighting machine in my company, how could I be anything but secure? Lotus is amazing.

The ropes are still in place dangling from the two Joshua trees above. There's a moon hanging over the desert casting a subdued glow over the rocky canyon below. Lotus and I stand for a bit and I get a lungful of the first clear air I've inhaled since plunging into that foul, dank tunnel.

"Short climb to where the guys should be waiting, Lotus. Unless there are more of those Arabs up there, we're in tall clover now."

"You go on alone, Dan. I have unfinished business in the citadel."

"No, Lotus. You've done more than any of us could expect. You led Jim out of there, pulled my fat out of the fire. Let the pros handle the rest. We'll get the map to them and they can take over at what they do best."

"There is one more task I must finish. Only I can do this. Hurry. Bring the force with you. I will be waiting." She hands me the folded map.

She helps me sling the two automatic weapons on my shoulders and I shove the flashlight into my pant leg pocket. Lotus gives me a final sweet smile, touches my cheek and slips back into the tunnel.

Feel like a pack horse with all this extra weight. But this is a climb I can make on adrenaline alone. A light breeze swirls around me, cooling my face and reminding me how sweaty and grungy I am. Feel like a recycled Rambo. All I need is a headband and a big knife to clench in my teeth. I make a mental entry in my 'do not' list. No more sand dunes or tunnels after tonight, Cooper.

* * * *

This is one tough haul. Getting too much age on me to be running around out here kicking sand and climbing over cliffs. Got another ten feet to scale, and it's getting harder with every pull.

"Hang on. We'll haul you up."

I lift my head and manage to make out a form at the top of the canyon wall. Jud!

"Pull away, dude. I'm about tapped out."

When I'm safely over the lip of the canyon, Jud and Pat reach out to help me shed my cargo and get on my feet.

"You had me worried, pal," Pat tells me. "I heard gunshots down there. We've been hiding in the ditch back there waiting for you. Saw two people go down, but they were armed to the teeth so we didn't challenge them."

"It got ugly for a bit, guys. Two Arab women. Jamila and Laila, they called each other."

Jud winces. "Ouch. I met one of them earlier."

Pat chimes in. "Me, too. That Jamila is a tough cookie."

"Not any more. You wouldn't believe the moves Lotus has. Put both of them out of commission. Permanently."

"What now, Dan?" Jud asks as we head for the jeep.

"First tell me. Where's Jim?"

"Oh, he's sleeping it off in the vehicle. Got some stale sandwiches in him and he went right off to slumber land." Jud grins and hefts his rifle. "This is a real killing machine. The bad boys better watch out now."

We leave Jim peacefully sawing away in the back seat, carry away the brush covering the jeep and pile aboard. It balks at climbing out of the ditch, but Pat and I give a shove while Jud steers and it clears the hollow.

Pat cautions, "Leave the lights off. We could still run into guards out here. Don't know how big a protection force they have."

"I can think of at least four that won't be helping them," I answer.

"Hope we don't hit any gulleys ahead. I can't see a thing," Jud snorts. We dip down, hit bottom and back up suddenly. Jim pops straight up in the back seat. I hear rocks and dirt falling. The echoes come from far below us.

"Who's the idiot driving this buggy?" Jim cries out.

"Jud Earnhardt," our fearless driver replies. "Shut up and hang on."

CHAPTER 59

Dan Cooper

All four of us are on nervous alert. The way armed Arabs keep popping up everywhere we've been, there won't be an easy breath drawn until this little put-putt clears the McCullough Range. Jud is hunched over the steering wheel watching for bumps like the one that almost dislodged Jim from his seat; Black's whistling under his breath but that doesn't fool me. We're about as jumpy as a crop of spring time frogs. That includes tadpole Jud.

When we find a gravel road leading out of the hills it looks like we're going to make it away without a fight. You can almost hear the collective sigh when we turn onto paved road and turn south. I look back at Jim and break my silence.

"Jim, that was some special lady that busted you out of that place. She's pretty but very deadly."

"You're right on both counts, Dan. That girl can make moves I'd swear break the laws of gravity. The little bastard that threatened me has treated her like trash, though."

"Who is he?" I ask.

"Kim Yung, the Korean that's in charge. He's the mastermind behind this whole terror plot. She told me how he's abused her. Lucky for me she decided to fight back about the time I showed up. She confirmed all my suspicions about what they're cooking up in that hole in the ground."

"Don't tell me she fell for your boyish charm, Jim. You been taking lessons from Studley Jud, buddy?"

"Nothing like that. She wants him taken down every bit as much as we do. Kim has this master plan involving biohazards released in high density locations to provoke mass epidemics—nasty crap like anthrax and smallpox—only he's built super strains even quicker and more deadly using nanotech." Jim stops talking and looks off into the distance.

"Don't stop now," I prompt.

"It's a long, scary story, Dan," Jim replies.

"Hey, we have all the way to Vegas to hear it. Unload."

By the time Jim gets through his spiel about bionasties and nano machines I'm looking at Pat and Jud like a kid at the horror flicks. Pat's eyes are about the size of saucers and Jud is twisting around like Jim's words are making him very uneasy.

Then Jim puts the capper on it. This Oriental maniac has Kenny and others working on a cure for his life-threatening ailment, and along the way he's hatched a scheme for body cell repair using nano machines that could be the closest thing ever seen to making a human being immortal. Any other time I would dismiss it as a madman dreaming or science fiction at its worst. Unfortunately, what Jim and Jud have already dug out about New Day and the fact that Kenny is about as smart a nano expert as anybody around gives the whole tale credibility.

"We may be up against a smarter enemy than we counted on, folks. And if this Yung character succeeds, we may be—to use a Korean term—in deep, deep *kimchi.*"

The silence is deafening. Every man aboard this sand buggy has his head down and his lips sealed. Don't know if there's a group prayer session going on or we're just too overwhelmed by the task ahead of us to speak. Either we stop the threat right here in the desert or it could be over for all of us.

* * * *

Everybody is so deep in thought we almost miss a creepy melody coming from somewhere near.

"You guys hear that? Did we go over the edge into the twilight zone or something?"

"Oh, damn!" Jud blurts out and reaches for his leg pocket. He pulls out a cell phone and answers in his characteristic manner, "Nekkid."

A slight delay then, "Yes, it's Jud. Cee?" He slows down and pulls onto the shoulder.

"Right." He says. "All four of us. On our way back to town. Not to I-15 yet. Great. Hold on a second."

He turns to me and says, "Celia and the storm troopers have landed. They're at McCarran Field about to saddle up. What do I tell her?"

"You remember the general store next to the exit for Primm?" I ask. "Tell her how to find us there. I have a map of the target's layout and an idea."

He continues his conversation. Jud tells her about the map then goes off into his own world like we weren't even here. I'm about to call him off when he flips his phone shut and says, "Hold on, gents. We're going to Primm to meet the real warriors."

For all his jolly exterior, though, there's something wrong. A clear worry line and he's staring down the road like he could take a bite out of something.

"Time to share, pal. What did she say that has you so upset?"

"It's Kenny. They have Kenny."

"What?" Pat thunders. "Who has him?"

"Somebody nabbed him from the hospital along with Celia's Senator buddy. Seems he's a long time family friend who was there to talk to Kenny after he came out of his dengue funk. They're being tracked on their way to fly out somewhere—could be back to Mister Yung's neighborhood."

Pat growls. "Now I'm sure as hell gonna be with those guys when they hit the underground. Haven't made like a Ranger for a long time, but if he causes Kenny to be hurt again I intend to personally wring Kim Yung's neck."

I look around at Pat and see the grimmest expression I've ever witnessed on that big, lovable guy's face. He's normally even-tempered to a fault, but right now O'Leary is definitely ready to chew glass.

Jud is driving like a wild man toward Primm. His head is somewhere else—most likely on the other end of that phone conversation. Big galoot. He's way too vulnerable.

"Jim," I start, "you must have come out of the citadel a different way for us to run into you and Lotus where we did. Maybe there are multiple routes into that place."

"Not an option, Dan. They'd never shinny through the spaces she put me through wearing their protective gear and carrying weapons."

"Okay, then we're left with a head-on assault and a strike through the tunnel. What I want to propose to Celia's team is that we nab the van from the Primm office and use it to access the front way in. I know they have their own ways of doing things, but it's an idea they may want to consider."

"Sounds good to me," Jim says. "Are you guys all going back with them?"

"If they allow it," Pat says. "This is one party I don't want to miss."

CHAPTER 60

"Ali Hassan, why have you entered my *dojang* uninvited?"

"The prisoner is gone, Kim. He has escaped."

"At last it is clear to me, Ali. You harbor deceitful snakes in our midst."

"Why must you abuse me with your words, Kim?"

"Your vaunted *al-Qinaa'* is a fraud. One of them has aided this Jim Barnett in leaving. He was the only link I had to learn how much is known by outsiders of our operation here. Your failure to bring me his friend as well made sure of that."

"Wait. You don't understand, Kim. My men and women are loyal. It is your own beloved Lotus who has betrayed you. She came to visit Barnett before I reached him and now he is gone."

"Liar! Lotus is devoted to me. I am her master and the only one she serves."

"There is no other explanation. She has taken him and fled the citadel. I have blanketed the area with my warriors. They will bring them back."

"I do not believe you. And what of Kenny Grant?"

"My messengers have succeeded in capturing the young fool. They are even now arranging to bring him to you. *Al-Qinaa'* has served you well, Kim Yung. You will see who is to blame when the bitch is found with Barnett."

Kim can not constrain himself. He lashes out and strikes the insolent Arab. "You will not insult her in my presence. I will bring her here and let you see your error." Kim presses the button on his pager. Lotus has never failed to answer a summons.

"Now tell me about Barnett's friend you lost in the desert. Have your guards not found him?"

"He is in our hands," Ali says, not looking Kim in the eye. "He had wandered a great distance. They are returning on foot. Please be patient, Kim."

Kim knows that's a lie of the worst order. He can look into Ali's soul and see he is trying to deceive. What can he possibly gain by stalling?

Minutes pass before a melodic voice sounds from the *dojang* doorway.

"Sah bum nimh, I am here." Lotus appears in attire that hugs her every delicious curve. Her waist length hair falls loosely behind her. She is a vision of loveliness.

"Now you must retract your words, Ali," Kim declares. "One of your own guards is to blame. I will expect him before me for judgment within the hour."

Ali's expression turns into one of contempt and defiance.

"So, if that is the way you wish it, yellow dog. I have taken my last order from you, devil of devils. Now you will listen."

At last Kim understands who the snake is among them.

"Have your say," Kim counters. "Then make your peace. This act of insolence finally seals your fate."

"Perhaps not, Kim Yung. Doctor Warren is under my control. He is locked in his quarters and closely guarded."

A chill goes through Kim. Warren is the other half of the team of brilliant scientists who will effect the cure for his deadly illness. His medicine and Grant's nano machines will repair the diseased cells, heal Kim's body and keep him ever young.

"I can see your concern," Ali spits. "He has confided—after some persuasion—the role he and Kendrick Grant play in your personal survival. They are both my prisoners. Without their help you will die."

Kim is stumped for only a moment. Then he sees through Ali's bluff. Su Lin has already informed him she is on her way to the flight that will bring her here with Grant. And Kim can set Warren free. Ali is holding an empty hand.

"You would bargain with me? For what?"

"I seek no trade. I hold your life in my hands, Kim. I will dictate my own terms to the world leaders while you experience a lingering death."

"No, Ali. It is you who will die."

With a lightning move Kim seizes Ali's arm and snaps the elbow, rendering it a useless limb. The Arab screams in pain and stumbles away from a follow-up kick. Ali reaches behind him with his good arm, produces a glistening dirk with a slender blade and waves it at Kim. The Korean is amused.

"Excellent. You will make it sport for me to finish you." He eyes Ali warily and calls out to Lotus, "Observe, *chagun kkot.* Watch the warrior and the serpent. The outcome is unworthy of a wager. His time has come."

Kim drops his arms and invites Ali's attack. He hesitates, debates his move.

Ali feints and probes, slices the air with his knife. Kim whirls and kicks but Ali draws back the hand holding the knife and grins his defiance. Then he mounts his own offense; leaps high into the air to come hurtling down upon Kim. Yung is too quick for him. His body uncoils into Ali and they meet in mid-air, their limbs coming together with the slap of flesh on flesh. They both crash to the mat and Kim places his foot beneath Ali's chin, seeking to press until his neck is snapped. Ai manages to wield the knife and slash Kim's foot. It only enrages the Korean. He springs up on his unharmed foot.

"Observe, Lotus. I will apply a lesson from an ancient master."

Kim bears the pain and leaps off both feet, hurling like a cannonball directly into Ali's middle. Ali flies backward and sprawls on the mat. With his unwounded foot Kim pins Ali's knife-wielding hand then rubs a bloody insole over his face. He strikes the bridge of Ali's nose with his heel sending bone fragments into the Arab's brain. Ali lies broken and silent.

Kim takes a long, pointed metal pike from the wall and walks to where Ali lies. Raising both arms above his head he sends the pike downward through Ali's body into the mat below.

The victor looks at Lotus. "The serpent is dead, precious one. The fool sought to overthrow me and take the glory for all that I alone have accomplished. But I *am* the leader and he is no more."

She says nothing.

"The attack teams have been dispatched, Lotus. They left the citadel no more than an hour ago. Soon four cities will reap a bitter harvest for the American conceit. One member of my inner circle is with each team to ensure the Arabs carry out their missions. I will pass the word that the American prisoner has caused the death of their leader Ali Hassan. His radical followers will consider their actions as retribution."

Her eyes show wonder at Kim's strength and resolute confidence.

"Ali sought to implicate you in the escape of our prisoner," he tells her.

"Escape?" she says. "Barnett is gone?"

"Ali said you had helped him elude the guards. Let me hear you say that is untrue."

"Surely you do not doubt my loyalty, *sah bum nimh.*"

Her slender fingers clutch the zipper ring at the neck of her jumpsuit. She moves it downward until it parts like a second skin and begins to fall away. Lotus glides toward Kim, her face aglow.

"Once again you are victorious, master. Now you shall have the reward you have earned."

CHAPTER 61

"My teams are ready, Major."

Celia and the team stand on the ramp at the back edge of McCarran Field. Six jeeps from Nellis Air Force Base are standing by along with four unmarked super cab pickups. Major Thomas is herding everybody up into their pre-arranged elements. The men stow gear in the pickup beds and place the decontamination suits in position for ready access.

"I want one three-person decontamination team in that pickup and the other group over there," Thomas says. "We'll leave here one vehicle at a time and take I-15 west to the Primm exit. Drivers will rendezvous off that exit."

The whole operation is a well-oiled exercise. These are professionals. Celia can only hope they can respond to whatever the terrorists throw at them later.

She moves with her two teammates to the designated vehicle, helps off load their equipment, and they take their seats. Thomas follows and slides in next to the driver. "Okay, sports fans, this is kickoff time." He smiles and they're on our way.

Very little conversation ensues as they cut across town and hit the Interstate. A feeling of intense nervousness seems to hit the whole group. Celia imagines each of them is doing exactly what she is right now. Every step of her decontamination plan is flashing through her head. Once they're inside the underground, timing will be critical. Every second they waste gives the defenders another opportunity to unleash a biological counter attack against them. They are in for a very tense time.

Celia checks her watch a dozen times as they motor out the Interstate. Must have been over an hour ago they landed back there. Her thoughts are elsewhere at the moment as they have been ever since that frightening call from the command post. Not knowing what's going on with Kenny is tearing her up inside. She can't seem to concentrate on the task ahead when what is really important to her is totally out of her control back in Virginia.

Mary takes notice of her agitation and nervous twisting in her seat. She touches Celia's arm and asks, "Are you going to be all right, Celia?" That shakes her out of her deep musing.

"This could be a long night for me, Mary."

"Hang in, Doctor. Kenny can take care of himself. Learned how from you."

Celia sits up straight and gets back to something she can manage. She tells Mary and Sam, "One more time, folks. Let's step through the sequence. I want it to go like clockwork when we reach the area we have to debug."

* * * *

Just off the Primm exit is a service station on the right with a lighted parking area. There is a jeep full of people sitting under the lamp post.

"Pull in there." Major Thomas points and the driver swings over. "That must be our contacts." He turns around and calls out, "Latrine break, folks. Our convoy will be drifting in over the next few minutes. We'll do a final briefing then."

Celia is already exiting the back door. The dusty jeep has four grimy passengers that look almost familiar through the layers of sand and dirt.

"Pat," Celia calls out as the Irishman hops out and starts toward her. He's dirty and haggard but he's a comforting sight. And the others look like they've been dragged across the dunes, but at least they're all safe.

"Hi, pretty lady. Fancy meeting you here," Pat quips. She hugs him then steps back.

"All you fellows need is a machine gun on that jeep and you'd look like the rat patrol."

Pat roars. "Slighty grubby, ain't we?" He takes her hand and guides her over to where his three partners are waiting.

"I think you know Larry, Curly and Moe the three Nevada prospectors."

Dan and Jim give her cheery hellos. Jud can't contain himself. He grabs Celia in a big hug and kisses her before he realizes what he's done. He looks a little embarrassed but she gives him a quick peck in return.

"I don't know what you four have been up to," she tells them, "but it's stirred the pot. We have thugs coming out of the woodwork back in Virginia."

"They haven't tried to harm our families, have they?" Dan fires back.

"As far as I know, only mine. I'm waiting for word on Kenny. He's recovered but now he's been kidnapped from the hospital."

Jud takes a step backward and reacts. "God, I'm sorry, Cee. We've been yanking some cords out here, but we never intended for that to happen."

"Sorry, Jud. I didn't mean it to sound like I was blaming you guys. All the help you've given Kenny and me is great. I'm just torn up over this latest turnaround."

Jim speaks up. "Celia, whatever Kim Yung has going in the citadel—and I think I'm aware of what that is—Kenny's talents are absolutely critical to him. They won't harm him because Kim can't succeed without him."

She looks at Jim with a deep frown. "You don't mean to say my Kenny is helping him?"

"Not consciously," he answers. "I think he finally discovered what Kim was planning. That's why he bolted from the fold. Kim has a life-threatening disease, and the work Kenny Grant is doing is essential to his cure."

Dan passes a map of the underground to Thomas. The major spreads it out across a jeep hood, and he and his team leaders pore over it.

Celia fills in Kenny's friends on the plan to take down the New Day sites.

"This is a tuned effort. With what you fellows have uncovered and the info Kenny's passing along now that he's improving, we have all the players on board. They've set up a command post to direct simultaneous raids on the mountain and the Los Angeles and Tampa plants."

"Sounds like we stirred up a hornet's nest," Dan laughs.

"Roger that," Jud chimes in. "Bunch of troublemakers, ain't we?"

"This is as serious as it gets," Celia tells them. "If these terrorists get their attacks launched, we're talking major panic and death. Defense, Homeland Security and the FBI are all involved now. They take at face value the intelligence you've passed along. This is a situation that doesn't allow time for delay or error."

"Didn't mean to sound flip, Cee," Jud replies. "Nobody understands how serious this is better than me and my pals. Sometimes we have to joke to keep from letting situations scare us."

Major Thomas comes walking over with his satellite radiophone. He hands it to Celia and says, "Friend of yours has a message, Doctor Grant."

"Hello. Doctor Grant here."

It's Gerry Crandall's voice. "Celia, Kenny's safe." Her heart races.

"Frank Kane was following us," he says. "He caught up at the Leesburg Airport. Two of our kidnappers are dead and the other one is corralled."

"Oh, thank you Gerry. Where is Kenny now? Can I talk to him?"

"He and Frank are on their way to, uh...the city nearest you. He's doing fine."

"Are you all right, Gerry?"

"Nothing hurt but my pride, Cee. Give them hell, lady and...my thoughts are with you."

"Oh, and there's more good news, Gerry. The four men you sent to check on New Day are all right here with me. They've been to, you know, that place and checked it out. Let me turn you back to the head man here."

No matter what else happens tonight it will be okay now that Celia knows Kenny's safe. She hands the phone back to the Major. The tremendous tension she's built up overflows in a torrent and she cries like a baby.

Jud folds his arms around her and asks, "What is it, Cee? Can I help?"

She turns her face up to him, gives him a broad smile, wipes her eyes and answers, "Everything is fantastic, Jud. Kenny's safe. I'm ready to roll."

In a matter of minutes the rest of the convoy has caught up. Major Thomas has been busy laying out his attack plan with the team leaders. He gathers everybody around, points at the four COBB guys and tells his men, "These four civilians have laid some excellent groundwork for us. They've already scouted the area. They even brought us a map of the underground layout."

Thomas opens the map and points out the important locations to the assault teams. "I've drawn in the back tunnel here." He taps on the map. "And there's an opening to the outside Jim told us about up here that's maybe a hundred feet above the cavern floor. The bio agents are in this store room right here."

He checks his watch. "Time hack. Twenty three oh four. When I give the signal we fan out. We'll be conducting a three-prong assault, front and back. We'll have two waves from the back and one from the front entrance. Ingress team one blows open the overhead, rappels down their rigs, takes out the watchtowers and attacks the guard quarters right here. Team two enters the store room through the rear tunnel and Doctor Grant goes to work on the decon procedures. Team three approaches the front gate in a New Day van we're picking up, takes out the guard post and does a frontal assault. Teams one and two will need about twenty minutes to complete their approach. When we hear the explosion set by the first team we all go in."

He turns to Celia and says, "Doctor Grant will go over the decon plan one more time."

She begins, "One three-person decontamination element will enter the main bio agents storage area from the tunnel with ingress team two and secure the area. Any containers will be covered with a strong sealant to guard against leaks. The other decon team will accompany ingress team three. You have your lightweight protective gear to get into before breaching the entrances. My people will be in heavy suits for prolonged exposure. That's about it."

Thomas thanks her and says, "Chill it here till we run a little errand in town. Cooper knows where we can find one of the bad guys' own vans for cover. When he gets back we'll launch."

CHAPTER 62

Dan Cooper

Thomas sends two of his men with me across town. We swing by the New Day office and find it dark. No van outside. I pull out my slip of paper with the contact numbers for the Primm New Day staff and punch in the numbers for a Harry Williams. A voice comes on line.

"You Williams of New Day?" I ask.

"That's me. Office is closed. We open at nine AM."

"Wait, sport. I can see you're closed. Got a delivery for you from New Day in LA. Says top priority. Got delayed on my way over. Man, I have other stops to make, so I need to hand this off to you."

Williams sounds seriously annoyed. He blusters and cusses under his breath then says, "Okay, I'm on my way. Park around back and I'll meet you."

A few minutes later a white van pulls around the corner and whips in behind the building. A man steps out and slams the van door. Looks around for us.

The two troops box him in and one barks an order. By the time I draw alongside, the driver's face is stark under the overhead spotlight. Looks like it's drained of all color.

"Look," he says. "I don't keep any cash or valuables inside. Got nothing you'd be interested in unless you want a used van."

"Get that back door open, one of our men tells him. "Have a little chore and a ride for you."

Doesn't take them long to convince Williams to call the mountain and tell them he has an important shipment to deliver. He's careful of his words since there's a Glock 9mm firmly planted in his ear.

In minutes we're on our way to meet the team with an additional set of wheels and driver to give us an element of surprise.

Thomas tells his men, "I want the six of you in my element of team three in the back of the van. O'Leary is with us, too. He's a former Ranger, guys, so he understands these actions. The civilians will ingress after we clear out the guards. Make it happen, team."

We take the mountain road and roll up to a curve in the gravel road maybe a quarter mile from the front entrance to the citadel. Lights are off and Major Thomas radios for the teams to split away. Drivers of teams one and two swing wide left and right in an arc up the hillside. My watch shows it's just past midnight. In our favor a haze has settled in over the desert and clouds drift overhead dimming the moon's glow. Gives me a creepy feeling.

Jim goes with team one to find the overhead opening. The explosion impact to open that entry will be our cue to assault from the tunnel. I have the job of guiding team two to the Joshua trees and getting them into the tunnel as quickly as possible before that happens.

"There are the trees," I tell the team leader. "Entrance is twenty feet down."

"Piece of cake," he says. We circle the trees and he directs, "Okay, you mountain goats, do your thing."

One of the troopers takes a look at our ropes still hanging around the trees, snorts and quickly does his own setup. Rigs slings on slip ropes with pulleys to manage the descent. The troopers are in their cover-ups and masks and the decon team has full protective gear. Celia's talked Jud and me into donning a couple of backup suits. Feel like I'm setting out on a moon walk. Two by two we slip over the canyon lip on the new ropes and work our way down onto the ledge below. Jud and Celia follow us down.

Team leader cautions us, "Total silence from here in. You civilians keep it zipped."

No problem here. I clamp my jaws tight and listen for any sounds of bad guys.

We begin the trek back through the musty tunnel with me right behind Thomas. I remember how uptight I got the last time in here. Of course, that had a lot to do with two narrow escapes. Without Lotus I would have been dog food for hungry coyotes or, maybe worse, at the mercy of a couple of wild-eyed Arabs. That little slip of a thingis an amazing woman. I think about her now and wonder what 'unfinished business' could have been so important she risked her neck by going back into that den of thieves.

"What?" the major blurts out.

I see him point his weapon then drop it down and move forward. He's found the two female guards.

He stoops to check and I hear him mumble, "Son of a bitch. Both necks snapped." He looks back and shines his light on me, but I just shrug.

We inch along in the narrow passageway, seven pros and five very edgy civilians. Jud and I have been in some strange situations since we hooked up again, but I can't imagine how spooked Celia and her medical folks must feel. And my monkey suit is getting hot and stuffy.

Farther down the tunnel there is another abrupt halt. Thomas is nudging something with his foot. The coyote carcasses are lying off the path where the side tunnel branches off. He plays the light beam back at me and motions. I point to confirm we keep going straight ahead.

Another five minutes of sweaty progress and we've reached the entry door. By now I'm frying inside this chemical garb. But it beats breathing in what lies on the other side of that door.

Thomas crouches and runs his hands over the stone surface. Looks back at me and takes on a puzzled look. I motion him aside, find the key and feel for the keyhole. Insert the key and turn, then open the door an inch or two.

"My treat," I tell him. Can't hear his reply clearly, but his expression say 'wiseass'.

We all kneel in ready position and await the blast from above that will signal it's time for us to enter the building.

CHAPTER 63

Jim Barnett

"It should be somewhere along here," I tell my team leader. "When we drove out we went through a dip and I heard rocks falling. Think we almost went through the roof."

One of the men calls out, "Believe I found it, sarge. Ought to open up nice and wide with a minimum charge."

"That's it," the leader says. He peers down into the hole and shines his flashlight. "Sizable drop. Rig a hundred-foot length and we'll go one at a time." They scope out the situation and pack explosives around the hole.

I open my big, stupid civilian mouth. "Won't the sound bring the guards? Can't they pick us off before we get inside?"

"Don't worry. Besides, chum, you ain't going," the sergeant says. He gives me a nasty look. Hold up my hands to show I'm backing off and he grins.

Wow! I don't know what these guys are using, but there's little more than a pop when the explosives do their thing. The sound of rock falling is louder than the explosion, but there is a distinct earth tremor as if the ground shifted under us.

Sergeant holds his men back until he listens for response from inside. Then he signals to go. They disappear through the hole one at a time and scale down the rope.

I wait and listen. A couple minutes pass after the last man rappels down. Then there is rapid gunfire and the assault is on. Nothing left for me but to take a seat in a jeep and wait.

* * * *

Dan Cooper

"Feel that jolt? That's it, boys and girls. Showtime!" Thomas calls and shoves the store room door open. I follow him in, careful not to bump anything or snag my chemical suit.

The room is dark except for the beams our own lights throw. The team members fan out behind us and move across the room. I've cautioned them to avoid jostling anything in here for fear we'll set off a deadly spray of some sort. Thomas leads them to the far door and they file quietly into the hallway and close the door. They leave one man as our cover while we take care of this room.

Jud, Celia and two other decon folks are scattering. Celia and her helpers are already working their magic to contain and secure the canisters. Jud crawls up next to me and says, "Got candy, GI?" Nut case thinks this is fun.

A burst of gunfire in the hall breaks the silence. Then another.

Celia's folks methodically check each container for leaks, move them to one corner of the room and cradle them. They're spraying some kind of sealant over the cans and covering them with a cloth that appears to shrink to form an airtight cover over the whole mess.

I hear continued spurts of gunfire and a lot of shouting outside the door. Our armed escort, Jamison, stands with his burp gun pointed, ready to drop any and all that try to get in here. So far we're unchallenged.

Celia removes her headgear and signals to the rest of us to do likewise.

"We should be safe now. Just keep your suits on until we're sure. Let's go out that way and seal the door behind us."

Jamison steps out into the hallway and takes a scan. Then he motions for us to move forward. Celia applies something to the door perimeter. Checks to see it's secured. Just as we turn to head into the next room, Jamison's gun sounds off with a sustained stream of fire. We all dive for the floor and wait.

"All clear," he reports. "If I shout cover, find a place to hide."

We work our way past a body and begin to search through a large complex of lighted rooms. There are several people in lab coats in the area. All of them look dazed, in shock at what is unfolding around them. They stand back and try to make themselves invisible. No resistance here.

"Must be Kim's collection of prize scientists," I remark to Jud.

"Yeah, neither fighters nor lovers, pal. Just geeks afraid for their own hides."

Celia is giving the lab setup a close inspection. I can see she's more than mildly curious; in fact, she appears quite impressed by what she's seeing. Jamison rounds up all the cowering scientists and locks them in one of the smaller rooms. I find Celia and intercept her.

"State of the art, huh?"

"Cutting edge, Dan. There's a fortune invested in this facility. I know some medical people that would sell their souls for an operation this elaborate."

I do a little exploring on my own. The next group of rooms has everything an aspiring nanoscientist could ever desire. There is even a rig with a metal plate identifying it as a Scanning Transmission Electron Microscope. I've heard of STEMs. They're the very latest in optical scanners. With one of these a scientist can view materials all the way down to angstrom level. That's less than the size of a hydrogen atom. The lab equipment blows me away. I start to rummage around, but Celia stops me.

"We may not be out of the woods yet, Dan. Lids on, everybody," she orders. Back into the steam oven goes my head.

She and her folks give the rooms a thorough scrubbing for potential dangers. Check every container whether open or closed. Run their detection instruments over every surface they can reach. We wait and wonder. Finally, she lifts off her helmet and starts to unzip.

"Suits off, everybody," Celia calls out. I shuck my suit like a bad memory and emerge sopping wet.

Jamison checks the hallway and returns. "Okay, our job is done. We wait here till the gunners finish cleaning house. They'll find us back here. Put my mark on the door to show this area's secure."

We sit and chill out—literally. I'm relieved to be free of that suit and drying off in the air conditioned lab. Jud and the other three are wandering around taking stock of the expensive toys these mad scientists have been playing with in a big hole in the ground. Jamison keeps a wary eye on the hall door and checks his ammo supply.

When Celia and Jud find me again she fires a set of questions at me. Wants me to relate what happened in that tunnel the last time I went through. Tell her how I found the way into the store room. And she wants to know the story behind the human and animal bodies all over the place.

"I can answer all your questions with one word, Celia. Lotus."

"A flower?"

"No. A veritable killing machine packaged in the most deceiving female form you could imagine."

"A woman caused all that destruction?"

"You had to be there," I say and grin. "The guy that runs this operation thinks she's his personal sex slave, but that little lady is a nuclear explosion with a hair trigger. She felled those two guards like it was child's play. She disposed of the rabid animals with her bare hands, according to Jim."

"How did you hook up with her?" Celia asks.

"She's the one that led Jim out of the tunnel. Lotus is somewhere down here now. Just hope she doesn't get mistaken for one of the bad guys. Jim and I owe her our lives."

CHAPTER 64

Pat O'Leary

"You look a little uptight, O'Leary."

One of Thomas's sharpshooters is alternating between checking his gun and giving me rather amused sidelong glances.

"Oh," I mutter and come out of my semi-conscious state. "Sorry. What was that?"

"Said you got a funny look like you're wondering how you got mixed up in this rumble we're about to start."

"No. Thomas probably told you I have Ranger experience. Been on more of these bashes than I care to remember."

"So do you feel nervous about sharing the ride with me?"

For the first time I take a close look at him. Under all that lamp black he looks Middle Eastern. Has no accent I can detect. He watches my puzzled expression and smiles.

"Eddie Amir. Born in Muncie, Indiana. Both parents immigrated from Iran."

"Sorry, Eddie. It just stopped me for a second. I mean, you do know there are...

"Arabs in this hole in the ground? Sure, I know. We got a full briefing on what we'd encounter. Jimmy Park and I are here because he speaks Korean and my Arabic is fairly good. Could need the edge."

"But doesn't it make you a bit...uncomfortable?

"Hey, those are fanatics in there. They're an embarrassment to me and all my Muslim friends. They corrupt everything we stand for. And the Korean guy, I understand, is a real nut case. All I'm gonna see is enemy."

"Thanks for straightening me out, Eddie." I shake his hand.

"So you're all right with sharing the ride with me?" he says and beams.

"That was never my problem, Eddie. I was thinking about the first time I was in this van."

"You've been in the New Day van before tonight?" Now his expression changes from mildly annoyed to completely puzzled.

"Yeah. Couple of their dirt bags drugged me and carted me out of a Vegas hotel four days ago. Had a bit of a tight squeeze for awhile."

"Then how come you're here now?" he asks.

"They drove me out here in this van, but I fought my way loose damn near in sight of the front door. See that block of wood next to the wheel well? It has some of my blood on it. I spent a long time in a shallow desert ditch till my buddies came along and found me."

Captain Vance, our team chief, gets a call that the boys up above are ready to blow the peep hole. Jim must be watching a real show up there.

"Stand by," he says. "Wait till you hear gunfire then cut a chogie to the front gate with all horses grinding. We'll make some excitement up ahead."

The New Day van fires up and rolls down the grade toward the entrance. Captain and driver are up front. Vance has a civilian cap pulled down low. There are five of us in the back, four sharpshooters and one slightly out of place former Ranger. We're wearing light weight biological cover-ups and masks, but I feel like I'm back in uniform again. It's a rush.

A gate sentry holds out one hand and says, "Why so late?" That's all he gets out before the captain nails him with a spray from his automatic. Must be two of them in that gate house. A second burst and Vance says, "I've got the door switch," and bounds out of the cab.

We scratch off and speed through the front door. Shouts in some foreign language. Vance must be on the front bumper. Rat-a-tat then quiet. We pile out and circle the van.

Calm and still for the moment. Overhead lights but only two of them still burning. Vance takes care of that and throws the scene into pitch black. We all lower our infrared goggles so we can see if there's any movement ahead. Not a sign so far.

"Take the door two abreast," Vance shouts and the men move forward.

I expect we'll be in for a firefight beyond those doors and, for a few seconds, I'm right. Our gunners belch out a deadly stream of fire and I hear scattered returns but it's mostly screams and people falling.

"Scatter and patrol," Vance barks.

No sign of further resistance and no movement in the rooms we pass. I'm beginning to feel loose and confident; wondering if things are going this well with the other two teams. Must be a great experience for any of the guys that haven't been through a drill like this. All we have to worry about now is keeping our eyes open for strays and hoping there are no germ clouds loose in here.

Then I hear a word that hasn't chilled me in years.

"Grenade," somebody yells and I dive for cover. There's a closed door on my right. I do my best to punch it open with my shoulder.

CHAPTER 65

Dan Cooper

Major Thomas and his advance force double back looking for us.

"Everything's secure in our section," he says. "Team one reports no losses and they cleaned up back in the guard quarters. Seems they caught the whole off-duty force sound asleep. Most of those that woke up didn't last long enough to regret it. The rest are corralled back there with two of our guys playing jailers. Unfortunately, we also had one civilian casualty. One of the scientists curiously ran out into the hallway. He got in the line of fire."

"Who was it? Pat asks.

"His badge said Doctor Fred Warren."

Jud and Celia are in the far corner having a smoke. They seem to be in deep conversation. She gets up and approaches Thomas.

"Our work is finished here, Major. We sealed off all the canisters in the store room and covered them with something they can't eat through. Nothing suspicious in the labs. No detectable leaks according to our instruments. Their detection gear makes ours look obsolete and it doesn't pick up any problems, either. The store room has an airtight door. I've double sealed it against intruders."

"Great work, Doctor. How would you like to do this for a living?"

"Not on a bet," she zips back at him.

"Any word on team three, Major?" I ask.

"Don't worry. Your friend O'Leary can handle himself. Has more experience than most of my own guys."

"We heard an explosion from somewhere up front. Had us worried," I tell him.

"Now that we know you're safe, I'll take the fellows and locate that element. I heard the boom and it concerns me, too."

"Wait," says Jud, "where is Jim? Didn't he go up top to show the team where the opening was?"

Thomas smiles. "Probably still up there. They wouldn't let him make the drop with them. Bet he's getting lonesome and wondering how we're doing underground. We'll make a pass through the facility. Then I'll send one of my guys to pick up your friend and bring him back."

He starts to leave then turns around and tell us, "You may want to go over next door. Looks a lot more comfortable. Must have been the head guy's hangout. It's plush."

"We'll do that, Major," I tell him. "Just want to look around some more. This is impressive equipment. Jud wants to get at their data base, too."

The five of us stay busy for quite a while looking over the biological and nanotech platforms they've built for what is obviously world class work. Jud and I are deep into inspecting that STEM when there's a ruckus in the next room. We rush in to find Pat with a large scowl and a bandage on his shoulder.

"You okay, Pat?" Jud blurts out and heads for him. Pat holds up the arm on his uninjured side and says, "Don't touch me, Jud. I'm seriously torqued and this shoulder hurts like purple hell."

"Gonna tell us what happened?" I ask him.

"Everything up front was under control till some Arab rolled a grenade down the hall. I heard the alert and hit a door like a pile driver. Think I widened the opening a foot or two with my shoulder. That's one of the two holes in the wall. The other is where the grenade ripped the wall next to where I'd been standing. Think I better have my military disability reappraised. This is not work for old men."

Jud turns to me and says, "Looks like a six-pack wound to me. Let's go see if those plush quarters have any real class—like a bar and some brewskys."

As we start to leave the room Pat scans around like he's counting noses. "Somebody's missing," he says. "We laid it on the line to snatch him and now I don't see Jim in this happy little group."

"Went up top with team one to show them the opening. Probably did the rope trick with them."

"Not in your wildest dream, buster. That's scary stuff," Pat snaps.

"Don't worry. Thomas says they'll pick him up in a bit."

"Well, if they don't hurry up," he says and grins, "He's gonna be at least one round behind. Lead on Jud."

While we walk I'm getting the skinny on their part of the operation. Sounds like they took care of eight or ten 'night watchman' Arabs along the way. Cleared out the front half of the fortress. Secured all the common areas, storage and utilities. As Pat puts it, they even 'kicked the motor pool tires and knocked over a few stacks of stored goods'.

That leaves only one unanswered question. What happened to Lotus?

CHAPTER 66

Jim Barnett

It's been quiet down there for awhile now. Heard a lot of yelling and some gunfire then it just went still below. Let's see if there's a spare emergency lamp in one of those jeeps. Good. Now if I can take a look without falling through the hole.

Mighty black down there. That must be a good sixty foot drop, maybe more. Not exactly my thing riding a rope. Hell, that climb out of my cell was enough to hold me for a long time.

"Get away from that hole!" somebody yells at me. I spin around to see one of the sharpshooters pulling up nearby.

"Can't have civilians on that rig. Too risky," he says.

"Oh, I understand. Just curious. How's it going below?"

"No sweat. Got the place contained. No injuries on our side. But a high body count of Arabs. Major said I was to fetch you."

"Do me a favor. Just for grins, show me how this harness works, sarge."

"I told you—oh, what the hell. Only take a minute."

He hooks the harness belt on me and explains how they connect and hold onto the rope. Step over the edge and play out the line at a measured pace to let down.

"So the hook goes here and I let the rope slide through my hand? What is it the paratroopers say in the old war movies? Some Indian's name."

"Yeah. If you were gonna do the deed. But you ain't. Hop in the jeep."

I snap the hook on and for an instant I imagine what it would feel like to drop through that opening. Then I start to unhook and stand aside.

"WATCH IT," he yells at me just as my foot slips from under me.

I'm plummeting down before I can recover. All I can think to do is hang on and holler, "Geronimo—oH-OH!"

For a quick ride it seems to take a long time. Whole episodes of my life are flashing before my eyes. I grab at the slip line with both hands and miss. Finally catch hold and yank back. I stop my downward flight with a jolt, though I'd swear my stomach is still moving. The rope sways and I ride it out thinking *I just had a once in a lifetime rush. At least I hope it was!*

The soldier is playing his light beam across me as I dangle in midair somewhere above the canyon floor. "You okay, Jim?"

"Depends on your definition of okay, I guess. Not the best idea I ever had."

He laughs out loud. "Look, you're probably twenty feet from the ground. Just let down—slower this time—till you feel solid ground underfoot."

"Got it," I call up to him. My feet finally touch something more than thin air and I take a deep breath.

Barnett, you stupe, of all the dumb stunts. Made it this far then almost splattered yourself.

"Can you find a way in from there?" sarge asks. "There's a new way into the guard quarters courtesy of our demolition man."

I scan along the wall ahead of me and see a familiar spot. A door is slightly open about where I met Lotus earlier. "Never mind. I know my way in."

Pick my way through the loose rocks and approach the door cautiously. The *dojang* is lit but there's no sound or movement. I push on the door and peer in then step back.

"Lotus. What's going on here?"

She doesn't answer. There is a body on the floor mat and she's standing in a trance-like state looking down at it. I walk toward her and plead, "Say something. Are you hurt? Talk to me, please." Still no reaction from Lotus.

As I get close she finally turns her eyes up to me and there is a spark in her eyes. She slowly raises a large sword and hefts it over her head with both hands.

"Lotus! It's me. Jim." She wavers, cocks her head to one side and brings the sword down point first into the mat. It's covered with blood.

"Ali Hassan," she says and points.

The body is a bearded Arab sprawled out with his limbs all akimbo. Embedded in his middle is a long metal pike that stands straight up as if it has been driven firmly though the mat into the floor beneath. My gaze works upward and stops at the metal rod's top. I recoil in horror.

A human head is jammed onto the pike.

Blood still drips from the neck where it has been cleanly severed from its body. But the Arab is still intact. What is this?

Lotus steps aside and for the first time I see a second body behind her, this one a headless torso, prone on the mat. One ankle is encased in a leather shackle with a chain anchored to the wall.

"Kim Yung," she mumbles and drops to the floor.

CHAPTER 67

Dan Cooper

The guys are always kidding me about my memory. I have this knack for seeing something once and having it etched on my brain—that is, if it's important enough. The map Lotus pilfered is laid out in my mind. I want to see for myself what this part of the fortress looks like.

We make a circuit through the common areas—sitting rooms, dining, recreation. There's a nicely equipped kitchen, movie theater, even a billiard room. No corners cut here. Kim clearly pampered his scientists and kept them content to stay underground with all the creature comforts they could want.

"This has to be where the scientists live," I remark when we find a group of suites near the labs. "Kenny was telling it straight when he said they have plush quarters."

I count eight apartments up and eight down in a two-story section that adjoins main level labs and upstairs offices. Each unit is spacious and extravagantly furnished. Large bedroom and sitting room with a private bath.

We've just about completed our tour when Celia lets out an almost girlish squeal and rushes into one of the units. Jud looks concerned and follows her in. Pat and I, along with Celia's assistants Mary and Sam, head off to see what the major meant about Kim's hangout.

"Whooee, look at this, guys. Thomas said this was comfortable. Talk about an understatement."

"Looks like a palace," Pat says.

The carpet is dazzling white and so is the leather furniture in the sitting area. Walls are papered in pastels with sketches of Korean people and animals. Everything else is Oriental style. Bamboo and burnished teak cabinets and frames. Jade pieces everywhere and the scents of fresh flowers. Closets full of expensive clothes from silk martial arts uniforms to suits that look like they cost a couple thousand bucks apiece. He may be a homicidal freak but this Kim knows how to live.

We step into Kim's office. It's a work of art as well. Massive polished desk and a conference table to seat ten. Awards and certificates on every wall touting the skills of Kim Yung in a variety of martial arts including several I've never heard of. I'm checking out his bookshelves when a yelp goes up from the next room that could only be Jud.

Pat and I rush out to see what's bit him. Find him in an area that contains a sparkling kitchen and a very staid dining parlor.

"Struck gold, chums." He swings open a set of double doors and shows off a large cooler stocked to the brim with bottles.

"Name a brand," he tempts Pat.

"Guiness. Park Ale. San Miguel," Pat fires back, laughing.

"Check—check—and check," Jud confirms. "Those and about anything else you can name. Time for international brew tasting, pal."

"Wouldn't happen to be a pair of Murphy's in there?" Pat asks hopefully. Jud searches long and hard but ends up shaking his head.

"Oh, well, can't have it all. You wanta sample them from left to right or top to bottom?"

"By the way, Jud, what was the upset with Celia?"

Jud looks stumped.

"She let out a squeak like she'd stepped on a mouse or something," Pat says.

Jud pops a bottle top and hands him a brew. "Oh, that. She found Kenny's room. He had her picture on the dresser. Kind of flipped out on me till I reminded her he should be here in just a few hours. But she's still in there trying to touch everything he's been near."

Major Thomas looks us up in Kim's suite.

"Well, everything's tidied up. We're in a holding operation till the feds move in and scrub this place down. They'll process the survivors and figure out where everybody fits in this pack of rats. Then they can decide what to do with the goodies we're finding and look for something more productive for these scientists to do."

I can't let that pass. "You know, Major, that we're talking about a bunch of technical heavyweights penned up back in the lab. There's more talent in that room than most research programs or foundations could ever afford. What they're doing could give us a real edge on the rest of the world."

"So I hear, Dan. Not my department. I just wrap them up and deliver them. Somebody above my pay grade decides what becomes of them." He turns to leave just as Celia appears.

"Stay and have a cool one with us. You earned a break. That was one well-greased operation."

"Thanks," He says. "But we have preparations to make. I'll check back in awhile. We'll all be here for the night. Did your friend get back? I sent one of my men for him a good while ago."

"Not yet. Hope everything is clear around the perimeter."

Thomas thinks about that and hurries off. I wander back into the office space and rummage around in general. Occurs to me if Jim was here he and Jud would be all over every computer in house snooping out secrets.

Hear a sound behind me and spin around to see a hidden door opening in the wall. Jim is leading somebody in here. Whoever it is looks terrible—beaten, rumpled and bloody. It's Lotus!

I run to help and we steer her to one of Kim's leather chairs.

"The unfinished business you mentioned must have been pretty brutal, Lotus." I look closer and see she's a mass of bruises. One eye is swelled nearly shut and she's bleeding from cuts in multiple places. She turns her palms up, and her hands are covered with blood.

I fix a stare on Jim without asking. He says, "You oughta see the other guys."

"Celia, we need you in here. Hurry," I shout.

The whole group comes running: Celia, Jud, Pat, Mary and Sam. Guess I did sound more than mildly upset by what I was seeing.

Celia and Mary take over and minister to Lotus. "She's had a rough time of it," I hear Celia say. "Nothing life-threatening I can see so far, but these marks will last awhile."

Jim leads me toward the adjoining room. I ask him, "How did you get in there? And what happened to her?"

"This room is—*was* Kim's private exercise place. I sort of dropped in on the back side of the building and found her standing in here in a daze. The most I could get out of her was 'the master taught his pupil too well'."

"Meaning what?" He flips a light switch and points. I step inside and take a closer look. The gory scene nearly makes me retch. Then I realize who the two cadavers must be and confess I feel a lot less upset.

Jud rushes in behind us and yelps, "Jeez, man, that Arab's been nailed. And I see you found Kim Yung over there...and there. Damn, he kind of came apart, didn't he?"

CHAPTER 68

Dan Cooper

Celia flops into one of the big leather chairs. She looks totally beat.

I ask, "Are you okay, Celia."

She lets out a long sigh and says, "Give me a minute. We took Lotus to her quarters and treated her wounds. She was in some kind of life and death fight with somebody and the effects were brutal. Mary volunteered to stay with her while she rests."

Jim takes that in and remarks, "You wouldn't believe what that little woman can do with her delicate looking body. You saw the results in the dojang. The master taught her too well. He paid with his life."

Celia comes straight up out of her seat. "Is she dangerous, Jim? Maybe I shouldn't have left Mary alone with her."

"Relax. Have a brew," he answers. "She's a gentle person. Just had this huge dose of hate to get out of her system. Son of a bitch had treated her like an animal. She'll be fine now."

Jud hands Celia a Heineken and asks, "Any word from Kenny yet, Cee?"

She looks nervously at her watch. "Surely they should be in Vegas by now. But we have an immediate problem." She peers around the room for reaction. Conversation has stopped and all eyes are on her.

"Problem?" I ask. "What now?"

"We need Major Thomas in here right away. Lotus told us something that could cancel out everything his folks have accomplished tonight. The attacks may be underway."

Pat doesn't waste a second. He's off and running to find Thomas.

Celia continues. "Lotus said Kim told her the messengers of doom, as he called them, had already been dispatched with their biological agents."

My heart skips. We were so close to shutting down this operation. They may have slipped us after all.

"Ohmygod, Celia! Can we stop them?"

"If we don't, this could be the biological equivalent of Armageddon, Dan."

The room is suddenly as quiet as a crypt. We're all sitting there minutes later in total shock when Pat returns with the major. Thomas rushes over to Celia and says, "Give it to me fast."

"Lotus has killed Kim Yung. The clincher that set her off was him telling her the bio attacks were already set in motion. There are teams of Koreans and Arabs on their way to release the viruses and bacteria in four cities: Las Vegas, Atlanta, Chicago and New York."

The major has been a rock throughout this whole operation but he's visibly shaken now.

"How long ago did these teams go out?" he asks. I can see the wheels turning. He's spring loaded and thinking on the fly.

"Best I can tell they must have maybe a ninety minute head start, major. Kim told her they left the citadel late this evening."

Thomas grabs the telephone on Kim's desk and dials a long sequence of numbers.

"CP? Sand Bird here. Give me control." A short pause then, "I know it's unsecure. Damnit, give me control now!"

He lays out the problem and asks for immediate action to blanket all highways and airports in the vicinity. I can tell he's running out of patience.

"Listen! I don't care who you are. If you were the freaking President I'd tell you the same thing. Get those forces out. Yeah, I know it's racial profiling. Would you rather see people drop like flies when those viruses hit them?"

He listens for a bit and starts to cool down. "Okay. We'll try to ID them by name. I'll head out to McCarran Field and stay in contact. You collar them, we'll sort them out."

Jud and Jim have a quick conversation then Jud starts prying open desk drawers. He holds up a sheet of paper and says something to Jim. Gets a head nod and an answer I can't make out. Jim is at Kim's computer calling up files. I don't ask. As usual they're way ahead of the flow.

Thomas hangs up the phone and says, "We need to find out by name who Kim sent out with the bio agents. Can't hold everybody they detain without some cause."

"Got you covered, major," Jud says. He holds up a list of names on a single sheet of paper from the middle drawer of Kim's desk. "These are the names of all the Koreans living here. Jim says he referred to them as the inner circle. Twelve names and four destinations should narrow down the possibilities."

Jim speaks up. "I'm printing out the names of the entire *Al-Qinaa'* guard force—thirty six names in all. We know some of them that died before and during the assault. Take this along as a starter. Leave us a satphone and we'll update you."

"You guys are great," Thomas says. "My people will do a check here and let me know who to cross off the list as either dead or captured. If we pull this off, I *will* have that cool one with you. Cross your fingers, toes and whatever else you can find. I'm taking twelve troops with me to fan out in all directions. We're off!"

CHAPTER 69

Dan Cooper

My old bones have taken about all the punishment they can stand for one day. My brain is saying 'give me a rest'. But how do I give in and crash now? If those bad guys slip through the net…can't even think about it.

The civilians in our midst are all gathered in the common area used by Kim's scientific force. They won't need it for awhile. Thomas's troops have brought all fourteen of them from the nanotech lab area.

"Those dudes could be anywhere from here to Phoenix to Los Angeles by now," Jud says. "We may already be fried along with the rest of the country."

"Come on, Jud," I chide. "You're the one that always sees the bright side. Don't whimp out on us now."

"Sorry, Dan. Another brew?" He heads off for the cooler again.

"No more for me. I want lots of strong coffee. Till we know the outcome of Thomas's foray I'm staying right here and wide awake."

Jud stops and sits down with a thud. "You're right, pal. This could be a nervous wait."

Celia is in the kitchen area with a couple of her folks. They're brewing coffee and heating water for tea. She's scouring the cabinets and cooler for food.

"How about some breakfast? Looks like we have eggs, bacon, sausage, even some canned biscuits."

"Going domestic on us, Cee?" Jud throws at her.

"Oh, I'm a lot more domestic than you might think, lanky." She gives him a little wink. "Besides, I'd rather cook than sit around and think about what ifs. Let the pros work the hard problems."

We try to get some food down and make light conversation, but our minds are obviously with what's going on outside this place. Hours have passed. The morning sun must be coming up outside by now.

Jud and I finally turn to comparing tonight's escapade with what we faced a few weeks ago on our first outing as amateur sleuths. "Looks like we went from bad to worse, Dan," he says.

"Well, old buddy, we gave this one our best. The stakes are about as high as they could get. Let's hope Thomas and his boys arrive in time."

Just then I hear that uncharacteristic girlish squeal form Celia again. She lunges for the door.

"Hi, Mom. We made it." Kenny is standing there looking fit and happy.

Celia checks him over like he's a delicate piece of china. Never saw a complete physical performed standing up. It's plain she is ecstatic.

I look at the doorway and see two other people. Pat hails the man. "Frank! Great to see you again. And who's this with you?"

Frank has a firm hold on a tall Oriental woman whose hands are behind her. She takes one look at Jud and says, "So, you win, Mister Black."

Jud exhales a long breath and says, "Su Lin." He starts to say something but looks at Celia first and thinks better of it.

When Celia finally shares her son with us, there are hand shakes and bear hugs all around.

"Kenny," Jim says, "that Sphinx routine was the key to our success here tonight. Hope you're back to normal now."

I add, "The heads up on that back entrance was the best edge we had in securing this place before they set off any of the dirty stuff. Your mom and her folks didn't miss a beat after that."

Kenny says, "Well, I'm great now that I know Mom's safe. You guys did a fantastic job of sitting hard on these terrorists. Thank God you were there for us."

"Don't get too optimistic yet," Pat tells him. "Not till we hear how the round up is going." He explains the mission Thomas and his troops are on to collar the attack teams. Kenny shakes his head and says, "Better pray they succeed, Pat."

* * * *

I've lost all sense of time. Check my watch and see it's after two AM. My body is asking, *"Okay, now tell me what day it is."* I'd give a million bucks to be sitting by the pool at home with Ellen. Seems like weeks since I saw her. If my addled brain hasn't short-circuited, I seem to remember it was Sunday when Pat and I crawled aboard that jet and headed west. This can't be later than Thursday or Friday, but I've had enough action and frustration for a month. Come on, guys, give us an update. The suspense is murder.

Pat takes a seat and gives me a pained look. "Dan, you look like I feel only worse. We stepped into some real trouble this time, didn't we? After this anything that comes along for COBB should be tame."

"Don't count on it, pal. Jud and I in particular seem to have a penchant for getting caught up in some pretty stinky messes. But it feels like the old days."

"Damn near fun, huh, Cooper?" Pat's got a huge smile.

"Well, Irishman, you gotta admit we're a kick-ass combine. We're either scary good or the luckiest quartet of amateurs that ever hooked up."

We're trying hard to keep our minds occupied with billiards, television, whatever works when Captain Vance comes charging into the dayroom. "Got big news, folks!" That brings all activity to a halt.

"They've bagged our quarry. You can take a deep breath. We're all clear."

We stand there dumbfounded. Must be half a minute of dead silence and shocked expressions. Then the celebration starts.

After a lot of hugging and high fives, back slapping and relieved whoops and hollers, Vance gets our attention again and fills us in.

"We kept in touch with the major and the others. Passed on the names of people we could account for here. They fanned out knowing exactly who they were searching for—four Koreans and eight Arabs by name. Stopped one of the trios at McCarran, another pair on the road across the California line, and one team on US 93 in Arizona."

"That's only three teams, Captain," I say tentatively.

The celebration ceases.

"I know. The other team had already arrived at the Venetian Hotel. Major played that one on a hunch from the feedback you guys had given him. That team was lying low with refrigerated canisters of something to hit the hotel. Could have been real ugly."

Jim interrupts, "We already know. It was nano spores of dengue and anthrax."

"Whatever," Vance says. "The Korean gave up without a fight. The Arabs tried to break their bio containers and kill everybody, themselves included. Our guys grabbed the canisters and put a hurt on the two Arabs."

CHAPTER 70

Jud Black

When the shouting is over we turn our thoughts to more personal matters—if anything can be more personal than survival. Anyway, I need a long talk with Celia. She's walking on air after getting Kenny back free and clear of his illness. I manage to borrow her and we walk off toward the wing with the scientists' suites.

"Cee, honey, I know you've had a lot to handle these past few days. We do need to talk."

She puts a finger to her lips and shakes her head. "Wait till we're alone." Takes my hand and leads me upstairs and into the first suite. We sit on the big couch in the sitting room.

"Jud," she begins, "you are a very special man. The first man in a long time I could feel totally comfortable with. There's something about you. You have a magnetism, an honesty I've seldom seen."

She reaches up and touches my cheek. Trains her blue eyes on me and I melt to goo. Then she leans in and kisses me. This is not just a kiss; it's like a thousand fans applauding my music, like getting the Nobel prize for my latest computer program…like my head is gonna explode any second.

When I can breathe again I start to mumble something profound but my brain fails me.

Celia gives me another of those smoky looks then smiles. "Don't. I need time to think, Jud. Give me a few days to sort out my feelings."

I've known a lot of women. Some of them I wanted in the worst way, at least for awhile. But there never was one like Celia Grant. This has to be the most stimulating woman I've ever met. She's beautiful, intelligent, everything I could ever want. No time to get heavy handed now.

"Take all the time you need, Cee. I'll be around."

She holds my hands in hers. There's something strange in her look. Or is it just my imagination?

* * * *

I'm sitting alone in the common area. Everybody's located places to bunk in for the night. The feds have arrived with their cleanup team, secured the site and hauled off the prisoners and the dead. The fourteen remaining scientists are all in custody at the Nellis base until the feds can determine which ones were a part of the terrorists' plans and which were only high-paid talent that just wanted to do valuable research with all the best tools at their disposal. Thomas and his troops left a little while ago after wishing us well and thanking us for our help. In the morning we'll on our way out of the desert. Probably spend a night in our soft hotel beds then be on our way home.

Celia and her teams, along with Kenny and Frank Kane, are spending the night upstairs in the abandoned scientists' quarters. Lotus looks to be in a much better frame of mind. Jim and Dan are ready to go to bat for her to see she's freed from any guilt. Dan, Pat and Jim are snoozing in first floor suites but I'm too troubled to sleep. Just sitting here staring at an old movie on the TV and not seeing a thing.

"Want to talk?" I hear, and feel a hand resting on my shoulder.

"Thought you were conked out, Dan. Sure. I'm just chilling."

"Since when did you and I keep secrets, buddy?" he asks. "We've been through too much for you to clam up on me now."

"It's Cee," I start, but the words aren't coming.

"From what I saw it looked like you two were getting on pretty well. Got a problem?"

"Dan, she's got to be the finest female I could ever hope to match up with. She has everything. I could leave the single life behind for somebody like her."

"That serious, huh? It is kind of scary to think about, isn't it? You should be happy, Jud. How does she feel?"

"That's the problem," I tell him. "She says the words but her eyes tell me otherwise. It's not gonna happen, Dan. We're too different."

"Look, pal," Dan says, "life's too short to get hung up on any woman."

"Easy for you to say. You have Ellen." Dan smiles happily at my gotcha.

"Other times, other places, Jud. Besides, think how many gals you'd be disappointing if you took yourself out of circulation."

"Maybe." I can't help but let a grin creep across my face. Dan's turned the tables on me, Now *he's* the one doing the 'be happy' pep talk.

"Talked to Ellen yet?" I ask, knowing he couldn't wait to reach her as soon as we got the all clear. "I know Judy and Susie have heard from the other guys by now."

"Everybody back there is fine, Jud. Ellen and Danielle are relieved. You know Ellen. She's figured out much more than I could tell her. Informed her we'd be picking up our things in Las Vegas tomorrow and flying home Saturday morning. She said to tell you the guest room in Trinity is empty anytime you want it."

"You're a lucky guy, Dan Cooper."

"Don't I know it."

"What now, Dan?"

"Let it go. I can't sleep. Let's tie one on. Saw a bottle of Bushmill's in Kim's suite."

Chapter 71

Dan Cooper

Saturday afternoon east coast time. The last day in Sin City was a toot. I knew it was too much to hope that this gnarly group would cool it and let me rest up for the trip home. The four of us ended up doing the Strip in royal fashion. We must have hit half the casinos in town and nearly that many bars. Turns out Jud's a natural at this gambling gig. He walked away with a bundle from one of the hotels. Then he wanted to hit a topless show.

Pat sneered and said, "Just a bunch of half naked women strutting around."

Jud rolled that around and answered, "So what's your point, O'Leary?"

Pat and Jim logged a good night's sleep at the citadel that left them ready for the last overnight in Vegas. By the time Jud and I got a snoot full in that day room, it was already nearly morning. The best I could do was flop in my nearly unused room at the Mirage until they drug me out for our assault on the Strip.

After making the rounds we rushed back to our hotels barely in time to stuff our bags and make our flight out of town.

Now we're about to get ourselves together again and the airliner is minutes from landing at Dulles. Pat, Jim, Jud and I are sitting four across in first class. Bought out the whole section so we could have some privacy. I don't know how much of our chatter the stewardesses have picked up. Probably wouldn't believe our story, anyway.

The head stew leans over and asks me, "How long have you four…uhh, gentlemen, known each other?"

"Not nearly long enough," I tell her. "We kind of go together naturally."

I hand her a fifty. "There must be at least a couple bottles of champagne somewhere on this airframe." She hesitates then slips away.

The stew comes back with two open bottles of bubbly and four glasses.

"I have a toast," I announce. She pours our glasses half full and we all take one.

"This is for all we've weathered together and all we'll share in the future. To the nuttiest, wierdest, most lovable group of guys I've ever known—and to COBB Eye!"

We slug down our wine.

Then, true to form, Jud has the last word. He leans over, puckers up, pretends to wipe away a tear and says, "Kiss me, fool."

Preview of

Then The Stillness

By

Don Otey

FOREWORD

The turbulent 1860's are perhaps the most richly recorded period of all United States history. Scholars of the Civil War have enriched our lives with accounts of the issues and actions that played out during the bloodiest years in our nation's existence. Our hearts go out for the suffering our forebears endured in moving a land born in the fires of revolution through the crucible of a white hot agony to forge the mightiest nation the world has ever known.

We have heard the story from the point of view of that day's prominent politicians and leading generals. From their lofty perches the struggle was a clash of ideologies, a divergence of economic goals, the issues of slavery and states' rights. But why did the common soldier fight? How did Billy Yank and Johnny Reb feel when they went into battle, braved the numbing winters and searing summers, times that promised little more than survival to face the next battle?

This story is dedicated to the brave men who offered up all they possessed, their mortal beings, to a cause, whatever it may have been in each man's mind. We can only pray that those who perished in the horrific slaughter of brother against brother have found their rewards in the great hereafter.

We will follow two soldiers through the war, one a Union troop and the other a Confederate. Owen Kearney and Ira Palmer are the names assigned to them, but they are, in fact, the typical common soldier of the North and South. Through these men's eyes we experience the battle, the tedium of camp, longings for home that filled the letters of so many of their companions during those dark days. They typify the nearly three million Americans in blue and in gray whose spirits were severely tested.

Then The Stillness portrays how they felt, their triumphs and defeats, their thoughts of family and loved ones. The reader will share the indomitable spirits of these two soldiers and so many like them. They suffered to heal a great division and weld our United States together for all time with their blood and sinew as the binding materials.

In so many ways these warriors established the pattern for the valiant American soldiers who have answered the call and preserved the world for freedom.

Bless you and your legacy of courage, brothers in arms.

With deepest respect,
Don Otey

CHAPTER 1

Sunday, April 6, 1862—Shiloh, Tennessee

The Confederates hold their gun line steady and press the attack. Cannon, dozens of them, rein fiery hell on the Federals in the woods and the blue coats are hard pressed to fight back. Shoulder-to-shoulder the rebels pass through the meadow. A smoky wall of gunpowder fills the air that only hours ago had welcomed a spring day and a peaceful rolling fog. The drummer beats his cadence as the attack moves across the meadow. From somewhere down the line comes the command, the drumbeat hastens and the rebels move to a quick time.

A shout billows up from the Confederate ranks. They charge the tree line. The din of musket fire crackles across the meadow, echoes off the trees, is answered from the woods. The hot metal of shot tears tree trunks, screams through branches and ravages human limbs. Cries of pain swell.

The advance is hard won. Men drop on both sides, but those standing are too intent on holding position in line to cast an eye toward the less fortunate. Thud of musket ball against flesh, more often than not accompanied by a shriek or a curse, then the line closes together and continues winding its way through the tall meadow grass. Men fire straight ahead, squint through the smoke and dust, hoping their aim is true, not wanting to know what human toll they may be taking.

In minutes the Confederates swarm through the trees with Federals only yards away. Fear fills the eyes of the defenders. Despite the tide of battle, even the victors quake with the cold fright of knowing they are part of a hell on earth unleashed against men just like themselves. Blue-coated soldiers drop their weapons, accept the inevitable, but there is little joy on either side other than the glow of having been spared the taste of death. Other days lie ahead, other battles await the human offering that will be laid on the altar of war.

The resistance breaks and what seems to be hundreds of the Union soldiers abandon their positions in full flight to the rear toward Pittsburg Landing. Rebels overrun their embattlements and fall upon them, taking prisoners at every turn. A great cry of jubilation finally swells up from the ranks as if it rises from a single throat.

A young Confederate soldier helps round up the prisoners. Jimmy has had his first taste of battle. Many of the captives look as green as he felt before this action began. The frenzy of combat is still in their eyes.

A hand touches Jimmy's shoulder, and he turns to see his tent mate Tom with a smile on his powder blackened face. Even after the skirmishes and pitched battles he's seen, there remains the same awestruck look behind his beard, the lingering shock and disbelief at standing where so many others have fallen.

"Well, Jimmy, you got your baptism of fire today. How's it feel, lad?"

"I'm not ashamed to say I was scared, Tom. Dumbstruck, weak-in-the-knees scared."

Tom reaches into his knapsack and fishes out a tobacco plug. Carves a piece away with his knife to offer to Jimmy.

"Don't chew, Tom. Never had the inclination."

"Well, now you're a hardened soldier. Been through live action and seen the elephant as us battle survivors like to say. You'll learn a good chaw is a mighty comfortin' companion on the musket line. Keeps your mind off what's happenin' in the moment. Little lump of tobacco's saved many a soldier from gnawin' off his tongue when the goin' got rough. Take a whirl at it, Jimmy boy."

The lad hesitates for a long moment then takes the tobacco and stands with his hand poised inches from his mouth.

"Go ahead, lad. You've earned the right to jaw like a man. Besides, next time when you get this close you can just spit in Billy Yank's eye."

Jimmy pokes the tobacco into his cheek with a thumb and two fingers and peers all around. Details search for wounded under the white flag. Men in blue wander the woods looking for friends smitten by cannon and musket fire. The fighting has raged all day at the Sunken Road, around the Shiloh Church, and in the place where fighting was so intense it was called the Hornet's Nest. Given pause to wash their wounds and seek water, men on both sides drifted to a small pond that turned red with the consequence of the battle and will ever after be known as Bloody Pond.

Now the day's struggle is over and night is falling. Here and there clutches of soldiers stand over a comrade beyond help. They offer what comfort they can. The dead and the dying lie thrown about like carelessly stacked cord wood across the bloody landscape. Cries of anguish and whimpers of resignation arise on every side. Shutting out those awful sounds is a task Jimmy finds beyond his capacity, so he withdraws to the tall grass. Sits heavily, head in hands, his back to the terrible scene in the woods, trying to make some order of this senseless loss of life.

But the lad's solitary lament is broken by a voice from the grass calling out weakly, "Jimmy?"

Lying a few feet away is a soldier who he had met only two days ago in camp. Now that youth wallows hopelessly torn asunder, a leg and an arm shattered by Minie ball, the life's blood slowly abandoning him. Jimmy moves to the man and calls out to a litter bearer. The medic looks down at the wounded youth, shakes his head then moves on. Jimmy stays and speaks in hushed tones until the soldier's eyes close and he sighs with a last labored breath.

The sun sets and stars fill the dark sky. One of them streaks across the heavens and dies over the horizon. Jimmy tries to remember the tale of what a shooting star means, but his mind and body are too weary to concentrate. The skies darken and a sharp report of thunder brings a sudden downpour with a new din not unlike the sound of cannon. The roar of thunder is welcome. It drowns out the pitiful cries of the wounded men that dot the landscape, soldiers who have proudly worn the blue and the gray for their very last time today. Jimmy closes his eyes and lets the rain wash his powder charred face.

When the thunder at length subsides an eerie calm blankets that steaming Shiloh meadow. The final pleas for help have ceased, and the survivors sit amid an uneasy quiet absent the sound of any voice. An unsettling numbness settles over the meadow. Jimmy shivers with its chill. His tears mix with the rain and pour down his powder-stained cheeks. He closes his eyes once again and listens as all sound departs.

Then the stillness. The terrible, all consuming stillness. A pall of hopelessness, of anguish, of death descends on the battlefield.

Jimmy, a son of the South barely eighteen years old, sleeps. His victory at Shiloh's Hornet's Nest will be short lived. On the day to follow, newly buttressed Federal troops will sweep the Confederates from the field and claim a bloody victory. Jimmy does not yet know this will be his last night on earth.

978-0-595-39560-6
0-595-39560-0

Printed in the United States
52497LVS00004B/259-309